HOMLAND

SAUL'S GAME

Also by Andrew Kaplan

HOMELAND™
SAUL'S GAME

ANDREW KAPLAN

wm
WILLIAM MORROW
An Imprint of HarperCollins*Publishers*

HarperCollins books may be purchased for educational, business, or sales promotional use. For information please e-mail the Special Markets Department at SPsales@harpercollins.com.

FIRST EDITION

Designed by Diahann Sturge

Library of Congress Cataloging-in-Publication Data has been applied for.

ISBN 978-0-06-231545-8

14 15 16 17 18   OV/RRD   10 9 8 7 6 5 4 3 2 1

For the real Anne,
the love of my life

AUTHOR'S NOTE

For readers interested in additional useful information on the characters, CIA acronyms, terminology and slang, organizations, agencies, and other entities portrayed in this novel, a list of characters and a glossary are provided at the back of the book.

TOP SECRET//X1: SPECIAL ACCESS CRITICAL//ORCON/ NOFORN/FOR DIRECTOR CIA EYES ONLY/100X1

[Polygraph Transcript: CIA Community Security Center/For Middle East Division/National Clandestine Service/Baghdad Station; Date: 20090621]
SUBJECT: Caroline Anne Mathison aka "Carrie"/ Operations Officer/Baghdad Station/MED/NCS
POLYGRAPH EXAMINER: [[*Name redacted—see comment at end*]]
NOTE: Includes Polygraph Examiner evaluations [[in double brackets]]. Polygraph audio transcript begins here:

EXAMINER: Your name is Caroline Anne Mathison?
MATHISON: Yes.
EXAMINER: You were born April 5, 1979?
MATHISON: Yes.
EXAMINER: You are thirty years old?
MATHISON: Yes.
EXAMINER: You are a CIA operations officer currently assigned to Baghdad Station in Iraq?
MATHISON: Yes.
EXAMINER: Have you had sexual intercourse in the last week?

MATHISON: . . . Yes.

EXAMINER: Have you ever heard of a CIA operation code-named "Operation Iron Thunder"?

MATHISON: I . . . Yes.

EXAMINER: Just yes or no. Have you ever heard of a CIA operation code-named "Iron Thunder"?

MATHISON: Yes.

EXAMINER: Were you, in fact, the lead operations officer for Operation Iron Thunder?

MATHISON: Yes.

EXAMINER: Did you terminate an Iraqi national named [[*redacted*]]?

MATHISON: He was going to [[*redacted*]].

EXAMINER: Did you personally kill him? Yes or no?

MATHISION: Yes.

EXAMINER: What about [[*redacted*]]? Did you have sexual intercourse with him?

MATHISON: Yes, but it was . . . [[*redacted*]].

EXAMINER: Were drugs, including ecstasy and/ or Captagon, also known as Zero One, and multiple sexual partners also involved?

MATHISON: No, I didn't participate. [[*False. Subject is lying.*]]

EXAMINER: You were acquainted with Warzer Zafir, an Iraqi employee of the United States embassy who also acted as a CIA operative in Baghdad, were you not?

MATHISON: Yes. We worked together.

EXAMINER: You knew him better than that, didn't you? You lived together and had repeated sexual relations with him. Is that correct?

MATHISON: Yes.

EXAMINER: Nevertheless, despite your relationship, were you also involved in the death of Warzer Zafir?

MATHISON: Are you out of your mind? Absolutely not. No. [[*False. Subject is lying.*]]

EXAMINER: Miss Mathison, were you, as part of Operation Iron Thunder or otherwise, involved in any way, in a [[*redacted*]] that [[*redacted*]]?

MATHISON: No. What the [[*redacted*]]?

[[*Evaluation redacted.*]]

EXAMINER: Just to be absolutely clear, you have no knowledge whatsoever about [[*redacted*]]?

MATHISON: [[*Redacted.*]]

EXAMINER: During Operation Iron Thunder, were you [[*redacted*]] and [[*redacted*]]?

MATHISON: Yes.

EXAMINER: And during that [[*redacted*]], did you reveal intelligence severely damaging to the security of the United States?

MATHISON: I did not. No. [[*False. Subject is lying.*]]

EXAMINER: Are you a traitor to the United States of America?

MATHISON: No, you son of a bitch! No. [[*False. Subject is lying.*]]

Remainder of examination redacted: FOR DIRECTOR CIA EYES ONLY. Examiner and all Human Resources Data/201 File/Aardvark HUMINT/ Redacted pursuant DCIA/M–20090624–2.

2009

ONE YEAR BEFORE
THE ARAB SPRING

CHAPTER 1

"*Mr. President. And Vice President William Walden too. I appreciate you both coming at this time of night.*"

"*What is this place? It's like a damn cave.*"

"*Special chamber, Mr. President. We use it for secure meetings with spook types like the vice president back when he was director of the CIA. It's right under the regular Senate hearing room. From an electronic eavesdropping point of view, it's probably the most secure location in Washington. And with Marines guarding the tunnel from the Dirksen Building, no one will ever know you were here.*"

"*Good, because this meeting never happened. Tim, my Secret Service guy, isn't thrilled about this.*"

"*You have my word, Mr. President. Speaking of which . . .*"

"*Let's cut to the chase, Senator. You can't hold your hearing.*"

"*Hang on, Mr. President. We're a coequal branch of government. The American people have a right to—*"

"*Bullshit. This is politics, pure and simple. Only I'm not a candidate anymore, Senator. I'm the president—and I'm telling you, you can't do this.*"

"Of course it's politics. What the hell did you expect? This thing stinks to high heaven. You can't cover this up."

"We sent you everything you asked for, Senator."

"You jumping in here, Bill? You sent us what my daddy used to call a giant wagonload of horse manure. The polygraph for this female agent, Mathison, for instance. You redacted damn near everything except her name. Surprised you didn't do that. This ain't gonna fly, gentlemen. We're going to have this hearing—in public. Full media, CNN, Fox, MSNBC, the whole circus. And if it embarrasses you, Mr. President, or you, Bill . . . well, tough shit."

"Senator . . . Warren, let's not pretend we like each other. I know you want to make political hay and see yourself on all the Sunday talk shows and maybe a stepping-stone to something bigger, but trust me, this is one hearing that isn't going to happen."

"You try to shut this down, sir, and as an old prosecutor, I warn you. Both you and the vice president are skating very close to articles of impeachment. I take this very seriously."

"So do I, Senator. That's why I'm here. But this hearing cannot go forward."

"With all due respect, Mr. President, I'm the committee chair. How the hell are you gonna stop me?"

"Because I'm going to give you the benefit of the doubt, that under all the bullshit—and yeah, we're guilty of it too, there are no virgins here—there's a patriot. Somebody who actually gives a damn about this country. Listen to me, Warren. This isn't politics. I am the president of the United States of America and I came here tonight for one reason only. This is critical for our national security. You can't do this."

"You're gonna have to give me a helluva lot more than that."

"That's why I brought Vice President Walden. Bill?"

"Senator, the president has ordered me to tell you everything. The whole truth and nothing but. Then you decide. I approved this operation. It was on my watch."

"What about this female agent? Mathison. Is she a traitor? I'm thinking seriously about dragging her in front of a FISA court, locking her up, and throwing away the key."

"We'll let you decide. But you're looking in the wrong direction. She's not the story."

"Then in the name of sweet Jesus, Bill, what is the story?"

"Funny you should say that. He isn't even a Christian. He's an Orthodox Jew. An Orthodox Jew who doesn't wear one of those yarmulkes on his head or follow any Orthodox Jewish practices. Go figure that one out, for starters. Let's call him Saul."

"What about this Saul?"

"You saw the docs we sent. It's in there. Now that the president's sitting here, I'll admit it's not full disclosure. We didn't send even a third—I'm sorry, Mr. President, but I couldn't—and maybe we fudged on what we did send, but, so help me, it's there."

"What? This . . . operation? Iron Thunder? Looks like a damn train wreck to me."

"Wow, you really don't get it. You are listening to Beethoven's Ninth. You're looking at the Mona Lisa, the Sistine Chapel, and you don't have a clue. Senator, this was maybe the most brilliant and successful operation in the history of the CIA—a work of genius—and you don't see it. This saved the Iraq War. Maybe the whole Middle East. If we hadn't done this, we were projecting more than ten thousand American casualties and a gigantic loss of American prestige around the world, and that was just for starters. We're talking about a worse disaster than 9/11. You should be handing out medals."

"Stop right there, Bill. Since you and the president want to make me one of the bad guys, why don't you walk me through it? Only let's be clear, I'm not making any promises. Where do we start? With this operation?"

"Well, since you brought her up, let's begin with the girl."

CHAPTER 2

Eastern Syrian Desert
12 April 2009
01:32 hours

The pair of Black Hawk helicopters flew low and fast over the desert. Skimming over sand and rock, less than seventy feet above the ground, barely forty meters apart in the darkness. The night sky was clouded over; only a single star and no horizon. For the pilots it was like flying blindfolded at nearly 160 knots and the only reason they didn't crash was the AN/ASN-128 Doppler radar that gave them the elevations of ground features: rock outcroppings, sand dunes, or buildings, although in theory, there weren't supposed to be any habitations in this part of the desert. It would have been safer to fly at a higher altitude, but that would have been suicide. Within minutes, seconds even, they'd be picked up on antiaircraft radar. Once the Syrian fighter jets scrambled, they wouldn't stand a chance.

Strapped into the hatch seat, Carrie Mathison tried to control her hands from shaking. It had been two days since she'd taken her meds. Clozapine for her bipolar disorder. She got them from the little pharmacy on Haifa Street in Baghdad's Green Zone, where if the owner, Samal, knew you, you could get any drug on the planet, no questions asked so long as you paid for it in cash. "American dollars, please, *shokran* very much, madam."

In the red glow of the helicopter's interior combat lighting, she could just make out the silhouettes of the Special Ops Group team in full combat gear, humped with packs, cradling M4A1 carbines with sound suppressors. Ten of them plus her made up the Black Hawk's normal complement of eleven. The distance to the target was inside the helicopter's 368-mile combat radius and the plan was to be back inside Iraq before daybreak. Through the window next to the hatch, where the door gunner stood manning his 7.62mm machine gun, there was only darkness and the roar of the helicopter's rotor.

They had crossed the border into Syrian airspace some fifteen minutes ago, taking off from Forward Operating Base Delta, a sandbagged slab of concrete in the middle of nowhere desert outside Rutba in western Iraq. Except for the occasional stop along Highway 10, much of the desert between Rutba and Otaibah was uninhabited but for a few smugglers' camps.

There had been smuggler routes in the region since before the Roman legions came tramping through these sands. When they had planned this mission, they'd figured that, in theory, the local tribesmen were the last people on earth who would make a cell-phone call to Syrian Security Forces. If the smugglers heard helicopters, they would assume they were Syrian army helicopters and hide. In theory.

She couldn't stop her hands from trembling. Shit. She had stopped taking her meds because she needed to be super-sharp for this operation. Already she was starting to feel strange, like an early warning. Focus, Carrie, she told herself.

How many years had she been chasing Abu Nazir, the leader of the IPLA, the Islamic People's Liberation Army, an affiliate of al-Qaeda in Iraq, and the CIA's most wanted man after Osama bin Laden? It had become very personal. Ever since U.S. Marine Captain Ryan Dempsey was killed outside Fallujah three years ago. Someone she had cared about very much.

She'd almost caught Abu Nazir back then, in Haditha, but he'd slipped away like some conjurer's trick. The man was a ghost. Still, they worked it. Her, Perry Dryer, the CIA Baghdad Station chief, and Warzer Zafir, presumably a translator for the U.S. embassy, actually her operative, and of course, back in Langley, her boss, Saul Berenson, the CIA's Middle East Division chief.

A year and a half after Dempsey died, Warzer left his wife. He showed up with a single suitcase at Carrie's apartment in the Green Zone. A tiny second-floor flat with a window overlooking the traffic on Nasir Street: black-market stalls under the palm trees on the street's center divider selling car parts, plastic jugs of gasoline, guns, even condoms to passing cars.

"I'm not Dempsey," Warzer told her that first night, the smell of someone cooking *masgouf*, fried fish, coming through the open window of her apartment. Standing there, hands in his pockets, looking like a boy on his first date.

"I don't want you to be," she said. She hadn't been with a man since Dempsey. She knew then she didn't love Warzer. But there was a gentleness in him, something she needed.

"I'm Iraqi. Of the Dulaimi from Ramadi. What I'm doing is *haram*, you understand? Forbidden. My mother cried. She turned her back on me. My own mother. My wife said, 'First finish with your American *sharmuta*. Even after, don't speak to me. I don't know if I can forgive. I don't know if I want to.' You understand, Carrie?"

She nodded. *Sharmuta*. Arabic for whore.

"All I know is I had to have you," grabbing her in his arms, the first time he'd ever done that. "The two of us. Alone in this war. This insanity. And Abu Nazir, who shames me as a Muslim, sick at what he makes of us."

And then there was only the two of them, Warzer with her, inside her, the first man she'd been with in so long, because that's what the hunt for Abu Nazir had done to them. The two of them like lost children in a storm, the sounds and smells of Baghdad coming through the open window of her apartment.

"Up and over," the pilot said, and the helicopter rose to clear an obstacle. They were flying dangerously low to the ground, but then, everything about this mission, three months in the making, was insanely dangerous. It was all on her. She was the one who had insisted on it, had forced the issue.

Putting together a CIA Special Operation like this had required approvals all the way up to the vice president and the national security advisor to the president. When it got to his desk, Vice President William Walden himself had yanked her back to Washington from Baghdad. She had gone into Walden's office in the West Wing with her boss, her mentor, the one person in the CIA she totally counted on, Saul Berenson; the first time she had ever been in the White House.

"Are you out of your mind?" Walden had said. "This is the riskiest thing anyone's ever brought to me. You realize if there's a screw up, a single mistake, a helicopter malfunction, a barking dog, a neighbor calls the cops, some asshole fires a shot at the wrong time, we're toast. The country, the Agency, everything. We'd be invading another country. What the hell, Saul, you don't think anyone would notice?"

"It's Abu Nazir. It's him. We've been chasing him for years. We got him," she said.

"How do you know? This Cadillac? I don't trust it, Saul. I can't

go to Higgins with something this risky." Mike Higgins was the president's national security advisor.

"It's actionable, Bill. Ninety percent probability. You know she's right," Saul said.

Cadillac was the code name they'd assigned to Lieutenant General Mosab Sabagh, second-in-command of the Syrian Army's elite Presidential Guard Armored Division. Sabagh was a trusted Alawite clan relative of President Assad and a member of the ruling military inner circle in Damascus.

Reeling him in had been Saul's op. He had long ago identified Sabagh as a potential CIA asset. So when a watcher tracking Sabagh at the London Club in the Ramses Hilton in Cairo signaled that the Syrian had gotten in over his head at the tables, Saul made his move. Sabagh had gone to Cairo while his wife, Aminah, was off with President Assad's wife, Asma, shopping on the rue du Faubourg Saint-Honoré in Paris. Her trip was something a lieutenant general's salary could never afford, so Sabagh had tried to win the money. "A dubious idea even in Las Vegas, much less at Egyptian tables," Saul had remarked.

When the watcher reported how much money Sabagh was losing, Saul needed someone to close him fast. He sent an emergency Flash Critical message via JWICS, ordering Carrie to grab the next flight from Baghdad to Cairo to make the approach. JWICS was the Joint Worldwide Intelligence Communications System, the CIA's special Internet network designed for highly secure encrypted Top Secret communications.

Carrie had walked into the private high-stakes salon in a skin-tight dress, with eyes only for Sabagh, now Cadillac. She made brief eye contact with the target in the gambling salon, then tracked him to his hotel room, where he tried to solve his money problems with a bottle of Russian vodka, a pretty Ukrainian prostitute, who later had to be whisked out of the country, and a Beretta 9mm pistol that

Carrie had to pry out of his hand, finger by finger, never knowing till the last second which of them he was going to shoot, her or himself.

She packed Cadillac off back to Damascus the next day with his debts taken care of and $10,000 in American taxpayer money in his briefcase. In the six months since then, with his wife, Aminah, happy in Dior and, more importantly, in President Assad's wife Asma's good graces, everything Cadillac had given them, every piece of intelligence, had been twenty-four karat. He had become the CIA's most important asset in Syria.

Walden studied the file again, although he'd already read it.

"Okay, so Cadillac says blah-blah and the satellite shows a compound in Otaibah, a suburb east of Damascus. Could be Hezbollah? PFLP? Hamas? Could be President Assad's grandmother? Could be anybody."

"We've been watching it for two months by satellite and a local team," Carrie jumped in. "I was there two weeks ago myself at the makhbaz, *the local bakery, pretending to be a Circassian. You'd be surprised what you can learn just standing there in an abaya, listening to other women buying bread. There are approximately fifteen to twenty men with families in that compound. Police don't go on that street. Assad's security goons never come by. This, in the most paranoid, security-conscious dictatorship in the Middle East. Are you kidding me? Why is that?" she said.*

"Satellite infrared confirms the number of people inside," Saul said.

"Only nobody ever comes out of the compound except to go to the market or the mosque. There's no telephone landline, no Internet, and they never make cell-phone calls. Just whatever contacts they might have at the mosque or the market," she said.

"Still doesn't make sense. Why would Assad, an Alawite allied with Hezbollah and Iran, give sanctuary to Abu Nazir? Head of IPLA. It's Shiites versus Sunnis? They're deadly enemies. They hate each other," Walden said.

"Abu Nazir's doing it because it's next to Iraq yet it's the one place

he knew we wouldn't look for him—and he had to get out of Anbar because we were getting too close. We suspect Assad's doing it because, in exchange, Abu Nazir's willing to keep the Sunnis in Syria from what they're dying to do, which is assassinate him," Carrie said.

"How do you know this? Cadillac?"

She nodded.

"So forget the raid. Instead we go in with a drone. Low risk. Flatten the place. Complete deniability. End of Abu Nazir. Period," Walden said.

Saul leaned in on Walden's desk.

"We've had this conversation before, Bill. We can't get intel from a corpse," he said. "We need an SOG." He meant a Special Operations Group. Only ever used for the highest-risk missions.

"If you blast him to smithereens with a drone, they'll say he's still alive. He could become more dangerous dead than alive. Last week he had a suicide bomber in Haditha lure children on their way to school with candy and then blow them up into a million pieces," Carrie said. "Little children! We need an SOG to make sure it's him and to get the intel to finish this filthy war. So do it, dammit. Before the son of a bitch moves and we lose him again."

"Twenty-seven minutes to touchdown," Chris Glenn, the SOG team commander, said over the helicopter's roar.

They were going in light and tight, he thought. Possibly outnumbered by hostiles in the compound. Two UH-60M helicopters with ten SOG team members each. Total twenty men plus the CIA woman, Carrie. The only advantage, the element of surprise, and after thirty seconds, that would be gone and all hell could break loose, unless they were able to eliminate the guards silently and take out the rest before they woke up. The key was planning. And Carrie being right about Abu Nazir and where he'd be in the compound.

And one odd thing he wanted to check out himself. Something

opaque that had shown itself in the spy satellite infrared images. An underground cave or vault. They were hiding something.

Or someone. Or several someones, he thought.

"Keep it tight, guys. Nothing gets out. No light, no sound. Not even a fart," Glenn said, moving over to Carrie. "You good to go, Mingus?" Per her request, they'd code-named her after jazz bassist Charles Mingus. Carrie and jazz. Everybody knew it was her passion. Back at FOB Delta, it became a team joke.

"Hey, Mingus, what's wrong with Chris Brown?"

"Lil Wayne, yo."

"Katy Perry, dog!"

"I'm fine. You watch your own ass, Jaybird," she said to Glenn. His code name.

She clenched her hands on her knees so no one could see them trembling. She'd been off her meds going on sixty-plus hours. The only reason she wasn't flying either on a high or a low with her bipolar disorder was that her system was probably so hopped up on adrenaline from the mission, she decided, shaking her head to clear it.

Glenn and the machine gunner opened the cabin door to a roar of wind. Through the open door, with the night-vision goggles, she could make out scrub on the desert floor speeding beneath them; it looked almost close enough to touch with her feet.

They were supposed to be in Syria one hour flying time in, maximum forty-five minutes on the ground, one hour back to the Iraqi border. Total: two hours and forty-five minutes. Hopefully finished before daybreak and before the Syrian Army knew they were in-country and could react. Once they were back in Iraq, the administration in Washington could deny they had anything to do with it—and nothing left behind but some dead bodies to prove otherwise.

And they'd either have Abu Nazir in custody once and for

all or he would be dead. If Cadillac's intel was solid. And till now, he'd been a hundred percent.

"Ten minutes. Everybody on night vision," Glenn announced.

One by one, the team members put on their night-vision goggles and adjusted their helmets and communication gear. There was little talking among them.

For weeks, they had trained on a mock-up of the Otaibah compound in the desert near FOB Delta. Each team member had his specific assignment and every man had trained to back up the others in case they were hit. The keys to success were speed and silence in the middle of the night. Every one of them was a combat veteran, the elite of the elite, in incredible physical condition; hair-trigger-trained volunteers who had pushed themselves beyond what they ever thought they could do in order to do exactly this kind of mission.

"Five minutes to target," the pilot called back over the sound of the rotor.

"Selectors to burst," Glenn said as everyone moved their carbine safety selectors into firing position. Men started stretching their legs, getting ready to get up and move.

Carrie leaned over to look out the open door. Through the greenish field of night vision, she could see scattered structures on the outskirts of Otaibah. Small farms and shacks. These were poor people. Tribesmen who minded their own business. People who didn't make it in the wider Syrian society, who didn't want visits from the GSD, the brutal Syrian secret internal security forces. If this was where Abu Nazir really was, he had chosen well. She checked her watch one last time: 1:56 A.M. local time.

"Three minutes. Everybody ready for landing."

The men in the helicopter got ready to get up. They were

seated in the order they would exit from each side of the chopper. Carrie peered intently into the darkness.

And then she saw it. A pair of yellowish lights from a house on a street about a mile or two ahead. Was that the compound? What the hell were lights doing on at two in the morning? Then more lights. It looked like the compound was lit up. Oh God, she had led them into a trap! They were going in hot.

And streetlights too. Oh no! The satellites had shown no streetlights at night in this part of Otaibah. As if the government had deliberately neglected this part of the city.

The intel was bad. Cadillac must've lied. Or someone. It was all her fault. They would die because of her. She looked around wildly, trying to think of how to get the pilot to pull them out, to find some way out. But they were too low.

They were coming in fast now. Too late to think about it as they passed over a fence topped with barbed wire and over the compound's courtyard, bumping down in a cloud of dust.

"Go! Go!" Glenn hissed, slapping her on the back as she stumbled out of the helicopter.

Jumping out, she felt the team moving around her. Every nerve in her body was screaming, anticipating an IED going off or men wearing kaffiyehs letting loose with automatic rifles any second. Everything was a swirling green haze in the night goggles, the lights over the courtyard like something in a van Gogh painting.

She ran behind Glenn, his M4A1 in firing position, toward the main building.

CHAPTER 3

Brody was dreaming of Bethlehem. That first time with Jessica. They were in high school; she a sophomore, he a junior on the football team. He was a jock. Never a choice about that. Because the son of Marine chief warrant officer 02 Marion Brody aka Gunner Brody was going to damn well be a tough-as-a-mother son-of-a-bitch jock or he'd beat the shit out of the little knobhead prick until he was.

They were to meet outside the Brew on the corner of Broad and Main, the trees draped with lights for Christmas, the snowy streets toward Woolworth's crowding up with people, everyone waiting for the lighting of the big electric Christmas star on South Mountain that could be seen across the Lehigh Valley.

Jessica was the prettiest girl in school. The prettiest girl he had ever seen. But it was more than that. There was something about her. He wasn't sure what it was—he didn't even know how to explain it or express it to himself because she wasn't a slut or anything like that. Willing to explore. Curious. Willing. That was the word.

He knew she liked him and somehow he knew that it was more than sex. Although all they'd ever done was kiss. She really liked to kiss, closing her eyes and sticking out her chest just that little bit that made you want to grab her breasts, but he didn't. He held back, knowing somehow that although she wanted him to touch them, it was part of whatever high school Catholic girl thing it was for her that he not be like the other boys.

So he waited. But that wasn't the willing part. What he sensed was that she was the kind of crazy girl that if she loved you enough she would drive off a cliff in a car with you, which was something he thought about. A lot.

Because there was one thing he knew above everything else in the world. Surer than God, surer than money, surer than anything. He'd have to leave home as soon as he could, because either he'd kill Gunner Brody or Gunner Brody would kill him.

And then he saw her crunching through the dirt-webbed snow on Broad Street with her friends Emma and Olivia. She wore a red scarf, her cheeks rosy with the December cold, everyone's breath coming out in clouds, and the girls started grinning and nudging each other when they saw him and Mike. Yeah, Mike was there. His best friend, Mike Faber, had always been there since the day the Brody family had moved into the upper half of a duplex on Goepp Street.

They had come to Bethlehem from California when he was seven, because his father had gotten a job at the steel mill; Gunner Brody apparently being the last man in the state of Pennsylvania who didn't know that it was only a matter of another year or two before the plant closed and those jobs were gone forever. Except ex-Marine lifer Marion Brody didn't have that many choices after an official inquiry into the accidental death of an eighteen-year-old private at the Air Ground Combat Center in Twentynine Palms, California, involv-

ing an M224 mortar, revealed Gunner Brody with a blood alcohol level of 0.29. The finding put the Corps in the questionable position of either a highly visible court-martial of a Marine chief warrant officer with a chestful of medals or the Marine gunner's early honorable discharge, but without the full pension he'd been banking on. So they had moved from the Mohave Desert, where Nick had been born, to Pennsylvania.

But if nothing else, Marines know reconnaissance. From the minute they moved in, it took Gunner Brody less than twelve minutes to scope out the liquor store on the corner of Goepp and Linden. An hour later, Mike found Nick Brody squatting under the wooden stairs in the backyard of the duplex, his nose broken, lip split, ribs aching, and said, "I'm Mike. I live across the street. You want to come over, man? I got a Nintendo. You play Super Mario Brothers?"

Nick Brody looked at him like he was from another planet.

"Your lip's bleeding," Mike said.

"I fell."

"Sure." Mike nodded, tapping him on the shoulder with his fist, and just like that they were friends. "There's this girl," Mike had said that first day as they headed across the street. "Her name's Roxanne, but everyone calls her Rio Rita. Sometimes she leaves the curtains open. When she turns around to put her bra on, you can see her ass."

"Gosh, I can't believe it's almost Christmas," Jessica's friend Olivia said, the girls joining them at the corner for the Christmas star lighting.

They wound up at Olivia's house. Olivia produced a bottle of her parent's J&B scotch, the music was Whitney Houston and Janet Jackson, and somehow it was just the two of them, Jessica and Brody, in Olivia's sister's bedroom, on a tiny single bed, kissing so hard it was as if kissing was the only known form of sexual expression, and then she pulled off her skirt, telling him: "I'm not wearing any panties." She handed him a Trojan still in its wrapper from her purse. And all he could think was, she had thought it all out, this was her idea.

He remembered how excited they had been on that narrow bed, how beautiful she was in the slanting light coming through the venetian blinds from the streetlight outside, the exquisite feel of her—when suddenly blinding light and someone shaking him hard.

For an instant, he thought he was back in the house on Goepp Street and it was Gunner Brody, smacking him, shouting at him, "Thought you could sneak your report card past me, you little maggot jarhead." But it was his guard, Afsal Hamid, shaking him awake, hissing, "Wake up, you American piece of shit! Do you know what's happened? Of course you know. Because of you we have to go. Because of you, you motherless bastard."

"What's going on?" Brody asked.

"You know why, you dog. We have to leave because of you," unchaining Brody and throwing clothes at him.

"You pig-faced son of a whore!" Afsal kept saying. For a minute it was like six years ago when they first captured him. That time they kept beating him until they nearly killed him. And Brody remembered at one point in those first weeks screaming back at Afsal through bloody teeth, "You think you hit hard, you raghead prick? The Marine gunner used to hit me harder with his service belt every freaking time he got drunk, just because he wanted to make sure I didn't grow up to be a pussy. Harder than that every day, you son of a bitch. I'm immune to you, you bastard. So hit me harder! Harder! Harder! Harder!"

"What are you doing?" Daleel, one of the others, said to Afsal. "We have to leave. Get him ready." By now, Brody had learned enough Arabic to understand some of what was said, though not all the nuances.

"This isn't over," Afsal hissed, pulling Brody close. "First we leave. But today, I promise. Today is the day you die, American."

He quickly dressed and washed, hurried along every minute by Afsal saying, "You fool the others, pretending to be a Muslim, Nicholas Brody. But you don't fool me. This will be the last time you will be a problem for us."

What had gone wrong? he wondered. All around him, everyone was moving, stripping away everything they owned down to the walls—clothes, furniture, pots, bedding, laptop computers, weapons, explosives—and packing them away into a caravan of pickup trucks and SUVs lined up in the street outside the compound. All the lights were on and Brody didn't know why they were leaving so suddenly and in the middle of the night.

"Ahjilah! Ahjilah!" Hurry! Hurry! everyone kept telling each other; all of them, men, women, even the children, moving with purpose.

At the last minute, Abu Nazir himself came in and everyone had a quick communal breakfast. Only hot tea and pita bread. When someone started to clear the breakfast dishes, Abu Nazir told them to leave it and headed out to the lead SUV. Afsal and Daleel stayed with Brody.

When they got to the SUV, its engine running, Afsal took out a pistol and put it to Brody's head. He ordered Brody to turn around so Daleel could tie his hands with plastic cuffs. Although it was the middle of the night, the street was bright from the headlights of the vehicles lined up and Brody could see the heads of people watching from the windows of nearby buildings.

"Is this really necessary, Afsal? I don't even know where I am," Brody said over his shoulder.

Afsal didn't answer, but instead pulled a black hood over his head so he couldn't see.

"Somebody help me with this infidel," Afsal said, and Brody felt himself being heaved up and shoved on his side. They squeezed him into the back of the SUV, the compressed air pressing the hood against his face as they slammed the hatchback shut, banging his skull.

It made his ears ring and he felt dizzy, maybe concussed. And blind inside the hood. For a second or two, he might have blacked out. Then the SUV started up. He could smell the exhaust. They were moving through the streets. Through it all, something told him, this time they weren't going to hold Afsal back. Why? What had changed? Why did they have to leave? Wherever they were going, he had the sudden realization that he was extra baggage, deadweight they could no longer afford to carry. This time, they would kill him. But it had always been that way with him.

Living on a bayonet edge with Gunner Brody, the worst of it, knowing he was a coward. He had known that ever since one night when he was twelve. Something he had never told anyone except Jessica—and she couldn't see it. But he could. And nothing could fix it. Not becoming a Marine, not Parris Island and Iraq. Not combat. Nothing.

That night. The night he learned who he was. It was three days *after his twelfth birthday. Gunner Brody had bought him a BMX bike, and for a few minutes, it was almost like they were a real family.*

"Who's the best dad in the world?" Gunner Brody had said when he gave him the bike.

"You are, Dad," Nick had said, wanting it to be true. Then,

seeing a sudden dangerous glint in his father's eyes because his father always insisted on being treated like a Marine officer, added, "Sir."

Three nights later, Gunner Brody had fallen dead drunk asleep, his .45 service automatic just sitting there on the kitchen table next to the cleaning kit he hadn't even started to use before he'd fallen asleep, head on the table, mouth open, spittle drooling from the corner of his mouth. Brody's mother, Sibeal, was doing what she always did; keeping the bedroom door closed. She slept curled to make herself tiny as a snail in a corner of the bed, as far away from her husband as she could get.

Gunner Brody had been celebrating the six-week anniversary of his unemployment benefit checks running out after he got his pink slip from the steel mill. ("They promised me I'd have a job no matter what," he roared to his best friend, one-hundred-proof Old Grand-Dad. "I got the Silver Star. What'd they ever do, those jerk-offs? They promised me!") Before he'd passed out, he'd used Sibeal for a punching bag, telling her if she hadn't gotten pregnant with the little jarhead shit, he wouldn't be in this stupid fix.

And Nick finally couldn't take any more. He grabbed his Little League bat from the closet and, coming from behind, swung it at his father, hitting him across the shoulder. Gunner Brody staggered, howling in pain. He turned around and rushed Nick, kicking him in the groin, followed by an elbow jab to the face and a leg takedown.

"Hit your father, you little maggot!" he screamed. "Hit an officer, you little jarhead prick! I'll teach you!" Banging Brody's head by his hair against the floor, again and again.

"Gunner, stop it! You'll kill him! Stop! You'll kill him. Your own son!" his mother screamed. "Marion, they'll put you in prison. Is that what you want? For the love of God, stop. Sweet Mary, Mother of God, stop!"

"You don't get it, you little maggot," Gunner Brody said, leaning close and whispering in Nick's ear as he lay there on the floor, helpless, utterly beaten. "When I hit her, she likes it."

Later that night, something told him to wake up. Wincing, he tiptoed on bare feet to the kitchen, where he found Gunner Brody dead drunk asleep, the loaded .45 and the cleaning kit on the table in front of him, and for more than nine minutes, as he later told Jessica, he stood there in his underwear, holding the gun with both hands less than three inches from Gunner Brody's head, trying to get up the guts to squeeze the trigger.

"Because I hate him enough," he told Jessica years later, the two of them walking together after class, walking down Center Street, in a quiet tree-lined neighborhood once you got away from the high school. "I don't hate anybody in the whole world like I hate that son of a bitch. I want him dead. It's the only way out for my mom and me. I came close, Jess. I started to squeeze the trigger. I swear to God. My hand was shaking and I squeezed. Another fraction of an ounce of pressure and it would have gone off. Only I couldn't do it. And I don't know why!" he screamed, running down the street as hard as he could toward the river, Jessica running after him, yelling, "Brody, wait! Wait!"

A block or two later, he just stopped, standing on the sidewalk outside somebody's house. A real house with a lawn and white columns like it had been plunked down there from a different world, but he wouldn't look at her.

"I'm a coward," he said, knowing it was true. He should have pulled the trigger. A chance like that wouldn't come again.

"It's because you're a good person, Brody. Because you didn't want to ruin your life. You were only twelve. A kid," she said, holding him close.

She took his hand and they walked down toward the tree-lined path beside the Lehigh River. He loved that she thought he was good, but he knew it wasn't true.

What was true were the nine minutes.

But Afsal Hamid, that al-Qaeda piece of shit, he knew, Brody thought, lying there, his hands tied, head covered with the hood in the back of the SUV. Dizzy from the ride and being hit, for a moment it was as if he had lost all sense of reality because he heard a distant sound of helicopters, and for one crazy second, he could've sworn they sounded like U.S. Black Hawks. But that was impossible.

He must be hallucinating, Brody thought inside his hood in the SUV. He tried to think. They're on the move. Why? Had to get out of Dodge. Must be a long trip, though. It seemed like it was taking forever.

He froze. They were talking about him.

"What about the American, Afsal?"

"Shut up, brother."

"He's a Muslim. He prays with us."

"Your mother! He's an American. A Christian crusader. He only pretends to be a Muslim."

"Why'd we keep him so long?"

"He has his reasons," Afsal said, and Brody knew they meant Abu Nazir. "He always has his reasons."

Now he understood. Afsal meant what he said. This time they were going to kill him. So why did they take him with them?

Because they didn't want to leave the body behind. Not with his red hair and pale white skin and Made in America face. Might raise too many questions. Better to bury the body out in the desert where it would never be found. Like Tom Walker. His Marine Corps buddy, his scout sniper teammate. Oh God, Tom. I didn't mean it. At first, they just said, "Hit him!" Hit him again. And again. And again. Crying as he did it, shouting, "I'm sorry, Tom. I'm sorry. Jesus. Help me, Jesus." Until his hands felt like they were broken and he couldn't hit anymore and Tom Walker was dead.

Now finally, they were going to kill him too, Brody thought, lying there in the back of the SUV. Something else he learned on that ride, along with the endless bumping and heat and smell of gasoline. You can doze off, even in your last few precious hours on earth. Because he only woke up when they stopped moving. His last thought as he heard them open the back of the SUV was: I'm sorry, Jess. I tried. Six years a prisoner of war. I really tried.

"Get out!" Afsal barked.

Hands grabbed him and Brody stumbled out. He fell to his knees and they lifted him up and pulled off his hood. He was blinded by the light and had to squint to see.

It was no longer night. The SUV had pulled about two hundred yards off a concrete road through a sandy desert. The convoy was gone, their SUV the only vehicle in sight.

Afsal pushed Brody to his knees and took out his pistol.

"Now we finish. Finally," he said.

"Can I say the *shahadah*?" Brody said, looking up. The desert was utterly empty. The early-morning sun was just rising over a distant dune, turning the sand and everything to gold, even the faces of the men who were about to kill him. O Allah, this world is so beautiful, he thought.

"Let him. It is required," Daleel said as Afsal stepped behind Brody and pointed the pistol at the back of his head.

"Ash-hadu an laa ilaaha illallah." I bear witness there is no God but Allah. *"Wa ash-hadu anna Muhammadan rasulullah,"* Brody said. I bear witness that Muhammad is the Messenger of Allah.

He braced for the shot, his eyes open, aching to see the beauty of the sunrise till the last instant.

CHAPTER 4

The compound in Otaibah was deserted. As the SOG team searched, it was clear that although it had been recently occupied, everyone was gone. Left behind were the odds and ends of hasty departure: bits of food, crumpled clothes, empty AK-47 magazines.

"Mingus, look," Little D, a six-foot-four Texan, said, leading Carrie to what looked like the main dining room, with two long wooden tables. He handed her a crumpled Arabic newspaper they found on the floor. Although most of them could speak some Arabic, she was the only one on the team who could read it. She held it up to the light. *Al Bawaba*, a Damascus newspaper that only came out in the afternoon, she remembered. It had yesterday's date. So at a minimum, Abu Nazir or at least some of his people had still been here as of yesterday afternoon.

Glenn came out of the kitchen.

"Check this out," he told her, and touched her hand to the teapot. It was still a little warm, as was the kitchen stove. "We just missed them."

"By how much?"

"Two, three hours."

"Of course. It was dark. They left the damn lights on," she said. "Let's get airborne. There's at least fifteen, twenty of them, plus women and children. There has to be cars, SUVs, pickup trucks. They'd stay together. A convoy. Maybe we could spot them from the air."

"We can't," Glenn said, shaking his head. "For all I know, somebody in a house across the street is on the phone calling the local cops right this second. Clock's ticking, Mingus. We go airborne to look for these guys, I've got to get high enough to spot them. We light up the radar—we're just sitting ducks for the Syrian Air Force. They scramble jets, and in a couple of minutes, bam, every last one of us is dead. And Washington has to pick up the pieces."

Carrie didn't say anything. The mission had failed. She felt nauseous.

"Anybody find anything?" she asked.

"Just some clothes and stuff. Ammo magazines. What looks like Muslim Brotherhood and al-Qaeda propaganda."

"Take all of it."

"Already taken care of. We'll fine-tooth-comb it," Glenn said.

Time was becoming critical, so he didn't mention the underground concrete cell he'd found. The spot from the satellite recon. A six-foot enclosure with an iron door and chain shackles where they had obviously kept a prisoner. He'd make a note in his report. At the moment, all he could think about was getting his men out of Syria.

"Time to perform the classic military maneuver of getting the hell out of here," he added.

Lousy way to end my career, Carrie thought, standing there

in a dimly lit al-Qaeda kitchen, feeling like she'd been kicked in the stomach, her brain ping-ponging a million miles all over the place. She wasn't sure whether it was because of what was happening in front of her or because she hadn't taken her meds, but this was a game changer. No way to paper this one over. It was total mission failure. And they had only missed by a couple of hours.

How was that possible? How could Abu Nazir have known?

She watched Glenn signal his team to get ready to pull out. Covering each other, they began to move outside and back to the choppers, rotors still slowly turning. She ran to a dark corner to strip off her clothes, changing out of her combat gear and into a full-length black abaya, complete with the hijab head scarf and veil.

Time to initiate the fallback plan she and Saul had worked out, the worst-case scenario. She wasn't going back with them.

She racked her brain. Who had tipped Abu Nazir off? Because it had to be a tip-off, and very recent. No one walks out of a compound they've been living in for a couple of years in the middle of the night just hours before a CIA raid from another country unless they've been tipped by a source they consider pretty damn solid.

Cadillac? Was he a double?

Possible. True, Cadillac had given her the lead, but he hadn't been told about the SOG raid on Otaibah. Zero. He had no knowledge of any kind about what they might do with his intel about the compound or anything else. Certainly not how or when. He couldn't possibly have known. If someone had tipped Abu Nazir, it wasn't Cadillac. Not to mention that it wasn't in his interest to do so.

Because it wouldn't have been hard for Carrie to burn him to the Syrian GSD. And then it would have been Cadillac screaming his guts out in some prison torture cell, and Assad's bully boys would do it whether his wife, Aminah, was a shopping girlfriend of President Assad's wife or not. So if not Cadillac, who the hell was it? And how could they have possibly known that the raid was set for tonight?

Who knew? Could it have been someone in Rutba? FOB Delta? Could one of the SOG team . . . ?

Unlikely. None of them knew the target before they arrived at FOBD—and once they did, standard protocol was no talking about the mission with outsiders, or even among themselves, except as necessary. They were isolated. Out in the desert, in the middle of nowhere. She didn't believe it. Not the SOG team. Once at FOB Delta, there was no interaction with the locals. That was part of the protocol, although she was sure Saul and Perry would have analysts go over every second of security camera footage of their time at Delta just to make sure.

She'd have to try to figure it out later, she realized. Hurry, Carrie. Change and get moving, she told herself, putting her combat outfit and gear into her assault backpack.

That left either Langley or Baghdad Station, she thought, heading outside. They had kept it tight at Baghdad Station. Perry had strictly limited who had knowledge of the raid. Still, you couldn't run an op like this without some coordination. But it had been very closely held. Maybe ten people. Mostly Americans. But a couple of Iraqis. Including Warzer. God, she didn't want to put Warzer under any suspicion. He was having a tough enough time as it was, working both sides as a Sunni double for her and dealing with an increasingly hostile Iraqi government.

Standing in the courtyard, her abaya flapping under the draft from the rotors, she handed Glenn her assault backpack. At the last second, she handwrote a quick note for him to send via JWICS when he got back to Rutba. A number quartet and just four words. The number was the private IP address of a computer at Langley whose location was untraceable—if a hacker tried, each time he would find a different inaccurate location in the world. The computer belonged to Saul and the four words, with letters scrambled in a way that only Saul would know how to unscramble, read:

"We have a leak."

Carrie hid in the shadows of a house a block away, watching as the Black Hawks rose up over the compound. First one, then the other. No flying lights, their dark shapes barely skimming over the roofs of the houses, they headed east toward the desert, watched by one or two cautious heads peeking out from nearby open windows.

The sound of the helicopters faded, lost in the dark, starless sky. Carrie stood frozen, waiting, till one by one the curious windows closed.

She was alone.

She waited, counting minutes, until, certain no one would see or hear her, she began to walk, her footsteps sounding faintly in the dark, empty streets. She walked till she was well away from the compound, and then found a place to hide behind a shed at the back of a house with a yard and a chicken coop.

She was tired, but knew she couldn't sleep. She waited silently, not moving, till even the chickens that she'd heard clucking got accustomed to her presence. In the gray light before dawn, she used a compact mirror to put on brown contact lenses and used a brown tint to color her eyebrows. During her time in Rutba, she'd used enough sunscreen to get a slight tan beyond her normal reaction to sun: beet red. Enough for her face and hands, the only things that would show.

A little after dawn, roosters crowing, the streets started to stir. Wearing her veil, she walked to a nearby souk and bought a basket of fruit from a farmer just opening his stall. Carrying the basket and looking like a local Arab woman, she caught a *servee*, a battered microbus from the souk to the bus station. There she sat with several other women and a few students to wait for the morning bus. To the world, she was just another Arab woman running errands in the city. She boarded the bus, which took about an hour and a half to do the twenty miles to the central bus station in Damascus.

She was running the backup plan. What she and Saul had talked about and hoped they'd never have to do, because it meant something had gone very wrong.

From the bus station she caught a taxi to Martyrs Square, with its Ottoman pillar, palm trees, and cheap hotels bordering the square. Walking as quickly as she could without attracting attention, she doubled back, then went around several other blocks in opposite directions to flush any tails. When she was sure she was clean, she went to the safe house, a top-floor apartment on Al Nasr Street, a block from the Palace of Justice.

There she finally cleaned up and changed into jeans and a top—got rid of the contact lenses; no more abaya and veil, thank God—and took out her new cover ID from a book safe and went over the paperwork. It was all there: driver's license, passport, visas, entry stamps—which, if anyone checked, would be in the Syrian immigration and security computers; the Company, as they called the CIA, was always very good about that—were in order.

She was now Jane Meyerhof, a travel agent for Midwest Continental Travel, out of Cincinnati. She called and booked a room at the Cham Palace Hotel, then used the drop to contact Cadillac.

It was a dual-contact approach. First she called his work from a pay phone at a tobacco kiosk. She left a message from a Captain Maher Dowayih asking him to call, but gave no return phone number. That was the emergency signal to Cadillac to urgently check the drop within two hours.

The drop itself was a rug shop in the maze of the Al-Hamidiya Souk, the immense iron-roofed market that bordered the legendary Umayyad mosque. The shop was owned by an asset Saul had pinched from the Israeli Mossad, a one-legged Syrian Kurd, Orhan Barsani, who sat in his shop all day, smoking an apple-tobacco *shisha* and playing *tawla*, a form of backgammon, with his fellow merchants, and anyone else he could sucker into playing, because, as rumor had it, he never lost.

Now, as she sat in a Damascus café on a sunny afternoon, sipping coffee, nibbling a slice of baklava, and watching people walk by and the honking cars on Al Nasr Street, one thing was becoming crystal clear: a leak like this, that involves a Top Secret SOG mission that suddenly gets delivered to IPLA, doesn't happen by accident. Either somebody talked out of turn or something far worse.

They had a mole.

She took a taxi to the Al-Hamidiya Souk, first walking past the rug shop to make sure it was clear to approach, then coming back. Orhan had an antique Persian-Kurdish yellow rug thrown on a chair; the signal it was clear to approach. She went in and poked around.

Orhan was playing *tawla* with a cigarette-smoking Syrian businessman in sunglasses and a mustache. Orhan threw the dice, made his move, then stood up and said to Carrie in accented English, pointing at the yellow rug:

"Please, madam, so beautiful lady. It is of the genuine Kurdish-Persian antique. This is tribal and handmade, of very finest of the Bidjar quality. Here, let me turn it over for you to see the knots of handmade, madam." Showing her.

"Very nice," she said. "I have a friend who likes such things." Hoping he understood she was talking about Cadillac.

With his eyes, Orhan indicated that Cadillac hadn't come in. Not yet.

"Please sit"—he gestured—"dearest beautiful lady madam. Would you like tea? Café? Perhaps a cold *gazooza*, yes?"

She sat, her back to the businessman, her back blocking his view. Checking the front of the shop to make sure no one was watching, she slipped the black flash drive into the brass pot under the table

Two minutes later, despite Orhan's entreaties—"We have many, many carpets, dearest lady, of finest Isfahan, so many"—she left the shop. With a shrug to his businessman friend, Orhan went back to his game.

That evening, back at the apartment on Al Nasr Street with all the lights out, Carrie stood, peering from behind the edge of the heavy drapes with binoculars at the sidewalk café across the street. At this point, she was ready to pull the emergency eject handle on this one. The black flash drive she had left at the drop at Orhan's shop in the Al-Hamidiya Souk contained a bunch of videos, cute stuff about dogs and children. Anyone who looked at it would see nothing unusual. But inside one of the videos, she had embedded a Word file that only the CIA software she'd given Cadillac would find. On the Word file were instructions to meet her at the sidewalk café, which was, although Cadillac didn't know it, directly across the street from the safe house.

She had arranged to meet Cadillac at the café at 7:15 tonight, and included the sentence "I saw your cousin Abdulkader at the Jaish versus Horriya football game," the code words "cousin Abdulkader" meaning "extreme urgency." Just in case, she had also sent him an email about the soccer match, supposedly coming from the same mythical cousin Abdulkader, using code to give him the name of the café on Al Nasr Street.

She'd picked that café so she could watch it herself from the relative protection of the safe house before she went there, because operating in Syria was always dangerous and that was even before the mission failure at Otaibah. Take it easy, Carrie, she told herself as she watched people going inside the café or sitting at the outside tables. Whatever was going on, she was alone, deep in the red zone.

She checked her watch one last time: 8:21 P.M. Cadillac wasn't coming. And she had no way of knowing if he was still operational.

Game over, she thought. She should report to Saul and get back to the hotel, the posh Cham Palace. But even that wasn't simple. Nothing in Syria ever was, she thought, grabbing her jacket and shoulder bag. On an impulse, she decided to give it one more try. She would go to the café herself, on the off chance that Cadillac had sent someone else. It nearly cost her her life.

She walked up the long block to the corner by the Palace of Justice and crossed over to the other side of Al Nasr. She started coming back down the street toward the café when suddenly two black Toyota SUVs raced past her. Instinctively, Carrie froze, then, looking around, went over to a shop window, where she pretended to examine the display. Men's shoes.

The Toyotas screeched to a halt in front of the café. A

man's body was thrown from the front vehicle onto the street. A woman screamed. The doors of the second SUV opened and four men in suits came rushing out.

The men ran to the sidewalk café and began grabbing customers, shouting and demanding to see their identity cards. One young man—he looked like a student in a windbreaker—began to run and one of the men took out a pistol and shot him in the leg. The young man went down. They grabbed both him and the young woman he had been sitting with and hustled them into the lead vehicle. The two SUVs drove off into the night.

No one said a word. This was Syria.

Everyone who had been sitting in the café hurriedly left. The owner of the café had his employees take the chairs and tables inside and closed up the place. No one approached the dead man lying in the street. Cars slowed down and drove around the body. No one stopped.

Carrie walked carefully down the street toward the café, scanning the buildings and cars for security cameras and watchers. She was taking a huge chance, but there was no choice. The needle was way over the red line on this one. Langley would have to know. She had to know the dead man's identity.

Just a few feet closer, she thought. If she could just get a look at his face, her eyes darting everywhere, because there were sure to be watchers.

The body was lying on its side, a hand outstretched as if asking for something. It was difficult to see clearly in the dark. Then the headlights of an approaching taxi lit the man's face for an instant and there was no mistake.

Cadillac. Mosab Sabagh. Her agent. There were cigarette burns on his face and something funny about the fingers of his hand. Was that nail polish? Jesus! They had cut off the ends of his fingers.

She wanted to throw up, but kept walking. She had to get away, fast. The lights and shadows of the street around her were a blur. She wanted to look around, but didn't dare. If there were GSD agents nearby, they might take her into custody any second. As the taxi slowed to go around the body, she signaled for it to stop. It was all so surreal. People were acting normally a few feet from a dead man. Everyone was afraid. Neither she nor the driver acknowledged that there was anything unusual, even though he had deliberately slowed to circle his taxi around the body.

She got in and told the driver to take her to Leila's.

"Yes, madam," the driver said.

Leila's was a popular restaurant in the Old City that overlooked the famous Umayyad mosque. At the moment, Carrie didn't give a damn about Leila's, but she desperately needed to call Saul and figured it would take the driver some time to negotiate the traffic and crowds in the narrow streets of the Old City.

Although the ride might take twenty-five minutes, once she started the call, she probably had only three or four minutes before the Syrian GSD and military security would start GSP-tracking the cell phone call. After that, she would have only another two or three minutes before they took her into custody.

The Syrian Security Forces, the army, the Mukhabarat, and the GSD monitored all calls, land and cell phone, and Internet in Syria, especially those to places out of the country. This one would certainly raise red flags all over the place for them, especially once they realized that it originated near Cadillac's body, that it was being scrambled, and that they couldn't decipher it with their normal decryption tools.

They would quickly understand that it was a foreign intelligence service—automatically jump to the conclusion it was either CIA or the Israeli Mossad, because that's how their minds worked—and there would be teams of GSD agents racing toward her cell phone's location as fast as they could go. The only question was how long it would take for them to latch on to it.

The trick was to keep the call short and sweet, use no names, and get rid of the cell phone's SIM card as fast as she could, before she arrived at the restaurant.

She dialed Saul's number, thinking, Please pick up. Please. Please. She checked her watch. It would be around 2:45 in the afternoon on the East Coast. Saul should be in his office in Langley. Someone picked up.

"Hi, it's me," she said. There was no time for passwords. This was all about recognizing voices.

"I got your message. Are you okay?" Saul's voice, flooding her with relief. Thank God. Just hearing him made her feel a little safer for the first time since the Black Hawk had lifted off from FOB Delta. He was letting her know he'd gotten the note about the leak from Glenn.

"I'm okay. I'm in Damascus. I love it," she said, nearly choking on that last bit. Make it fast, she told herself. The Syrians will be onto this sooner than you think. We don't know what they got out of Cadillac or how much. And she hadn't even had a chance to check on Orhan yet. Oh God, Orhan.

"I'm a little worried about the car," Saul said. Cadillac.

"You should be. It's pretty bad. I don't think it's going to make it," she said.

"How bad?" She could hear in his voice just how bad this news was. First the failed SOG mission, now Cadillac down. This was shaping up as a total disaster. Was the network blown?

How to let him know in such a way so that the Syrians—if they managed to decipher their conversation—wouldn't understand?

"Remember last Christmas?" she asked. Saul had flown into Baghdad. They'd all gotten together, her, Perry, Warzer, some of the other key CIA personnel, in his room at the Al-Rasheed Hotel in the Green Zone, everyone getting plastered and telling stories over Scotch and Russian Standard martinis and Mrs. Fields cookies.

When it was his turn, Saul had told them about growing up in the only Orthodox Jewish family in Calliope, Indiana, and how when he was a kid, on Christmas Eve, when his parents were asleep, theirs the only house without a tree or lights or presents in the whole town, he would sneak down and watch the black-and-white movie *A Christmas Carol* on TV. "The one you told us. Do you remember the first line of that story?" Come on, Saul. The first line of the Charles Dickens story: "Marley was dead." "That's how bad," she said, hoping to God he'd get her meaning.

For a moment, he didn't answer. Please say something, she thought, the seconds ticking. Please. With every second, she could feel the GSD closing in on her, imagining Toyota SUVs, tires screeching as they surrounded the taxi, blocking off the street any second now.

"Are you absolutely sure?" He got it. God, he was smart. She loved that about him.

"A thousand percent," she said grimly, trying not to think of Cadillac's body, what they had done to him, what they might do to her.

"Any idea what might have caused it?" he asked. She had nothing, only speculation. He wanted to know if she'd spotted something, someone. But in her heart, she knew. Cadillac, the deserted compound, just missing by a few hours. None of it was a coincidence and it wasn't the SOG team. They'd had nothing to do with Damascus. There could be only one possible explanation.

"I'm thinking maybe it was an animal." Come on, Saul. I'm all alone and we're getting killed out here. What the hell do you think it is? Because I'm thinking a mole. A small furry animal that likes to dig, doesn't he, the miserable worm-eating son of a bitch?

"I'm thinking the same. You'd better get going," he said.

She was right, she thought, exhaling, not realizing she'd been holding her breath. Saul agreed with her. They had a mole. And he was also telling her to get the hell out of Syria. Now.

"I will. Just have to check on something," she said. Orhan.

"Take care," he said, and hung up.

She checked her watch. Four minutes. Too damn long. The GSD would be onto her. They would be closing in on her taxi any minute. She opened the cell phone and, with her fingers fumbling and sweating, took three tries to take the stupid SIM card out of the cell phone. Come on, Carrie. Come on, she told herself.

The taxi's back window was half open. She checked the driver's eyes in the rearview mirror. He was watching her.

"Keep your eyes on the road, please," she told him, and waited to see that he did. She looked to see where she was. All around were the older buildings of the Old City, TV satellite dishes sprouting on the roofs like mushrooms. Still plenty of traffic despite the hour. When she was sure the driver wasn't watching, she tossed the SIM card out the window. Ahead, she could see the dome and minarets of the Umayyad mosque.

"I changed my mind," she told the taxi driver. "I want to go to Naranj, not Leila's."

"Naranj, madam? On Straight Street?" Naranj was a famous restaurant. As for Straight Street, it was the oldest street in Damascus, maybe in the world. It was mentioned in the Bible.

"Yes," she said. "Go around the mosque."

"It's better if I turn around and go back, madam," he said.

Yes, and get stopped by the GSD, she thought, her nerves drawing tight as violin strings. God, was her bipolar kicking in? Not now, please, feeling her heart rate skyrocket. Take it easy, Carrie. She had taken a clozapine. It just had to kick in.

"I'm not in a hurry. Go the back way," she said, waiting till they had gone four or five blocks before she dropped the empty cell phone—minus its SIM card—out the window, hearing the faint plastic click as it hit the cobblestone street.

Now there was nothing to connect her to the call except the driver, she thought as they drove behind the Umayyad mosque, which supposedly contained the head of John the Baptist, as well as the tomb of Saladin, the great Muslim warrior who defeated the Crusaders. They zigzagged around the outside of the mosque to Al Sagha Street, then over to Straight Street. Somewhere behind them, she heard the sound of police sirens.

She didn't like the way the taxi driver looked at her when he dropped her off in front of Naranj, a platoon of Mercedes and Porsches parked in front of its high arched windows. If questioned, that taxi driver would remember her. Maybe because of Cadillac's body. Not good. She had to get away from here as quickly as possible, she thought as Naranj's doorman bowed and opened the door and she went inside.

Damascus was becoming too dangerous. But she had to find out if Cadillac ever made it to the drop. And if he had left something for her. And what had happened to Orhan. Because if the GSD had finished with Cadillac, there was a good chance that Orhan was next. And the clock was ticking.

As always, Naranj was crowded and noisy, the two-story, high-ceilinged restaurant filled with the most important people in Syria, from political leaders to TV stars. At first, the maître d' looked at her oddly, a woman alone, just standing there, but then, taking a good look: an attractive American woman, long blond hair, not wearing evening clothes, but still, borderline, perhaps somebody important's mistress, best not to offend till one was sure.

"Are you meeting someone, miss?"

"Yes, but I just saw his wife's Mercedes, that lying son of a whore! Is there a back way out?" Carrie whispered, slipping him a twenty-dollar bill.

"Of course." The maître d' smiled, pocketing the bill smoothly as he motioned to a waiter and whispered instructions. He gestured for Carrie to follow the waiter, who led her to a corner of the crowded atrium toward the back of the dining room, the thick smell of kebabs wafting from the kitchen. The waiter led her to a side door and outside to a sidewalk terrace and the street. She had gotten turned around, but now she realized where she was. They were on a side street opposite the big St. Mary's Greek Orthodox Church, lit up a bright white in the night behind an arched facade.

She tried to tip the waiter, but he refused any money. He stepped out into the middle of the street and refused to leave until he had waved down a yellow taxi. The waiter opened the taxi door for her.

"God willing, all will be good, madam," he said, as if he knew she was in trouble.

"God willing," she murmured back.

"Where to, madam?" the driver asked.

Time to decide, she thought, her throat dry, unable to swallow. It was incredibly high risk. Every second she stayed in Syria, the danger increased exponentially. By now the Syrians had to know about the Black Hawk incursion into their airspace. Plus Cadillac had been tortured and killed. There was a damn good chance he had told them about the drop location, in which case the GSD would be sitting there, waiting for whoever showed up.

A female CIA agent would be an unbelievable catch for them. What was in her head could blow everything Langley had going in the Middle East wide open. The downside risk was enormous. If they got their hands on her, the GSD would open her like a can of tuna.

What a coup it would be—not just for them, but also for their patrons: the Iranians and the Russians. And what a disaster for the CIA, for the United States, for Saul.

On the other hand, there was a chance that before he was picked up, Cadillac left something for her at the drop. If she could do a quick in and out before the GSD got to Orhan's shop, she might be able to salvage some intel out of this whole mess. And what about Orhan? If Cadillac hadn't revealed the location of the drop under torture before he died, she could warn Orhan, maybe save him.

Time to bet. Only the stakes weren't just her life, she was risking her country too.

"Where to, madam?" the driver asked again, his finger tapping impatiently on the wheel.

"The Al-Hamidiya Souk. Hurry," she said.

CHAPTER 5

Al-Hamidiya Souk
Damascus, Syria
12 April 2009
19:14 hours

"This amber necklace is made for you, madam. It brings out the gold of your hair, the blue-green of your eyes, like the sea," the merchant said, his hand tracing the curve of Carrie's hair in the air. He was the same mustached businessman in sunglasses she had seen playing *tawla* with Orhan earlier in the day. There was a good chance he had just saved her life.

"How do I know it's real amber?" she said.

"Many ways." He smiled. "Feel it grow warm in your hand. Real amber is alive. Rub it with a piece of soft cloth or fur. It will become charged with static electricity and attract lint and dust. Did you know the ancient Greeks called amber 'electron'? The word 'electricity' comes from amber." Again he smiled. "There are simple tests for true amber. Put it in salt water. Real amber floats. The fakes, plastic, glass, they all sink. Or rub a drop of alcohol or nail polish on it; doesn't bother real amber, but the fakes turn nasty. Hold it in a flame. Real amber burns nicely with a wonderful pine aroma."

"I wouldn't want to burn this," she said.

"No, miss. Allah forbid. Not this necklace."

They were in his shop in the Al-Hamidiya Souk, an Aladdin's cave of jewelry and expensive handicrafts, handmade gold, silver, and amber jewelry, Damascene silk brocades hanging from racks, copper engraved pots and vessels, mother-of-pearl-inlaid tables. "One of fourteen shops I own," he told her.

Carrie had been walking fast toward Orhan's shop in the souk, checking for watchers, but seeing nothing out of the ordinary. Despite the late hour, there were still plenty of shoppers and a few tourists wandering the lanes of the souk; some young people gathered at an ice cream stand. Most of the shops were open, but strangely, many of the shopkeepers were not at the front, beckoning people inside as they normally did. True, it was late, nearly time to close, but still, not normal.

Internal alarm bells began to go off. Her skin began to prickle all over, like before one of her descents into depression, the opposite of her bipolar "flights," when she wasn't on either lithium or clozapine. The black times when she could barely move, when she would sit for hours, days even, catatonic; the only ray of light, the terrible beckoning seduction of the small Glock 26 pistol in her handbag. Lift me out, it seemed to call to her. Why go through it all when you can end it with a little squeeze of the trigger? Trying to tell herself, it's not me, it's the bipolar talking. It's not you, Daddy, because sometimes it was the voice of her father, Frank. And it's not me.

Something was happening. The souk seemed normal enough. The strolling water vendors, the side streets open to the night, the women in hijabs with plastic shopping bags. But was it her imagination, or were two shopkeepers talking furtively to each other as she approached the turn that led to Orhan's shop? And there was a man in a suit jacket talking

into a Bluetooth headset while standing next to a shop selling
women's shoes. Shit, she thought.

The question now was whether they had arrested Orhan
already. The needle was off the chart on this approach. She
decided to get near enough to see if his shop was open and then
leave by a side street.

"Do you remember me, lovely miss?" The merchant who
had been with Orhan earlier in the day had stepped out of his
shop into the passageway. Then coming closer, he whispered:
"The rug dealer is dead. Come inside."

"You were playing with Orhan," she said, stunned, as
though she'd walked into a wall. She stepped into the merchant's shop and looked around. Delayed reaction, she told
herself. Like when you just miss getting hit by a truck. For the
moment, they appeared to be alone. She said the first thing
that came into her head. "You know he cheats."

"So do I," he said, offering her a seat on a chair with an in-
tricate inlay of mother-of-pearl. Clapping his hands, the merchant told a teenage boy who suddenly materialized from the
back to bring them tea.

"Bring *baklawa* and *ghraybeh* cookies too," he added. As the
boy left, he introduced himself. "Aref Tayfouri, miss. Businessman; also import export."

"And what game are we playing now, Mr. Tayfouri?" she
asked, exhaling. Suddenly realizing she'd been holding her
breath all that time.

He leaned closer.

"Listen, miss. I don't know what this is. I don't know what
Orhan's done. I don't know you. I don't want to be involved," he
whispered, at the same time showing her an exquisite honey-amber
necklace with a gesture that would not have been out of place from
a courtier presenting a crown to a queen. "Lovely, isn't it, miss?"

"Why are you helping me?" she asked, her eyes darting to check out passersby, then looking at the necklace. It looked very expensive. If Orhan had been arrested, the souk must be thick with GSD agents, she thought.

"I don't know. Here." He handed her a copper-and-honey-amber brooch. "A gift."

"I can't," she said, pushing it away.

"Please," he insisted, pushing it back to her. "It's from your friend. For you, lovely miss. Perhaps to match the beautiful necklace, if you would like to buy," he said loudly, then whispered urgently: "Truly, I thought of throwing it away. But what if they traced it to me? Ah, good, the chai," as the boy brought the tea and pastries on a copper tray. "Please," gesturing for her to enjoy.

Carrie took a sip of the tea and a bite of *baklawa*. She wasn't sure how far to trust this Tayfouri; clearly he was scared and out of his depth. Or pretending to be. Making sure no one was watching, she pinned the brooch on her blouse based on the theory of hiding in plain sight. But first she needed to confirm that it had come from Orhan and when.

She fingered the amber necklace. It looked expensive.

"Lovely," she murmured. "When did he give it to you?"

"The brooch is mine, madam. It has a clasp that opens. I thought it best, understand?" he whispered back.

She nodded. There was something concealed inside.

"Barsani came to me barely an hour before they came for him," he went on. "How he knew they were coming, I have no idea. The rumor in the souk is that when the security police came for him, they found him wrapped in his favorite yellow Bidjar rug. The rug was soaked red with blood. He had cut his own throat, the knife still sticking in it. Can you imagine?"

He took out a pack of Marlboros and lit one, his hand shaking. He angrily snapped the lighter shut. "I have a wife and three children, miss. I don't need this."

Two Syrian policemen armed with submachine guns walked by the entrance to the shop and looked inside. Carrie had to grab her teacup with both hands to keep it from spilling. After a moment, the two policemen walked on. Now that she thought about it, the souk had grown suddenly empty. Her nerves, never her strong suit, were screaming. She had to get away from here soon. But she was a trained operations officer. She couldn't take this at face value. She had to know why Orhan, no matter how desperate, would risk giving something for the CIA to Tayfouri.

"Why did he come to you?" she asked.

"I don't know. We're both Kurds. Do you know what that's like in this country?"

"No." She looked at him. "Tell me."

"Like walking barefoot on broken glass, miss. Carefully. Only you smile. And smile. And smile," gritting his teeth.

"So he came to you because you're both Kurds? Or maybe because you both cheat at *tawla*? What do you import-export?"

He hesitated. "That depends."

"On what?"

"On who's asking."

Strange why people do things, thinking of what it must have been like for Orhan in those last few minutes, making his choice about who to trust with whatever was in the brooch.

"I'm beginning to understand, Monsieur Tayfouri." She leaned closer to whisper. "The sooner I leave Damascus the better for both of us. Can you be of assistance?"

He thought for a moment. "Do you know Aleppo?"

After leaving Tayfouri's shop in the souk, she took three taxis and a *servee* microbus, all going in opposite directions so that she had to run from one vehicle to another, to make sure no one had followed her from the souk before she risked going back to her room at the Cham Palace.

Back at the hotel, there were the usual low-level GSD watchers sitting and looking bored in the lavish lobby and atrium, but no one seemed particularly interested in Jane Meyerhof, she thought. She went over to the concierge's desk and asked him to make arrangements for a bus trip to Aleppo.

"You will like Aleppo, madam. It is famous for its mother-of-pearl inlaid boxes. Many important sights, although not like Damascus, of course," the concierge said.

"Of course. Thank you," she said, paying him for the tickets and heading for the elevator.

Once in her room, she locked the door and took her time going over the room and bathroom, checking for bugs and hidden cameras. The room was clean except for the normal GSD bug in the room telephone, which she left alone. She used that phone to call room service to order a sandwich and a mint lemonade and got to work on her laptop.

Inside the amber brooch was a compartment containing a thumb drive. She hefted it grimly in her palm. Orhan—and maybe Cadillac too—had died to get this to her. She plugged the drive into her laptop, turned on the sound, and suddenly she was watching people dancing at a wedding led by the young couple, the bride in white, swaying in front of a multi-tiered cake.

She lurched to turn down the sound and close the laptop, because right then there came a knock at the door. She grabbed her pistol, holding it behind her back, and moved to the door.

It was a waiter with her sandwich and drink. He brought it in. She waited till he had gone, then started the video again, this time with the sound turned low. Whose wedding? she wondered. Then she saw Cadillac and his wife among the guests. They had taught Cadillac well, she thought wryly. Looking at this video, the GSD would assume it was just an ordinary wedding video. They'd watch it, but never see it for what it really was.

Next, she ran the NSA software that parsed out a file hidden in the video. The software pulled millions of bits together to create an .avi file, which she titled "Damascus sights." She put in her earplug and, placing her pistol beside her on the bed, sat down to run the file.

The video lasted less than a minute and thirty seconds. After she ran it, she sat there, stunned. It changed everything. A whole new ball game. All she could think was, I have to get this to Saul ASAP.

Her instincts had been screaming for her to leave Damascus. With the SOG team incursion and the deaths of both Cadillac and Orhan, right now she was in the bull's-eye of the red zone. She couldn't risk trying to communicate with Saul from here. Her only chance was to get out of town and send the intel to Saul from Aleppo.

The video had been taken with a hidden camera. In all likelihood, the one concealed in the sunglasses Carrie had personally given to Cadillac at their second meeting in Beirut. It had to have been taken by Cadillac himself.

It was in two parts. The first locale was obvious. One of the restaurants clustered on the ridge of Mount Qasioun, the mountain that loomed over Damascus. In this most ancient of cities, it was said that it was on these slopes that Cain killed Abel.

She could tell it had been shot close to sunset, the lights just coming on in the city spread out below and the lamps of the restaurant on, but despite the shadows, still enough sunlight to see, although not clearly. It showed two men talking at a table, with a breathless voice-over by Cadillac. One of the men was an Arab in an expensive suit. Because of the angle from which the footage was shot, she could only see the Arab's back and, just for one second when he turned, part of the side of his face. My God, Carrie thought. Could it be him? Abu Nazir? Was it possible this was an actual sighting? There was no way to tell who the Arab really was. Nothing definite; a man's back. But still, something told her Cadillac had delivered something important. A shiver went through her. Seated at the table with him was a European in a striped shirt worn outside checked wool trousers, talking while he ate a slice of pizza.

The voice-over was by Cadillac. Added later, she thought.

"The man in the suit is Abu Nazir," Cadillac's voice said in Arabic. It could be him, Carrie thought. It absolutely could be him. "I don't know the name of the man he is with, but I've heard him referred to as 'the Russian.' But here's something interesting. Seated at the table next to them." As Cadillac spoke, the video moved to the next table, where three Syrian men were sitting, all wearing white shirts and ties.

The three men were eating little dishes of *mezze*. One of them was smoking a *shisha* water pipe and watching the next table with great interest.

"I know the one smoking the *shisha*," Cadillac said on the voice-over. "His name is Omar al-Mawasi. He is definitely GSD. All these guys are GSD. They're calling the guy with Abu Nazir 'the Russian.'"

And then Cadillac must've pointed the pen with the hidden microphone at Abu Nazir's table. It caught a jumble of voices in Arabic and a bit of the man Cadillac said was Abu Nazir and the Russian speaking in English.

". . . will change the course of the war," Abu Nazir said. The voice, even with the poor quality of the recording and the noise of conversations, was somehow familiar. She stopped the video and played it again. And again. She'd heard the voice before somewhere, searching her memory for where. She played more of the video.

"Your action will change everyth—" the Russian said, the rest drowned out by someone at another table saying something in Arabic about a car accident on Al Katheeb Road.

". . . regret the necessity of having to leave . . ." the Russian said amid a jumble of voices, including one of the GSD men at the next table talking about getting reimbursed.

"An inconvenience. We always planned for such a . . ." Abu Nazir said, the rest lost in background noise. And then she had it. Back in 2006. The ruins of the porcelain factory in Ramadi and the recorded conversation and the voice of the man who had interrogated her agent, Walid Karim, code-named Romeo. It was him! Abu Nazir! It was his voice. She was certain of it.

That section of the video ended and it left Carrie's mind reeling. It confirmed—at least tentatively—that Abu Nazir had been hiding in Syria, and for some time, with the connivance of the Syrian government. The Syrians were playing both ends against the middle. But who was the European, the Russian? What did he have to do with it? Or with IPLA? More important, what was Abu Nazir planning that would change the course of the war in Iraq?

The date of the recording had been automatically imprinted on it by the camera. Two days ago. Two days! Could the Russian have been warning Abu Nazir about the SOG team op? My God, was that it? Did Cadillac actually see it happen without knowing it? Because the timing was unbelievable.

It was a breakthrough! Proof positive of a leak. And even better, a lead. The Russian. Saul would go nuts over this, she thought, racing to finish the video. That was a mistake.

The second part of the video was gut-wrenching. It was jerky footage shot by Cadillac while walking on a wide, busy Damascus street, probably 17th of April Street, near his office. The video was nothing special; people and cars going by. The part that killed her was Cadillac's voice-over.

"Billie . . ." The cover name she had used with him—for jazz singer Billie Holiday. "I think I'm discovered. I got your captain message and the Cousin Abdulkader emergency message. I will try meeting you at the café tonight, but I have to tell you, I think I am done. Today, I saw my commander, Tariq. He and I go back many years. But this time, instead of the normal way he usually looks at me, or nods, he looked away.

"I have never in my life felt as I felt at that moment. My whole body began to sweat. We say in Arabic, as if someone is crying on my grave.

"So I said something to him about 'those idiots in the petrol depot. They got the amounts wrong again.' This is something we both always complain about. But instead of agreeing, or calling them 'asses' as usual, he just looked at me. Such a look, Billie. It turned my blood to ice. He said nothing, just walked on. This man is my friend, Billie.

"Then in my office. Not a single phone call. No new emails. Nothing. No junior officers. No colleagues stopping by. It is like the word has gone out. I am *haram*. Forbidden. I left work early. I will try to get this to the drop in the souk now if I can. I will come to the café tonight, but I feel it coming. The noose is closing around me. Please, if you get this, help my family. Get them out of Syria. Don't let them be refugees, Billie. You can do this. I know you can do this. *Allahu akhbar*, Billie."

God is great, she translated numbly to herself as the video ended.

Damn, damn, damn, she thought. And then Cadillac had

led them right to Orhan. A shiver went down her spine. And they almost got me . . . closing the laptop and sliding the pistol under her pillow as she got into bed.

She woke up sweating in the middle of the night. In the darkness, she had no idea where she was. A sense of panic closed in. Then she remembered. Her hotel room. Still in Damascus.

She went to the window and peeked out from behind the curtain at the city, the strangely yellow streetlights and the minarets of mosques. Her mission sense was prickling all over her skin like a terrible itch. I have to get out of here, she thought.

CHAPTER 6

Aleppo, Syria
13 April 2009

In the year 1123, Baldwin II, king of Jerusalem, made what was for him a rare tactical error and was captured in battle by the Seljuk Turk Belek, who held him prisoner for two years in the Citadel castle in Aleppo. The massive white-stone castle still gleamed in the afternoon sun on its acropolis, an outcropping of rock over the Aintab plateau that had been used as a fortress since long before history. But it held little interest for Carrie, except for a few cell-phone snapshot photos that she would need.

Coming from the bus station, her only real interest in Aleppo was the Internet café someone on the bus had mentioned. They said it was on Noureddin Zinki, a street that radiated north from the Citadel castle, which could be seen from all over the city.

Once in the café, she sat next to a young Syrian college student. She got online, plugged in the flash drive, and uploaded Cadillac's video file via a CIA cover website. The site, presumably for a freight forwarding company, was actually a server in Hamburg used to bounce files to a Vimeo-like international video website.

Once the video was on the website, she sent an encrypted email to Saul's private IP address. She sent her report in a file encrypted within photo JPEG files of the Aleppo Citadel castle that she attached to her email.

The email ended: "Can you believe it? I think I saw an aardvark. Hope to see you soon. Hugs and kisses." "Aardvark" was CIA code for Flash Critical; the highest possible urgency.

After she pressed Send, she plugged in the separate NSA flash drive that deleted all traces of everything she had done, all evidence that she had even been there, not just on the Internet café's computer, but on the servers it linked to across Syria. Once Saul read her report, he would retrieve the video file from the Vimeo-like website and then have the NSA delete it from the website without anyone ever knowing it had been there.

She had gotten it to Saul, she thought, relieved, coming out of the café. Walking down the street with its palm trees, feeling the late-afternoon sunlight, smelling falafel from a street vendor, she felt lighter, better.

Now Saul will take care of it, she thought. He would come up with a game plan and we would get the mole that prevented us from capturing Abu Nazir. Someone must know who this mysterious Russian was. Maybe the CIA's Moscow Station had intel on him? Now she would go to ground and wait till she received instructions from Saul. Thank goodness he was there in Langley, putting all the pieces together.

She had no way of knowing that at that moment, Saul was about to get fired.

CHAPTER 7

"Wait a minute, Bill. This Saul, this genius master spy. This super-star. Mona Lisa and all that. You were going to fire him?"

"I came close, Senator. Damn close. Look at what happened: Our Middle East operations had been in trouble for some time. Abu Nazir's IPLA knew every damn thing we were going to do before we did. We took a humongous risk and invaded Syria with an SOG team and came up empty. An operation he pushed, that was strictly on his dime. Not only that, we had our top asset in Syria dead, tortured; our network in Syria completely blown to hell. Abu Nazir had disappeared, and after years of work we were back to square one. He's our Middle East Division chief! The buck has to stop somewhere. What would you do? It was a complete and total balls-up. You know how it works around here. Somebody's head had to roll."

"What about the girl, Bill? This female operations officer. He took a helluva risk with her."

"That's another thing, Mr. President. He put a female CIA operations officer into a hostile red zone completely on her own. Alone, with no backup. To handle an unbelievably dangerous operation without any support. What if she had been killed—or worse, captured? He put all our operations in the Middle East at risk."

"What do you mean all?"

"Carrie Mathison was out of our Beirut and Baghdad Stations. She knew everything. I mean everything. Our assets, networks, codes, contacts, every one of us. Everything. What if the Syrians had captured her? What if they had turned her over to Hezbollah or the Iranians? Or the Russians? Think what they could have squeezed out of her. It would have been . . . well, I'm not sure how we would have recovered, but one thing's for damn sure. A lot of very good people would have died. And as far as the war in Iraq was concerned, we could've quit right there. Game over. Do you blame me?"

"What did he say when you confronted him about her?"

"You want to know, Senator? He said, 'She's a big girl. She can take care of herself.' Like it was nothing. No big deal."

"I'm wondering, Bill, she'd come up with this lead about a Russian. Didn't you factor that in?"

"We didn't know about it. Not then, Warren. I had called an emergency, early-morning meeting in my West Wing office. Me; the CIA director and deputy directors; David Estes, director of the Counterterrorism Center; Saul. But it was mostly me, yelling at him. And him, sitting there, looking like a rabbi who forgot his yarmulke."

"What did he say?"

"That I was jumping the gun. That we had to wait for Mathison's report."

" 'We don't even know if she's alive!' I said. At that point we didn't. The SOG team barely made it back to Rutba. 'We're losing assets,' I said. To hell with firing him. I wanted to punch him in the nose. And him. Just sitting there like a bearded Yoda, blinking behind his glasses.

" 'She's operational,' he said.

"'How the hell do you know?' Estes asked him. You know what he said?

"'She's good.'

"That was his answer. She's good. Like it was a mantra. Do you believe this shit? We all looked at each other. I was on the verge of firing him on the spot. I swear I almost did it right there and then."

"Why didn't you?"

"Two things, Warren. Two things every one of us should never forget. Remember Congressman Jimmy Longworth?"

"Longworth of Missouri. Who could forget Jimmy Longworth? You should've known him, Mr. President. Unbelievable character. What about him?"

"When I first came to Washington, I got into a pissing contest with one of the agencies. Jimmy stopped by my office with a bottle of Jack Daniel's and two glasses and said, 'Billy Boy, in Washington, if you learn nothing else, remember one thing. You can make life miserable for an Old Hand, but you never ever want to fire him.' When I asked, 'Why not?' he said, 'Because Old Hands know where the bodies are buried. You fire one of them, they'll go. They won't say a word. They'll make damn sure they got their pensions nice and clear. Then six months later, you'll find yourself talking to some smartass reporter from the Washington Post or maybe a grand jury on something that'll bring down the whole administration including you. And you're done for the rest of your life. That's why.'"

"What's the second reason?"

"My predecessor as CIA director. He told me something I never forgot. 'Saul's biggest problem is morality; but he's not only ten times smarter than you think you are, Warren, with all your Harvard Phi Beta bullshit and all, he's also the smartest Jew son of a bitch you'll ever meet. So after you finish yelling at him—and believe me, sooner or later everybody wants to—listen to what he says. Carefully.'

"So I stood up at the meeting and told Saul that he was going on administrative leave, effective immediately. And you know what?"

"What?"

"He just looked at me, Warren, with those glasses, and said he thought that was a good idea and just got up and left. We all sat there scratching our heads wondering what the hell just happened."

"So that's it? Then how on earth did we come to this mess?"

"Really, Bill. What happened?"

"Simple, Mr. President. He got the Aardvark report from the girl, Carrie. Twenty minutes later, he walked into my office. Then I got to meet the real Saul."

CHAPTER 8

That morning, Saul Berenson, CIA Middle East Division chief, publicly reprimanded at a meeting the previous day by the vice president of the United States, William Walden, and on official administrative leave, woke from a dream he hadn't had since childhood. He was alone; the house silent, empty.

His wife, Mira, was gone. Back to Mumbai, India, two days earlier. If anyone asked, it was because of her mother's illness, and to deal with the issues of Human Rights Watch, the charitable organization chapter her family ran. In reality, it was because she and Saul barely spoke anymore. There's the official and the unofficial story in marriages like everything else, Saul thought as he dressed and packed for the airport.

Sandy Gornik, an angular, curly-haired up-and-comer from the Iranian desk, took time from the office to drive him to the airport. During the drive, Saul let it slip that he was going to Mumbai to spend some time with his wife and her family.

"Have you been there before? India?" Gornik asked. He had heard about Saul almost getting fired. Nearly everyone in the NCS (National Clandestine Services), certainly everyone on the fourth floor at Langley, had heard about it. The story was topic A in the cafeteria. In fact, Sandy suspected he was probably not doing himself any good, careerwise, driving Saul to the airport.

But Gornik was one of Saul's Save-the-Dead-Drop band, a tiny group, some four or five wise-ass, mostly single-rotation ops officers who picked up crumbs of tradecraft Saul dropped as he scurried through Langley's anonymous corridors going from what he called "one moronic meeting to those where the Washington art form of wasting time reaches absolute mind-destroying perfection."

"Once," Saul said to Gornick. "Indian families are . . . well, it's like getting into bed with a tribe of octopuses. No matter which way you turn, there are arms everywhere. Trust me, it isn't simple."

"I'm sure your wife and her family will be glad to finally spend some time with you," Gornik said, hoping that came out right, that he didn't sound patronizing or like he knew Saul had been involuntarily pushed out to pasture.

"I'm not so sure," Saul said.

It caught Sandy Gornik, who always knew what to say to catch the female GS-8s and -9s trolling in Georgetown pubs, but not the real thing to someone who until yesterday had been not only his boss's boss, but something of a force, if not yet a legend, in the Company, off guard.

"Sorry," he said, face reddening.

"So am I," Saul said, looking out the window at the traffic on the I-395, and that was that.

Cover established.

Saul thought he would prep for his next meeting during the two-hour flight from Reagan International to Tampa, but instead he kept his laptop closed. Officially, he was on leave.

Officially, I don't exist, he thought, looking out the plane's window. Below, there were only wisps of clouds, and far below, the rolling green and brown hills of North Carolina.

Suspended in midair. Disconnected. A perfect metaphor.

He wondered if he would ever see his wife, Mira, again, because he certainly wasn't going to India. He wasn't even sure he would ever see Langley again. None of that mattered now. All that mattered was Carrie's intel. It had changed the equation. It was about to change everything the United States was involved with in the Middle East.

The dream.

It had come back. For years, he'd had it almost every night as a child. And then one day it stopped. The day after he told his father he didn't want to go to the old Orthodox synagogue in South Bend, the nearest to Calliope, anymore. He didn't want to be Bar Mitzvahed. And his father just looked at him, took his mother in the car, and, leaving him standing there, they drove off to the shul in South Bend without a word. Nothing. As if to say, Have your own war with God, Shaulele. You think because you say so, this is the end of the matter? You think God has nothing to say too?

Not a dream. A nightmare. He was a little boy in a ghetto somewhere in Europe. It was like some old black-and-white World War II movie, only it didn't feel like a movie. He was there. It was night and he was hiding in an attic. The Nazis, the Gestapo, were hunting him. He had heard someone talking, and even though he didn't understand the language, he understood they were informing on him. The Nazis knew he was there.

They were searching the lower floors of the house, coming closer. He could hear their dogs, German shepherds, panting, coming closer. Closer. He didn't know where his parents were. In the concentration camps. Gone. Alive? Dead? He didn't know. He didn't know where anybody was. All the Jews were gone. He had been alone for days, weeks, without food. Living like a rat. Scavenging food from trash in the alleys at night; licking water from dirty pipes in the coal cellar. But now somebody had told on him and they were coming for him.

The Nazis were talking in German, a language he didn't know, although it was close enough to Yiddish that he got a sense of it. He was so afraid he couldn't move. One of the dogs barked twice, very loud. It was close. Too close, just on the other side of the closet door. Suddenl, the door opened and light spilled in.

"Heraus!" one of the soldiers shouted. The soldiers had rifles, but the ones he truly feared were two men who wore black leather overcoats with swastika armbands and death's-head insignias on their caps. The soldiers yanked him out and smacked his face so hard he saw flashes of light and the room spun. They were shouting and yelling at others as they hauled him down the stairs.

When they got outside in the street, they kicked him and stood him facing a brick building with two others, a young woman with blond Veronica Lake peekaboo bangs, wearing a jacket with a yellow Jewish star on the pocket over a nightdress. She was shivering. Next to her was a little girl. The young woman and the little girl held hands. The little girl was crying.

The three of them stood in the only light, the headlights of an army truck. A stream of exhaust came from the tailpipe of the truck.

One of the Gestapo men in a black leather overcoat came over to the young woman. Saul noticed for the first time how pretty, no, much more, stunning, she was. Like a movie star. The German took out a Luger pistol.

"I'm pretty. I'll do anything you want," the young woman said.

"Yes," he said, and shot her in the head. The little girl screamed. He shot her too, but it seemed to Saul that her scream didn't stop. Although she was dead—he knew she was dead. She had to be; he *could see the blood streaming from her head on the cobblestones—her screaming went on in the dark street.*

The German came to Saul and pointed the pistol at his head. Saul could feel the muzzle just touching his hair. The German started to squeeze the trigger. Saul couldn't help himself. He began to pee. It was always at that moment that he would wake up, the bed wet, smelling of urine.

He never told anyone about his dream. Not his parents, not even when they scolded him about the bed-wetting. His parents never spoke about the war, the Holocaust. Once, when he was eleven, he started to ask. His mother just turned away. His father pretended not to hear.

The second time he asked, his father told him to come with him. They were going on a trip.

They drove all the way to Gary, Indiana, to the big steel mill on the shore of Lake Michigan. There was a platform where visitors were allowed to stand and watch the molten steel being poured from the giant bucket. They watched the fiery display of sparks and felt the heat of the blast furnace on their skin. His father held his arm tight like a vise.

"You see that fire, Shaulele? First you stand in that fire. That fire. Then you ask me about the camps, *farshtaysht*? Because in that place, Shaulele, the place you're asking, there was no God." They drove home in silence and never spoke of it again.

So he didn't tell them about the dream. He never told anyone. Except Mira.

He told her the night when, as a young CIA operations officer in Tehran in 1978, the Revolution turning too dangerous for her to stay in Iran any longer, he sent her back to the States.

They argued. She didn't want to go. She accused him of wanting to be apart from her, of wanting her to go. She knew better. It was all around them. Even their friends talked about what was happening every day. What Saul couldn't tell her was that his friend and best intel source, a former SAVAK officer, Majid Javadi, had warned him that it was time for all foreigners, especially Americans, to get out of Iran. Still she refused to go.

That night in Tehran in 1978, for the first time since he'd been a child, the dream, the nightmare, came again. He had been moaning in his sleep, Mira said. That's when he told her.

"I forgot. You were the only Jews in this little town in Indiana, surrounded by Christians. Were they mean to you?" she asked, putting her hand on his arm.

"Sometimes. Sometimes kids called me 'dirty Jew' and 'Christ killer' or they would look at me funny. One of the teachers said something and they left me alone. I spent a lot of time alone."

"Little Saul, by himself on the playground," she said.

"Look, it's not like Hindus and Muslims in India, Mira. The Christians didn't try to run us out or burn crosses on our lawn. I was an American kid. That's all I ever wanted to be. The fear came from someplace else. My parents never spoke about what happened to them in the Holocaust. Never," he said.

"Why are you telling me this?" she asked.

"Because last night, for the first time since I was a child, I had that dream," he said.

"What does it mean?"

"You have to go now. It's a warning. Something terrible is coming," he said. As soon as the words came out of his mouth, he knew it was true.

Barely speaking to him, she got on the plane. A month later, it was Javadi himself who would teach him how terrible—and how true.

A very fit-looking African-American in his early forties in pressed slacks and a well-fitted casual shirt, hair cut short in a military high-and-tight, stood waiting in Tampa Airport by the luggage carousel. He was dressed as a civilian, as Saul had requested.

"Mr. Berenson, sir?" he asked.

"You are?" Saul asked.

"Lieutenant Colonel Chris Larson, sir. Can I take your bag?"

"I'll take it. They told you to look for the guy with the beard?" he asked as they walked to the parking lot.

"Something like that, sir." Larson smiled.

As they got into the car and drove on the airport road, Saul asked:

"Will it take us long?"

"It's not far. You'll be sitting in the general's office in nine and a half minutes, sir."

"The general likes it precise, does he?"

"He does, sir."

They drove to the gate at MacDill Air Force Base, and nine and a half minutes, almost to the second, later, Saul was able to park his suitcase in the outer office and was sitting next to his carry-on in the office of four-star General Arthur Demetrius, CENTCOM commander, famous for having implemented the surge in Iraq, the current commander of all U.S. military forces in the Middle East, and in charge of all military-related activities and negotiations including the Status of Forces Agreement and the military resolution of the war in Iraq.

Demetrius was about Saul's height, six feet. Lean, very fit, about fifty, with an intelligent horsey face, tanned from spending time outdoors. Not just West Point, Saul reminded himself. He had an M.P.A. from Columbia and a Ph.D. in political science from Princeton. He remembered Bill Walden's description of General Demetrius. "He's not just some military hard-ass. He listens."

"So, Mr. Berenson, you know my problem?" Demetrius began, leaning forward on his desk, fiddling with a ballpoint pen. Behind him, Saul could see a bit of the air force base and a palm tree through the office window's partially closed venetian blinds.

"Your problem is that Abu Nazir, IPLA, knows everything your troops or the Iraqis are going to do before you do. So do the Shiites and the Iranians. They're always one step ahead of you. Your problem is that the U.S. is on the verge of an economic meltdown and the Congress and the country think the war in Iraq is over, only nobody told the enemy. Meanwhile, we, the CIA, have been playing Whac-A-Mole with IPLA and AQI, al-Qaeda in Iraq, not to mention the Shiites, and have been of little or no use to you. That's your problem. Oh, call me Saul, General," he said.

"Finally." Demetrius smiled, putting down the pen. "Somebody from Langley capable of telling something that resembles the truth."

"There's more," Saul said, and told him about the SOG mission to Otaibah and Carrie's intel. When he talked about the SOG mission, Demetrius went to a wall map and they followed the mission on the map and then Carrie's route in Damascus and to Aleppo.

"So the Syrians gave sanctuary to Abu Nazir?" General Demetrius asked. "Why?"

"So that Sunnis in Damascus don't start strapping on suicide vests or RPGs with President Assad and his generals as the target," Saul said. "Anyway, Abu Nazir's gone. He's not in Syria anymore."

"So where is he?"

"Probably back in Iraq."

"Any idea where?"

"Could be anywhere, could be south, even north."

"Why? The Kurds'd have him for breakfast."

"Hard to say. The one thing we've learned is not to underestimate him."

"But you'll find him?"

"Eventually. Right now that's not my priority," Saul said, moving his chair closer to the general's desk. "Or yours either. You're leaving very shortly, aren't you?"

General Demetrius nodded, looking at him sharply.

"How did you know that?"

Saul pointed to himself. "CIA, remember? Listen, I came to you because it's vital."

Demetrius put down the ballpoint pen and leaned forward, his chin resting on hands clasped together as if he were praying.

"I'm listening."

"I've been suspicious of something for a long time. Our ops officer in Otaibah and Damascus came through with intel that confirms beyond the shadow of a doubt that we have a mole. The likelihood is that it's a very high placed mole somewhere within the Coalition Forces or top echelons of the Iraqi government. But I need to be absolutely honest and clear. It could also be inside the CIA's Baghdad Station or even at Langley. It could even be inside your own command, General. It is one hundred percent actionable intelligence."

"Inside my command?"

"Or mine, General. I don't think it's likely that a CIA agent or an American soldier would do such a thing, and none of us likes to think it's possible, but you and I both know, sir, it's been known to happen."

General Demetrius stood up. He began pacing up and back in his office, then turned to Saul.

"What the hell am I supposed to do? We're on the verge of making critical decisions to finish this war. I have to trust the people I work with, that I give orders to."

"It's worse than that. The same actionable intel also indicates that Abu Nazir is planning a major 'action,' something that may finally trigger the civil war you have been doing everything in your power to prevent, General," Saul said, rubbing his beard.

"Do you know what it is?"

"Not yet. But I will. Very soon."

General Demetrius glanced at his watch.

"We have three and a half minutes, Saul. Then I have to go." He leaned against his desk. "Why don't you tell me why you're really here?"

Saul smiled. "They said you were good, General. I have to get going too," he added, standing up and lifting the handle on his carry-on. "I need a favor."

"And that is?"

"A counteroperation to block Abu Nazir's action is being set up. I may—repeat may—have to come to you at some point for some Special Forces–type resources. Not sure if and not sure how much. Anyway, just in case, the name for this counteroperation is 'Operation Iron Thunder,'" Saul said.

"And flushing the mole is part of this operation?" Demetrius asked, heading for the door.

"You could say so," Saul said, following him to the outer office, where a half-dozen officers stood ready for the general. "You could definitely say so."

General Demetrius stopped.

"And do you know where I'm going now?"

Saul smiled. "You're flying, along with some additional resources, on your specially fitted C-17 to CENTCOM HQ in

Doha, Qatar. Actually, I'm headed to the Middle East myself. Only not to Qatar."

"Would you like a lift? I think we need to continue this conversation," General Demetrius said.

"I was hoping you'd ask," Saul said as a master sergeant grabbed the handle of his suitcase and pulled it after them outside the office toward the general's waiting staff car.

The C-17 was bigger than any aircraft Saul had ever flown in. Both sides of its cabin aisle were fitted with rows of screens and electronics, which enabled the dozens of officers and men working at their stations to track the latest data from land, sea, and air operations from all parts of General Demetrius's widespread command across the entire Middle East and South Asia. For several hours out of MacDill, an F-16 fighter jet flew escort, then peeled off when they were well out over the Atlantic.

Saul sat toward the rear, in an area of seats that were set in rows like business-class seats in a normal passenger jet. He worked on his laptop, doing tradecraft, setting up basic drops, codes, locations, for Operation Iron Thunder. He used special CIA encryption software that was unique to CIA Top Secret Special Access files; it could not be decoded by standard NSA, DIA, or other agency decryption software, not even by other CIA decryption software.

Two hours out, Lieutenant Colonel Larson, looking much more in his element in a Class-A uniform, came and asked if Saul would like to join the general for coffee. Saul followed him forward past the men and women working at their screens, talking through headsets to their counterparts in various commands, to the general's office. It was completely closed off. Inside was a desk, conference table, armchairs, and a lounge area with a stocked bar, all of it modernistic and made of stainless steel; it had the odd feel of a men's club for robots.

General Demetrius was sitting in a swivel armchair, sipping coffee and reading a copy of the *Economist*, which he put down when Saul came in. He poured Saul a cup of coffee.

"How do you take it?"

"Milk and sugar; you take yours black, thanks."

General Demetrius swiveled toward him, hands on his knees like a sumo wrestler about to pounce.

"You're setting up a separate operation outside Langley, aren't you? That's what this little trip is all about, isn't it?"

Saul sipped his coffee.

"Good coffee. I'm here so you could ask me that." He looked around the partitioned office. "No bugs I hope."

General Demetrius shook his head.

"You *are* worried. Who else knows about this?"

"The director of the CIA; the vice president, Bill Walden. Took him by surprise, but he finally agreed. Facts are facts. The national security advisor, Mike Higgins. The president. Now you."

"Where are you going to run it from?"

"I'll be moving around. But I'll have something in Bahrain," he said. "The capital, Manama. For obvious reasons."

"Middle of the Persian Gulf. Not that far from Iraq. Or CENTCOM. Or Iran, for that matter. Like the real estate people say: location, location, location. Or do you have some thing or some one particular in mind, Saul?"

"Both maybe. Manama's a crossroads. A place where people come to do business, clean and dirty. And close enough to your headquarters in Doha, General, although I suspect you won't be there that often." He put down his coffee.

"You know damn well I won't be sitting on my ass there," General Demetrius growled. "There's a battle shaping up in Basra right this minute—and we don't have shit there."

"It's not just IPLA. The Kurds, the Shiites, the Mahdi Army, the Iranians . . ." Saul ticked them off. "Abu Nazir is trying to light a match. There's plenty of tinder lying around."

"How soon and where?"

"I'll let you know very soon," Saul said, looking at the map of Iraq on the general's laptop screen. "There are some things I have to do first."

General Demetrius looked at him.

"Operation Iron Thunder?"

Saul nodded.

"Where do you start?"

Stand in the fire of a blast furnace to get the answer in a place where there is no God, Saul thought, for some bizarre reason thinking of his father. "By sending my best operations officer into the enemy's camp with a big fat target painted on her back," he said.

"What?"

"Sorry. A stupid metaphor. We don't just know we have a mole who's feeding IPLA, General. For the first time, we also have a lead that might help us nail who it is. There's more. The Iranians. They may be also be getting intel."

"You've been reading my DIA reports. There's something going on with the Iranians. The Shiites in Iraq have suddenly gone quiet. Too quiet. If our withdrawal from Iraq were to come under heavy enemy attack, it could be a bloodbath," General Demetrius said grimly.

"What if we were to come under attack from both sides, the Sunnis and the Shiites at the same time—and they know everything you're going to do in advance?"

"You must be a mind reader. What the hell do you think has been keeping me up at night?"

"I have a plan," Saul said.

"Iron Thunder."

"Exactly. I understand you play Go. Something of a fanatic, they say," Saul said, taking a board and a box of black and white stones out of his carry-on. "You can be black. If you like, I'll take a modified *komidashi*."

General Demetrius studied him. "Are you hustling me, Saul?" He glanced at his watch. "Are you sure? The game'll take at least a couple of hours."

"No," Saul said, waiting for the general to play his first stone. "Not that long."

CHAPTER 9

Tal Afar, Iraq
15 April 2009

It was raining, gray clouds bundled over the city. Brody followed Daleel and five of the others, weapons concealed beneath their robes, in a single file through the narrow street. They were going to the mosque for the noon *Dhuhr* prayer. The street was muddy, the pavement cracked and rutted. Every shop and building was battered, shot through with bullet holes from the heavy fighting that had taken place there two years earlier between Abu Nazir's IPLA joined by elements of AQI and the U.S. 82nd Airborne.

Although Tal Afar had been officially proclaimed a "Coalition success" and it was a majority Turkmen, not Arab, city, you could still hear the sounds of one or two rocket attacks and IEDs almost every day. But Brody wasn't thinking about any of these things. He had a decision to make. His life depended on it.

The young Turkmen woman in the *makhbaz*, the bakery shop where he bought the flat bread for some of the group, spoke English. One morning, three weeks ago, when Afsal had walked outside to talk privately with Mahdi and, for a moment, they were alone in the shop, she looked at him and asked, "What is an American doing with these Sunnis?"

For some reason, maybe because it was the first time a woman had spoken to him in English in six years, or because she wore a braided female Turkmen's cap that meant she wasn't an Arab, wasn't in any way like his captors, or maybe because her black eyes held a hint, though it was hard for him to believe, that she looked at him the way a woman looks at a man, he told her: "I'm a prisoner, an American Marine. They captured me." Then, louder, "*Bikam haadha?*" How much is that? Because Afsal and Mahdi had just come back in.

After that, each time he went into the *makhbaz*, she glanced at him. Even Mahdi noticed.

"What's going on with you and that Turkmen girl?" he said.

"Nothing. We say salaam, hello, that's all, and I buy the bread, thanks be to Allah," Brody said.

"You think she likes you? A foreigner? You think she'll be like American girls, who all you do is look at them and they spread their legs?"

"I'm a married man. I have a wife and two children," Brody said.

"But you want the Turkmen girl too?"

"No. Why? Do you want her?"

"Pah! Turkmen women grow mustaches on their upper lips. Too bad you can't have a soft Arab woman, American," Mahdi said.

"I told you, I'm married," Brody said as they took their shoes off at the entrance to the mosque. But even here, one of them, Afsal, who had been next to him all along, stayed behind with his AK-47, scanning the street for IEDs or any cars or carts that might come along with a bomb, or worse for IPLA, an Iraqi army patrol—more dangerous now because recruits in the new Iraqi Army were nearly all Shiites.

So they watched him even closer, Brody thought as he bowed his head to the floor in unison with the others in prayer. Except ten days ago, it happened again. Abu Nazir himself had driven by and called Afsal and Mahdi out to his car, leaving Brody and the Turkmen girl—her name was Akjemal—alone in the bakery. She motioned him to the side of the counter and spoke quickly, showing him a beautiful round bread with star patterns baked on the top.

"My uncle Jeyhun is the sheikh of our neighborhood," she whispered quickly. "He doesn't want to risk anything here in Tal Afar, but he is willing to smuggle you to Mosul under sacks of flour in his truck. Mosul is not far, maybe sixty kilometers. He knows American soldiers there. He says you can be turned over to the U.S. First Cavalry in one hour. Will you come?"

"They watch me closely. If they catch me, they'll kill me. You and your uncle too," he said, glancing at the shop window. Afsal and Mahdi were still talking by the car.

"I'm a Turkmen woman. I don't fear these Sunni dogs," she said, her cheeks reddening. He understood then that she did like him and that everything hinged on what he said next. Out of the corner of his eye, through the window, he saw Afsal coming back into the shop.

"I'll let you know," he said, moving away from her. "That is beautiful bread, *al anesah*, but we will have the usual order, please."

That same afternoon, Abu Nazir called for him. They sat over small cups of tea in the main room on the top floor of a large stone house, one of several connected by underground tunnels in the Old City, where they were staying. Although Abu Nazir spoke softly, the whole time Afsal stood by the door, a 9mm pistol in his hand. Through the row of arched windows, Brody could see the roofs of stone houses in the city, many of them showing scars from the fighting, and on a hill in the distance, an old Ottoman castle. Abu Nazir told him they would be leaving Tal Afar soon.

"It's been hard for you, hasn't it?" Abu Nazir said, putting his hand on Brody's shoulder.

Brody found it hard to breathe. It all came back. The capture. The beatings. Killing Tom Walker. Digging his grave in the sand. Then more beatings. Again and again till he couldn't take it anymore. His tiny concrete cell that he called his tomb, because he came to think of himself as dead. No more Jessica, no more Dana, his little girl, no tiny Chris, his own son. The endless beatings and taunts from Afsal and Mahdi. Afsal the worst, his personal demon, until he thought he would go insane, and there were times in the cell and even when he was praying with them—at first just to try to mitigate things a little and because he was so desperate for any kind of human companionship, anything—even then, even when he was saying the *shahadah* with them, he knew all they wanted to do was kill him and he thought he was going insane.

Because he was afraid. Like acid, drop by drop eating his soul away. He had been afraid all along. He had lived with it all this time. He had lived with it all his life.

Nine minutes. Gunner Brody.

And then, when they had left Syria in the middle of the night, they took him out to the middle of the desert. There was nothing there. Only emptiness and a hawk against the golden sky. And God, he thought. Finally, Allah. He was sure of it.

Afsal put the gun to his head. They were going to kill him and leave him there; his bones never to be found. For Jessica, he would be MIA, missing in action, forever. Would she wonder sometimes, years later, probably married to another man, what had happened to him?

Jessica. What had happened to her? It had been six years. Did she still think of him? Had she found someone else? Did she get a divorce and remarry? What of the kids? Dana would be thirteen now. What was that? Eighth grade? A teenager. Starting to think about boys maybe. And Chris? His baby boy? He would be seven. Going into second grade!

He should have died then and there in the desert. Only right at that exact moment, Abu Nazir had driven the flat sand in his SUV and pulled up perhaps fifty meters from them. He had leaned out a window and shouted: "U'af!" Stop!

So they had come to Tal Afar. A city seared by war. Many of the houses empty, where the only movement at night came from cats or rats that you sometimes saw in the streets or on the top of a broken wall, eyes gleaming like dimes. And another room, this one he had to share with Afsal, who would sneer at him, "Infidel! American! Because you say the *shahadah*, do you think you are fooling anyone, you piece of camel shit!"

Now in his dreams, sometimes it was Gunner Brody beating him and sometimes Afsal from when they first captured him and he couldn't tell the difference. He wished he would die. Get it over with. Do it. I don't understand why my body keeps living when I don't want to. What do you want from me, Allah? Tell me, because I don't think I can do this anymore.

"Why didn't you let them kill me in the desert?" Brody asked Abu Nazir.

Abu Nazir turned the teacup in his hands.

"Truly, I don't know. Before we left Syria, I gave the order to Afsal. You must understand, Nicholas Brody. You are a soldier too. This is war. But there, in the desert, when the moment came—truly, I don't know why. They tell me you have become a Muslim. You pray *salat* with the others. Is this so?"

Brody nodded.

"Yes, but why? You were born Christian, yes?"

Brody hesitated. He looked at the open window, at the gray sky. After all this, would being honest cause Abu Nazir to kill him? And if he was honest with himself, did he even care anymore, or had the Turkmen girl finally given him a glimmer of hope?

"I understand," Abu Nazir said. "You are afraid. But say the truth. It will be good. Why did you become a Muslim?"

Brody put his face in his hands.

"I don't know," he muttered. "At first, I needed to be with other people. I didn't want to be alone." He looked up. "But then, I couldn't live without it."

Abu Nazir nodded. "It is so," he said. "Sometimes we find Allah. Sometimes Allah finds us. Where are you from in America, Nicholas Brody?"

"Alexandria, Virginia."

"Is that where you were born? Where you grew up?"

Brody shook his head. "I was born in Twentynine Palms in the Mojave Desert in California, but I grew up in Bethlehem. It's in Pennsylvania."

Abu Nazir stared at him. "Bethlehem? Like Jesus?" He stood up and folded his arms across his chest. "You? From Bethlehem?"

"I didn't know Muslims liked Jesus so much," Brody said.

"You are ignorant," Abu Nazir snapped. "Muslims honor Jesus. He is a messenger of Allah and the Messiah, of a virgin born."

"So why do you hate Christians?"

"Christians are fools. They say Jesus was the Son of God, that he was also God his own father and conceived himself with the Virgin Mary his own mother. This is both impossible and obscene. Allah is One. He makes no perversions.

"Then these same Christians come into our lands and make war on us. This they have done since the Crusades. Our war is with America and unbelievers, not Jesus," he said, and motioned for Brody to leave. But it was strange. After that, Afsal treated him differently. Mahdi and the others too. Almost as if he were one of them. And they let him sleep alone in his room at night.

Now, walking in the rain back from the mosque, he glanced at the *makhbaz* shop as they passed. There were two of the round breads with the star patterns in the window. It was the sign Akjemal had said she would put there to let him know her uncle and his truck would be ready that night if he could get away.

An hour down the highway—just one hour, after six years—and he would be in Mosul and free. Free.

Except the previous evening, Abu Nazir invited him to dine with him. They were alone, just the two of them, eating chicken with rice and raisins, no Afsal with his gun, watching beside the door.

"We are leaving Tal Afar, Nicholas," Abu Nazir told him. "Very soon."

If he was going to try an escape with the Turkmen girl's uncle, it would have to be tonight or never, Brody thought.

"Why? What's happened?"

"Many things. We never intended to stay here. And there are things that are about to happen. The Americans think their war in Iraq is finished. They have foolishly handed Iraq over to the Shiites and the Iranians, thinking they can walk away like children who tire of a toy. They are about to learn their war is not over. As a Muslim and an American, your loyalty will be tested," Abu Nazir said, leaning forward. "What will you do?"

"I'm a prisoner of war. I want it to be over, *inshallah*," Brody said. God willing.

Abu Nazir clasped Brody's hand and held it tight. "You have so much to learn, Nicholas. This is a very old war. If you let me, I will teach you. But we must be honest with each other."

His dark eyes peered at Brody as if he could see straight into his mind.

"Why did you save me in the desert? I have to know," Brody said.

"Truly, at the time, I did not know. All I knew was that I felt a sudden urgency that I had to stop it. I sense the hand of Allah in this, Nicholas. We shall see." He frowned. "When we get to our new destination, I have something important to ask you."

That night, he lay awake calculating his chances. If he failed, they would kill him and probably the girl and her family. If he succeeded, Abu Nazir would, at a minimum, bomb the *makhbaz*, killing her and whoever was in or near the bakery. Probably go after her family too. But he would be safe and out of this hell.

Could he live with that?

He'd killed Tom Walker. He was already living with it, he told himself. Guilty of murder. The girl, Akjemal, what did he owe her? And what about Jessica—and his kids? He owed them something too, didn't he?

He'd kissed Jessica good-bye so long ago. She must think I'm dead. My kids; my mother; my buddy, Mike; and Mike's wife, Megan; they must all think I'm dead. What did he owe her and the kids now? He had no choice, even if it meant Akjemal's life. He had to try. Even though there was a good chance they'd catch him. In his mind, he could picture Abu Nazir's face, what it would look like, when he told Afsal to kill him.

He stood up from the pallet on the floor that was his bed and pulled on his pants. He picked up a kaffiyeh head scarf in which he'd bundled his shoes and the rest of his clothes. If anyone stopped him, he was going to the toilet. Barefoot, he made his way down the dark hallway, feeling his way along the wall.

It had to be the balcony; there was no other way. They were on the second floor. There was always someone on guard at both the front and back doors and at a secret basement tunnel to the next building. But there was an iron drain pipe that ran from the house's tile roof down to the alley below. The pipe was about a meter from the side of the balcony. In his mind, he had reached over and climbed down that pipe a thousand times.

This time he would do it.

The balcony was in a bedroom shared by Daleel, his wife, Heba, and their two children. He tiptoed into the bedroom. Daleel was snoring as he crept past them to the balcony door, luckily left open for air. It had stopped raining. The air smelled of rain and there were a few stars out. The stone floor of the balcony was cold and wet under his bare feet.

He tied the kaffiyeh bundle of clothes around his neck. It was awkward, but it would only be until he was down on the ground, he told himself. As he lifted his leg up onto the balcony ledge, he felt his foot graze something. Oh God! He had dislodged a piece of tile. He heard it scrape and fall. Please no, he thought, his blood freezing inside as he heard the tile smack into pieces on the stone of the alleyway below.

Instantly, he dropped on all fours. Heba stirred. Daleel snorted and stopped snoring. Brody began crawling through the bedroom on his fingers and toes.

"*Maadha?*" What? he heard Heba say. "Did you hear that?"

"What?" Daleel said.

Brody was moving quickly to the dark rectangle that was the doorway to the hall. O Allah, he thought.

"I heard something. Was it the children?"

Brody heard her getting up, but by this time, he was in the hall. Now upright and moving fast on bare feet, he walked back to his room, stripped off his pants, and slid back on his pallet. Less than ten seconds later, a flashlight was shining in his face.

Brody raised up on one elbow; one hand shielding his eyes from the flashlight. It was Afsal.

"Did you hear that noise?" Afsal said.

"I don't know. What happened?" Brody said.

"I don't know. I thought it was you."

"No. Maybe a cat. They're all over," he said, dropping back on the pallet.

An hour later, his arm over his eyes, he thought about trying again. If it was risky before, it was ten times riskier now. He could see Jessica receding from him, the way it was at the bus station when he first joined the Marines with Mike, looking back from the bus watching her and Dana grow smaller in the distance.

I tried, Jess, I tried. And then, the finality of it. There was no other night. No other chance. The girl, Akjemal, had left the two loaves in the window for him. If he didn't do it tonight, he would never escape. He would die a gutless prisoner.

He would do it tonight, he decided. He would kill whoever was guarding the front door and just run all the way to the bakery shop. One way or another, his captivity would be over tonight. All he had to do was wait one more hour till everyone was back asleep.

An hour later, just as he was about to leave, he heard Afsal get up. His nerves screaming, he could only wait. A minute or two later, Afsal came back and turned on the light. Brody closed his eyes. Afsal poked him.

"Come. He wants to see you," Afsal said.

Brody pulled on his pants and followed him to Abu Nazir's bedroom, which showed signs of activity, weapons and suitcases out. Abu Nazir looked at Brody.

"Nicholas, get ready. Much has happened. We are leaving Tal Afar," he said.

CHAPTER 10

He was waiting for her by the ship's rail. For some reason he always seemed taller, thinner than Carrie remembered, but at the sight of him the knot that had tied up her stomach for days was gone. No, better than that. She felt safe. Saul.

"The seagulls aren't flying over the rocks," she said. Code that she hadn't been followed in the taxi to the dock where she'd caught the ship's tender.

"I know, or you wouldn't be here," he said, putting his hand on the rail. They stood side by side at the ship's rail looking at the city, savoring being together—Saul and Carrie—then he turned to really look at her. "How are you?" he asked.

"It got a little hairy there—actually, damn hairy—but I'm okay," she said. "It's good to see you."

"You were alone. There wasn't another way." Despite his words, he was smiling, beaming almost, as if he couldn't stop himself if he wanted to.

He wore a windbreaker and had a canvas, messenger-style bag slung from his shoulder. Behind him was the seascape of the harbor in early morning. Container ships at the dock and other freighters like theirs moored offshore. Beyond them, looking north along the curve of the coast, she could see the palm-tree-lined, white sand beaches and hotels of the tourist area the locals, in imitation of the Côte d'Azur, called "the Blue Beach," where she'd waited for him to arrive.

It was a beautiful sunrise, she thought. The sun was split by a cloud edge over the hills like a painting, the sky a dozen shades of blue. They were aboard a rusty Malta-flagged Turkish freighter, *MV Denkaya II*, bound next for Famagusta, in the Turkish portion of Cyprus.

"We have a mole," she said.

"I know. I've suspected for some time," he said.

"What about those assholes upstairs?" Langley. "Do they know?"

He nodded. "The director does. So does Bill Walden. It's being closely held. I'm running a special op; completely separate from Langley. We're calling it Operation Iron Thunder."

"Who else knows?"

"Besides Walden? The director; Higgins, the president's national security advisor; the president; General Demetrius; me—and now you." His voice almost lost in the sound of the ship's anchor chain rattling up and an increased thrumming of the engines.

"Interesting," she said, swaying and grabbing on to the rail as the ship's horn sounded and they began to move.

For a time he didn't say anything. They waited as the freighter maneuvered out of the harbor. After a few minutes, they became accustomed to the movement, the sway and splash below at the waterline. Standing by the rail, they watched the city recede. The cranes and buildings at the harbor's edge and the city, a jumble of buildings along the coast, began to merge with the horizon.

"Carrie," Saul began, "I'm not sure I have the right to ask you to do this. Especially after this last one."

She felt vaguely nauseous—and wasn't sure whether it was the movement and noise of the ship or the idea that he might have lost confidence in her. It felt a little like when she was coming down from one of her "flights," when she was off her meds.

"Saul, what are you saying? That I can't do this?" she said, almost panicked.

"I'm not saying anything of the kind," the wind tugging at his hair and beard, so that for a second, she thought he looked like an Old Testament prophet. "I don't want to lose you." He held on to the rail and looked into her eyes. "You're good, Carrie. We both know it," he said, the words thrilling her. He'd never said anything like that to her before. "I know you've been in some pretty hairy spots recently, but you have to trust me on this. This op is—will be—by far, the most dangerous thing you've ever done. I don't want to minimize the danger."

She put her hand on his arm, nearly falling on him as the ship's motion began to increase. The swells were bigger now. They were getting into rougher seas.

"Why are you trying to talk me out of it, Saul? What's going on? Guilty conscience? In case something happens to me, you want it on some kind of karmic record that you tried to talk me out of it?"

"It's not like that and you know it." He frowned. "Two minutes—and we're already fighting. Why is that—with the people I really care about—I always end up . . . ?" He leaned against the rail.

"What is it? Tell me." She touched his arm with her fist, relenting.

"You deserve better. What you've been through, it isn't fair.

You've earned better," he said. "I don't want to have to put you through this again. You'd think there'd be someone else, dammit."

She looked around. They were truly out to sea now. The coast, the city of Latakia, was distant. The freighter's engine throbbed through the ship, the motion rocking them through ink-blue waves that raised and lowered them at each heavy swell. The wind had come up too, whipping her long blond hair.

"Does this bother you? Do you want to go inside?" Saul asked, tilting his head to indicate the salt wind, the sea, the ship's sway.

"In a minute. I like it," she said.

"I know. So do I." He smiled. "I want you to know, you don't have to say yes. Say the word, I've got something waiting for you at Langley. You'd have your own team. A promotion in grade with a nice jump in pay. It's a good position. I'm not just saying that. It's damned important. It's not a placebo, Carrie. It's an important job that could use someone like you."

"Come on, Saul. Who are you trying to sell? You or me?"

He leaned back against the rail next to her, the way he used to do, the two of them side by side, leaning on his desk at Langley.

"Both of us, I guess. I had to at least try."

"Saul, it's me." She looked at him. "What are you trying to tell me?"

"A life. Find somebody, Carrie. A good guy. Have some kids. Have a life, a real life, for chrissakes."

"Jesus, Saul. Who the hell do you think I am?" The wind whipping her blond hair about her face, and behind her the rolling sea. Do you really want to get into this, Saul? she thought. What life is like for a single woman? Much less one who's a CIA spy and has a bipolar mental condition to boot? The nights alone, just me, my laptop, and a bottle of tequila because it's better than Singles' Night in downtown anywhere. The times when you walk into a bar, ready to pick up any man who isn't physically repulsive and doesn't smell like taking out the trash, just because you need to hear the sound of a human voice other than your own. Believe me, that isn't a road you want to go down, Saul. "You want me to bake cookies? Maybe in five, ten years, Saul. But not today. Not today, not when we've got a son-of-a-bitch mole. Tell me the truth. Why don't you want it to be me?"

"Because it has to be you." Again he frowned, turning to her. "Everything I just said was bullshit and we both know it. It has to be you."

"Why?"

"Because you're good and you're the only one I can trust. I said all that other crap because there's a real chance you won't come back from this one. And I hate that, Carrie. I can't even begin to tell you how much I hate that. That stuff about you with a husband and kids, that's my fantasy for you. That's my Jewish guilt talking," he said.

"Yeah, well, Catholics know a thing or two about guilt too. The sisters at Holy Trinity High made sure of that. Speaking of marriage, how's Mira?" she asked, pulling up the zipper on her jacket.

"I'm supposed to be in Mumbai right now. On leave, spending time with her and her family." He grimaced. "I let it slip to Sandy Gornick that I was actually going to India to try and patch things up. That's the cover."

"Oh Saul, that bad?"

"Worse." Shaking his head.

"I'm sorry," she said, nudging him with her arm.

"So am I," he said, patting her arm. "We have a problem with 'the Russian.'"

"Why? Wasn't the image on the—" she began.

"Image was fine—for the Russian. There's no clear sighting of the guy you said was Abu Nazir, but for that we had Cadillac's comment, plus your voice recognition on him. Image of the Russian was wonderful," he said angrily. "Trouble is, nobody knows who the hell he is."

"That's impossible," she snapped. "We have . . . Do we even know if he's Russian?"

Saul shook his head.

"What about Moscow Station?" she asked.

"Nothing. Walden's got two teams back at Langley on it. One's headed by your old boss, Alan Yerushenko. The other by David Estes. Also Chase Jennings."

"Who's he?"

"The new Moscow Station chief."

He turned to face her. The sea swells had started to ease. The sun glittered on the water so that he had to squint behind his glasses. "Officially, I'm on administrative leave. Unofficially, everybody back at Langley thinks my career's over. I'm history. RIP," he explained, smiling, but his eyes weren't smiling.

For a time the only sound was the slap of the waves on the hull. "If anybody can find out about this Russian, it's Alan and his people," she said, then burst out: "It's impossible, dammit. Human beings don't have meetings with important terrorists out of nowhere. The Russian's our only lead. With all these people looking, are you saying nobody has anything?"

He shook his head.

"Are you kidding? The whole CIA? Nothing?"

"One thing," Saul said. He dropped his head and closed his eyes. Shit, she thought. It was a habit of Saul's when it was something bad. It was coming now. Why he had tried to talk her out of staying on this operation.

He pulled the messenger bag off his shoulder, opened it, and took out his laptop computer. After it fired up, he entered the password and found what he was looking for. It was a photo image of two men meeting at a waterside restaurant. It was shot at a ninety-degree angle so the person taking the photo caught two men at a small table in profile, the water with a part of a boat or a launch with people on it behind them. Carrie recognized one of the men instantly. The Russian.

"Where was this taken?" she asked.

"We've nailed it down with ninety percent probability. It's one of the waterfront restaurants in Istanbul. Probably in Büyükada. It wasn't taken that long ago either."

"Where'd it come from?"

"It didn't. The source was Israeli. Mossad. The NSA poached it from them electronically. Someone on Alan's team found it in an NSA intercept. The Israelis have no idea we have it."

"Who's the other man? Have you been able to identify him?"

He nodded, his glasses reflecting the glare of the sun. "Abd al Ali Nasser."

"Who is he?"

"You won't like this."

"Saul, stop trying to protect me. Who is he?"

"He's the head of the Syrian Mukhabarat." The ruthless Syrian intelligence service, she thought, feeling queasy. Head of the Mukhabarat; probably the most dangerous man in the Syrian government. That's why Saul had given her the song and dance about the job back in Langley.

Saul turned so he could look at her without squinting into the sun. Behind him in the distance, she could see a distant brown finger of land on the line of the sea. The northwest tip of Cyprus. They would be getting in soon. Not a long trip, but at least she was out of Syria. The red zone.

"Carrie, we don't have a lot of time. I'm not sure whether your raid on Otaibah forced Abu Nazir's hand or whether what he was planning was already in motion, but General Demetrius and I are agreed. The Iraq War is hanging by a thread and Abu Nazir is about to cut it."

They heard a loud clunk from below in the ship's hold. Something with the cargo. Unexpected things happen, she thought. It felt like a warning.

"And the Russian? Operation Iron Thunder?"

He frowned. Her skin went prickly like a million needles all over. It was her bipolar. Even with her having taken the clozapine, something inside her was arching its back like a frightened cat. "You have to go back to Damascus."

"They'll arrest me for sure. They almost got me last time. It's Syria, Saul. You know what they do," she said.

"I know," he said.

CHAPTER 11

They sat over drinks on the terrace of the Bloudan Grand Hotel. The sun was shining, but because of the altitude, the air was cool and clear. The view looked out over the manicured grounds and the swimming pool, on down the slope to the red-roofed houses and trees, the orchards and vineyards of the Zabadani plain.

"I'm not sure why I'm here," Carrie said, pulling her jacket around her.

"You would prefer a cell in Adra Prison? Handcuffs and leg irons?" Abd al Ali Nasser, head of the Syrian Mukhabarat, said with a half smile in clipped Oxbridge English. "A war story to tell your CIA colleagues, if you survived."

He was a big man, trim, attractive. The kind who looked after himself at a gym, she thought. Salt-and-pepper hair cut short and a neat mustache that was virtually a requirement in the higher echelons of the Assad regime. He wore a polo shirt under an expensive suit, dark sunglasses, a black-faced Rolex on his left wrist, and seemed perfectly comfortable despite the cool temperature. He didn't try to conceal that he considered himself attractive to women; part of her wondered if this was some bizarre kind of seduction.

"I can't tell if you're joking," she said.

"I have the same problem," he said, signaling to the waiter for another Bombay Sapphire martini. For a moment, neither of them said anything. She toyed with the lime wedge on her margarita.

"I often come here in summer to get away from the heat of the city. Now in spring, it's not so crowded, but believe me, a couple of months ago, people were skiing on that slope over there. Pretty, isn't it?" he asked. His gesture encompassed not just the slope behind the hotel but the orange-yellow hotel itself with its commanding view of the mountains on one side and on the other, the green plain below, stretching into the distance.

Beautiful, she thought, if you could forget the dozen or so armed Mukhabarat agents hovering just out of sight. Or the room upstairs, where other Mukhabarat thugs were holding Cadillac's—Mosab Sabagh's—wife, Aminah, and her ten-year-old son, Jameel.

The only thing keeping all three of them—herself included—from the Adra torture cells was the slim thread Saul had given her to play.

"It's lovely," she said. It was. The hotel, with its marble-and-polished-brass colonial lobby and porters in white uniforms, was from another time. One might expect to see Lawrence of Arabia or Winston Churchill strolling out of the bar.

"The hotel is historic," he said, lighting a cigarette for himself after she declined one. "Did you know the Arab League held its first meeting here in '42?"

"Fascinating," she said, because if this was a tennis match, it was her turn to hit the ball. She leaned in sexily, showing him as much cleavage as she could, motioning him closer. "But to tell you the truth, *Assayed* Abd al Ali Nasser, I don't give a shit who met who here or how pretty it is. I only have one question: did you bring me here to fuck me, interrogate me, or are we going to do serious business?"

The smile disappeared from his face as if it had never been there, and for a second, Carrie thought she had gone over the line. She saw the real man, his face like a skull with Oakleys instead of eyes, who could, she knew, murder her brutally without a second thought and never have to answer to anyone. Either way, she thought, the moment balanced like a spinning ball on the tip of a basketball player's finger. It could go either way.

Then the skull disappeared. The smile was back.

"It seems I have the same problem. I can't tell when you're joking." Putting it back in her court.

"Trust me," she said, nudging aside her margarita, which they'd made too sour, "I'm not joking."

You better be damn right, Saul, she thought, because she was about to play the only card she had.

She and Saul had talked it over in her cabin on the Turkish freighter before they docked in Famagusta. On the small cabin bed was a Tumi roller carry-on. Inside was a brand-new cover identity, complete with clothes, papers, credit cards, and passport to match. And a Glock 26 pistol.

She was Anne McGarvey, a State Department cultural attaché on temporary assignment at the U.S. embassy in Damascus. Classic cover for a CIA agent and both she and Saul fully expected the Mukhabarat and the GSD to be all over her every move from the instant she landed at Damascus International Airport.

She checked in at the U.S. embassy on Mansour Street, a white concrete compound, outer buildings facing the street surmounted by a wrought-iron fence on the roof. Although she was ostensibly there to arrange a cultural exchange program, the only cultural thing she did was a ten-minute "Don't expect to see me, but I'll be borrowing an apartment and a car" with Dale Crosby, the deputy chief of mission. Her next meeting was with Lieutenant Robert Anderson, the officer overseeing the U.S. Marines guarding the embassy, to set up the call-in procedure.

If she failed to make a one- or two-sentence call-in every four hours to either of two embassy phone numbers, the Cultural Center or the emergency number, and use the code word "Alabama," the Marine on duty was to send a blank JWICS email to a CIA front company in Zurich with the subject "The San Francisco ballet company can't change the schedule." If she was arrested, captured, or under duress but still able to make the call-in, she would use the word "complain," as in "This is Anne. Everything's fine. Can't complain."

The call desk in Zurich was a CIA freight-forwarding front company, manned 24/7 by personnel whose appearance and cover were so good that not even other companies on the same floor of the office building they were located in or walk-in customers had any inkling of their real activity.

Once the call was received, the person on duty would forward it via the company's ultrasecure phone-switching technology that would bounce it a dozen different ways around the world to make it untraceable before forwarding the message to a cell phone Saul kept on him at all times strictly for that purpose. A tenuous safety line, but as long as it existed, Carrie felt in some way connected to Saul.

It had been the most harrowing twenty-four hours of her life.

Step one, as Saul laid it out in the Turkish freighter cabin, involved two problems. Had Cadillac left anything behind? The only person who would know was his wife, Aminah, who would be closely watched. The second, how to make the approach to the Syrians convincing?

Soon after arriving, she called Aminah and set up a meet, introducing herself by way of telling her that her company had done business with her husband, General Sabagh, and there was bonus money due him. On the phone, Aminah sounded frightened, cautious, but by the way she responded, Carrie got the impression that she was desperate for money. That wasn't a surprise. The Assad regime had discovered her husband was a CIA spy; they weren't about to pay a pension to the wife.

Using a borrowed embassy Ford sedan, Carrie headed for the address. In less than a minute, she had company. Two white Toyota sedans in the rearview mirror, and up ahead, a black Renault with four men inside. Front and back tail. GSD, she thought grimly.

She drove down Beirut Road, the greenery of Tishreen Park on her left. The objective was to lose the GSD tails, but not entirely. She would need as much time inside Cadillac's apartment as she could get; although she had to assume it was under surveillance. At that moment, there were just the three cars, though there might be more. Impossible with all this traffic and possible distance and GPS surveillance to know for sure.

She kept the two Toyotas in the rearview mirror as she pushed the Ford harder, weaving in and out of traffic. They stayed with her till she came to the big Umayyad Square traffic circle. Four lanes of dense Damascus traffic swirling around the water fountains in the big center island. Perfect, she thought, cutting in front of a red car, nearly denting its fender, then swerving back in front of a Citroën, causing its driver to slam on his brakes and raise his fist to curse her and her offspring for a hundred generations. She made a sudden right turn onto Ibn Barakeh Avenue, one of the main avenue spokes emanating from the big traffic circle, losing the black Renault, which had gone too far and had no choice but to continue around the circle.

She gunned the car up Ibn Barakeh, honking like a maniac Damascus taxi driver, then made another sudden sharp right for one block and right again, headed back to the Umayyad traffic circle.

In the rearview mirror, only one of the white Toyotas was still with her, about a half-dozen cars behind. The black Renault was gone, presumably following on Ibn Barakeh Avenue. This time, she went around the circle three times, switching lanes with each revolution. On the third go-round, she cut in front of a car to her right, then turned off the circle and onto the exit road that ran by the Sheraton Damascus Hotel. The white Toyota, caught in an inner lane, was unable to make the exit. Hopefully, it would give her the minute or two she needed.

She drove to the hotel parking lot and parked in a long row of cars. Looking around, she didn't see any watchers as she walked to the hotel entrance and caught a taxi just pulling up.

So far, no Toyotas, black Renaults, or anyone else she could spot following her. She told the taxi driver to take her to the Fardoss Tower Hotel. When they got there, she told him to go around to the back entrance because the Fardoss was close to the Cham Palace, where she was afraid someone might recognize her.

For the moment, she was clean. She walked as calmly as she could through the Fardoss Hotel lobby to the front entrance and took another taxi to Aminah Sabagh's apartment.

The building was a six-story apartment house in the upscale Malki district in north Damascus, with balconies that looked out on other elegant high-rises on tree-shaded streets. The kind of neighborhood where nannies pushed Bugaboo strollers past parked Lexuses and Mercedes.

Getting out of the taxi, she saw no obvious watchers in the street. No parked vans with someone sitting in them. The roof lines were clear. Then she saw it as she glanced back one last time from the entrance to the building. The movement of a drape at a window on the third floor of the building across the street. She took a deep breath. The clock had started. God, Saul, you better be right, she thought, pushing the buzzer for Aminah's apartment. She had ten, fifteen minutes at most. And ten to one every word she said in the apartment would be listened to and recorded.

Aminah let her in and offered her tea. Her son, Jameel, came in, said the obligatory *"Aleikem es salaam"* to Carrie's *"Salaam aleikem,"* and went back to playing video games in his room. Aminah was an attractive, dark-haired woman in her late thirties, early forties, who looked like she was trying to hold it together. But there was a spot on her blouse that Carrie suspected she never would have allowed when she was buddies with President Assad's wife, Asma. She had gained weight since her glory days shopping on the rue du Faubourg Saint-Honoré, Carrie thought. She was the wife of a traitor now.

After the usual preliminaries about the weather and "Where did you know my husband from?" Aminah tiptoed around to the the subject of the money.

"If it's permissible, God willing, you mentioned something about bonus money that was due for my deceased husband, Mosab?" she asked.

"Please," Carrie said, looking at the phone on the coffee table, where there was almost certainly a bug, and God knows how many cameras and other bugs were on her this second. "We don't have much time. Your late husband, General Sabagh, asked us, me, that if anything ever happened to him, we help his family. I'm from the American embassy," taking her diplomatic passport from her handbag and showing it to her. "I have one question: do you want to come to the United States? If you do, I can arrange it for you," she said, glancing at her watch. Not much time, she thought. Please let me have a few minutes in the apartment.

"I don't know," Aminah started, and began sobbing, her face in her hands, rocking back and forth. "I'm so sorry, miss . . ." she sobbed. "Since Mosab . . . You don't know . . . Jameel and I, even at his school, we don't exist."

"I know," Carrie said, sitting next to her and putting her hand on her shoulder. She glanced at her watch again. "Listen, when Mosab worked at home, where was it? Did he ever keep anything private? Something maybe he didn't want anyone to know about?" Of course, it was a million to one. The Security Forces would have gone over the apartment, Sabagh's safety deposit box, every relative's house, everywhere, with a fine-tooth comb, especially this apartment.

Carrie stood up and went to the window and looked down at the street, four stories below. There were two white Toyotas—she couldn't tell if they were the same two—and a black Mercedes double-parked in front of the building. They would be at the apartment any second. She grabbed Aminah's arms.

"They're coming. Do you know anyone he might have gone to?"

Aminah shook her head wildly. She looked terrified. She'd probably been interrogated by the Mukhabarat and the GSD before. She clutched at Carrie, her fingernails digging into her arms.

"Save us!" she cried. "For the sake of Allah, save us!"

There was a loud pounding of fists at the door and men shouting in Arabic to open up.

"Open up! *Shurtat!*" Police! "Security Forces! Open up at once or we'll break it in and shoot!"

"Don't! Please! I'm coming!" Aminah said, running to the door and opening it. As she did, Carrie slipped her passport back into her handbag and slung the bag over her shoulder, holding it tight under her arm.

The door flew open. Six men rushed in. Two of them grabbed Aminah, threw her to the floor, and handcuffed her.

"I'm an American State Department official! I have diplomatic immun—" Carrie started to shout, when she was knocked to the floor and handcuffed. "I have diplomatic immunity!" she shouted. Someone kicked her in the stomach. She felt a hand between her legs, poking, prying.

A man with garlic breath whispered: "Shut up, you American *sharmuta!*" Whore! They dragged her and Aminah down the elevator to the cars. She couldn't see what happened to the boy.

A half hour later, she was alone, sitting on a stool in a concrete interrogation room, her hands still handcuffed behind her. Her handbag was on a metal table. Something was wrong, she thought, getting a bad feeling. They hadn't taken her to the Al-Jehad police headquarters, but instead to an unmarked building near the old Al-Hijaz train station.

She could hear the sounds of someone being beaten and screams coming from another room nearby. She couldn't tell if it was a man or a woman. Please God it wasn't Aminah. The last thing she had wanted in all this was to bring added trouble to Mosab's family.

Three men came into the room. Two of them, big, muscled, in work shirts, stood there watching. The third, in a gray-striped suit, shirt open at the neck, came over and studied her as if she were a painting in a museum.

"As you can see from my passport in the bag, I'm an American diplomat," she said, looking up at him. "If I don't call into my embassy in less than an hour from now, you'll be hearing from people so high up in your government, you'll wish you were never born."

He came closer. She could smell his sweat and unwashed body odor. He backhanded her across the face, knocking her to the floor. He hit her so hard she thought her jaw was broken.

"Strip her clothes off," he told the other two men, who tugged her pants off. She squirmed and kicked at them, but they pinned her legs and pulled her panties down.

"Bastards!" she screamed, kicking. "Sons of bitches!"

She was naked. The man in the suit pulled her up by her hair to the stool and sat her on it. He started to unzip his fly.

"You American women like it in the mouth," he said. "You all do."

The other two men came closer. They were smiling.

"Do it and I'll bite it off," she said, her heart pounding.

He took out a pistol and put it to her head.

"You even start to think of it," glancing at the others, "I blow your whore head off. Now, all three of us, me first."

He started to free his erection from his trousers.

"Before you make the biggest mistake of your life, do one thing," she said. "Call your commanding officer. Make sure. Look in my handbag. You will see a photograph of Abd al Ali Nasser himself. Go and look at it, you fool!" she shouted in Arabic. "Look for yourself! He's the head of the Syrian Mukhabarat. Trust me, if he finds out what you've done, he'll kill you himself. All three of you, you stupid assholes! So will Abdulkader Salih, head of the GSD. Call him. Call your own commander. Right now. Make sure. Don't make the mistake of your life. Go look! Look! See if I'm lying. See the diplomatic passport. See the photograph. Look for yourselves, you fools!"

The smile had faded from the two men. The man with the pistol no longer had an erection. He glanced at the others, who looked at each other.

"She's lying," one of them said in Arabic, but without conviction.

"Easy to find out," the other said. He went and brought the handbag. They found the Glock pistol and looked at Carrie. Then the passport. Then the photograph of Abd al Ali Nasser and the Russian she'd printed on a printer at the embassy from a file on her laptop.

"Is this him?" the man in the suit asked. "Nasser?"

The other two men shrugged.

"Ask your boss?" Carrie said. "Or his boss? If I don't call into my embassy very soon, you'll be hearing from some very important people in the Syrian government. More important than your boss or his boss, I promise you. Are you sure you want to risk it?"

"Shut up, whore," the man in the suit said, grabbing her by her hair.

"Don't be stupid. Call your boss," she said, her head twisted by his grip.

He looked at the other men. "Just to make sure," he said, and went over to the table and called.

Carrie couldn't hear what was being said from the other end. The man in the suit kept saying "*na'am,*" "*na'am,*" "*na'am.*" Yes, yes, yes.

When the man in the suit finished he brusquely told them to untie her and let her get dressed.

It took two more interrogations, in nicer offices, but similar men and the same questions, till they came and brought her in a BMW sedan to the hotel in Bloudan outside Damascus.

Now, sitting there with Abd al Ali Nasser, watching the shadows of the mountains creep across the trees and the plain in the late afternoon, she put the photograph of him and the Russian on the table between them. He had, of course, already seen it, or they would never have met.

"So, how do we do this? Are we trading? Do I throw you in Adra Prison till we wring everything out of you and send what's left of you back to the CIA in exchange for something we might or might not want? What is it about this photograph, which may or may not be real or Photoshopped, that is so important?" Nasser said.

Here's the tricky part, Saul had said. Terra incognita. Put your pieces out one at a time. But nothing is sure. Not for you. Not for him. Start with what you know.

"Assume the photo is real, because it is and we both know it," she said. "It was taken at a waterfront restaurant on Büyükada Island in Istanbul."

"May I know the source?" he asked.

"What if I said Mossad? Israeli," she asked.

"But you are not Mossad, I hope," he said, and for a moment, she saw traces of the skull. Strange how that happened. "I would have no choice, Anne, is it? Although of course, we both know that's not your real name. Because if you were Mossad, dear Anne, pretty as you are, pleasant as this is, I would have to kill you." Pointing his finger at her like a gun. "I would do it personally. Today."

"You know I'm not or you would have done it already," she said, holding her breath. She tapped the photograph. "Tell me about the Russian."

"What makes you think he's a Russian?"

"Who is he?"

"You mean his real name? Haven't the foggiest. Don't know yours either. Sort of how we do business, we spies, isn't it . . . Anne?" He smiled. The seducer again.

"Where do you think he's from?"

"Eastern Europe. You're probably right about that. Not sure where. Not even sure about that."

"Who did he represent?"

"Himself mostly. Don't we all?" He glanced at her. "Is there a point to this?"

She nodded. "A very important point."

He exhaled a long stream of cigarette smoke. For a moment, she watched the smoke swirl against the backdrop of the nearby trees like mist. Whatever he said now would decide things, one way or the other, she thought.

"We're enemies, you and I," he said. "Syria is surrounded by powerful enemies: Turkey, Jordan, Israel, the American Army in Iraq. You want something from me. Me, in particular. And you went to a lot of trouble to get to me. Leading GSD men on a chase through Damascus, and losing them—this by someone who presumably has never been in Damascus before—nicely done, by the way. Why? This man? Why is he so important?"

"This man." She nodded. "And Abu Nazir." Taking an educated guess that the reason for the meeting between Nasser and the Russian in Istanbul had something to do with Abu Nazir and sanctuary for him in Syria. "We were surprised you permitted IPLA, a radical Sunni group, to establish itself here."

"You Americans!" he snapped. "You make blunders out of unbelievable ignorance. You are not like a bull in the china shop, you are like an elephant. You are so big, you break things even when you don't want to." He tapped the table with his finger. "My country, Syria. You think we are bad guys. I'm bad.

Assad is bad. But let me tell you something, Miss whatever-your-name-is. This is a big majority Sunni country. If the Sunnis were ever to rise here, even if we were stupid enough to have a real election, every Salafi, every lunatic jihadi in the world would be drawn here like moths to the flame.

"What would happen to the Christians in this country, then? The Kurds? The Druze? The Assyrians? The Palestinians? And us Alawites? And even Sunnis who just want to live like normal people, like it's not the Middle Ages? What if they were to win completely? You think it would be like some fine Constitutional Convention with Benjamin Franklin and George Washington? This is the Middle East. There would be a bloodbath in this country greater than the Holocaust of the Jews in Germany.

"And it wouldn't stop here," he went on. "They would expand their terrorism to Lebanon and Turkey and Europe. And then America, miss. A thousand times worse than your 9/11. You know why? Because they would have weapons captured from the Syrian Army. Serious weapons. That is the al-Qaeda way. And you Americans would stupidly blunder into it, the way you did in Afghanistan and Iraq, never even knowing what you did," he said, shaking his head.

"I think we can help each other," she said. "I think we have to."

"Why should I help you? Why should I even let you go? I should let you rot for the rest of your life in Adra Prison. You're a CIA agent conspiring with the wife of a traitor. What do you want?"

"Why did you give Abu Nazir sanctuary?"

"Not sanctuary. We ignored his presence. The way we ignored the presence of two helicopters that invaded our airspace near Otaibah recently." Staring at her. Shit, she thought. She didn't think they knew that.

"Why did you ignore him?"

"Because the alternative would have been pitched battles between Hezbollah and al-Qaeda in the cities of Syria. Right now Abu Nazir's interest is Iraq. Maybe he'll be killed there. We wish you Americans would do it for us."

"Is he back in Iraq now?"

Nasser didn't answer. The sun had gotten low enough that he took off his sunglasses and she could see his eyes. They were pale blue and gave nothing away. She understood why he didn't answer.

"It's a poor merchant in the souk who offers a customer tea and little gifts and she doesn't buy," she said.

He smiled. "Well, at least you are not completely ignorant," he said, motioning to the waiter hovering in the distance for another drink. "Do you want another?"

"Tell him not so sour this time," she said.

They waited till the waiter had gone.

"Is Abu Nazir back in Iraq?"

"*Kos emek,*" he cursed. "It's none of my business. He's not in Syria. Now it's your turn. What are you offering?"

He mustn't see it as a quid pro quo, Saul had cautioned her. He'll walk away. In Go, it's called *ko*. It's a threatening move. If done correctly, Saul told her, it should do more damage to your opponent than the value of losing the *ko* itself.

"The 2005 assassination of Rafik Hariri in Lebanon. We've identified two Hezbollah operatives who were responsible: Mustafa Rabi Badreddine and Salim Ghaddari," she said.

"So you say," he growled. "This is slander, propaganda."

"No. We have evidence, hard evidence."

"Have you?" he said. Looking as if he was about to kill her.

"There's more. We've tied an approval for the Hariri assassination and the RDX explosive used to one of your own

Mukhabarat agents who was working with the two men, Badreddine and Ghaddari, on the attack. I'll write his name down for you in case someone's recording this conversation," she said, taking out a pen and a small pack of Post-its from her handbag. She wrote the name on the top one, peeled it off, and stuck it on the table so he could read it.

The Hariri assassination had created an uproar in Lebanon that even four years later hadn't gone away. A United Nations tribunal was investigating the matter with the spotlight on Hezbollah and Syria. There was a serious possibility of international sanctions and renewed civil war in Lebanon if the tribunal ruled that Hezbollah and Syria were responsible.

His expression didn't change. He picked up the Post-it, looked at it, rolled it into a tiny ball, and stuck it in his pocket.

"And what were you planning to do with this?" he asked.

"Tell you. It's why I got myself arrested," she said as the waiter brought their drinks. She sipped the margarita, letting him go through the permutations and work out the trap Saul had lured him into.

"I could kill you," he said. Staring coldly at her, blue eyes, no Oakleys. She had no doubt he was seriously considering it, working out the pros and cons. "There would be no body. We would have no knowledge of what happened. People, women disappear all the time, even in America."

"Doesn't even the score. Not even a little. And your foreign minister's probably already gotten a phone call about me. Don't be stupid. We can help each other."

"All this, just for this man?" Tapping the photograph of him and the Russian.

"Who is he?"

"I told you, I don't know. Ask the Mossad, since according to you, they were there."

"We did. If they knew, I wouldn't be here. Did he give you a name?"

He hesitated briefly before he spoke.

"He called himself Haroyan. Marcos Haroyan. An Armenian name. He was apparently trying to mislead me. I'm a Syrian. Believe me, I know Armenians. This one was no Armenian."

"Who is he? Who does he work for?"

"I'm not sure. I got the idea that he was working for a third party, but I'm not sure who. But he's connected. This I know."

"How do you know?"

"Because he can deliver."

"Deliver what?"

"Anything. He's a fixer, a kind of broker."

"So you agreed to meet him in Istanbul sight unseen? Out of thin air? Who vouched for him?" Suddenly it hit her. "You'd heard about him before, hadn't you?" she said. "Maybe you didn't know his name or who he worked for, but you'd heard about him. Where? Who told you?"

He looked at her oddly.

"What is it?" she asked.

"Don't you know? *Ya Allah*, you don't know!" he said.

He leaned toward her. The sun was setting, turning the plain and houses below rose and purple. Lights in the hotel and the landscaping and in houses had been turned on. The view was magical. It was getting cold. In a minute, they would have to go inside. But Carrie didn't want to break the moment. This was what it had all been about. Wait for it, her instincts told her. Wait for it. "What about the UN Tribunal?" he said finally.

"The information on the Hezbollah agents directly involved, Badreddine and Ghaddari, will be turned over to the tribunal," she said.

"And the name that was on the Post-it?"

She didn't answer.

"So. Blackmail. I don't think so, Miss CIA Agent." Looking away. Lighting another cigarette.

"When your men—or GSD, who cares—first arrested me, they almost raped me. Three of them," she said, staring out at the lights and the darkening plain.

"Were you afraid?" he asked.

"Yes." Turning to look at him. "I was."

"Every government uses brutes. The problem is, they act like brutes," he said, taking a drag on his cigarette, then stubbing it out like it had a bad taste.

"Who was it who first told you about the Russian?" she asked.

"An ally of yours. English. A diplomat we assumed was an MI6 agent. Don't you people ever talk to your allies?"

"Do you tell the Iranians everything?"

"Of course not. Dealing with your friends can be more dangerous than your enemies," he said, and they both smiled.

"What happened?" she asked.

"We expelled the Englishman from Syria. Which, my dear Miss McGarvey, is what I am afraid we are going to do with you. You have twenty-four hours to leave the country." He stood up and looked at her. The skull was back. "Don't ever come back, miss. If you do, God willing, you will never leave. As we Arabs say, not in this life."

CHAPTER 12

Ibiza, Spain
20 April 2009

Saul was tired. So tired he'd fallen asleep in the taxi from the airport to the little village of Roca Llisa, not far from Ibiza town. The taxi driver woke him when they arrived at the villa. A concrete-and-glass slab, white as bone in the sun. The property was surrounded by a wrought-iron fence and was set amid a cluster of expensive villas and condos clinging to cliffs overlooking the sea.

Saul tried the gate. It was open. He hadn't expected that and wondered if he was making a mistake. He'd been wondering this a lot lately.

He'd just come in from Baghdad, where he'd met with Perry Dryer, CIA Baghdad Station chief, Virgil Maravich, the CIA "Black Bag" technical expert Carrie trusted above all others, and Lieutenant Colonel Chris Larson, whom General Demetrius had assigned as secret liaison on Operation Iron Thunder.

Although it was April, Baghdad was already turning hot, even at breakfast time. They met at his hotel room at the Rimal Hotel in the Karrada district on the east bank of the Tigris River.

They each arrived separately, a little uncertainly. It was the first time they had all met. He had deliberately chosen a hotel outside the Green Zone, one rarely used by U.S. personnel or journalists, even freelancers used to low-rent digs, to help preserve secrecy.

They understood that Iron Thunder was a separate operation, outside normal CIA channels. No reports or communications of any kind were to go to Langley.

"Everything through me. Only me," Saul told them. "And none of your subordinates or colleagues can know. No little winks or 'Sorry, can't say,' at the Al-Hamra." The Al-Hamra Hotel, everybody's favorite watering hole since they'd closed the Baghdad Country Club in the Green Zone.

"General Demetrius wants to know about a GO and if so, what classification?" Larson said.

"Yes. It has to be official. And Top Secret," Saul said. Issuing a General Order would make it an official military order. Top Secret was the highest U.S. security classification.

"But won't that—" Larson started. If the mole couldn't learn about the Iron Thunder General Order, wouldn't that defeat the purpose, was what he was going to ask.

"No. That's the damn point," Saul said, i.e., the mole already had access to Top Secret intelligence.

"There've been two bombings in Baghdad in the last two days. Back home, everyone thinks this damn war is over. We have indicators that the Mahdi Army is gearing up for something big here in Baghdad. Frankly, Saul, I'm not sure my reports are making it into the PDB," Perry said. The President's Daily Brief. The summary the president of the United States saw every day of the most critical intelligence issues.

"I know. The general is very worried. We are signing this damn agreement with the Iraqis. We are locked up," Larson said. He looked at Saul. "Do we have any kind of lead?"

Saul scratched his beard.

"You know the battle of Cannae? Hannibal?" he asked.

"Of course. Classic battle. We studied it at West Point," Larson said. "Hannibal defeated the Romans. He used a deceptively weak center to lure the Romans into attacking his center. Then, as they advanced into the trap, he attacked them on both flanks simultaneously in a classic double pincer move, completely destroying them. It's considered one of the greatest tactical victories of all time. Why?"

"Because that's what we're doing. Two flanks at the same time. One to deal with IPLA and the Sunnis; one to deal with the Iranians and the Shiites," Saul said.

"And us, the people in this room?" Perry asked.

"The deceptively weak center." Saul smiled. In the distance, they heard the sound of an explosion. They looked at each other. Baghdad.

Like Baghdad, Ibiza was also hot, but it was sunbathing hot, putting-on-sunscreen-after-an-hour-in-the-sun-so-you-don't-burn-too-badly hot. The kind of heat that gets people thinking about cold drinks and daytime sex.

Walking up the gate to the villa, all Saul could think of was that the blade he was about to use for the second flank cut both ways. He pressed the doorbell, but it didn't sound. He knocked, but when no one came, tried the door and it opened. He walked inside.

The stone-paved entryway led into a spacious room with glass windows, open to a broad teak deck with recliners and an infinity pool, framed by palm trees, and at the edge of the cliff, a breathtaking view of the Mediterranean and the island of Formentera. A man clad only in a towel around his waist was standing out on the deck, facing the view. As Saul came closer, the man whirled around in perfect shooting position, a 9mm Beretta pistol aimed directly at Saul's chest.

Dar Adal. The CIA's go-to person for Black Ops; the kind no one talked about, not even inside Langley.

"Jesus, Saul! Don't sneak up on me like that. I almost killed you. You set off a dozen damn sensors," Dar said. A thin, swarthy man, bald, goateed, with intense, intelligent eyes.

Two men rushed in from opposite sides of the house behind Saul. One was big, at least six foot four, muscular, in jeans and a T-shirt. The other was Spanish, about eighteen or nineteen years old and exceptionally good-looking. The kind of looks you might see on a male model in a perfume ad. He was wearing a silk bathrobe. Both men were holding MP5 submachine guns.

Dar waved them off. The good-looking young man, holding his MP5 like a banjo, smiled at Saul and went to another room. The big man, holding his MP5 like a soldier who knew exactly how to use it, stared at Saul suspiciously, then left.

"You want sangria?" Dar asked.

"Sangria? Are you kidding? What time is it? Ten A.M. Coffee," Saul said.

Dar went over and pressed the reheat button on the coffee maker.

"The young man's name is Antonio. He's twenty. And don't say a damn word," Dar said.

"I didn't say anything," Saul said.

"You didn't have to. I could see that little rabbi inside your head spouting some Talmudic bullshit on the evils of homosexuality without you saying a goddamn word. You always were a little *Yiddische* prude, something Mira, coming from a culture that invented the *Kama Sutra*, should've thought of before she married you," Dar said, sitting on the edge of one of the recliners. "How is she?"

Saul, sitting on a recliner facing him, didn't answer.

"Like I said, she should've given it more thought," Dar continued. "They don't teach that in college, do they?"

"Not at my alma mater. Part of my revolt. Back then, it was 'sex, drugs, and rock and roll.' My Orthodox Jewish parents came to visit just once when I was in college. Never even got to the dorm. They saw some Christian group sign-up tables outside the Student Union—and fled like the devil was after them."

"An orphan, like the rest of us. How the hell do you think we all got in this business?" Dar said, motioning to the young man, Antonio, who had reappeared dressed in linen slacks and a black Ninja Boy T-shirt.

Antonio brought Saul a cup of coffee and Dar a sangria with an orange slice, then smiled at them both and went back into the villa.

"What about you?" Saul said. "What were you running from? A little Druze boy, growing up with a gun in his hand in the Chouf in Lebanon?" Saul said.

"You're right," Dar said. "I went to the school of Kamal Jumblatt and the LNM. I learned to tape explosives and gouge fingernails at an age when most American kids are still learning how to spell *C-A-T*. The PLO, the Palestinians, were my teachers. The Maronites too, when they captured me once. They taught me things I'll never forget," he said, balancing the Beretta pistol on his thigh. "Look around, Saul," gesturing at the villa and the view of the blue Mediterranean Sea. "We're a long way from Mount Lebanon and the Chouf. What do you want?"

"We need to talk privately," Saul said.

Dar shrugged. "Go ahead."

Saul shook his head.

"I need to be sure I'm not being listened to, recorded, any of that," he said.

"You have a dirty mind," Dar said.

"I thought you said I was a prude. Where can we go?"

"You are. Prudes have the filthiest minds in the world. Come on," Dar said.

Still carrying the Beretta and calling for Hector, the big man, he grabbed a T-shirt, a pair of running shorts, and keys and dressed on the way to the front of the villa. They went outside. Dar and Saul got into a red Audi. Hector, carrying his MP5, followed in a Range Rover.

They drove along a winding road through the interior of Ibiza, the hills green from winter rains. Saul glanced at the side mirror. Hector was still behind them.

"I knew someone from Langley would come knocking. I wasn't going to be in exile forever," Dar said.

"Rawalpindi," Saul said. "You were supposed to provide cover. People were upset."

Dar drove around a sharp curve. The road sign said PUERTO DE SAN MIGUEL 10 KM.

"You know what happens when you're dealing with hordes of people and chaotic situations like a revolution. Mistakes happen. You should know that better than anyone," Dar said.

Like a punch to the solar plexus. Tehran, 1979. Four bodies laid out in a neat row in the safe house on Saidi Street near Mellat Park. Each with his hands tied behind him and a bullet in the back of his head. Sanjar Hootan. Tal'at Basari. Milad Rasgari. Ferhat Afshar. All courtesy of his onetime source and supposed friend Majid Javadi, Saul thought as they passed a roadside memorial. Crosses and wilted flowers for someone who died. You saw these markers everywhere in Spain. He looked back over at Dar.

"Well, they better not happen on this one," Saul said.

Dar turned off to a side road and drove along the top of a cliff. Even from the road, Saul caught glimpses of the sea. They drove past a hotel and then stopped near a sign that read LAS CUEVAS DE COVA DE CAN MARÇÀ.

A gated entrance led to stairs on the face of the cliff going down to the caves. Below them was a beautiful cove with a sandy beach and aquamarine water.

"Don't worry, we're not going down there," Dar said, indicating the stairs as they got out of the car. Instead, they hiked a rocky path to the top of the cliff overlooking the sea.

Saul looked around. Except for Hector, sitting in the Land Rover about a hundred meters away, there was no one around. Nothing but sea and sky, the cove below, and the sound of the wind. As listener-proof as this world was ever going to get. They looked at each other.

"This is a Special Access Critical operation. The focus is Iraq . . . and Iran. Code name: Operation Iron Thunder. It's being run by me outside Langley. Completely separate operation and very, very tight," Saul said.

"Son of a bitch," Dar said. "You've got a mole." Amazing how quickly he had figured it out, Saul thought. People forgot that about Dar. They focused on his ruthlessness, his effectiveness, forgetting how smart he was.

"Dar, no killing. We need intel, not bodies," Saul said.

"You're too damn squeamish for your own good. You always were."

Saul smiled. "Not according to the Kamal Jumblatt school-of-warfare playbook?"

"He took me in, you know. After the Phalange raped and murdered my mother. My father had been blown up . . . oh, years earlier," Dar said, shrugging at the memory. "Old Kamal himself. Him and his son, Walid. I was one of a number of orphans he groomed." He looked out at the sun sparkling on the water below. "You're wrong about my education, Saul. I'd done one year at the American University in Beirut when the civil war finally exploded and he called me back to fight. That was '75. Where were you?"

"Africa. Burundi."

"Another shithole."

"It's where I met Mira," Saul said.

Kirundo Province. Both of them working with refugees. An amazing time despite the nightly Rwanda-Burundi cross-border killings between Tutsis and Hutus, because in that tent with her for the first time in his life, Saul felt alive. Her from India, him the Jewish boy from Indiana; beings from two different planets. And yet, Mira.

Dar nodded. "Old Kamal. Intellectually, he was a communist. He used to quote Marx, Lenin, Trotsky, to us."

"Really? Like what?" Saul said.

"His favorite saying was a line from Trotsky: 'You may not be interested in war, but war is interested in you.'"

CHAPTER 13

The French were putting on a show. Petits fours, napoleons, pâtés, cheeses, champagne, jazz on loudspeakers, a video show with scenes from Paris, the Loire châteaux, and Provence. There was even a Marcel Marceau–like mime, circulating among the local diplomatic corps, Turkish officials, and to Carrie's eye, at least three MIT (Turkish intelligence service) agents. She had come here on the trail of the Englishman Abd al Ali Nasser had told her about, the only lead to the Russian. The reception was being held in the *très* old fashioned French consulate building on Istiklâl Caddesi, just a block or two from Taksim Square.

"A froggy mime! And piss to drink," Gerry Hoad said, pouring his champagne into a potted palm. "I hate the bloody French." He was middle-aged, rumpled tweed, shirt collar out in back—no woman in his life to see that he's presentable, Carrie thought—and his longish hair was in need of a haircut. He looked like a midlevel academic hanging on for tenure instead of what he was, a diplomat whose career had driven into a ditch.

"It's their turn to do the DD. The mime's perfect, actually.

Repulsive, but he makes no noise," Sally Rumsley said. She had dirty-blondish hair longer than she should; a woman of what the French call "a certain age." Still attractive, slim, angular, but she'd reached the stage that when it came to men, she'd have to be more the hunter than the hunted, Carrie thought.

She was feeling good. Maybe too good. She hadn't taken clozapine in thirty-six hours and it was starting to show. Getting a twitch there, Carrie, she thought. Wanting a man between your thighs maybe? Missing Warzer too. Where the hell was he? Doing something for Saul? It had all happened so fast once the Otaibah mission got approved, she'd barely had time to say good-bye.

Only Warzer to see her off in that utilitarian little departure building at Camp Victory before she'd left for FOB Delta and the Otaibah raid. One hurried kiss and then the helicopter lifting off and a reminder from the air of all the damn palm trees in Baghdad, the view of the Tigris River, and once they'd gained altitude and cleared the city, only desert.

"What's the DD?" Carrie asked.

"Diplomatic Dervish. This month France heads the EU, so it's their turn to reject any overture from the Turks while simultaneously telling them how much we value their cross-cultural contributions, whilst at the same time showing them how much they have to learn from us superior Europeans. It's rather like kissing someone while kneeing them in the goolies. You just have to keep on spinning," Sally said.

A heavyset man in his fifties, Savile Row suit, hair in a comb-over, smiled and waved at someone as he approached.

"Why aren't you two circulating? And this is?" Indicating Carrie.

"Sorry, Simon," Gerry said. "Miss Anne McGarvey, this is Simon Duncan-Jones. Our Consul General, Head of Mission,

Ruler of the Keep, OBE, CMG, etcetera, etcetera." Making a circular semigenuflecting motion with his hand. "Mr. Simon Duncan-Jones, Miss McGarvey of the American State Department."

Duncan-Jones looked at him. "Don't be deliberately dim, Gerry." Then peered at Carrie. "Are you for real or is Langley sending us another damned spook? Heard you got booted out of Damascus. You two have something in common." Pointing at her and Gerry. "I hope it's not incompetence."

"I don't plan to be in Istanbul long, Mr. Duncan-Jones. Just here to get the lay of the land," Carrie said.

"The lay of the land is that this country is in crisis. The Islamists mean to finish off the generals and the secularists with this Ergenekon trial and there's talk of coups and civil war. We don't need our Americans cousins screwing things up here as in Iraq," Duncan-Jones said.

"Don't worry, Mr. Duncan-Jones. I wouldn't screw you for anything," Carrie said to Gerry and Sally's muffled sniggers. Oh Lord, she thought. Did I just say that? She was starting to fly. Really fly. She'd better take a clozapine the next chance she got.

Duncan-Jones glared at them.

"Circulate, you two," he said, and walked away.

"Whose cousin is he to get this job?" Carrie asked, lifting a glass of champagne from a passing waiter and taking a sip.

"Didn't need one," Sally said. "It's the bugger-all Eton, St. Paul's, Oxbridge mob. Good old Simon Duncan-Jones just put one plodding foot in front of the other. You Yanks have your Dems and Republicans cock-ups, we have our class wars. You wouldn't know I took a First at Lancaster, not that it matters. Those nobs wouldn't know a college even existed out past Blackpool. Gerry, darling, Anne and I are going to the loo." She pulled Carrie aside.

"Ace. I'll wait here and wave the Union Jack, if anyone gives a shite," Gerry said, grabbing a piece of cheese with a toothpick stuck in it from a passing waiter and waving it like a flag.

Sally led Carrie out of the noisy entry hall and down a long hallway to the *toilettes des dames*.

Inside, Sally leaned against the sink, pulled out a hashish pipe, tapped down the black paste, and lit up. She took a deep drag, then offered it to Carrie, who took a drag. It hit her at once. Between that and the champagne and the no clozapine she was feeling no pain.

She smiled at herself in the mirror. She looked good. Nice dress. Her one and only LBD. Pretty Carrie. No, she was Anne. Starting to lose it, Carrie? Remember cover. Saul, long ago at the Farm, telling them: "Cover isn't just some temporary identity; it's who you are." She dug into her handbag, turned away, found the clozapine, and took one with a sip of water from the sink in her cupped hand.

"What's that?" Sally asked. "Anything interesting?"

"Diabetic," Carrie said. She'd learned long ago that saying anything else, tummy, headache, anything, might prompt the other person to ask for one.

"Ah. So, love, what really happened in dreary Damascus?" Sally asked, taking a big hit from the pipe and exhaling a dank-smelling stream of smoke.

"No good deed goes unpunished. Tried to help someone. Next thing, I'm officially slapped on the wrist and sent here to mull over my sins," Carrie said.

"Lucky it's only your wrist they slapped," Sally said, eyeing her.

"Yes." Thinking of that concrete interrogation room near the old Al-Hijaz station, the man in the suit's penis, then blinked to shake it off. "What about Gerry? This a way station for him too?"

"Gerry, is it?" Sally smirked. "Didn't think your taste ran in that direction, darling. Still, between us girls, trying to find a decent cock, circumcised or the very rare uncircumcised one in these parts, that doesn't stink of kebabs, is damned near impossible. Much less trying to find the owner of one who actually knows what to do with it. And you've got to be bloody careful. How you dress. How you move. Especially with Turko males. Just shake hands with one and he thinks it means you want him to bang your bum," she said.

"What about you guys? How's Istanbul for you?"

"It's the same for us as for you. Let's not kid ourselves. Istanbul may be a world city, but this is still just a la-de-da consulate, a diplomatic backwater. The embassy's in Ankara. That's where the action is. And it's not the big time. It's not Washington or Beijing or Moscow. It's bollocks really. Mmm, you have lovely skin," she said, coming close, touching Carrie's cheek. "I used to have skin like that. Now I'm like a bloody tortoise. It's a wonder men don't crawl away at the sight of me."

Carrie looked at her. She had beautiful china-blue eyes.

"You're still an attractive woman," she said, holding Sally's arms. For a moment, they were almost on the verge of kissing and Carrie wondered whether it was the hashish or the lack of clozapine that hadn't kicked in yet or everything that had happened since Syria.

"You're a liar," Sally said. "A very pretty, young, American liar, but thank you anyway, darling. Anyway, it doesn't matter. For me, Istanbul's the last stop on the FO pension train. It's not bad, actually, except for the Turko males groping your bum everywhere you go. Wonderfully exotic. Food's a marvel. Not a prob. I'll go back to Lancaster or Leeds, suck some lucky gent's cock till he says 'I do,' and be one of those old ladies who tell scandalous lies about their wild days to the little girls. Except of course, in my case"—she winked—"they won't be lies."

"What about Gerry?" Carrie asked.

"Gerry's PNG. Gerry's bloody finished."

"PNG?"

"Sorry, persona non grata. Our little world has its own language; sorry, sorry."

"What did he do to get PNG? Get thrown out of Syria? In America, some of us regard it as a badge of honor," Carrie said.

"Haven't the foggiest. Everyone assumes he's MI6, but of course, naughty to talk about that. It wasn't Damascus, whatever happened there. No, dearest, Gerry's train ran off the rails before that," she mused. "Of course, Simon D-J absolutely loathes him. The only thing no one understands is why he hasn't cashiered him already." She looked sharply at Carrie. "Why the hell are you so bloody interested all of a sudden? He's not rich, darling, and he's not exactly dishy, our Gerry, is he?"

"No biggie, really." Carrie shrugged. "Apart from a couple of people at our consulate, you two are the only people I know in Istanbul. Why?"

"Gerry's a sod." Sally made a face. "Bugger Gerry."

What happened there? Carrie wondered. They each took another hit on the hashish pipe and went back out to the entry hall. Gerry joined them at the guest-book table. He looked like a boy, ready to escape school any way he could. Carrie looked around. Eleven P.M.; early by Istanbul standards. The gathering was still going strong.

"Have you been enjoying the soirée, *mes amies?*" a young dark-haired Frenchman behind the guest-book table asked.

"Wonderful," Carrie said. "Best party of the season," she wrote in the guest book.

"Formidable," Gerry said, signing. *"Incroyable."*

"Simon of Duncan-Jones will be cheesed at you leaving so early," Sally said.

"Excellent," Gerry said. "He can mime telling me off in the morning. He can practice with the bloody frogs."

"You're such a prick, Gerry," Sally said, turning and going back into the main room.

Carrie hesitated for a moment, then followed Gerry outside. The two of them stood in the crowded street outside the embassy, light spilling from nearby shops. There were electric lights strung over the street and they had to get out of the way as a red-and-white tram came clanging by.

"I believe our Sally's going to try her luck with the Frenchman at the table," he said.

"Why is she so pissed at you? Did you kick her out of bed?" Carrie said.

He didn't answer, just began to walk. She stayed with him.

"Jeez, that's it, isn't it? She wanted to screw you and you said no, you shit. Is that it?"

He stopped and looked at her. People, mostly Turks, walked around them, ignoring them.

"I like Sally. She's at the curling-together-by-the-fire stage, so she won't be that old woman in the tattered sweater who lives alone with thirty cats, but *entre nous* I don't fancy her that way. Where to?" he said.

"There are ways of doing it," Carrie said. "There are ways."

"Well, why don't you bloody well teach me? Because I've had plenty of women slam the door in my face and they didn't seem to mind the least little bit." He looked at her closely. "You seem lost. Where do you want to go?"

"I'm not sure," Carrie said. "I'm pretty high."

Almost unconsciously, they moved with the flow of the crowd toward Taksim Square.

"Do you want to get a drink? There's a semidecent Irish pub in Taksim Square."

"No thanks. I've had enough obnoxious Brits for one night," Carrie said, swaying and walking unevenly. Then, aware of how that came out, "Sorry, I didn't mean you."

"Of course you did," he said. "It's all right. We were obnoxious. We sit in our own grand consulate stew, poisoning each other with our own juices."

Carrie stopped walking.

"No, I didn't mean you," looking at him, his unruly hair haloed by the haze of electric lights over the street. "I meant your asshole of a boss, Simon Dunkin'-Donuts or whatever the hell he calls himself." She touched his arm. The whole purpose of her coming to Istanbul was to get him alone and talking. "I want to go to your place."

Something in his face changed. His eyes, the lines in his forehead; he looked younger, more attractive. She became conscious of all the people in the street. The city had an electricity about it, like New York or London, she thought. A street vendor selling *simit*, Turkish-style bagels, in the crowd was calling out, "*Simit! En iyi!*"

"Does that mean you want to sleep with me?" he said.

"I haven't decided. Do you have something to drink? Something decent?"

"Just a bottle of Yeni raki. Look, I haven't done this . . . it's been some time. If you're not sure, there's a rooftop bar not too far from here."

"My God, when it comes to sex, Englishmen are unbelievable. No wonder Sally's ready to hump the furniture. If we have sex, we have sex. We have to talk," she said.

"Regarding . . . ?" He smiled.

"Vauxhall Cross," she said, referring to the location of MI6 headquarters in London, and his smile disappeared.

He had a studio flat on the top floor of a building in the Eskişehir neighborhood in Beyoglu. From his window he showed her, over the roofs of buildings on down a hill, you could catch a fragmentary glimpse of the minarets of the Dolmabahçe mosque, lit up at night against the darkness of the Bosphorus.

They sat on the bed against the wall, with glasses of raki, mixed with water and ice from the fridge. Carrie, her legs curled beneath her, was feeling, not better, but more normal now. Not so buzzy. The clozapine had kicked in, thank God.

Between them on the bed were the photos and flash drive with the video she'd shown him on her laptop of the Russian, first with Abu Nazir, then with Abd al Ali Nasser.

"His name's Lebedenko. Syarhey Lebedenko," he told her, pointing at the photo of the Russian.

"You know him?" she asked.

"Too bloody well. Biggest catch of my life—and he ruined it. My life. And it wasn't even his fault."

"So why didn't MI6 tell Langley who he was when we inquired?"

"Oh, Carrie, darling, you are naive about us Brits. The one absolute rule that VC holds sacred above all others, that must never ever be broken, is 'Never expose the holes in our undies to the Cousins.'"

"Meaning us Americans?"

"Indeed."

"And this was a hole?"

"Like your Grand Canyon is a ditch," he said, finishing his raki. He got up to refill their glasses.

"How'd you meet?" she asked.

He looked sharply at her. "None of this gets back to Vauxhall Cross?"

"Not even Langley. Just you, me, and the only man in the whole damn Company I trust," she said, crossing her heart like the little Catholic girl she once was.

"We were running a honey trap," Gerry said, nodding. "This was Skopje. Piss-all god-awful stinking Macedonia. Gorgeous country. Mountains, forests, but sweet mother of God, the bunghole of the universe. New Year's Eve, 2003. You Americans, and we Brits right behind you, were banging the war drums to charge saber tips up into Iraq. All on bullshit intel, but that, as you'll see, is part of our bedtime story. Because this, my darling Carrie"—she'd told him her real name; part of the deal, as Saul had indicated she might have to, for him telling her the gospel truth and nothing but—"is a love story."

"Who was the target? Of the honey trap?" she asked.

"A UN pooh-bah, down from Pristina, Kosovo, for the sex. In those days, there were whole towns of Macedonia that were brothels pure and simple, a giant neon stop on the sex trade motorway. The op was equally slimy. VC, that is, Vauxhall Cross, was pushing us to 'persuade' UN types to support our upcoming attack on Iraq. All on bullshit intel from MI6 and the CIA."

"Not our finest hour," Carrie said, half to herself.

"Well, we weren't exactly Churchillian either." He nodded. "The girl, Mariana, pretty little thing. Honey-blond hair. Like a little angel. She'd been trafficked from Moldova; sold for four hundred dollars American. We'd paid off her Albanian pimp, a miserable piece of human fecal waste named Agron, gave him an extra hundred euros to shut his blowhole, and told her if she played along with us, she'd be back in Chişinău—or the UK, if she wished—by the following night. Poor girl just wanted to go home."

"What happened?"

"A rumpus. Banging, screaming. On the floor above us. Sounded like someone was being killed. Of course, we were in the next-door room, peeking at our dirty little video screen, me feeling like a perv, when little Mariana comes running in, clad in nothing but her undies, Pooh-bah with his pants down, the honey trap ruined, and she's begging me to come help.

"She's sobbing, pulling at me desperately. Something about her best friend, Alina. So up we go, me with my Beretta, and my backup, a big off-duty Macedonian copper named Boban, who grabs—no joking—this big brass knuckle-duster with a knife, looked like something from World War One—and we run upstairs, expecting to save some sexy young thing, Alina. Sir Galahad to the rescue, eh?"

"I actually like that." Carrie smiled. "What happened?"

"It was that scum, Agron. He had a bloody nose and banged-up eyelid, but he and one of his mates, who had a length of iron pipe, were pounding on a poor sod, who kept trying to punch Agron, screaming, 'Where is she, you bastard? Where is she?' Then the mate hit the aforementioned sod a wicked blow to the arm that broke it—you could hear it—then punched him in the side of the head, and he was down, stunned, helpless, but still demanding to know where she was.

"Agron pulls out a switchblade, grabs the guy's head, and is about to stab it in his eye when I put the Beretta to Agron's head and suggested he reconsider. Boban is less gentle with the mate."

"And the poor sod?"

"Lebedenko. I didn't know it, but he was the biggest fish of my life. Not Russian, by the way. From Belarus. Minsk. More about that in a sec."

He poured refills for them both, added the water from a pitcher, then stirred the raki with his finger, drained it, and looked at her.

"You really are the damnedest woman. Pretty too. Suppose I shouldn't say that. Am I a total fool?"

"Not total. Everyone's lonely," she said quietly.

"The damnedest woman," he muttered. "Where were we?"

"The fight," she said.

"Right. Turns out Lebedenko had paid Agron four thousand euros to pay off this sex slave Alina's quote-unquote 'debt' to him. But when he came to pick her up, she was gone. Agron had sold her to—we later found out—a Bosnian trafficker from Mostar, figuring to kill Lebedenko and so get paid twice for the girl.

"We put Agron and his mate in the boot of Agron's Volks-wagen, took Lebedenko with us, and drove—it wasn't far, the brothel was out past Mother Teresa—into the forest going toward Vodno. We stopped in the middle of the woods, took them out, tied them to a tree, persuaded them we were about to kill them, and basically got everything we could out of them. Which was, among other things, the name of the pimp they sold the girl to and where to get hold of him.

"We patched up Lebedenko as best we could. He and I spent the rest of the night drinking Russian vodka in a bar right next to the brothel. Bar was a bog of a place, but it stayed open all night just for us. He showed me a photo of Alina. Carrie, even in a photo, she was a stunner. Long dark hair, unbelievable blue eyes. Sure she was less than half his age. Maybe more. He didn't give a rat's arse. Lebedenko was over the moon for her.

"You know how it is, sometimes, those of us in this game. Even if we're enemies, sometimes we just connect. I used MI6 resources to help track down Alina. Because Lebedenko was an incredible find. His firm, Belkommunex, was a front company. They weren't subtle about it either. I mean, bloody hell, it was located in Minsk on Nezalezhnostsi Prospekt, right across the effin' street from KGB headquarters.

"It was Lebedenko's company that sold Saddam Hussein the mustard and sarin gas he'd used on the Kurds. They were also involved with certain key instruments for Saddam's Osirak nuclear reactor, the one that the Israelis destroyed. Lebedenko knew more about WMDs in Iraq than Saddam himself. That night, after we'd killed a couple of bottles of Russian Standard between us, both of us nine-tenths pissed, he told me Saddam was bluffing. There were no WMDs in Iraq."

"You knew? Before the war?"

He nodded. "When I sent that report to VC, they buried it—and me. I had forgotten the most elementary rule of government service: 'never tell your masters what they don't want to hear,'" he said.

"And the girl?"

"Total cock-up." He grimaced. "She got packaged and repackaged. Wound up getting sold to some Saudi princeling. One of the many, many offspring. Nasty rich and swinish as it gets. Private parties outside Riyadh. Apparently auctioned off her virginity a couple of dozen times. Men wanted to believe. She was that drop-dead gorgeous. After that, sometimes twenty, thirty men a night. By this time, the price for buying her out had gone up, way up. At one point, it was a hundred and thirty thousand pounds sterling. Poor Lebedenko couldn't compete.

"Eventually, she got AIDS. Her looks began to go. The princeling sold her to somebody else. But here's the thing. Lebedenko still loved her.

"No matter where she was—and I made sure to keep him posted—he would scratch up the money, get on a plane, put on a condom . . . see, it really is a kind of what? Compulsion? Love? You tell me," he said.

That word, she thought. Love, the undefined country.

"What about her? Alina? How does she feel?"

"Who the hell knows?" He shrugged. "After all that happened to her? Her family's starving, like the rest of her whole bloody country, so according to Mariana, she applies for a job as a waitress in a restaurant in Italy. Next thing she knows she's being gang-raped and sold as a sex slave in Macedonia. You know the rest. Lebedenko isn't older than her. He's decades, aeons older than her. How the devil can she feel? On the other hand, he's the only person in the world who's trying to help her. Six years he's been trying to free her. You tell me how she feels?"

"You're right. Who knows?" Carrie said. "Where is she now?"

"Bahrain. Manama. Private club."

"And Lebedenko?"

"He needs forty thousand American dollars. He's got eighteen. If someone were to stake him . . . ?"

"You mean for twenty-two thousand we could—Lord!" She stared at him, sitting there, all angles on the bed, like an aging graduate student.

She had to get this to Saul, she thought. This could be the ball game. Then something hit her. There was a catch. There's always a catch, Carrie.

"Wait!" she said. "You said he was a big fish. That he was connected. Sold sarin gas to Saddam. What else? Abd al Ali Nasser in Syria said you vouched for Lebedenko. What are we talking about? And if you were able to schmooze with al Ali Nasser, why'd they kick you out of Syria? What's missing here?"

"Clever girl, Carrie. Idiots like Simon, what-did-you-call-him, Dunkin'-Donuts, don't see any of it, do they? *Très* good." He smiled. "Because what al Ali Nasser may have forgotten to mention was that our little friend of the working girl, Syarhey Lebedenko, wasn't out of the poison-sarin-gas business. He was selling tons of it to Syria through the Mukhabarat. Outing me, a British diplo-slash-MI6 agent so they could chuck me out made Lebedenko look aces to al Ali Nasser, made al Ali Nasser look even better to President Assad, and made me look like royal shit to VC, which is what they pretty much thought of me anyway," he said.

"So that's why MI6 didn't tell us about Lebedenko or you. It's worse than holes in your undies," Carrie said. "MI6 had intel there were no WMDs that might've stopped us from going into Iraq and never passed it along to us. No wonder you're P—what's the expression?"

"PNG, Carrie. Persona non grata. I'm the family embarrassment. They don't want me around. They can't get rid of me. They can't let anyone know I exist. I'm the perfect metaphor for the modern Englishman, the Invisible Man."

"Ah, but we had other sources. Moscow Station should've known about Lebedenko. He was KGB. Right across the street from the KGB office in Minsk, you said. So why couldn't they find him?"

"You're warm. You're burning. I told you he was a jolly big catch, didn't I? If he was being run—and let's face it, Belarus is not an independent country no matter what they pretend; when Russia sneezes, they get pneumonia—then one must ask the question of the day: who the bloody hell was running him? Remember, our lover boy, Lebedenko, has been around awhile. So who ran him, eh? Back in the day? Before the SVR? Back in the bad old KGB Cold War days? Maybe someone who's moved up in the world. Way up."

"Holy shit, Gerry. Are you talking about the president of Russia?" she said.

Gerry smiled.

"Of course," she said. "He would have had all those KGB records about him destroyed. Anyone who would have said anything would have been either gotten rid of or . . . no wonder the CIA's Moscow Station came up empty."

She finished her raki and put the empty glass, along with the photo and the flash drive, on the nightstand, then stood up and pulled off her top.

"It's getting late. Turn off the light," she said.

He did, then undressed. They fumbled on the bed, pulling off clothes, groping at each other, trying to find room on the bed and a comfortable way to fit together.

"Is this really happening?" he said, cupping her breasts with his hands.

"Wait. Back in Macedonia. What happened with the girl, Mariana?" she asked.

"I sent her back to Chişinău. Gave her whatever cash I could spare. Not much. A hundred quid, but it was something. They have nothing there."

"And the Albanians?"

"Put 'em back in the boot. Boban tossed 'em in the local lockup. A double win for old Boban. He got to keep the money they had on them plus credit for the arrest, plus he got to take over their share of the brothel and their girls in addition to his own. Told you he was bent. The entire country's a bolluxed-up bunghole. Oh God, that feels good."

"And Lebedenko?"

"He reconnected with me after Damascus. Business is business, old chap; you know the drill. I suppose it was his way of apologizing."

"Or more likely, his way of still using you," she said.

He got up on one elbow and looked at her.

"You are good. Damned good."

"Lebedenko," she said, touching him. "He's 'the Russian,' right?"

"Uh-huh . . . Last I heard, he was leaving Iraq. Told me something was going to blow there very soon. I'm giving you straight intel, Carrie. Everyone thinks the bloody war there is over. Focusing on the financial crisis and the politics in America. Lebedenko knows Iraq. Since the days of Saddam. But he says it's all going to change very soon," Gerry said.

"Where's he now?"

"Can't you guess? Oh yes! Oh, that's good."

"Bahrain. And needing money? For her?" she said.

"God, yes. Please, yes. Yes."

CHAPTER 14

The heat. And the humidity that wrapped itself around him like a hundred steamed towels the second he stepped out of the air-conditioned terminal. Saul and Dar looked at each other in the taxi coming in from the airport on the Prince Khalifah Causeway.

"I always forget how hot it is," Saul said, using a handkerchief to wipe the sweat off his glasses, checking his cell-phone app, which showed the local temperature at 112 degrees F.

"Thank God it's April, when it's still cool. Glad we're not doing this in July," Dar said. He told the driver to turn off the causeway on Avenue 22, near the U.S. naval base. Bahrain was headquarters for the U.S. Navy's Fifth Fleet in the Persian Gulf.

The taxi took them past the U.S. base. Sand-colored buildings surrounded by chicken-wire fences topped with barbed wire. It was nearing dusk. Lights and neon signs were coming on in buildings set against a purple-gold sky. Now they were going through backstreets in the Juffair district. Around them were cars and taxis full of sailors and Marines on a forty-eight-hour pass, Arabs in white flowing *thaubs* on motorcycles, and a passing minibus packed like sardines with migrant Indian workers. Evening in Bahrain.

Turning onto Shabab Avenue, they saw a parade of prostitutes, mostly young Asian or Filipina girls in barely there miniskirts or skintight short-shorts, high heels, and bikini tops lining the street in front of the shops, buildings, and restaurants, interspersed with Gulf women in head-to-toe abayas, only their eyes showing, sailing by the prostitutes like black ghosts.

"You picked a helluva spot. I thought Exhibition Avenue was the place for street whores in Manama," Dar said.

"I guess business is expanding," Saul said, turning away.

He wasn't thinking about the prostitutes. Bahrain had become the Las Vegas of the Arab world, only instead of gambling and entertainment, it sold alcohol and whores. On the weekends, the King Fahd Causeway, a seventeen-mile bridge from the Saudi Arabian mainland to the small island kingdom, was jammed with traffic that made L.A.'s 405 at rush hour look like an empty country road. Every car and SUV was filled with young Saudi males flush with oil money, anxious for what they couldn't get at home: all the booze they could drink, the music they could dance to, and the girls they could buy.

The only problem was the competition: male tourists from other Arab countries, American sailors and Marines from the Fifth Fleet, and civilian contractors on TDY allowances. But the prostitutes triggered thoughts in Saul about the intel Carrie had sent him from Istanbul about Lebedenko and his infatuation with the girl, Alina. Maybe it was true. "The rose grows among thorns," his father had taught him, quoting from the Talmud. He glanced over at Dar, busy checking for tails, eyes flicking at the taxi's mirrors and the cars behind them. He was there, just in case.

The taxi pulled up in front of a ten-story apartment build-

ing, set back behind a row of shops and a pizza restaurant on
Road 4020. They got out with their suitcases. Dar looked up at
the roof as they walked toward the entrance. The windows in
the building were rectangles of gold from the sunset.

"Did you rent this place by the hour?" Dar said.

"Might as well've," Saul said, pulling his suitcase behind him.

They went up in the elevator. The apartment was on the
top floor. As they got out, a young American woman, packing
a baby in a BabyBjörn and pulling a two-wheeled shopping
cart, smiled at them as she got in the elevator.

"Navy wife," Dar muttered as they went down the hallway
to the apartment.

"Dar, nobody gets hurt here," Saul said, and knocked twice,
then twice again. Virgil, gun in hand, opened the door.

"How are we doing?" Saul asked, coming in and looking
around.

"We're good. JWICS set. Computers. Cameras. Bugs. Cell
phones. I've already programmed them for us." Passing out
prepaid cell phones to them for local use. They would be disposed of quickly so they couldn't be easily tracked. "I set up a
small dish on the roof with a wire drilled through to the apartment. It's pretty well hidden. I don't think anyone'll spot it. If
they do, we'll be gone."

While Dar checked the rest of the apartment, Virgil spread
out on the table two SIG Sauer 9mm pistols with sound suppressors, an H&K MP5 submachine gun, magazines of am-
munition, and an H&K FP6 short-barreled shotgun and a box
of shells.

"A shotgun? Is that necessary?" Saul asked Dar, coming
back into the room.

"Better for close work," Dar said, loading it with twelve-
gauge shells.

"Where'd we get these?" Saul asked.

"Courtesy of the Navy," Virgil said, nodding in the direction of the navy base.

"How'd you manage that?" Saul asked.

"Well, I didn't ask." Virgil smiled. He went to the refrigerator and came back with three bottles of Stella beer. They sat around the table, sucking down the cold beer.

"What do you think?" Saul asked them.

Virgil shrugged. "What does Carrie say?"

Dar looked at him sharply. "You value her opinion that much?"

He's never met her, Saul thought, deciding he wanted to keep it that way. Virgil nodded.

"Fifty-fifty," Saul said. "Maybe it started as an infatuation, but five years as a sex slave is a long time. And we're getting this from a KGB, now SVR spy who sells poison gas for a living as told by a soggy Brit who's hanging on by his fingernails. She likes this Gerry Hoad. Thinks he's worth more than he's being given credit for, but she also thinks maybe he wants to believe because it keeps him in the game. On the other hand, the story about MI6 hiding him from us because of the screw-up on 9/11 rings true."

"Because . . . ?" Dar said.

"Because they bury their mistakes the same way we do. That's what intelligence services are for. To lie to each other whenever needed," Saul said, wiping foam from his lips. He pointed his beer bottle at Dar.

"I hope you're not planning on using that thing," indicating the shotgun. "We don't want a bloodbath. This isn't the O.K. Corral."

"No. This is for emergencies only. For security I have someone special," Dar said.

"Good," Saul said, picking up the SIG Sauer and awkwardly loading the magazine. "Because I haven't fired one of these since the firing range during training. Probably blow my damn foot off."

In the evening, Saul sat uncomfortably on the chair in the hotel room, waiting. The cash he had brought, $22,000 in hundreds, was in a paper bag on the coffee table in front of him. He was aware he was being watched. He had spotted two hidden cameras, one at an angle to the bed, as well as a bug, before he sat down. He was also wired for sound. Dar, with a mobile listening device and an FP6 shotgun, was listening in the room directly across the corridor. Virgil, also listening, was in an SUV, parked across the street to cover the hotel entrance.

The room was on the top floor of a ten-story hotel two blocks from "American Alley," the street leading from the main gate of the U.S. naval base. It was lined with Burger King, McDonald's, Avis, Chili's, and other American franchises. The first two floors of the hotel were filled with nightclubs and bars that throbbed with clashing types of music on loudspeakers: Filipino Pinoy, Arabic, and throbbing American hip-hop blasting so loud it could be heard even on the top floor.

When they finished wiring him up and doing a sound check, just before he had gone into the room, Saul stuck a stick of Black Jack gum, soft from the heat, into his mouth.

"You still do that for luck?" Dar said.

Saul nodded.

"Where'd that start?"

"Can't remember."

Dammit, Dar, did you have to bring that up, Saul thought. Now he couldn't help thinking about it. "Little Saul, all by himself on the playground," Mira had said. If she only knew. At home, Jewish ritual and silence, his parents always listening to the news on the TV. "Did you hear? The Syrians shelled Israel again, those momsers. Wait, it'll be war again."

At school, he was not only the only kid who wore a yarmulke, he was the only boy the other kids had ever seen wearing one. The white-bread Indiana kids treated him like someone from another galaxy. The only thing he knew was that he was alone and that evil, unspeakable things had not only happened, they were lurking somewhere just out of sight, waiting to rise again like Godzilla.

1961. The year Roger Maris went for sixty-one homers, Mickey Mantle right behind. He was eight, and like everyone else that year, it was all about baseball. He hung around the Little League field until they finally let him shag flies or field grounders, one hand holding on to the yarmulke on his head, the other going after the ball, but he couldn't play. They started every game with a prayer that ended "in the name of Jesus Christ, Our Lord, amen." His father would never sign the form to let him play.

One day, he went to the batting cages on Highway 933. A bunch of kids chased him, calling him "kike" and "Jew boy." They caught him and pulled his pants down. Three of them held him down while a fourth kid, a big bully who everyone called "Gull" and whose father sold cartons of illegal cigarettes out of the back of his pickup in the lot behind the drugstore, raised a brick and said he was going to smash Saul's face in, but an older kid, freckle-faced, with wild red hair, a popular kid named Terry, stepped in and stopped them. "Leave him alone. I seen him at the Little League," Terry said.

And when they wouldn't stop, Terry said, balling his fists, "If you hit him, you're gonna have to hit me."

The next day, Saul forged his father's signature on the release. The first three games, they sat him on the bench. The last inning, the score tied, two men on, two out, the kid who was supposed to bat had *to go home. Saul was the only boy left on the bench. They had to put him up. As he was about to bat, Terry came over and handed him a stick of Black Jack gum.*

"Chew it. Helps you relax. I seen you at the cage," Terry said, rapping his shoulder with his fist. "I know you can hit."

Saul hit the second pitch into left field for a triple.

Black Jack.

Terry O'Leary became the best friend he ever had. Terry's family had moved to Calliope from Cincinnati. Terry was a rabid Cincinnati Reds fan, so Saul rooted for the Reds too. His idol, of course, was Frank Robinson. Incredibly, the Reds beat the Dodgers to make it to the Series, Saul and Terry yelling and jumping up and down like crazy people. But that year—with Mantle, Maris, Berra, Howard, Kubek, and Whitey Ford—nobody was going to beat the Yankees. Saul was a junior in high school when Terry was killed in Binh Dinh Province, Vietnam.

Someone was blasting loud Arab music from a nightclub loudspeaker. Something that sounded a lot like *"Habibi, habibi, habibi,"* Saul thought, waiting. Young prostitutes, Chinese, Thais, Filipinas, Russians, wobbled on high heels down the hotel corridor with slips of paper in their hands, knocking on doors. Two had mistakenly knocked on Saul's door and he sent them away. A stained piece of paper inside clear plastic by the phone in his room explained the slips of paper: a price list, listing girls by nationality, the price in Bahraini dinars, and an in-house phone number.

The third time there was a knock at the door, when Saul opened it, he saw her. Alina. Absolutely Alina.

He recognized her from the photo Carrie had sent him that she had gotten from Gerry Hoad. She looked younger than he expected and he had to remind himself she was barely twenty-two. Long dark hair, mouth lipsticked fire-engine red, long legs, pretty, with sea-blue eyes that showed nothing. She was dressed in high heels and a pink see-through baby-doll nightie that concealed nothing.

"You Mr. Smith?" she asked in English with an Eastern European accent.

Saul nodded. Credit me with originality, he thought.

"Where's Lebedenko?" he asked.

"He's coming, baby. First we make good time, you and me," she said, sitting on his lap and reaching for his crotch.

Saul stiffened.

"What is this?" he said. "Where's Lebedenko?"

"Please, baby," she whispered in his ear. "I have to do this for my pimp. I don't, he hurt me." Showing him a bruise on her thigh as she slid off him. Kneeling in front of him, she tried to part his knees and open his fly. "Just quickie suck, baby. One hundred BD," she said. A hundred Bahraini dinars. About $250.

"I mean it. Where's Lebedenko?" Saul said, pushing her back and standing up.

"You got cigarette?" she asked, sitting on the side of the bed.

Saul shook his head.

"You gonna be sorry, baby. These guys, not nice guys." Shaking her head.

"What makes you think I am?" he asked, glancing at the door. They would come any second.

"You got good eyes. You know how many got good eyes, not just want stick something in me? Zero," she said, making a circle with her thumb and forefinger.

The hotel room door opened. Saul recognized the man who entered from the video in Damascus and the photo from Istanbul as he stepped quietly inside, a satchel in one hand, a pistol in the other. Lebedenko. Where was the girl's Thai pimp? Lebedenko was supposed to have set up the meet. Was he trying a double cross?

"I thought you two would be in bed," he said with a thick Russian accent. No wonder Cadillac had called him "the Russian," Saul thought.

"He don't want," Alina said, swinging her crossed legs from the edge of the bed like a schoolgirl.

"You're supposed to make him want," Lebedenko said. "That's your job."

"I thought you wanted her out of this. I thought that's what this was about," Saul said. Then he glanced at the girl and got it.

"Look, make simple. She get undressed. You get undressed. One photo. Everybody happy," Lebedenko said, motioning with the pistol at the paper bag. "Otherwise I take money anyway."

"A honey trap for a CIA officer, is that it?" Saul said. "A little leverage? A double cross? Plus you get Alina away from her pimp and some intel at the same time. Is that the game?" Thinking, okay, Dar. You can show up anytime, now. We can just reverse this. Except where's the damn pimp?

He barely had time to complete the thought when he heard the sound of the door lock opening again—they must mass-produce the master card key—and two men with guns, both Thais, burst into the room. Lebedenko turned, gun in hand.

The first Thai, a muscled man with an odd half mustache, the middle part missing, in jeans and a Florida Marlins T-shirt, motioned for Lebedenko to drop the gun. Lebedenko looked at the two of them, both aiming their guns at him and carefully put his down on the floor. The second Thai was bigger, more menacing. The muscle. He had a mashed boxer's nose and his pistol never wavered from Lebedenko.

The half-mustached Thai went over to Alina.

"You suck him?" he asked.

"Not yet," she said, wincing.

He punched her in the stomach, then turned to Lebedenko and Saul.

"You got my money? Forty thousand?"

Saul pointed to the paper bag.

"There's twenty-two thousand there. He," indicating Lebedenko, "has the rest. You have her passport?"

"I got everything." The Thai slapped his jeans pocket. They watched as Lebedenko started pulling stacks of U.S. bills from a satchel he'd brought with him. He put the money on the table next to Saul's paper bag. The Thai moved to take it.

"First her passport," Saul said, and indicating Lebedenko, "Give it to him."

Lebedenko stepped forward and held out his hand.

"Passport," he said.

While the big Thai aimed his gun at Saul, the pimp grabbed Alina by her hair and dragged her toward the door.

"*Kos emek*," the half-mustached Thai said to Lebedenko, using the Arabic curse involving the Russian's mother. "This whore bring me one thousand dinar a day. You think I sell that for forty thousand American, you suck dick, you *neek* Russian? And where you find stupid American?"

Lebedenko reached to the floor for his pistol. Before Saul could react, the half-mustached Thai shot Lebedenko in the chest. Alina screamed as Lebedenko collapsed onto the floor, bleeding, gasping.

The big Thai aimed his pistol at Saul. At that moment, Saul had no doubt he was about to die. He heard a faint clink of glass and two quick thunks from the direction of the room window. The two Thais collapsed to the floor; each of them with a bullet hole in the forehead.

Alina screamed again. She ran for the door, but Saul grabbed her arm. A second later, Dar was there in the doorway with his shotgun. He slapped Alina across the face, then put the shotgun under her chin and walked her back into the room.

"Don't move," he told her.

Saul ran to the window. He just caught a glimpse of a shadow going up a climber's rope to the roof. There was a neat circular hole in the window through which the shooter had fired. The window glass had been cut earlier and pushed through just before the shooter fired. The shooter must have hung on a belay from the rope from the roof, watching from the outside of the building until the time came to shoot. Unbelievable, Saul thought. He turned to Dar.

"Who the hell was that?"

"I told you, I had someone special. A protégé, if you like," Dar said, going over to Lebedenko. He had stopped breathing. His eyes were open. Dar put his fingers to the Russian's neck to feel a pulse and shook his head.

"Who's the shooter?"

"One of mine, Saul. Not yours," Dar said, pulling on a pair of latex surgical gloves. He took the pistol from Lebedenko's hand, put on a sound suppressor, and went to the room window. He stuck the pistol through the circular hole, pointed it up at an angle toward the sky and fired two shots, then put the pistol with the sound suppressor back in Lebedenko's hand.

"Is that supposed to fool ballistics?" Saul said.

"Ballistics?" Dar said. "Where the hell do you think you are? Downtown Manhattan? Trust me, this gun will never see a lab."

"I told you no bloodbaths. Look at this." Pointing at the three bodies. "Not to mention the idea was to get intel. Tell me," pointing at Lebedenko's staring eyes, "how much are we going to get from him now?"

Dar pushed the girl at him and began gathering up the money and throwing it into Lebedenko's satchel.

"They were going to kill you. There was no other option," Dar said, going through the pockets of the two Thai pimps, pulling out a thick roll of dinars from the back pocket of the half-mustached one and throwing that into the satchel as well.

"And all this mess?" Saul said, holding Alina. She was trembling.

"Leave it. Three pimps fighting over whores. In this place? No one will care." Dar stood up. "No passport," he said, walking over to Alina.

"Where's your pimp's room? And Lebedenko's?" Dar asked her.

She pressed her face against Saul's chest.

"All right, you be the good cop," Dar said.

"We better get going," Saul said. "Somebody might've heard."

"Are you shitting me? With all this freaking Pinoy music and hip-hop bullshit? Everybody's too busy humping. I could set off a bomb."

Dar went over to Lebedenko's body and started going through his pockets and putting everything into the satchel.

"Take everything," Saul said.

"Don't worry," Dar said. "We'll find something."

"I hope so," Saul said.

CHAPTER 15

"Let's get this straight, Mr. Vice President. We had this so-called brilliant undercover operation that frankly looks to me like a total balls-up. It happens in the territory of a Persian Gulf ally, Bahrain, practically next door to our own damn naval base. We have a bloody shoot-up with three people dead, one of them a Russian SVR agent—which often has, as you know, repercussions—and the only notation you sent us is . . . wait, let me find it. Quote: 'Ancilliary op in Manama derived from operative Mathison's Istanbul contact resulted in a critical lead. Also termination in Manama of an agent from an unfriendly power with associated collateral damage, two local nonnational criminals.' That's it?"

"Terse, Senator. But accurate. And technically, Lebedenko was Byelorussian, not Russian."

"What difference does it make?"

"To the Kremlin, a lot, apparently. Look, begging your pardon for the language, Mr. President, but while the exchange took place in what some might call a hotel, for all practical purposes, it was a whorehouse. As far as the local Bahraini cops were concerned, the *bodies were a trio of pimps fighting over who owned some whores. Good riddance, as far as they were concerned. And since Bahrain advertises itself as 'fun in the sun,' the last thing in the world they wanted to do was to call attention to the seamier side of the real business they're in. So they buried it. As for the Russians, it was one less embarrassing reminder of where their president came from, so good riddance and the less said the better for them too."*

"Still, a screw-up."

"Really, Warren? Saul and his Black Ops partner, whom we didn't name, but who is a senior CIA officer, were faced with two double crosses and imminent threat to their lives. The Byelorussian, Lebedenko, tried to honey-trap Saul and the Thais tried to kill them both and keep the money and the girl. It could have been a serious blow. Instead, our people came out clean as a whistle. No blowback on the U.S. No harm except for some dead criminals no one will miss, no foul."

"You know, Bill. I never fully realized till now what a dirty business you people are in."

"With all due respect, sir, to protect ourselves from our enemies, who the hell do you think our people have to deal with? The Dalai Lama and Nelson Mandela? Only when we have to kill, usually, as in this case, in self-defense, it's one at a time and close up, in a room or a dark alley. When you or the senator do it, thousands die. You know what Saul says? The reason he does what he does?"

"No. What?"

"To keep our brave politicians, who never go into combat themselves, from pulling the trigger on much bigger killings."

"Get down off your soapbox, Bill. Let's get back to Iron Thunder. With Lebedenko dead, where could they go?"

"Funny thing, there are people who think Saul is soft. Some kind of fuzzy liberal. Boy, do they not get him at all. Saul is stainless steel. For him what mattered was the intel Lebedenko left behind."

"*Which was what?*"

"*Solid gold, Senator. What we were looking for. It wasn't just Lebedenko's laptop and cell phone and his room at the Intercontinental. It was the girl. Alina.*"

"*What about her?*"

"*He got every last ounce out of her. Every bit. Saul is good at that.*"

"*Are you saying it was a romance, Bill?*"

"*Lebedenko and Alina? Who the hell knows, Warren? The day you figure women out, I wish you'd let me in on it. I don't think she loved him, because apparently in addition to everything else, Lebedenko was running her. When she belonged to this sex-fanatic Saudi princeling, it turned out the prince was high up in the RSSMF food chain. She was Lebedenko's pigeon, feeding him stuff on the Saudi missile bases, which he passed along to the Russians.*"

"*A whore and a spy. Basically a slut.*"

"*That's not how Saul saw it, Warren. Or how he got intel out of her. And this is the thing about Saul that will drive you bananas — and at the same time makes him the best—let's call him for what he is, 'spymaster' in the business. He said that in spite of the age difference and that he had screwed her and used her, Alina cried for Lebedenko. You know why? He was the only man who ever gave a shit about her.*

"*And when I said, 'So she cried. So what?' Saul just looked at me in that infuriating way of his and quoted some damn thing from the Talmud, this Jewish stuff that, believe me, once it's in your head, you can't get it out. He said: 'Do not make woman weep, God counts her tears.'*"

"*And our agent, this Carrie? What about her?*"

"*That's just it, Warren. Things were about to explode in Baghdad.*"

CHAPTER 16

It began with a single boy, Kasim, looking flushed and listless and complaining of a sore throat. Within two weeks, more than a hundred of the boys at the madrassa had come down with chicken pox. One of them was Abu Nazir's son, Issa.

They brought Brody into Abu Nazir's house to help with the chores, because, as he had assured them, he had already had chicken pox and was immune. The house was in Abu Nazir's compound, a cluster of stone houses surrounded by a high wall topped with broken glass. The compound was in a wadi outside the town of Aqrah, whose square stone-and-concrete houses climbed up the steep face of the mountain. The wadi was green with trees and scrub. There was water from wells and a brook that ran over rocks and eventually went underground to become part of a tributary feeding the Great Zab River to the east. There were houses and trees along the narrow wadi road, its infinity point disappearing into the barren plain of the northern desert.

This was Kurdish territory. Mostly KDP. And many of the houses on the mountainside put blue tarps on their roofs or painted the roofs blue to ward off evil. But in the wadi, there were Christian Assyrians, with small stone chapels with crosses, set amid the trees. So because they were Sunni Muslims, Abu Nazir's people had to be careful.

Strung out at the very end of the wadi, stretching into the desert, were the houses of the Sunnis. Here, every man carried an AK-47, even to go to the outhouse to relieve himself. And women wore abayas. Along the Baradash Road, a paved two-lane, there were shops, even a gas station, and the madrassa with a playground for the children in an old stone building that hundreds of years earlier had been a synagogue, a Star of David carved into the stone over the door that somehow still survived.

While cleaning dishes and sweeping the floors, Brody thought about his own childhood chicken pox. He'd had a severe case with blisters over his entire body, his palms, his eyelids, even his penis. It burned intensely and his mother had put mittens on his hands so he wouldn't scratch the blisters and make them worse. His father brought him a present: a Marine M7 bayonet.

"Thanks, Dad, sir," Brody had whispered, eyes feverish.

"Maybe you'll use it when we go camping," Gunner Brody had said, smiling, and that night Brody fell into a fitful sleep, trying to ignore the pain all over his body and thinking maybe Gunner Brody had changed, imagining camping and roasting marshmallows around a fire with his dad. Except not long after the boy had gotten better, Gunner Brody had gotten drunk and nearly killed him and his mother with the M7 bayonet. The next day, Brody buried the weapon in the backyard where Gunner Brody wouldn't find it. He and his father never did go camping.

In a way it was strange that illness had come to this place, because Aqrah, isolated from the rest of the world by the desert, was like no place he had ever been. The town was magical, with its green wadi and stone houses on the mountain, like a town in a fairy tale. There were times when Brody imagined he would not have been surprised if birds began to talk or people were to greet dead ancestors in the market.

One night, while he was reading his Quran in the kitchen, Abu Nazir's wife, Nassrin, came in.

"How is the boy?" Brody asked.

"Better, thanks be to Allah," she said, wearily rubbing her eyes. She hadn't left her son's bedside for days.

"I admire how you watch over him, tend him."

She looked at him oddly.

"Who doesn't love their child?" she said.

My father, Brody thought.

Everything was different here, Brody thought. For the first time they were treating him almost like he was one of them. He had his own room in a separate structure in the compound. The only person who hadn't changed was Afsal, who watched him constantly.

"Did you think we didn't see you with that Turkmen woman?" Afsal told him. "Did you really imagine you could fool us? As if a Turkmen whore could outsmart an Arab!"

During the day, when he wasn't doing chores, he was allowed to read his Quran, picking his way through the Arabic lettering, and wander around the compound grounds and in Abu Nazir's garden, always with Afsal watching, his AK7 ready. Something was going to happen here, Brody thought. He just didn't know what.

At night, Brody dreamed. Aqrah was a place for dreaming.

One night, he saw Jessica, as real as if she were there in his room.

The way she looked in her negligee that night on their honeymoon. Two nights in that B&B in Albrightsville in the Poconos, little hearts quilted on the comforter, the old lady proprietor, Mrs. Jenson, smiling over breakfast and turning off the a/c the minute they left the room. Or Jessica sitting up in bed after Dana was born in the hospital, looking at him with wonder, little Dana in her arms, him commuting from a miserable forklift job at that warehouse in Allentown.

And the worst, the look on her face in their tiny apartment when he told her what he had done, Mike there, hanging back the way he always did, because they'd done it without telling her. He and Mike had been going over it again and again over Budweisers the previous night at Woody's Tavern.

The dot-com recession had killed what few jobs were left. Brody couldn't afford to go to community college anymore and what was the damn point? Nobody was hiring anyway.

Except the military. For Brody, son of Marine chief warrant officer 02 Marion Brody, the choice about which service branch was nonexistent.

"So it's the Marines?" Mike had said.

"Semper fi." Brody raised his brew and drank.

"Well, shit, you're not going without me, bro'," Mike said, hitting him in the arm. "The only question is, how do we tell our wives?" Because by that time, Mike had married Megan.

Jessica standing there after they had come from the recruiter. She was crying.

"Without asking me, Brody? You did it without even asking me?"

"It's a paycheck, Jess. And health coverage." Holding her as she sobbed. "Bethlehem's dead. Everything here is dead. There was nothing else, Jess. Nothing."

And her pulling back, her eyes wet, her nose red. Even then, still the most beautiful girl he had ever seen.

"The military takes care of its own, Jess," he told her, looking to Mike and Megan for confirmation.

"And if you're dead, Brody. Who takes care of us?" Then a loud shriek and they all turned to little Dana, she must have been five, screaming and crying in the doorway.

He woke up shivering. He was in Aqrah; he understood now he would never go home. He would never see Jessica or his children again. He was an utter failure: as a man, as a husband, as a father, as a Marine. Surviving all this time as a prisoner— for what? Who was he? What had he become?

He fell to his knees, then bowed his head to the stone floor in prayer. O Allah, I can't do this anymore, he prayed. I don't know if you're there. I don't care. Then he remembered. There was a way out. The last time he'd been walking around the compound he'd spotted something on the ground and picked it up.

A piece of barbed wire.

He had it now and scraped it across his wrist, ripping at his veins as hard as he could. He immediately felt pain and the wetness of the blood. He switched hands and used the barb, sawing back and forth at his other hand, crying out at the pain, to cut the other wrist.

That's all, he thought. Let me go, Allah. I can't do this anymore. I was born in the desert, the Mojave. I'll die here in the desert. My whole life has been a desert. He started to feel dizzy, hazy.

He was remembering Jessica in that print dress at the base, the last time he saw her, when they shipped out. He was in his MCCUU cammies, the two of them clutching at each other like they knew it was the last time. The Marine Corps band was playing "Halls of Montezuma," Dana and Chris holding hands, Chris all twisty and crying. A two-year-old not liking any of it, and his little girl, Dana, looking at him, eyes sadder than anything he'd ever seen and he didn't know what to say to her, so he just said good-bye. The last thing you ever said to your daughter. Good-bye, like you were going to work and you'd see her in a few hours. And then running to join his company to board the plane, because the truth was, that's where he wanted to be. Looking back just once at the three of them near the buses. Jessica. Dana. The toddler, Chris, he barely knew.

They brought him, bleeding, to Abu Nazir, who bound his wounds, telling him, "Oh, Nicholas, you must not do this. Self-murder is the worst of all sins for a Muslim. It is *haram*. Forbidden. Nicholas, you cannot do this." Abu Nazir put him to bed in his own house, despite bloodying the sheets. Holding him.

"I can't take it anymore," Brody mumbled. "Let me go. Please."

"No, Allah wants you to live. You have submitted to him. Don't you see? That is Islam. This isn't the end. It is the beginning. Allah has not abandoned you. But you must never do this again, Nicholas. Now it begins. Your new life," Abu Nazir said, holding him in his arms, rocking him like a child while Brody cried.

When he woke, he was looking at Nassrin. She was a beautiful woman. Older, with a strong nose and brown eyes, wearing a hijab even though she was inside the house.

"You will stay here now," she said, helping him sit up. She served him hot tea from a cup. "You have been through much."

"Why are you helping me?" he asked.

Her eyes searched his face.

"We must learn each other, you and I."

"Why?" He looked around the room. Simply furnished, but he was clearly in a house, Abu Nazir's house.

"Because I must know if I can trust you," she said.

That evening, she brought him dinner and they talked. She asked about his family.

"Your wife? Is she beautiful?"

"Very."

"Do you fear she has gone to other men in this time?"

He nodded. "She probably thinks I'm dead."

"No." She shook her head. "I am sure of it."

"How could you possibly know?"

"Nicholas, things of the heart, a woman knows."

The next day, Abu Nazir asked him if he would teach his son, Issa, English.

"I can't," Brody said. "I don't know how. I'm not a teacher."

"You can do this, Nicholas. This is the way back. And, Nicholas, you must never do that other to yourself again. It is the one thing Allah, who is merciful, Nicholas . . . but self-murder, even Allah cannot forgive."

That night, Nassrin served them dinner. Brody sat with Abu Nazir and the boy, Issa. Near the end of the meal, Nassrin whispered to Brody, "I am trusting you with what is most precious in all the world to me, Nicholas."

The next day, he began with Issa. He pointed at things and said what to call them in English. The boy was ten, and although introverted and shy, he was very smart, picking up on the words almost immediately. As Brody was pointing at a lamp, three men and Abu Nazir walked by, in tense conversation.

"What's going on?" Brody asked. First in English, then his clumsy Arabic.

Issa didn't answer and looked away.

"I overheard them say something about Baquba," Brody said. He remembered from his orientation when his Marine unit first got to Iraq; Baquba was a city about fifty kilometers north of Baghdad.

"We mustn't talk about such things," Issa whispered.

That evening, Abu Nazir came to him.

"You know about Baquba?" he asked.

Brody nodded. Of course Issa had told his father.

"Are you with us, Nicholas?" Looking at him with those dark eyes. Brody understood if he said the wrong word now, he would die.

"I will say nothing."

Abu Nazir nodded. "Of course. It is too soon. For now, just saying nothing is as much as can be expected."

He sat down across from Brody.

"Listen, Nicholas, we are at war. It is jihad. The rest of the world, the Americans, they have their tanks and their F-15s and their cruise missiles and their CIA. And we, Nicholas, what do we have?" He smiled. "Only a few rifles, and our little brains, and Allah. And do you know, Nicholas? It is enough. We will win."

"And Baquba?"

"The Americans are planning a Top Secret operation in Baquba called Iron Thunder. And look, Nicholas. Top Secret! Here we sit, in our wadi at the edge of the desert, and already I know. Who will win, Nicholas? Don't you see? They have already lost."

CHAPTER 17

"Look, I'll tell Walden to shove it up his ass. You have priority," Dar said as he finished throwing things into his carry-on.

The room was on the fifteenth floor of the Hala Arjaan, a businessman's hotel near the Abu Dhabi Mall. The window looked out at a long line of tall buildings and traffic on Tenth Street. Just going by the view, they could have been in New York or Chicago.

"When's the drone attack?" Saul asked.

"Soon. We should've done it while the media was blabbing about that North Korean rocket. Now we'll be in the news cycle instead of that crazy Kim Jong-il? What about Lebedenko? Did he get off anything about Iron Thunder?"

Saul nodded. "The software found a deleted sent email."

"And the girl? Anything?"

"Him and the girl. He was a regular. Same hotel. They'd meet in the room. Sex and a laptop. Love in the twenty-first century."

"We have a lead? Baghdad?"

Saul nodded again.

"So the lead in Baghdad has it. Want me to do something?" Dar said quietly.

"Nobody does anything. Nothing."

Dar stared at him.

"Is this one of your crazy-making Talmudic riddles?"

"We don't know what this is yet. Might be a bridge agent. Might be a false cutout. Might be Mary, Mary, quite contrary."

"Don't bullshit a bullshitter, Saul. You worked the girl?"

Saul nodded.

"You should've been a damn therapist instead of a CIA division chief. So you know. The lead is either for real or it isn't."

"It's real," Saul said.

"So pull the trigger. You got a mole. End it. I'll be happy to do it."

Saul got up and went to the window. He looked out at the buildings, one of them still under construction, then looked back.

"The object of the game isn't to capture a single piece. The object is to win the game. Moles are operatives. They work for *someone*. We need to know who." He paused. "Walden needs you for the ISI?"

"When the drone hits, the Pakistanis will go ballistic. They'll close the passes to Afghanistan. As it is, our troops are barely hanging on by a thread. It'll finish 'em." Dar looked at Saul. "Lot of pieces in play. If you absolutely need me, I'll stay."

Saul shook his head. He sat on the side of the bed.

"You'll handle Islamabad?"

"General al-Kayani and I go back a ways. That son of a bitch owes me."

"Be careful. He might decide it's cheaper to terminate you," Saul said.

Dar's eyebrows went up. "Beirut style? I was born in the

Chouf, remember? I've taken steps. He knows better than to play those games with me," Dar said, zipping up the carry-on. "Let's say good-bye here. I hate airport send-offs. Might as well hang out a neon sign. 'I am a CIA agent. This person is my freaking contact!'"

"See you back at Langley? Usual place? Walter's?"

"Why mess with perfection?" Dar said, leaving.

"Waffle plain, no whipped butter," Saul said as the door closed.

He waited forty minutes, checking his watch, then went downstairs and took a taxi to a restaurant in the Abu Dhabi marina. Squinting against the sun glare, he went into the restaurant, nearly empty before the lunchtime crowd. The place had a blue-greenish tinge from sun-tinted glass windows. It was like entering an aquarium. The air-conditioning was turned up to arctic frigid. A young Filipina waitress started toward him, but Saul waved her off. He had spotted a Middle Eastern man with a trim beard sitting alone at a table, his back to the view of the boats in the marina, reading a copy of the *Khaleej Times*.

Saul went over and sat down.

CHAPTER 18

They were taking bets around the swimming pool at the Al-Hamra Hotel. Some of the journalists were in the water, playing a hard-edged version of water polo using a sealed empty Jim Beam bottle for a ball. A match that had, according to the old-timers, been going on at the Al-Hamra since Saddam's days. Nearly all the reporters were stringers from smaller papers and magazines, who remained behind after the major metro journalists had left now that Iraq was no longer front-page news.

The bet was on which hotel would get hit next with a car bomb. Right now top money, being wagered by a drunken Peruvian mercenary wearing nothing but a Speedo, who—after parking his FN submachine gun against a palm tree—kept yelling for "Pisco!," was on the Palestine Hotel. The Al-Hamra was number three.

Number two was the Sheraton Ishtar Hotel.

"That's not fair," Carrie said, keeping her eyes on the big South African plowing his way through a double Johnnie Walker Gold that he'd poured into a glass of Guinness. He was the reason she had come back to Baghdad. "They're both on Firdos Square. It's the same thing."

"Ah, but the question is," Marius de Bruin, the South African said, "which hotel sustains the most damage? Five thousand American on Palestine," taking a thick wad of U.S. hundred-dollar bills out of his jeans pocket and banging it on the poolside table.

Hanging on to the South African's arm in a slinky black top and shorts was an auburn-haired Ukrainian with super-model looks named Dasha. She looked bored, except for her red nostrils and dilated pupils. High on some kind of speed, Carrie thought. The kind of young woman who might do anything, no matter how insane, just to feel something.

She wasn't the only arm candy. There were a number of good-looking women, Iraqis, Asians, Europeans—and they weren't there for the journalists. There were a few high-powered businessmen and politicians along with two low-level members of the Coalition Forces diplomatic corps. Nibbling like feeder fish around the edges of the pool were more than a dozen young Chinese prostitutes in bikinis pretending to drink from plastic cocktail glasses. Lanterns strung from palm trees around the pool area lit the scene with a party glow, creating shimmering reflections on the water.

"How did Chinese girls end up in Baghdad?" Carrie had said to de Bruin earlier. One way or another, the mission had come down to getting close to him.

"How does anyone? That's an existential question," he'd said, looking at her like she was next on the menu after the Ukrainian supermodel. By the way he looked at her, she wondered if maybe he wanted both at the same time.

De Bruin was a big man. He oozed physicality. His hair was shortish brown. He had a solid, boxer's build and an oddly charming smile that reminded her a little of that actor, Russell Crowe, in the Roman gladiator movie. Carrie couldn't take her eyes off him. "Be careful, Carrie. Ignore the charm, the smile," Warzer had warned her. Although she took what he said with a grain of salt after they'd argued at her apartment. "Even powerful people in Baghdad are afraid of him. No one says anything. Not good, not bad. Nothing."

Carrie had sensed it too. No war stories. When you mentioned de Bruin's name, people's faces got a look that conveyed *stay away* and they changed the subject. His South African and Peruvian security guards were feared. There were whispers that not all the headless bodies with holes in them from power drills that turned up in the Baghdad morgue every day came from Sunnis and Shiites having at each other.

"I'm not sure you going straight at him is a good idea. It's too dangerous," Warzer had said. Virgil, who was there, nodded his agreement.

"There's no other way," she said. Saul had told her she had to get in close. Lebedenko's last call had been to a cell phone linked to de Bruin. It would be a tightrope walk. But with the timing, Abu Nazir and Iron Thunder all happening, at this point, he told her, do whatever it takes. It was on her. She knew what it cost Saul to say that to her. Only she couldn't tell either Warzer or Virgil; those orders were strictly for her from Saul.

Another secret. They all lived with secrets from each other, even the people they were closest to. "As for danger," she had told Warzer and Virgil, "where the hell do you think we are?"

Baghdad. The war had wound down but the desperation stayed, she thought. Part of the landscape like the palm trees.

The Al-Hamra Hotel had become the watering hole of choice after the Baghdad Country Club in the Green Zone had closed and the Palestine Hotel had been badly damaged by a car bomb. The Al-Hamra was in the Jadriya section of the Karada, a peninsula that stuck out like a thumb from the east bank of the Tigris River, forcing the river to make a sharp loop around it.

Although Carrie couldn't see him, she knew Warzer was sitting there near the pool, watching her. At that moment, the argument they'd had earlier came back.

"You can't go, Carrie. I forbid it," Warzer had said when they were alone in the apartment on Nasir Street.

"Forbid," Carrie said. "You're telling me 'forbid' in my own apartment? You can leave anytime you want." Waving her finger at him. "You forbid nothing."

"And if it means him having you like one of his whores? And drugs, Carrie? He's a dealer. Zero One. Heroin. Guns. Women. Everything. Everyone knows. And I'm supposed to watch?"

"Then don't watch," she had snapped back.

"What does that make you, Carrie? A sharmuta? *How different from any street whore? How?"*

"No different. Is that what you want to hear? I'm a whore, all right? That's what you left your wife for. A whore. You can go back now."

"And if I let you, Carrie? If I just watch? What does that make me? Who am I?"

"A pimp. You're a pimp and I'm a whore," she said, sinking to the kitchen floor, her face in her hands.

When she'd first come back to Baghdad from Istanbul after getting the lead on Lebedenko from Gerry Hoad, which led her back to Baghdad and de Bruin, she'd been so happy to see him. Warzer, with his puppy-dog eyes and shy smile. Like when they first started their affair. Then a silly dinner. Laughing and talking and bad Chinese food at the Freedom Café and sex late that night. And when she couldn't fall asleep, knowing she was lying to Warzer, that she liked him but she didn't love him, until finally, she fell asleep to the distant loudspeaker sound of the dawn call to prayer

Then the argument before leaving the next evening for the Al-Hamra.

"Stop. Please. This is pointless," she had said, getting dressed.

"Why?" he asked, coming closer.

"Because if I don't do this, bad things will happen."

"We do bad things too, sometimes."

"Yeah, well, we don't kill little children, okay? So if you're not going to be on my side, leave. Just leave," she said, getting up.

Now she watched de Bruin work his magic on two men, one an Iraqi, with a Saddam-like mustache, she thought was a senior Iraqi government official smoking a water pipe, and the other, a man in a black T-shirt who looked like a Turk, or more probably a Kurd.

Two attractive young women in low-cut cocktail dresses, one an Iraqi who looked like she'd had a nose job, a good one; the other, Vietnamese, very sexy, hovered close by. Ready to move in the second de Bruin signaled to them to attach to the Iraqi and the Kurd. He's always selling, she thought. Well, don't we all?

De Bruin was head of Atalaxus Executive, one of the top two PMCs, private military companies, still in Iraq, now that many of the American companies had scaled back. Atalaxus brought in heavy-duty military TCNs, third-country nationals, ex–South African Special Forces and former Peruvian NIS officers who'd honed their brutal skills against Shining Path guerrillas, at a third the cost of the American companies. The Peruvians were said to be so ruthless that even hardened al-Qaeda jihadis recoiled at some of their tactics. "The rest," as Warzer had overheard de Bruin say to someone in a suite Virgil had bugged at the Al-Rasheed Hotel, "is profit."

All at once de Bruin got up from his table and came over to her.

"Your drink needs refreshing," he said, pouring in enough Johnnie Walker to float a destroyer.

"What about your deal? Who are those men?" she asked.

"The Iraqi is Mustafa Abdul-Karim, deputy minister of roads and transportation. The Kurd is, well, let's call him Bayar, from the PDK. Cheers," he said, clinking his glass against hers and drinking. She did the same.

"And what are you selling them tonight?" she asked.

"The same thing I always sell," he said, touching his finger to her shoulder and letting it slide down her arm. "The chance to make a lot of money." He came very close. She could smell his aftershave. Cartier? Mingled with the smell of Johnnie Walker.

"Zero One? Heroin? Guns?" she whispered.

"Even you, if the price is right." He winked, his hand going around her waist, slipping down to her buttocks and pulling her tight against him. She could feel his erection.

"What about your Ukrainian girl?" Carrie said, looking right at Dasha. She was watching the two of them, her eyes unmoving, like a hawk.

"She's very open-minded. She'd like you almost as much as I would," he said.

When Carrie tried to move away, he twisted her arm behind her and pulled her tight. He was not only a big man, he had strong oversized hands, like a miner or a boxer, but without the bruises. With her free hand, she slapped his face.

Just as quickly, he slapped her face back.

"So?" he said.

They stood there, looking at each other, as if both were surprised at the turn things had taken. He was swaying slightly from the drinking. He let her go.

"I didn't mean to offend. I know you're interested," he said. "That's the one thing I know in this life," retrieving his drink. "When someone is interested in me. The rest isn't worth knowing."

He started to weave away, back toward his table. There goes the mission, the war, she thought, her face burning. Warzer was, she knew, watching her with binoculars from a hotel room overlooking the pool area. She hoped, as she stood in a lantern's shadow, he couldn't see her face.

"I didn't say I wasn't interested. I'm not a slut," she said.

De Bruin turned around and came back halfway.

"That's just where you're wrong, dear Anne, of the American embassy, is it? You *are* a slut. I'm a slut." Pointing at himself. Waving his arms. Now he had everyone around the pool's attention. "Everyone here is a slut. Why the hell else are we in Baghdad? If not to raise our skirts to make money?"

"What do you want, de Bruin?" she said.

"You know what I want." Looking at her breasts, her face. His glance flicked over at Dasha. "Say the word, I'll send her away. But I prefer not. You know why?"

Carrie shook her head.

"She has a gift. She never says no. No matter what I tell her to do." Coming close again. "A girl in a million."

"She's very pretty. What do you need me for?"

"Besides sex?" he said. "To talk. You've got a brain. Sex and a brain in"—gesturing at the night—". . . this anus of the world." A touch of an Afrikaans accent slipping into his English. He came closer again. Noise and lanterns around the pool behind him. "Can you believe civilization started here? In this shithole? What does that say about humanity? Something, doesn't it? Come, I'll show you a Baghdad you didn't know existed."

"You'll show me a bed and drugs. I've seen it before, King of Baghdad," she said, giving it what she hoped was the right touch of derision.

He nodded. Touché. "I'll show you more than that, American girl from the embassy who's been seen in the company of a certain Iraqi translator named Warzer Zafir, known to have worked with the CIA."

He held out his hand. She hesitated.

From somewhere close by in the darkness came the sound of a single gunshot. For a moment, everyone stopped and listened. When there were no further shots they went back to their conversations. Baghdad.

"If you want to tango, Lady Anne, you have to get up when the music plays," he said.

CHAPTER 19

Khafat, Baghdad
23 April 2009

De Bruin's house was a fortified villa in the Khafat district of west Baghdad, south of the Abu Ghraib Expressway. The villa was contemporary in design, white with cantilevered levels. It was surrounded by twelve-foot blast walls, zigzag car-bomb barriers, a steel gate, and had at least twenty or more heavily armed Peruvians on round-the-clock shifts.

Inside, the grounds were exquisite. A glass opening to an indoor-outdoor pool, flowers everywhere in the landscaped garden, and, painted on the interior walls, a mural of nineteenth-century Baghdad, the Ottoman Baghdad of horses and carriages and palm trees by the Tigris River.

What was unexpected were the guests: famous Iraqis, a painter, a poet, a glamorous television star, among others, and the food: a spread of *mezzes*, along with the best *masgouf* and *kofta* Carrie had ever tasted. In the background, a trio of musicians on the *oud*, piano, and violin played traditional Iraqi *maqams*.

"And when the war ends . . ." Eric Sanderson, deputy chief of mission at the U.S. embassy, eyeing Carrie when she walked in with de Bruin and Dasha, was saying.

"You keep saying that, but it is your war that will end," Shaima Yassin, the television star, said, tossing her long wavy hair. "America will go home to its baseball games and its endless self-contemplation. You'd think Americans were Buddhists instead of Christians the way they study their own navels as though the rest of the world doesn't exist, but the war you left us will go on for a hundred years."

"Now you set her off, Mr. Sanderson. Suffering is the new Iraqi art form. It infects every conversation," Abdul-Jabbar, an archaeologist noted for his deciphering of Sumero-Akkadian tablets, said.

"And despair. And ugliness," the painter, Msayyiri, said.

"*Ya Allah*. And what was under Saddam?" Shaima said.

"Grandiosity. Stupidity. And banality. The triteness alone made you want to shoot yourself," Msayyiri said.

"And fear," Carrie said.

"And fear," Msayyiri, looking at her, agreed.

"And now?" Sanderson asked.

"Sewage, Mr. Sanderson. And dead children. I hope it was worth it," Msayyiri said, getting up and pouring himself some champagne from a bottle chilling in a silver bucket.

"You're the artist?" Carrie asked.

He nodded.

"It's odd, sometimes there's beauty too. You see rockets exploding or red tracer bullets arcing across the sky at night; it can be beautiful," Carrie said.

"Like Yeats," al-Tariq, the poet said. "A terrible beauty."

Later, in the bedroom with Marius de Bruin and Dasha, overlooking the garden and an outdoor pool so still it reflected the stars, and flying on ecstasy, Carrie had some of the best sex of her life; the three of them intertwined, no way to tell where one ended and another began.

And in the morning, first light, floating naked in the pool. Alone, with only the flowers and the birds and there was no war anymore and nothing except the sense that she had done it.

Because she had gotten up in the middle of the night and used the thumb drive sewn on the inside of her clutch—and a good thing she had taken care to conceal it, because when they first walked in, she was frisked by one of de Bruin's people, Estrella, a tiny Peruvian woman from the Andean highlands, obvious Indian blood, no more than five feet tall, with sharp dark eyes and a suspicious moon face, who opened her clutch and poked through everything, even her lipstick. But the little woman didn't find the drive. Carrie connected it now to de Bruin's cell phones and laptop to upload the NSA software that Virgil and Saul would use to GPS-track de Bruin's every move and capture every word, every keystroke he typed from now on.

And while she walked around in the darkness, still stark naked and a little buzzy from the ecstasy and the sex, checking to see de Bruin and Dasha were still sleeping and then looking to see if there was something else, a safe or place he might keep papers, suddenly there stood Estrella. A dark small shadow in front of her, like an imp. Holding something Carrie couldn't see, but it could well have been a gun.

"What are you doing, señorita?" the little Peruvian said.

"Looking for the bathroom," Carrie said.

"No, you weren't."

"Go back in your hole, little *rata*."

Going back to the bedroom, Carrie thought, We know each other, little *rata*. Because when Estrella had first searched her purse, she'd kept Carrie's cell phone, with an email attachment detailing Iron Thunder on it, including General Demetrius's planned military attack on Baquba. Nibble on that, little *rata*, Carrie thought. Nibble on the poison.

Then, after dawn, floating in the pool, she watched the sky turn blue. De Bruin watched her from the sliding-glass bedroom door, a towel wrapped around his waist, and after a minute, Estrella came in, talking to de Bruin and pointing at Carrie in the water. De Bruin dropped the towel and came over to the edge of the pool, naked. With him was one of his Peruvian guards with an FN P90 submachine gun and Estrella, her eyes triumphant.

"Coffee?" De Bruin asked.

"Please," Carrie said.

CHAPTER 20

"There's something I don't get, Bill."

"What do you mean, Warren?"

"Saul got the lead about the mole, this de Bruin, from what Lebedenko left behind? His cell phone? Laptop? The girl, Alina, whatever, right?"

"Actually more than that. A number of leads. Including an influential member of the Salmani tribe, who had taken the kunya, the code name, Abu Ghazawan, after a companion of the Prophet. We were able to track this Abu Ghazawan from a location in northern Iraq to Karbala, which proved critical. Also, they found a gmail address that the NSA was able to tie directly to de Bruin with repeated contacts that closely matched the dates Saul had previously determined to be when the intel was passed."

"Including the raid on Otaibah?"

"Yes, exactly."

"So this de Bruin character was what? . . . Head of Atalaxus Executive, Pty, a PMC, a private military company. So the question is, how in the name of all that's holy does someone like that get his grubby hands on Top Secret American intelligence?"

"Really, Warren? We're sitting here with the president, and you, the head of the Senate Select Committee on Intelligence, ask me that with a straight face?"

"Wait a damn minute, Bill. This is a helluva breach of security. If the senator doesn't get it, I need to know. How did this de Bruin get his hands on our Top Secret stuff?"

"We handed it to him, Mr. President. On a silver platter. Happens every day. It's happening this second."

"I don't understand."

"Excuse me, Mr. President? You know as well as I do, you can't fight large-scale overseas wars like Iraq while maintaining a global military presence with an all-volunteer military. For political reasons, the American people decided after Vietnam, no draft. Your army isn't big enough. Something's got to give. So either we can't fight a war or we do what the ancient Romans did. We hire mercenaries. Only nowadays we call them PMCs."

"Yeah, but—"

"Come on, guys, they do everything from cleaning up the garbage to training and security. Except they can't do what we pay them to do without giving them intel, even if we have to remove the shiny 'Top Secret' wrapper. De Bruin was at the highest level. He met with CENTCOM's top officers, the inner circles in the Coalition and the Iraqi government. He met with everyone every day."

"In other words, we outsourced everything in the war, except our casualties."

"You hire people who do things for money, Senator, you really shouldn't be surprised if they do things for money. Including buying and selling inside information."

"There's still something bugging me. I just don't get it."

"What's that, Warren?"

"This business with the female agent, Carrie Mathison, and the Iranians? Why put her in harm's way again? What for?"

"You mean, why bother?"

"Exactly. Why bother? Saul already knew about de Bruin, right? And whatever this Abu Whatever person was doing, Saul had identified the mole. And Carrie had seen to it that de Bruin got the intel about Iron Thunder. Why didn't Saul just shut the son of a bitch down?"

"What you're really saying, Warren, is that's what you would've done. And to tell you the truth, maybe that's what I would've done. But what I've been trying to tell you both—and believe me, I would never tell him—is that when it comes to this game, we three are amateurs. We are not the genius Saul is."

"What do you mean?"

"Look, the Iranians were part of this from the beginning, because from the minute we toppled Saddam, like it or not, Iran became a major player in Iraq. Saul understood that intel wasn't just leaking to IPLA and al-Qaeda. The Iranians had been acting all along like they were getting a piece of the mole's intel too. Yes, boys and girls, de Bruin was a businessman. As we were to learn, he was getting paid twice for the same goods. Saul suspected as much. But he knew if he simply leaked Iron Thunder to the Iranians through de Bruin, they would be suspicious. It was critical to the success of Iron Thunder that they believe it. The only way they would believe it without any shadow of a doubt was if they thought they had gotten it for themselves."

"You mean . . . ?"

"Yes, Warren, the second arm of Saul's Cannae double-flanking strategy. Stop the Iranians by making them think we were going to launch a massive attack against them in Baquba. And they would believe it—"

"Because they would have gotten the intel for themselves."

"Exactly. Iron Thunder."

"It's brilliant, Bill."

"*I thought so, Mr. President. More importantly, given the circumstances we were facing, it was necessary.*"

"*And Saul? Where was he when this was happening?*"

"*Working the end game with General Demetrius, Warren.*"

"*To get the mole and complete the implementation of the Status of Forces Agreement with the Iraqis?*"

"*No, Senator. To save a war everyone thought was over.*"

CHAPTER 21

Ramadi, Iraq
24 April 2009

They met in a two-story house in the Warar district, a few kilometers from the U.S. military base at Camp Blue Diamond. Like nearly all the houses in Ramadi, this one was surrounded by a high security wall, but from the comfortable second-floor room, its windows left open to catch a breeze, Saul could see the Euphrates River. There were overgrown green fields between the house and the river, and on its banks, U.S. soldiers keeping watchful guard around the house. The river was bordered with reeds and palm trees shimmering in the heat and, on the far side, a shepherd in a kaffiyeh and dark *thaub* robe, with his flock. It was like something out of the Bible. Saul wished his father could have seen it.

Ramadi was nothing like the way Carrie had described it to him back in 2006, during the worst of the fighting. Driving through the paved streets in an MRAP armored vehicle with General Demetrius, he had seen combined patrols of U.S. Marines and Iraqi ISF vehicles, men in white robes, women in black abayas with baskets, and girls in blue uniforms on their way to school. There was construction and rebuilding everywhere. The transformation was astonishing.

"You heard about the suicide bomber who lured children and then blew them to pieces in Haditha?" Sheikh Ali Hatem al-Rashawi said. He was a thin man with a goatee and dark sunken eyes, wearing a white kaffiyeh and *thaub* trimmed with gold thread suggesting his status as the leader of the Albu Mahal tribe.

Two of al-Rashawi's aides and Lieutenant Colonel Larson sat in chairs beside the door, all of them carrying weapons. Beside the table where they sat sipping cardamom tea, a fan hummed a small breeze to help relieve the heat.

After the death of his brother, assassinated by Abu Nazir, Sheikh al-Rashawi had rallied most of the Sunni Dulaimi tribes of Anbar Province to join with the formidable "Sons of Iraq" tribal fighters to battle Abu Nazir's IPLA. He had even brought some of the Salmani tribesmen, once the deadly rivals of the Albu Mahals, over to his side against al-Qaeda.

"Abu Nazir is trying to retake Anbar. Only now you Americans went and made the Sons of Iraq part of the ISF, the Iraqi Security Forces, General. For us Sunnis, this is a problem. The Shiites always play politics. This must be dealt with," al-Rashawi said.

"It's worse than that. Abu Nazir has mobilized for a series of attacks and assassinations he anticipates will force the Americans out. He wants civil war," Saul said.

"What would he gain?" al-Rashawi asked.

"You know the Chinese saying? Out of chaos, opportunity. Otherwise, IPLA is dead. But if there were a civil war, where does it leave the Americans?" Saul asked.

"Caught in the middle. Flat-footed. In the middle of a drawdown, pulling out—according to Napoleon, the most vulnerable time for an army—only worse, because we're tied hand and foot by the Status of Forces Agreement and I have no support at home for additional military action in Iraq. We'd be sitting ducks. You know this for certain, about Abu Nazir?" General Demetrius asked, looking sharply at Saul. This was new intel.

"There are a lot of moving pieccs. If IPLA is moving, so is Iran. As we speak, they're mobilizing to put weapons and Revolutionary Guards Al-Quds brigades into Baghdad. Possibly to link up with the Mahdi Army. It's full-scale civil war," Saul said.

"*Allahu alam*, but this is evil news," Sheikh al-Rashawi said. He turned to General Demetrius. "Give me more of your good American weapons, General, and I will push al-Qaeda all the way to Afghanistan."

"Saul, these attacks and assassinations, do you have locations? Targets? Timing?" General Demetrius asked.

Saul nodded.

"Not a hundred percent. But we've got a pretty good idea and we're narrowing in."

"What are they?"

"Abu Nazir and IPLA are moving on both Karbala and Baghdad."

"The Shiite shrine?" al-Rashawi said, looking at the others. From their glances, it was clear he and the general understood the implications immediately.

The Imam Hussein Shrine in the city of Karbala housed the remains of Hussein ibn Ali, grandson of the Prophet Mohammed. Hussein and his followers were killed at the battle of Karbala in the year 680. It was the killing of Hussein that caused the final rift between Shiites and Sunnis that exists to this day. After Mecca, the shrine in Karbala was the holiest site in the world for Shiites. An attack that caused significant damage to the shrine or Hussein's tomb would prompt violence across not only Iraq, but the entire Muslim world, with an end game impossible to predict. An Iranian counterattack would be almost inevitable.

"How do you know, Saul?" General Demetrius asked.

"We've traced intel from a mole who has been feeding Abu Nazir and linked it to one of Nazir's commanders, a Salmani tribesman who uses the *kunya* Abu Ghazawan."

"Abu Ghazawan?" al-Rashawi said through gritted teeth.

"Yes," Saul said.

"It was some of his men, dressed in uniforms like INP police, who came into Haditha and beheaded any man who did not have a beard and ordered the killing of the children. Like Abu Nazir, he is capable of any evil," al-Rashawi said.

"We're able to track his movements," Saul said.

They both looked at him, surprised.

"Where is he now?" General Demetrius asked.

"Karbala."

None of them spoke.

"How much time do we have?" General Demetrius asked, finally.

"A week, maybe. Not much more," Saul said. "There are a couple of pieces missing that I still have to fill in."

Al-Rashawi turned to Saul.

"You have come to us before, Sha'wela, our friend Saul. What is best now?"

General Demetrius looked at the sheikh.

"You trust Saul so much?"

"Listen, General. Years ago, in the first American War—"

"Back in '91. Operation Desert Storm," Saul put in.

"Yes. After the cease-fire, there was a revolt by the Shi-ites and the Kurds against Saddam. You Americans had beaten his army easily, but you stopped. You had not destroyed the Republican Guard. Many of them were Tikritis, of the Albu Nasir tribe, you understand? For Saddam Hussein, blood of his blood. The Americans, even their president, said, 'Rise up against the dictator, Saddam.' Secret emissaries came from the Shiites. 'Join us. Help us, fight.' In those days, before the Iranians helped them, trained them, they were weak like children.

"I was a young man," al-Rashawi said. "Ready for war. But the leader of our tribe was my uncle, Sheikh Abdul Jabbar Abu Nimr. A man respected across the Anbar among all the Sulaimi tribes. My uncle met with this man, General, Sha'wela, and asked him the one question we had to know before deciding about what to do about Saddam: 'If we fight, will the Americans help us?'

"You must understand, General. Saddam was a tyrant, but like us, a Sunni. Here was the great American army only a hundred, two hundred kilometers away, with nothing between them and us but empty desert. We had to know. And Sha'wela told us, 'No. The Americans will talk, but they will do nothing.' And he spoke the truth, General," al-Rashawi said. "So we did nothing too. Of course I trust Sha'wela now. What do we do?"

Saul leaned in. Unconsciously, the others did too.

"We end this. There's a Top Secret operation called Iron Thunder. General Demetrius will place a strong American force in Baquba to stop the Iranians. That's where all the arms and explosives are coming into Iraq from Iran. It will be the last operation of the war."

"Baquba? You're sure?" al-Rashawi asked.

Saul nodded.

"Also, actions in Baghdad," he added.

"And the Sons of Iraq? The tribes?" al-Rashawi said.

"They take all of Anbar, once and for all. Also, I need your help in Karbala. I need some of your best. Men you can trust. Four or five. Albu Mahals only." Looking at al-Rashawi's aides by the door.

"Would they be killing IPLA?"

Saul nodded.

"Yes, also protecting a female agent of ours." Saul tapped on his cell phone and brought up a photo of Carrie. He showed it to the general and al-Rashawi. "She is essential in this."

Al-Rashawi motioned to one of his aides, a lean, fierce-looking man, with eyes and a nose like a hawk. The sheikh pointed at the photo.

"This blond American woman, Ali. She is your sister. If any harm, or worse, dishonor comes to her, to her honor, it is a dishonor to you. Is it good?" al-Rashawi said.

Ali nodded. "If any man touching her," he said in clumsy English, "even of Albu Mahal," gesturing at the other aide, "he die."

"Yes," Saul said. "It's good."

"Still one more thing," al-Rashawi said, looking at the two of them. "I need more serious American weapons. Javelin anti-tank and Stinger missiles. MRAPs too."

"That's a problem." General Demetrius frowned. "With the Sons of Iraq being officially transferred to the ISF and us having signed the Status of Forces Agreement, I can't. It would be a violation."

Saul grimaced. "This isn't about al-Qaeda. You're thinking of the Shiites after we leave."

"You Americans," al-Rashawi said, shaking his head. "You come, you go. But we stay. We have been here thousands of years, since the dawn of Adam, praise be to Allah. You will have been a cloud that has come and gone. As always, Sha'wela knows my heart," nodding at Saul. "Yes, the Shiites and what is to come when you Americans leave." He looked at the general. "You want our help, General, you must also give it. Javelins. Stingers. Serious weapons. Ali has a list."

General Demetrius didn't answer. For a long moment, the only sound was that of the fan. The general looked sharply at Saul, who gave an imperceptible nod.

"I'll get you everything I can. There may be a little flexibility in the SOF Agreement," General Demetrius said finally to the sheikh.

"Good. Time for blood. *Inshallah*, we end this Abu Nazir," al-Rashawi said, putting his hand to his chest.

Later, in the MRAP, driving back to Camp Blue Diamond, General Demetrius told Saul: "I didn't want to cut you off at the knees in front of the sheikh, but I didn't agree with everything you said back there. And I'm not sure what, if anything, I can give them—or if I should. Even if I agreed—which, by the way, I don't; we shouldn't take sides in this mess—the secretary of defense or the president might reject it."

Saul smiled. "Of course not. Just give them something. A handful of Javelins. The important thing is we pulled in the Sunnis. That's half the battle."

"You lied to him. How many troops am I supposed to send to Baquba?"

"None. Zero. But you'll generate activity as if you're sending a strong force along with the ISF. Send some preliminary people up there for a day or two to scout things out. Pass the word to General Allenford. Maybe line up some units on Highway 4, tanks and APCs or something. Have your scouts up there inadvertently drop the word you might be there in force in a week. Maybe even you yourself. On the key day, we use Predator drones to hit their hidden weapons depots in Baquba. Not a single American is going to die," Saul said.

"A diversion?"

"Big-time."

General Demetrius turned to Saul. Behind him through

the window, sand-colored walls of houses and the occasional palm tree slid by.

"This is some game you're playing, Saul," he said. "And it's all on that female agent?"

Saul took off his glasses and blinked like an owl waking up. "Yes. Yes, it is."

"She better be damn good."

"She is. She has to be. For all our sakes," Saul said.

CHAPTER 22

Habibiya, Baghdad
25 April 2009

"You were spying on me," de Bruin said. He was sitting on the side of the pool, naked, his feet in the water. Estrella handed him a SIG Sauer handgun, which he put down beside him. Carrie was still in the water, holding on to the side of the pool.

"Of course," she said.

"For the CIA?" he asked.

Say the wrong thing now, it'll go very bad, something told her.

"As a woman. I've got competition," indicating the bedroom with a jerk of her head.

"Dasha?" he said, looking amused.

"She's beautiful."

"Very. Mmm . . ." He hesitated. "I wanted to . . . Maybe I shouldn't ask this?"

"Maybe you shouldn't," she said.

"Last night . . . Who—did you enjoy more? Her or me?"

Carrie pulled herself out of the water and sat beside him, naked, dripping wet. The sun coming up over the palm trees felt warm, good on her skin. At that moment, she thought, This is interesting. My sister Maggie's got the doctor's degree, and the nice safe life. The nice house and car and two great kids, but even if my head gets blown off in two minutes, maybe it's my disease and I'm crazy as a bedbug, but this is interesting.

"Do you know, I don't know. It all got mixed up," she said, standing up. She wanted him to look at her. Look at me, she thought. If you're going to kill me, look at me. At that moment, she felt sexier, more like a woman, than she ever had. "Women. We mark our territory. If we're interested in a man, we try to find out everything we can about him, by any means we can—and if you don't know that about us, at your age, you're a complete idiot."

She went back to the bedroom to find her clothes. De Bruin came after her. He grabbed her and turned her around.

"I went to a lot of trouble for you. You think arranging a soirée in Baghdad is simple? Every one of those people risked their lives," he said.

"I know. I'm here. What do you want with me?"

"I don't know." He frowned. "I have a meeting today. Big security conference with the Iraqi leadership and General Allenford, head of Baghdad security."

"That's interesting," she said, changing her plans that instant. "So do I. Same meeting."

He put one big arm around her, held her tight, and grabbed her face with his other hand.

"Don't try to jerk me around, Anne, if that's even your name. I think you're a spy. Whatever you are, you're trouble. I don't know whether to screw your brains out or get rid of you."

"I vote for the first," she said, looking up at him. "I'm not Iraqi, you know. I'll be missed."

"Have you any idea how much money is involved? This is Baghdad, Lady Anne. People who play games don't survive here very long." He shook his head. "What am I to do with you?"

"Did somebody say 'jerk off'?" said Dasha from the bed.

"Go play with yourself, *dorogoi*. Anne and I have to go to work." He let go of her. "See you there?"

"Wouldn't miss it," Carrie said, pulling on her clothes.

She said good-bye to Warzer in the car queue at the Qadisaya Expressway checkpoint. They were in the SUV, the one without embassy plates that he would be driving down Highway 8 to Karbala. His job would be to see if he could locate and, if possible, get a photo or an ID on Abu Ghazawan, Abu Nazir's man in Karbala. Carrie would join him there as soon as she could.

"You've got all your badges?" Carrie asked, feeling like a mother hen. Since the Iraqis had taken over control of the Green Zone checkpoints, various kinds of different-color badges were required to get through checkpoints that had sprung up all over the city.

"Or they won't let me back into the Emerald City? I won't get to see the Wizard?" Warzer half smiled. "And you? Will you let me back?" Looking so much like an Arab that morning, with his dark eyes and beard. All he lacked was the kaffiyeh and prayer beads. He tugged at her sleeve.

"What do you want, Warzer? I need to know," she said as they sat in the midst of a line of cars inching up to the checkpoint, where she would get out. She was supposed to meet Perry Dryer and Virgil later that morning. Virgil, who was tailing de Bruin (whom they'd code-named "Robespierre"), had already texted her as he followed the Mercedes.

"Where is he?" she'd texted back.

"lots of zigzag in g.z. and al qasim xway to lose tails. very pro. headed habibiya?"

So de Bruin was trying to lose any tails, zigzagging in the Green Zone and on the Mohammed Al-Qasim Expressway. Habibiya was a dangerous Shiite area south of Sadr City in

"New Baghdad," the eastern part of the city built by Saddam Hussein.

Sadr City was the headquarters of the Mahdi Army and had been the site of a major battle between American forces and the Mahdi Army only last year. Virgil's question mark meant he was wondering what the hell de Bruin was doing in a Shiite stronghold. A dangerous place for anyone who wasn't local.

"???" she texted back. She had no idea. It didn't add up. If de Bruin was passing American intel to IPLA, who were Sunnis, what the hell was he doing in the Shiite part of the city?

"??? sida sq," Virgil texted back.

Sida Square? That meant de Bruin was definitely in Habibiya, Carrie thought. And Virgil couldn't figure out what de Bruin was doing there either. Now what?

She and Warzer were almost at the checkpoint, which was blocking the entire road. It was manned by Iraqi ISF soldiers, who had erected barriers that squeezed the approach down to a single lane. Two U.S. soldiers watched from a Humvee by the side of the road. Time to say good-bye, Carrie thought.

She got out of the SUV and walked around to Warzer's side. There were taxis on the opposite side of the road, waiting to take people from the checkpoint into the Green Zone.

"Tell me what you really want," she said.

"Loving you is killing me. I want to marry you. I want to divorce my wife," he said.

Before she could stop herself, the words came out of her mouth.

"A free ticket to America. Is that what I am to you, Warzer?" she said.

"Is that what you think? *Kos emek*, Carrie," he snapped, cursing her mother. Not looking at her, he drove up to the checkpoint and stopped to show his badge to the Iraqi soldier, who barely glanced at it and waved him on. A lot easier getting out of the Green Zone than getting in.

"Warzer, wait! Please! Oh God, I didn't mean it!" she called after him, standing by the side of the lane as he drove away on the expressway, but she didn't think he heard.

She never spoke to him again.

"Who the hell is he?" Carrie asked.

She and Virgil were driving on Palestine Street in a Mersin delivery van, images of Iraqi cheeses and yogurts painted on its sides. They were four cars behind de Bruin's Mercedes. Because the neighborhood was conservative Shiite and hostile to outsiders, Carrie wore a full abaya, wig, and veil. The only part of her that was visible were her eyes. She and Virgil were the rear half of a front and back tail, tracking de Bruin's car after he had briefly stopped at a teahouse on Umal Street, a block from Sida Square.

Although it was morning, the day was already hot. Heat haze shimmered over the cars and streets, busy with women in abayas with shopping baskets, men working or sipping tea outside a shop, boys on their way to school. Everything seemed normal, but they were Shiites here. They had been persecuted and killed by Saddam for a long time and they knew who their enemies were.

Outsiders who came by for a look might find a young man smiling and saying *"Salaam aleikem"* to them while a confederate, unnoticed, stuck something on the side of their car, and twenty seconds later, there would be an explosion.

One of de Bruin's Peruvians had gone into the tea shop and came back out with an Arab in a Western business suit, no tie. He spoke briefly to someone—de Bruin?—and then the two men got into the Mercedes. The good news was that Virgil managed to get a few cell-phone snapshots of the Arab before he got into the car.

Virgil passed his cell phone to Carrie, who emailed the photos to a cover gmail account that got routed through several cutout servers to Perry Dryer, at CIA headquarters in the Republican Palace in the heart of the Green Zone.

Who was the Arab meeting with de Bruin? Identifying him was essential before the security meeting this afternoon. Carrie waited anxiously for Perry to respond.

Traffic was getting heavy, she noticed. They were driving on a wide three-lane street, ragged trees on the center divider. Come on, Perry, Carrie thought, getting jumpy. She was on her meds, back in Baghdad with all the clozapine she wanted from Samal on Haifa Street, but still, she was getting jittery.

This whole op—and now the thing with Warzer and de Bruin—was becoming more terrifying by the minute. It was the operation to end all operations. And there was something about de Bruin, his cunning and unpredictability. She sensed that she was getting in way over her head this time.

De Bruin's Mercedes made a sharp right at a big intersection, losing the front tail. He sped up Thawra Street, a broad boulevard with a wide tree-lined center divider, cutting in and out of lanes, then turned right again onto a side street.

What the hell is he up to? Carrie wondered, then realized what de Bruin was doing. They were in an area of two- and three-story concrete houses and empty lots. A poorer neighborhood that had gone even further downhill since the fall of Saddam. Dead easy to spot a tail.

"Shit. We've been made," Virgil said, going slowly, still on Thawra Street. "He knows he's being followed." He glanced at Carrie. "Now what?"

"Go slow. Stay on Thawra," she said.

"You realize this street takes us straight into the heart of Sadr City? A month ago, they were killing Americans on sight here," he said.

"I know." She called Perry back on her cell phone and said: "Anything?"

"Yeah, but not one hundred percent. Say eighty," Perry answered

"Cut the foreplay, Dallas-One," his code name. "Just tell me."

"Okay. A certain 'Victor Papa.' Someone near," Perry said.

Carrie tried to understand his reference. Victor Papa was the military alphabet for the letters *V* and *P*. VP. Vice president? Vice prime minister? Iraqi vice prime minister Mohammed Ali Fahdel? But he was a Sunni. A leader of the Sunni faction in the Iraqi parliament. Perry said "someone near." What the hell was someone close to Fahdel, a Sunni, doing with de Bruin in a café in Sadr shithole City, the stronghold of the Shiites? Who was it? A relative or an aide? No one else could be close to him.

"A helper?" she said into the phone. Was it someone who was an aide to Mohammed Ali Fahdel?

"Bingo. Think forty thieves," Perry said.

Forty thieves? "Ali Baba and the Forty Thieves," is that what he was trying to say? What was he trying to tell her? In her mind, she tried to think of people around the vice prime minister. Someone named "Ali." Of course, Carrie. Ali Hamsa, the senior aide to Vice Prime Minister Mohammed Ali Fahdel. But in Sadr City? What on earth would Ali Hamsa be doing here?

Then it hit her. She almost had it all. Almost. There was one other piece she couldn't quite understand. Oh, Saul, she thought, terminating the call. You clever, clever man.

Just then, they saw the Mercedes shoot out from a side

street back onto Thawra and turn right, heading toward the Imam Ali Overpass into the heart of Sadr City.

"There he is. Do we follow?" Virgil said, speeding up.

"Turn around," she told him. "We have to go back."

"Where?"

"To the teahouse. What an idiot I am."

"What are you talking about?"

"I'm saying forget about following them. We need to go back to the teahouse where they talked to that guy," she said. And checking her watch, she called Perry back on Virgil's cell phone.

"Tell you-know-who," she told Perry. Tell Saul.

"What about continuing? Maybe a third?" Perry said. Carrie understood. He was obviously worried that the two of them, Ali Hamsa and de Bruin, were on their way to meet a third party.

"Not enough time. Pass it along to you-know-who," she said, and ended the call. Saul had to be told that the person de Bruin was passing intel to and getting intel from was Ali Hamsa. And they had to move fast. De Bruin had told her this morning about his security conference with Vice Prime Minister Mohammed Ali Fahdel, General Allenford, and a few others that afternoon. And she had told him she would be there.

"Back to the teahouse," she told Virgil, checking her watch again. She barely had time to make it back to set up for the meeting.

Virgil turned the Mersin van around and headed back to Sida Square. He drove the roundabout to the teahouse and found a parking space about fifty meters away.

"I don't get it," he told her when they parked.

"Ask yourself, Why did they do the pickup here, in a Shiite neighborhood? Because Ali Hamsa met someone else here. These guys are even bigger crooks than I thought," she said, preparing to exit the van.

Now was the tricky part. In Iraqi society, teahouses were for men; women rarely entered. This business of being a woman in the Middle East made her job somewhere between difficult and ridiculous, she thought, taking the Glock 26 out of her handbag, racking the slide so it was ready to fire, and putting it back in her purse.

"Look," she told Virgil. "First they did a pickup and ride here in Habibiya so there was no chance anyone they know would see them. Not in this part of town. Any Sunni or Coalition type who shows his face around here is a dead man."

"Okay, that makes sense," Virgil said.

"But why here exactly? I mean, okay, he was waiting at the teahouse. But maybe he was here because our friend, Ali, whom we now know is some kind of mole, is playing more than one side. And maybe our friend, de Bruin, who'd cut his own mother's throat for an extra buck, is selling intel to both sides. IPLA and al-Qaeda on the one hand and the Iranians on the other."

"Shit, that actually makes sense. Otherwise, why risk coming to this part of town?" Virgil asked. As she started to get out of the van, he added: "Carrie, make it quick. The life expectancy of someone who looks like me isn't long around here. Someone's gonna attach a sticky bomb under this van any minute."

Pulling on her veil, she took a deep breath and walked into the teahouse. It was a long shot that the man Ali Hamsa might have met before de Bruin—that was still speculation on her part—was still here.

Inside the teahouse, men at bare wooden tables, some in Western clothes, some in *thaubs* and kaffiyehs fingering prayer beads, looked up at her. Mostly workingmen, she thought. An Iraqi in an apron came around from behind the counter.

"What are you doing here, madam? No women here," he said to her in Arabic.

"*Men fadlek*, I'm looking for my husband, Hussam Abdul-Zahra. He's a truck driver who comes here sometimes," she replied in Arabic, looking around the room as if for her husband. She saw no man by himself. Certainly, no one who might have been at a level to meet with the aide to the vice prime minister. But that meant nothing, she reminded herself. He might be right in front of her. He might have left. He might be a figment of her imagination.

"We don't know this man, madam. You're being here is *haram*. You must go," the counterman said, hustling her toward the door. On the wall, she spotted a framed photograph of a mosque with small Arabic lettering on the bottom. It looked like the kind of souvenir sold at shrines all around the country. She squinted to see it better as she reached the door.

The photograph was of a mosque with a gold gate, with a single gold minaret and dome. The Arabic lettering read IMAM REZA MOSQUE.

"A thousand pardons, brother. I seek forgiveness from Allah," she said to the man in the apron, and left, her head bent modestly, but her mind firing on all cylinders. She got into the van, motioning Virgil to go. As they drove off, she felt them being watched by a hundred eyes.

There was something about that mosque, she told herself. She'd seen it before. Something from long ago, from college, majoring in Near East Studies. What was it? She racked her brain. Where was that mosque? She tried to picture the page of the book she'd read in the Princeton library on a cold New Jersey afternoon, then she had it. It wasn't Iraq; it was Iran. That mosque was for a Shiite martyr, the eighth imam, Imam Reza. The men in the teahouse must be Twelvers, she thought.

The "Twelfth Imam," she remembered from her classes, was Muhammad al-Mahdi, the *Mahdi*, the Messiah. According to Shi'a Muslim tradition, he was born in AD 869 and supposedly never died. Twelvers believe that when the Mahdi comes out of hiding, he will wield the Sword of God and kill all the unbelievers on Judgment Day. The most hardline true believers of the Iranian Revolutionary Guard, the ones who were key in the Iranian power structure supporting Muqtada al-Sadr and the Mahdi Army in Iraq, were Twelvers.

That was the other piece, the thing Saul had figured out. De Bruin and Ali Hamsa. Getting intel right from the horse's mouth, U.S. and Coalition leaders and the top of the Iraqi government, and feeding it to both sides: IPLA and the Iranians.

She told Virgil to take them back to the Green Zone, pronto. If she was quick enough, she could watch it happen at the meeting where de Bruin and Ali Hamsa sat with the leaders of U.S. forces and the Iraqi government. She needed to let Saul know about this latest development ASAP.

That bastard de Bruin, she thought. He had been inside her, aroused her sexually to heights she'd never experienced before. And he was fascinating, the way a beautiful, dangerous snake was fascinating. The hell of it was, she admitted to herself, she was both attracted and repelled by him. He was killing people. What the hell was wrong with her? Pull me out, Saul. I'm looney tunes.

She tugged off her veil and pulled the hijab from her hair. Virgil drove on wide Thawra Street, eyes checking the side mirrors for tails. They headed toward the Al-Ahrar Bridge to cross back over to the Green Zone.

They passed the checkpoint and started across the bridge, its surface rumbling under the tires, the hot sun shining on the green water of the Tigris River. Something that was still bothering her suddenly registered. She turned to Virgil. Thank goodness Virgil was there. Someone she could count on.

"Who suggested the code name 'Robespierre' for de Bruin? It's really odd," she said.

"Warzer," Virgil said.

"Did he say why Robespierre?"

"He said he remembered a quote from him he learned in high school when they studied the French Revolution: 'Pity is treason.' That's some quote," Virgil said. He glanced at Carrie. "I think he meant it for you, Carrie. To warn you about de Bruin."

Pity is treason. Which side is everyone on? she wondered.

CHAPTER 23

"How is the fishing?" Saul asked.

Tal'at al-Wasi laughed. He was a small, middle-aged Arab in a white *thaub* and kaffiyeh, with a darker skin than most Arabs in Baghdad, a ragged Vandyke beard, and a belly. If his beard were longer, he'd look like an Arab Santa Claus.

"Nobody fishes anymore. Too much money in smuggling," Tal'at said.

They were sitting on the veranda of al-Wasi's villa overlooking the Shatt al-Arab waterway from an inlet shaded by a dense palm grove. The sun was brilliant on the coffee-and-cream-colored water, the heat intense, although it was still April. The temperature, according to a weather website on Saul's laptop, about 46 degrees Celsius, 115 degrees Farenheit. Out on the waterway, commercial steamers, motor launches, and the occasional patrol boat from the Basra Border Guard left V-shaped wakes that rippled past the rusting hulk of a half-sunken five-hundred-foot freighter.

The Shatt waterway, formed by the confluence of the Tigris and Euphrates rivers, was littered with wreckage left over from the

Iran-Iraq War in the eighties. In the distance, a flame from a gas flare stack at a Basra oil facility was visible against the bright sky.

"What do they smuggle?" Saul said, careful to say "they," knowing full well that as a leader in the powerful Bani Assad tribe in the Shatt al-Arab, Tal'at had to be at the center of the smuggling himself.

"Oil, weapons, cars, consumer goods, even people. I can get you a beautiful young girl now," Tal'at said, glancing over at Saul, who imperceptibly shook his head. "Of course not," Tal'at continued. "Oil is best. Most money."

"Who buys? The Iranians?"

"The Revolutionary Guards are making a fortune, those sons of pigs and whores." He shrugged.

"How? In barges?"

"How you Americans say, 'easy-peasy,' yes? They cut hole in the pipeline. Run big hose to the barge. Barge has many open tanks." He pointed to the sky. "No need for to close tanks. There is no rain. Barges go out into Gulf waters. The Iranians come. Pay money on the water." He slapped his hand. "Money first."

"How much?"

"Every day we get world price per barrel from Kuwait. They pay half world price, tow barges to Bushehr, load on tankers from different countries. Malta, Panama, who can say? They sell same day two dollars fifty per barrel under world price. We do maybe three, four barges a day. Half-million-dollar profit each barge. Everybody getting rich."

"What about Iraqi patrols?"

Tal'at laughed.

"Is joke, right? The ones who are not my tribe, Bani Assad, we bribe. Also, some die," he said, fingering his prayer beads. "The Shatt"—he sighed—"can be treacherous place."

"What about the Iranians? Don't they worry about pirates?"

"Those flea-bitten dogs?" Tal'at shook his head. "Once you are in the Gulf, Iranians come with missile torpedo boats. Peykaap class, very dangerous. Protect barges. For Iranians, in Gulf, anything within forty, maybe thirty kilometers from Kuwait, they say is Iran. Tomorrow, their border maybe twenty kilometers from Kuwait." He grinned like an impish schoolboy. "But drink, eat, my friend." He gestured at the tray of dates and almonds and glasses of chilled rose *sharbat*, each with a rose petal floating on the top.

Saul took a sip of the sweet rose *sharbat*, although even in the shade, the heat was so intense nothing was going to help.

"Where is your friend? The Lebanese?" Tal'at asked. Dar Adal.

"On other business," Saul said carefully.

"Hard, your friend, like pine nut," Tal'at said approvingly. "Where did you meet?"

"Somalia, 1987. The country was falling into civil war. We tried to do something," Saul said.

Saul and Dar met for the first time as they boarded a Black Hawk helicopter on the way to Galkayo in Somalia's central highlands. They were going to meet General Mohamed Farrah Aidid, leader of the United Somali Congress faction, formed after the military dictator, Mohamed Siad Barre, had massacred civilians of the Hawiye tribe.

They were considering offering American military support and training to help Aidid oppose the other rebel factions, which were all communist dominated, and see if they could establish a stable government in Somalia. After meeting Aidid, Saul decided not to do it. Something told him Aidid might be even worse than Barre. Years later, his fears were confirmed when this same Aidid became the warlord behind the deliberate starvation of tens of thousands of women and children and the killing of Americans in the Black Hawk Down incident.

Even then, he and Dar recognized the skills of the other. Even then, they argued over methods.

"Killing isn't always the answer," he remembered telling Dar, after they left Mogadishu following a car bombing that failed to kill the dictator, Barre. Saul had discovered the bombing had been carried out on the orders of someone from a militia faction Dar had connections to, only he hadn't warned Saul about it.

"Sometimes killing is the only answer," Dar had said.

"Did it work?" Tal'at asked.

"Nothing worked there." Saul looked up. "It was a long time ago."

"And we are older, my friend," Tal'at said, brushing a fly away from his *sharbat.* "Are we any wiser?"

"More cautious, maybe. No, not cautious. More careful," Saul said. He looked at the inlet, the palms overhanging the water. "Everything is precious."

"Here we say, the caravan passes. You and I, my friend . . ." Tal'at shrugged. "Only shadows on the sand."

Saul nodded. His cue. Time for business. *Tuchas affen tisch,* ass on the table, as his father used to say in Yiddish.

"About moving the woman into Iran, these people, can they be trusted?" he said.

"Who can be trusted?" Tal'at said, hesitating. A matter of delicacy. "Is this of importance?"

Saul nodded. "Very." What did the old buzzard want? he wondered and decided to preempt. "As you know, America doesn't interfere, although the Iraqi ISF has asked us to," gesturing out at the Shatt, where a barge carrying steel racks filled with new Toyota cars five stories high was passing by as it churned south toward the Persian Gulf, some twenty-five miles away. Ten to one destined illegally for Iran, Saul thought.

He was bluffing about interfering. The United States Navy was stretched to the hilt policing the Persian Gulf as it was. They weren't about to start tackling the smuggling trade too, which would involve their being shot at from both sides, Iraq and Iran. Of course, Tal'at probably knew that, but Saul was betting the old boy wasn't going to risk the sweet business he had going to test it.

Tal'at sighed and ate a date.

"On our side of the Shatt and as far as Bushehr, there will be Bani Assad. On this, my friend, Saul"—he touched his chest—"there is no fear. Once in Iran and on to the mountains and the flats of Borazjan, of the people to be used, some are Lurs, some Muhaisin of the Bani Kaab. Of these"—he brushed his hands together twice, a sign he took no responsibility for them—"who can say? The woman? Does she speak Farsi?"

"A little. She speaks good Arabic, also French, English," Saul said.

"And you, my *sadeeq*, do you know Iran?"

"Does anyone?" Saul said.

Tal'at studied him, the American with his glasses fogged from the heat and the sweat rolling down into his beard, clearly wondering, How far can he be trusted?

"Nothing is simple there," Tal'at said.

"No, it isn't," Saul said.

"Have you been?"

Saul nodded. Don't think about that now, he told himself.

"So you know." Tal'at raised both his hands as if to say, *This is the world. We are in it. What can we do?* He stroked his mustache and beard for a moment, deciding whether to say something. "We sent someone before. An *Eenglizi*." An Englishman.

Saul was instantly alert. Tal'at was trying to tell him something.

"How'd he do?"

"He was stopped by the VEVAK in Isfahan. After that . . ." Tal'at shrugged.

"Weren't you afraid he would lead the Revolutionary Guards to you?" Saul asked.

Tal'at shook his head.

"He was blindfolded. Knew no one's name who took him. Certainly not mine. Knew nothing of clans. For the woman, it must be the same or there is nothing, yes?"

"Of course. *Shokran*," Saul said. Thank you.

"Good. Understanding is good, my friend. That no one knows of the involvement of the Bani Assad is everything," Tal'at said, brushing away the fly again.

Saul stood up. He was being dismissed.

"*Ma'a salaama*," he said. Good-bye. One of the few Arabic phrases he knew.

"*Allah yasalmak*," Tal'at said. Allah keep you safe.

Saul rode in a Land Rover driven by a Brit paratrooper from the last British forces in Basra. He was on his way to the airport for a flight from Basra to Kuwait on Al-Naser Airlines, a private U.S. contractor.

"Bleeding hot, sir, isn't it?" the soldier said.

"Yes, very," Saul replied, not wanting to talk.

They motored past groves of palm trees. They seemed endless around Basra. Saul tried to concentrate on the road, or failing that, on all the different pieces of Iron Thunder in play. He couldn't stop his mind from thinking about Iran, now that Ta'lat had brought it up. Don't think about it, he told himself, because it was all tied up with Mira and Africa and Javadi and the Iranian Revolution.

Focus. Take your mind off it. Say a blessing. Because thanks to Carrie, we've gotten very far. We've almost got this done.

Don't screw it up now. "Blessed are you, Lord our God, Ruler of the Universe, who has granted us life, sustained us, and enabled us to reach this occasion," he prayed, but they were just words. It wasn't working. In his mind, he wasn't seeing the palm trees, but Africa. And Tehran.

It was a football game that changed everything.

He hadn't wanted to bring Mira to Tehran. It wasn't what they had planned. He was a young CIA operations officer, recruited out of the Peace Corps in Africa. When he had told his parents he was joining the Peace Corps soon after he graduated from college, his father took him aside.

"You want to save the black people, Shaulele? That's a noble thing. But it won't help you save yourself."

"I just want to help people, Pop," he had said.

"Zei gezunt. I'll give you money to go to Africa. People need help. But listen, Saul, even in Africa, no matter what happens, Ha Shem, Blessed is His name," he said, pointing at the sky. "God is watching. You think your battle with Him is over? Believe me, it isn't."

"What about yours, Pop? The camp! What about yours?" he had shouted back.

"Also," his father said. "Why else do we exist?"

Mira saved him. Right from the beginning, seeing her in his mind the way she looked the first time he ever saw her, standing alone by some tall papyrus, looking out at the brown water of Lake Rweru, part of the border between Burundi and Rwanda. Dangerous water in many ways, and that wasn't counting the hippos. The lake was vast. It was surrounded by marshes, with flocks of birds, meadows of lily pads, and floating islands covered with hyacinth. There was something about her. She stood there, slim as a reed in khaki slacks and a white shirt, dark flowing hair, and then she turned around and he knew.

"What's a mzungu *doing here?" she asked, using the Swahili slang word for a white man, rare in these parts.*

"There's been a coup in Bujumbura. Micombero's out," he said.

"Thank God," she said. "He was a butcher. He was a drunk and a filthy murdering bastard. Are they going to massacre Hutus again?"

"I don't know. We need to get your people out," he said.

Later, because he was CIA, he was able to stabilize things with Colonel Bagaza of the new regime. To celebrate, he and Mira had a picnic by the rock outside the capital, Bujumbura, near Lake Tanganyika, where Stanley met Livingstone. You could see where Stanley himself had carved the date, "25-XI-1871," on the rock. They sat on a blanket, just the two of them, in the midst of green hills and meadows, clinking bottles of Primus beer.

And that night, the best night of his life, finally he discovered joy, and inside her, home. And it was her.

Africa was what they wanted. Then Tehran came, Saul reflected in the stifling-hot, airless terminal at Basra Airport, waiting for the flight to Kuwait. Maybe it was fate, he thought. A chance encounter. A thousand people go by on a street. One stops for a minute to buy a soda and wins the lottery. Another comes by a minute later and gets hit by a bus. Here in the Middle East, they were all fatalists. "If you're fated to drown, a cupped hand of water is enough" was an Arab proverb.

Officially, he was *the assistant cultural affairs attaché at the U.S. embassy in Tehran. Unofficially, he was the ops guy and whipping boy for Barlow, an old-hand CIA station chief, and his smarmy deputy, Whitman, an aging Yalie with compadres in the SAVAK, the secret police, and a taste for the good life as dispensed at the shah's palace parties. I should've quit then, Saul thought. It would have saved me and Mira, our marriage.*

Or would it?

He and Mira talked about it in the tiny garden behind their apartment building in the Farmanieh district at night. Whispering, because they couldn't be sure that their building wasn't being bugged by either the SAVAK or their own people. Not anymore.

"Working to help this brutal regime against their own people. This isn't us, Saul. What about Africa?" she had said. He was ready to quit the CIA. They were agreed. He would submit his resignation.

So what was it? Blind chance? Luck? Fate? Or had his father been right all along? *You think your battle with Him is over? It isn't.* Had *Ha Shem*, God Himself, the Ruler of the Universe, finally decided to take a hand in the game? Because suddenly, what he and Mira and the CIA and the rest of the world wanted didn't matter. Only it wasn't just his life and Mira's that changed that day, Saul thought, sweating in the stifling airport terminal. It was everyone's.

Of all things, it was a soccer match. So odd that his life and Mira's, that the fate of nations, of the world, could swivel on such a seemingly trivial thing, a football game, made it even more incomprehensible. Only Mira, furious, ever said anything that tried to make sense of it. Afterward, when he had come back to Langley from Tehran and cried out in frustration and anger: "If only I hadn't gone to that game!"

And she said: "Maybe that's all we are, Saul . . . a game for your Old Testament God. The one who demands that fathers go up on a mountain to murder their sons just to prove their loyalty to Him, like some lunatic Mafia don! Unless you're telling me your Jewish God was just playing a sadistic game, which kind of proves my point, doesn't it?"

The football game.
Tehran, November 1977. Aryamehr Stadium. Packed to the

gills, one hundred thousand screaming fans, including the seventeen-year-old Crown Prince Reza Pahlavi, for the most important soccer match in Iranian football history. The World Cup qualifying match against a powerful Australian team.

Iran had qualified by winning the Asian Cup 1–0 against a weak Kuwaiti team. Australia had beaten tough teams from Hong Kong, Taiwan, South Korea, and New Zealand. Iran's chances hung by a thread. Only by beating the powerful Aussies would they qualify, for the first time in history, for the World Cup play-offs.

It wasn't just the stadium. The entire country had shut down. Every café and corner grocery, every home, had their black-and-white television tuned to the game. In the mountains and deserts, whole clans and villages crowded into the house of the one person in the village with a TV set. The streets of North Tehran, normally clogged with traffic this time of day, were empty. Not a single car moved. There were no police to direct traffic. Even prayers from the empty mosques were hushed. The only prayers were from the fans.

Saul was at the stadium. He had unbelievable seats, near midfield. Whitman had given him a pair of tickets from one of the top guys in the SAVAK. Mira didn't want to go, so Saul sat with Crocker, an Office of Trade Affairs attaché at the embassy, who was the closest thing to a friend Saul had there, so isolated had he become.

Saul had never been to a game like this. The entire country was roiling with discontent with the shah. Islamists had joined with communists, religious leaders, and democratic reformers. The harder the shah's SAVAK cracked down, the more the discontent grew. There were calls for the return of the Ayatollah Khomeini from exile.

No one knew what was possible. It was as if Iran's future, the future of the Middle East, hung on the outcome of this one match.

And then it started, and almost immediately the Australians proved they were no joke. Their midfielders ran around the Iranians, passed to the forwards, and a solid line-drive kick sailed right at the goal, an almost certain score. Except Iran's bearded young goalkeeper, Nasser Hejazi, leaped sideways and with his outstretched fingertips deflected it inches away from the goal. An incredible save. An instantaneous roar went up from a hundred thousand fans in the stands, gripping Saul up from his groin like nothing he had ever experienced before. A people screaming for its life.

The game went on like that. Muddled midfield play by the Iranians dominated by aggressive attacking by Australia's forwards, but time after time, Hejazi's brilliant saves kept them from scoring. At half time, the score was still 0–0.

And then, after the break, Ghelichkhani got the ball from an attacking Australian and passed it to Hassan Rowshan. He slipped by two Australians, and suddenly he had a shot. As everyone held their breath, Rowshan kicked and suddenly, impossibly, the ball was in the net. A goal! And an entire nation went insane.

The noise and vibration in the stadium was beyond imagining. Iranians who were too polite to even shake hands were hugging and kissing each other, their cheeks wet with tears. The shah's son, oblivious, began hugging everyone, total strangers, as though they were intimate royal family members.

Saul and Crocker hugged each other and people around them, complete strangers, dancing for joy. It was one of the most unbelievable moments of his life.

Of course, the match wasn't over. The Aussies were now desperate. They kicked, they played physical, but shot after shot was knocked away by the goalkeeper, Hejazi. Impossible saves, as though he had grown an extra pair of arms and the laws of gravity no longer applied to him.

As the final whistle blew, the stadium erupted again. The Aussie players ran for their lives as spectators swarmed the grass. Saul and Crocker were caught in a stampede and got separated.

The force of the crowd carried Saul from the stadium gate out to Ferdous Street. There was insanity everywhere. People were in the street, honking auto horns, cheering and screaming, and street musicians of every kind played music that couldn't be heard over the noise of the crowds.

Men and women embraced openly in the street, something never seen in Iran before or since. It was as if they had been dead and now they were alive. Suddenly anything was possible. Anything, even revolution.

An old man embraced Saul, his face wet with tears.

"The lions of Persia. I have lived to see the lions of Persia," he said.

"Bale, brother," Saul said, trying to squeeze out of the press in the street into a packed café. "I was there."

A honking convertible packed with joyous young men, screaming and waving team banners and their shirts that they had taken off, made its way through the crowd as someone accidentally pushed Saul and he fell directly in front of the convertible's wheels. He was about to be run over when a trim, well-dressed young man pulled him to safety on the curb as the convertible, oblivious, still honking, moved on.

Saul managed to get up. He turned to thank the young man.

"Mersi. Thank you, I think you saved my . . ." Saul began, then stopped. The young man stared at him as though he had seen a ghost.

"You were there, baradar?" *the young man said. Brother. "In the stadium? You saw?"*

"I was there," Saul said. "After meeting my wife, it was the greatest moment of my life."

The man embraced him tightly.

"Mine too. Was not Nasser Hejazi wonderful?"

"Beyond wonderful! The best!"

"You're American?"

"Bale. Yes, I am."

"Always I have mistrusted Americans. But as of this moment, we are brothers," the young man said.

Majid Javadi. A SAVAK officer, but even more importantly, one with links to revolutionary groups too. They became friends, Saul and Mira and Javadi and his wife, Fariba.

The strange mating dance of case officer and agent. Can I trust you? Is it safe? What's in it for me? What's the fallback? Tradecraft. Time and place for RDVs. "Chance meetings" that were anything but chance. Ciphers. Memorized phone numbers. Dead drops. The rituals of tradecraft; their own little CIA religion.

And Mira drifting away, growing ever more lonely.

With Javadi as an asset, Saul became the most important CIA case officer in the Middle East. Barlow and Whitman may have despised him, but the intel he was bringing in was too vital to let him go. No way to quit now. Although, there were times when Saul wondered who was running whom, him or Javadi? Like some kind of Iranian Zen koan. Who is the player and who's being played?

By the time he learned the answer to that question, it was too late.

It's done, past. The dogs bark; the caravan moves on. And we poor humans? Shadows on the sand, Saul thought as he boarded the Al-Naser flight to Kuwait. The white-painted skin of the plane was so bright in the sun he couldn't look at it, the ladder so hot he could not touch it as he climbed to board.

It would be a short flight. Maybe fifteen, twenty minutes.

Lions of Persia, remembering that old man as the plane rose high over groves of palm trees and the city clustered beside the brown waters of the Shatt. It was all on Carrie now, he thought. Her turn to enter the lion's den.

CHAPTER 24

Mansour, Baghdad
26 April 2009

"Did you see it?" Virgil said.

"I'm not sure," Carrie admitted. "Can we slow it down?"

She, Perry Dryer, and Virgil were in a private office off a conference room in the Republican Palace, watching a video of the security meeting between Vice Prime Minister Mohammed Ali Fahdel, de Bruin, General Allenford, Eric Sanderson, from de Bruin's party, representing the U.S. embassy, and other members of the Coalition and Iraqi government. Sitting next to the vice prime minister was his aide, Ali Hamsa, to whom Carrie and Virgil had assigned the code name "Arrowhead." He was a skinny man with a narrow face and a lean parrot's beak of a nose like an ax. You could cut wood with that face.

Carrie had attended the conference openly with Perry. But Virgil had been busy installing a set of hidden video cameras.

Perry Dryer presented evidence of increasing supplies of sophisticated weapons from Iran to the Shiite Mahdi Army coming in through Baquba. Not one word on Iron Thunder.

"Go slow," Carrie said. They were looking at the moment when the meeting broke up.

"There! See," Virgil said, freezing the image, then moving

it imperceptibly forward, a fraction of a second at a time. It showed de Bruin placing a pen on the conference table as he left. A moment later, Ali Hamsa picked it up.

"Run it again," Carrie said. "We have to be sure."

"It's in the bank, Carrie. That's a direct hand-over. Perry'll make sure we get this to Saul ASAP, right?" Virgil said to Perry, who nodded. "You know what's in it?"

"Ten to one it's the Iron Thunder intel from my cell phone that one of de Bruin's little Peruvian helpers lifted from me. Ali Hamsa—sorry, Arrowhead—is the missing link."

Leaving Virgil and Perry, Carrie went back to the conference room table where Ali Hamsa had been sitting. He had taken his notepad, but a glass he had been drinking water from remained. She picked up the glass with a tissue and brought it to Virgil.

"What's this?" Perry asked.

"Evidence," she said.

"What do we do with it? Fingerprints?"

"Everything. Fingerprints, DNA. Ali Hamsa's dirty. Let's do a complete work-up on this bastard," she said.

"So the leak's definitely coming from the Iraqi government?" Perry said.

"Some, not all. Remember, they didn't know about the raid on Otaibah. That was classified. But Ali Hamsa's part of the chain. He feeds intel from both the Iraqi government and de Bruin to IPLA, and as we now know, also to the Iranians via some Shiite in that damn tea shop, because otherwise he never would've been in Habibiya."

"What makes you so certain?" Perry said.

"Look, Ali Hamsa is a Sunni, aide to one of the leading Sunnis in the country. Yet instead of the Shiites killing him, he's sitting there, in a Shiite stronghold, sipping tea. He's probably passing it to someone high up in the Mahdi Army. All we have to do is follow him. See who he passes it off to," she said, getting up, their meeting over.

Perry returned to his office. Carrie went outside the Republican Palace, where she waited for Virgil to pick her up on a side road that ran alongside the palace grounds. He had to get a different car; they couldn't use the Mersin van again.

She waited by the curb near where the road intersected with Haifa Street. Standing there, glancing at the lavish palace grounds, the statues and green grass and palm trees, she felt they were getting close to shutting the network down. Arrowhead/Ali Hamsa was right in the middle of everything. Just squeeze him and they'd get it all.

She heard a car pull up from behind, but when she turned around, it wasn't Virgil. Sitting there was de Bruin's big black Mercedes. A back window rolled down.

"Get in," de Bruin said.

"I'm really busy. I can come by later," Carrie said, her heart racing, looking around to see if there was any way out. This was definitely not in the plan.

"It's not a request, Anne—or should I call you Carrie? Get in," he said, as a big Peruvian climbed out of the front passenger seat, aiming a large pistol at her.

She got in. De Bruin moved over to make room for her in the backseat. The big Peruvian got in and, as they drove off, turned and kept the pistol aimed at her. They drove up the wide Fourteenth of July Street, moving with traffic, not checking for tails, she noticed.

Not good.

"What the hell is this?" she said.

"It accomplishes two purposes. It gives Juan something to do and it reminds you of the stakes here," de Bruin said.

"Well, if this is your idea of how to get a girl back into bed, let me tell you, it isn't working."

"Don't play games with me, Carrie? We—you—need to decide some things, and fast," he said.

"Is that supposed to impress me? That you know my name? Took you long enough, King of Baghdad. Maybe we should demote you to duke or count?" she snapped, her mouth dry. This was going bad very fast.

He slapped her hard across the face. When she tried to slap back, he grabbed her wrist and twisted it.

"Stop. You're hurting me."

"Then be a good girl and behave."

"Go to hell, de Bruin. Beating up girls, is that what gets you off? Ecstasy and Ukrainian girls aren't enough anymore?"

He twisted her wrist further. She cried out in pain.

"If you twist it any more, I think it'll break," she gasped.

He let her go.

"*Loop kak*, Carrie," he cursed. "You're making things very difficult."

"Who taught you your negotiating technique? Hitler?" she said, rubbing her wrist and looking out the window. They were making a turn. Damascus Street. She recognized the dome of the planetarium.

Not good, she thought. She should be tailing Arrowhead, although she was betting ten to one Arrowhead was on his way back to Habibiya to pass details of Iron Thunder and General Demetrius's planned military action in Baquba to some Shiite bridge agent who'd get it to—whom? Close the circle. What about Muqtada al-Sadr, leader of the Mahdi Army? Sadr City, next to Habibiya, was his base. Or the Iranians? Or was that the same thing now? Saul would know. God, she missed being able to walk down the hall to talk to him.

What about Virgil? What would he do when he discovered she was missing? Try to find her or follow Arrowhead? Stay on

Arrowhead, Virgil, not me, she tried to will him mentally. For God's sake, stay on the son of a bitch, sensing that he wouldn't. That he would hit the panic button and go looking for her.

"There are things you don't understand," de Bruin snapped.

"Like what, lover boy?" she said sarcastically.

He made a face. "Shit, Lady Anne. You are not easy."

"I know," she said.

He exhaled. "I was a Recce, South African Special Forces. I built Atalaxus Executive from nothing, just me. Now you Americans are looking for the exit and everyone's scrambling, Anne or Carrie or whatever the hell you want me to call you. You'll walk away, you bloody Americans, and leave the rest of us holding the shit end of the stick."

"What does that have to do with me?"

"Don't bullshit me, Anne. We're past that," he said.

"What do you want, Marius? If you really want me, I have to tell you, kidnapping a woman and almost breaking her arm with a gun pointed at her head—tell that son of a bitch to stop pointing that fucking thing at me—isn't the least bit seductive," she said, looking out the window. They were passing the big Mansour gas station, cars lined up, as usual, for what seemed like a kilometer, waiting to get gas. "What is this about?"

De Bruin waved off the Peruvian with the pistol. The man turned around and kept his eyes on the street.

"Am I the target of a CIA operation? Is that what this is?" de Bruin asked.

"I have no idea," she said.

"The hell you don't. You're part of it."

"Am I? News to me," she said, seeing where this was heading.

"I can make you tell me," he said. "Trust me."

"Not if I don't know," she said.

For a long moment, neither said anything. Around them,

there was just normal Baghdad traffic on the wide street. People walking, vendors selling kebabs and fruit drinks, houses surrounded by blast walls, a small grocery store with vegetables in boxes outside in the hot sun.

"Bloody hell, Anne," he said, having settled on the name she'd first used when they met. "You're making this very hard."

"Hard to what?" she said softly.

"To keep you alive, dammit," he snapped. "Do you understand what is happening? We're like people on a damaged plane losing altitude. If we don't throw things overboard, we crash." Staring at her.

"Am I one of the things?"

"What do you think?"

Time to choose, Carrie, she decided, taking a deep breath. If he had already decided to kill you, he wouldn't be talking. He hasn't made up his mind. For some reason he doesn't want to.

What is it? That he likes me? The hell of it was, she had to admit she was attracted to him. He was sexy. Even the scent of him: Santos de Cartier and expensive whiskey. That means there's a play here. C'mon, you're a trained CIA operations officer. MICE. Money. Ideology. Compromised (circumstances). Ego. That's why people do things. Pick one and go.

"De Bruin, Marius, listen, I'm not what you think. But if I were, hypothetically, me disappearing would make things worse, not better," she said. "For both of us."

"Shit," he said. "You are CIA. This is an operation and I'm the target."

"I didn't say that."

"Yeah, Lady Anne," staring at her. "You did."

Neither spoke. They were driving past the vast open space around the massive Al-Rahman mosque, with its giant unfinished dome, a construction crane left there from Saddam's reign, surrounded by smaller domes that looked like missile silos. Every time she passed it, it reminded her of that poem by Shelley from high school, "Ozymandias." "Look on my works, ye Mighty, and despair!"

De Bruin shook his head. "Not that it matters now, *bokkie*, but for what it's worth, I thought you liked me."

She turned to him.

"I like you, de Bruin. I'd like to screw your brains out right now. And without Dasha, although I like her too. More important, I'd like to actually—" She stopped. Took a breath. Make it good, Carrie. If you want to live, you better make him believe it's more than just sex for you, she thought. "Do you have any conception of what it's like to be a single woman in this testosterone-fueled Middle Eastern lunatic asylum? I wish we had met . . . But not like this." Was it enough? Would he let her live? she wondered, and gestured at the Peruvian with the pistol, still watching her. "Not this."

He was looking at her oddly. She wished she could read him better.

"What I built here, I'm not giving it up. Not for a piece of . . ."

She put her hand on his arm, swaying against him as they made the turn on Ramadan. They were in the Mansour district, she saw, heading toward the Abu Ghraib Expressway. So that's where they were going? she thought. His place. Or if you stayed on the Abu Ghraib long enough, Fallujah. Where Dempsey died, she remembered, and for a second she couldn't breathe. It could go either way, she thought. At least try to make him believe you're a little on his side.

"I know. Sometimes you feel if you don't have someone to talk to, you'll go insane," she said.

"Well, we're all balls-out insane here," he said, motioning to the driver.

CHAPTER 25

Hart Senate Building, Washington, D.C.
29 July 2009
01:27 hours

"Are you shitting me? Really? The story about this colonel—what's his name?"

"Colonel, later General Namir Fahmadi, Mr. President."

"I don't believe it. It defies all medical science. It's impossible, isn't it?"

"Honestly, I have no idea. I'm not a doctor or a scientist. All I know is what was in Carrie Mathison's report. We take in data, Mr. President. We collect, we analyze, we cross-check, distill as best we can. We're like archaeologists, picking over bits and pieces, making educated guesses about what the hell we're looking at and giving you our best estimate in your daily PDB. Absolute truth, one hundred percent certainty, Mr. President, never happens in intelligence work. Never."

"Mine too, Bill. President of the United States or not."

"Maybe it's apocryphal, this colonel story. I'm not sure, in this case, that what is scientifically true matters in the least."

"What do you mean, Warren?"

"The point, gentlemen, is not whether or not the story's true in some pure scientific sense. The point is, these people believe it. No wonder they hate us."

"Wait a damn minute, Warren. We had diddly-squat to do with the excesses under the shah, and God knows, we've had no control over what happens in Iran in what—thirty, thirty-five years? Are you telling me the ayatollahs are better? Blaming us is what these people do so they can duck taking responsibility for what they've done to themselves."

"But it does bring up something else, Bill, which we haven't answered."

"What's that, Warren?"

"Why didn't this de Bruin fellow kill Carrie? She was his Achilles' heel. Presumably, given the way things are done in Baghdad, he'd probably be able to 'prove' he had nothing to do with it. So why didn't he simply eliminate her? Did she sell out? Is she really a traitor, like the polygraph suggested?"

"You know what Saul said, Warren? He said, 'De Bruin was like any man who couldn't stop thinking about a woman. Killing her wouldn't have solved his problem.'"

"Are you saying it was love, Bill? Really?"

"Who the hell knows? Look, for a field operative, the spy game is like being a soldier lost in a fog in the middle of no-man's-land. Sometimes you might encounter an enemy soldier and, if you don't kill each other, discover you have more in common with him than with some of the bozos on your own side."

"Seems a bit far-fetched, Bill."

"Yeah, Warren? Well, Romeo and Juliet were supposed to be enemies too."

"Wait a minute, Bill. Whatever his feelings were, are you suggesting that she, a trained CIA agent, loved him?"

"Love's a strong word, Mr. President. She admitted she was sexually attracted to him and maybe she liked him. Saul says it may be harder to kill someone you like than someone you love. Whatever else, it's clear de Bruin was attracted to her. Everything that happened afterward came from that."

CHAPTER 26

Borazjan, Iran
27 April 2009

"What happened between you and Robespierre?" Saul asked her. He'd called her via JWICS Skype from the U.S. embassy in Kuwait before she left Baghdad.

"Nothing. He knows we're onto him, but hasn't decided what to do," Carrie replied.

"Wants to see which way the wind blows?"

"I think so."

"What about you? Any problem with him?"

She thought about telling him how scared she'd been, then changed her mind.

"I can handle him," she said, wondering if that was true. With de Bruin, nothing was simple.

"Well, we figured Virgil and Perry were there and we knew his location at all times—" Saul said, then stopped. "Why didn't he . . . try to do something?" Kill her.

She took a deep breath and let it out. The Question of the Day, boys and girls.

"I don't know," she said.

"Yes, you do." Eyes blinking behind his glasses, patient, waiting. Saul.

"I think he likes me. Is that enough?"

Saul looked away, then back at the camera over the monitor.

"Do you like him?"

"If you mean, do I find him sexually attractive, yes. We're playing each other, Saul. I don't know who's going to win. He likes me enough not to kill me. For now," she said, feeling awkward, naked. This business was worse than being a stripper. You have to bare everything.

"Good," Saul said, scratching his beard. "We can use that."

She didn't tell Saul about what happened that last night in Baghdad with de Bruin, when he decided to tell the driver to turn the car around and they wound up spending the night, the two of them, in a suite at the Al-Rasheed Hotel.

She had hesitated at the front entrance of the Al-Rasheed, the sight of the high white stone lobby bringing it all back. The last time she'd been in the Al-Rasheed it'd been with Dempsey, a man she'd really cared about.

De Bruin saw it. For all that he was a big man, he possessed a sensitivity to women's moods that was almost female. Odd, but in a way she couldn't explain, sexy.

"What is it?" de Bruin said. "You don't like the al-Rasheed?"

Time to exorcise Dempsey's ghost? It's been three years since he died. Get a life, Carrie. That's what I'm trying to do, dammit. The fact that it was with de Bruin, whom she couldn't figure out, an aspect of him that reminded her of Dempsey, made it seem like if she couldn't do it now, she might never, she thought.

"Nothing," she said.

Still, it was strange seeing it again. The white hallways, the arched doorways of the Al-Rasheed. And then it didn't matter. The two of them were in a suite, undressing each other in the shower.

Afterward, the two of them drying off, both wearing only towels on the balcony, watching as the sun set blood red over the Tigris

River, reminding her again of Dempsey. Only now, somehow, the memory was bittersweet.

After dark, they talked and watched the lights of the city in the districts that had electricity, while from a nearby mosque came the loudspeaker call of the muezzin for the Maghrib *prayer. They downed Zero One capsules with vodka martinis and moved to the bed, trying all kinds of positions till she had to bite her lips to keep from crying out. She would remember this night for a long time.*

Later, she watched him smoke a cigarette, his arm around her, and thought, He's the enemy, and yet he's been as intimate with me as anyone I've ever known. Damn, this is a crazy business. Good thing I have bipolar. I was born to it; they ought to make being mentally ill a CIA job requirement.

"Why'd you change your mind?" she asked. Unsaid, that when he had picked her up outside the Republican Palace, he had intended to kill her—her body a hairsbreadth away from being one of so many headless things found floating in the Tigris River or laid in rows like ears of corn on the floor of the Baghdad morgue—and for some reason, decided not to.

"Interesting things are happening. We'll have to see how it plays out," he said.

"Meaning you want to be on the winning side, no matter what? I'm a bargaining chip."

"Like you said, bokkie," *turning on his side and grinning at her. "I'm the king of Baghdad, right? Somebody's probably looking for you right now. Probably right outside the door with a brassed-off Navy SEAL team or something."*

More likely just Virgil with a 9mm pistol, she thought. Except Virgil's smarter than that. He'd wait.

"Don't worry," she said, and kissed him. "I'll protect you."

"No, you won't. And I won't either, Lady Anne. If push comes to shove, I won't lift a finger. But I'd regret it," stroking her breast. "I would."

"Likewise. I wish you were on my side." She pressed the length of her naked body against his. "Can I go in the morning?"

"Not before we do this again," he said, stubbing out his cigarette and grabbing her.

When she woke up in the hotel room in the morning, he was gone. Just a handwritten note on hotel stationery: "Gone. Business. Don't leave Oz, Lady Anne. Pls."

Oz. The Emerald City. The Green Zone in Baghdad. *Don't leave Oz.* He was saying, 'Stay put. There's a shit storm coming.' *Pls.* Please. He's going out of town and wants me here for the grand finale, whatever it is, she thought.

Thirty minutes later, she was cleaned up, dressed, and back with Virgil, who had done exactly as they'd planned when she disappeared. They knew de Bruin might do something and programmed the what-if.

The first thing Virgil had done was alert Perry Dryer, back at the CIA Station HQ in the sectioned-off portion of the Republican Palace that was the U.S. embassy until the new fortresslike embassy building was completed. The key was that Perry and Virgil could track de Bruin because of the NSA software she'd loaded on his cell phone and laptop that night.

The real open issue was Ali Hamsa, Arrowhead, and who his contacts were. As they had decided, instead of trying to follow her, Virgil had tailed Arrowhead, who had gone back to the Umal Street teahouse in the Habibiya section of Baghdad, near Sadr City. That nailed it.

Through one of Perry's Shiite agents, they'd already learned that the owner's son, the man who had shooed Carrie out the door, was a courier for Muqtada al-Sadr, leader of the Mahdi Army. Al-Sadr was closely tied to Iran.

Circle closed.

As for de Bruin, after their night at the Al-Rasheed, the software told them he had gone to Baghdad International Airport, but by the time she, Virgil, and Perry had reconnected and checked the airlines' passenger rosters, de Bruin's flight via Emirates Airlines to Tehran had already taken off.

That's when Carrie debriefed on JWICS with Saul and he gave her the go-ahead for the next phase in their plan.

Iran.

Before she left, he gave her an update on Warzer. He had gone to Karbala to locate and track Abu Nazir's key operative, Abu Ghazawan, who they believed to be the IPLA point man for both de Bruin and Abu Nazir on the Sunni side.

According to Perry, Warzer had linked to a local IPLA cell in Karbala. He spent a lot of time hanging out near the Imam Hussein Shrine. The local cell knew of Abu Ghazawan, but so far as Perry knew, Warzer hadn't spotted him, or any IPLA jihadis Abu Ghazawan might have brought with him to attack the shrine.

"Except for one thing," Perry said. "A rumor in the teahouses that the Grand Ayatollah Ali Mohammed al-Janabi, the *marja'*, or leader of the Shiite authority in Iraq, is coming himself to speak at prayers this Friday at the shrine mosque."

"Only four days," Virgil said. "Should I go down to Karbala?" Perry shook his head.

"Leave it to Warzer. You'd stick out there like a sore thumb." He looked at Carrie. "Are you ready?" he asked.

"Iran," she said.

"With any luck, no one will ever know you were there," Perry said.

She caught an Air Force helicopter flight from Baghdad to Basra, then a taxi to a warehouse on the Shatt al-Arab in the pounding heat.

That night, two Arab men led her from the warehouse to

the dock. They took her belowdecks on a motor trawler and locked her in a small cabin.

After a long while, at least several hours, the motion of the boat changed. She felt waves, bumping, the boat moving and lurching through swells. They must be out in the Persian Gulf.

"You come now," a young Arab said, unlocking the door and leading her up the ladder, out on deck, a hood over her head. They led her stumbling, passed along hand to hand, onto another boat or ship. No way to tell anything with the hood on.

Someone, a man, his breath smelling of onions, led her down iron steps, She banged her head on something. Carrie shook her head inside the sack.

"Bebakhshid," the man said. Sorry in Farsi. The man led her down, one hand guiding her head. He sat her in a chair, where she sat rocking with the motion of the boat or whatever she was on. Sometime later—she had dozed off—she woke. The boat had stopped, no throb of the engine. They were tied up somewhere, she thought.

Someone led her up on deck, her backpack slung over one shoulder. They were outside. She could smell the change of air. Hands guided her off the boat and onto a dock. For the first time in hours, she was on land. A few minutes later, they put her into a vehicle, and as it began to move, someone pulled off the hood.

Although it had felt like days had passed, it was still night. She checked her watch. Four A.M. She was in an SUV with two men. One of them, with bronzed skin and speaking bad English, told her to lie down on the floor of the backseat. They drove through the port and stopped. She assumed they were at a customs gate, because the driver spoke Farsi to someone, probably a guard.

Two or three endless minutes later, Carrie holding her

breath while someone shined a flashlight on the interior of the SUV, they started to move again. The man who spoke some English told her she could sit up.

Now she could see where she was. They were driving along a coast road, the dark waters of the Persian Gulf on one side, the lights of the city on the other. She was certain now it was Bushehr. In the far distance on the coast, she could see the lit-up dome and the tall smokestack of what had to be the nuclear plant. Iran.

Soon they were speeding on a two-lane highway past outlying houses and a lone billboard advertising Zam Zam Cola, out into the desert.

"Sun will be up soon," the man who spoke some English said. "Will be hot. You have the sunglasses?"

She nodded.

"Good. Is hot, white on eyes, salt flats of Borazjan," he said.

"Thank you for doing this," Carrie said. "It's dangerous, even for Persians, *bale*?"

"I piss on the heads of Persians," the driver said. Carrie knew just enough Farsi to catch it.

"Be quiet," the man who spoke English said to the driver in Farsi. Then to Carrie: "We are Lurs. Between us and the Persians is no good." He made a motion indicating separation.

That's why Saul chose them, she realized. They hated Persians and, if captured by the VEVAK or the Revolutionary Guards, would tell them nothing. Not these men.

"Why do you hate them so much?" she asked.

The driver laughed.

"Namir Fahmadi," he said, and spat out the open window.

The sun was coming up. She watched it turn the sky gold, then blue. The desert was empty.

"Who's Namir Fahmadi?" she asked, the sound of her voice surprising her. Just something to say to fill the emptiness.

The man who spoke English shook his head.

"A name to frighten children," he said.

The two men glanced at each other and said nothing. For some reason, she had touched a nerve. The only sound came from the tires on the road. Around them, the land was flat and blinding white. Salt, she thought, putting on sunglasses.

"Where'd all this salt come from?" she asked.

"Long ago, in time of fathers' fathers, sea was here," the man who spoke English said. "Now only desert." Up ahead was a road sign with a city's name in Farsi and the flag of the Islamic Republic.

Borazjan. A small city filled, it seemed, with young men on motorbikes.

The road became a wide dusty main city street. It was late morning and the market was crowded with women shopping, vendors hawking their wares, and dozens more motorbikes. There was a big crowd in a square on the main street. Some men were shouting, but most of the crowd was silent. They stopped the SUV to see what was going on.

Carrie saw a young man stripped to the waist, standing in the bed of a pickup truck, his hands tied to a steel roll bar, being savagely whipped by a big man wearing a balaclava on his head. Everyone watched as the camel whip landed with a loud whack, again and again, on the young man's back, till it was striped red and bleeding. The young man screamed at each crack of the lash.

They got out of the SUV. Time for her to change into a black chador that would cover her from head to foot. The joy of being a woman in a part of the world where if you showed someone any part of your arm above the wrist, even accidently, you were a whore. But the public whipping that was still going on stunned her. She turned to the man who spoke English.

"What's going on?" she whispered.

"Wait," he said, and went over to a cluster of young men watching, spoke to them for a minute, and came back.

"Is okay. Not worry. This man," pointing at the man being whipped. "He drink beer. *Haram*. Forbidden."

Shit, she thought. I'm in the Middle Ages. And I've only got four days, Saul.

After Borazjan, they drove on a narrow blacktop road that snaked its way through the harshest landscape she had ever seen. Stark rock mountains. Behind the mountains, still higher mountains, fading to blue against the sky. There was nothing green anywhere. Not a tree, a bush, a single blade of grass.

Carrie was sweltering in the black chador that covered her from head to foot. She turned to the man who spoke English.

"Who is Namir Fahmadi?" she asked.

"Colonel Fahmadi," the man who spoke English said, "was in Borazjan in time of shah. Persian peoples don't like Medes peoples. Hate Lurs. They is hating anyone not Persian."

"What did this Colonel Fahmadi do?"

He looked at her.

"Not good," he said, turning away.

"Tell her," the driver said.

"I tell," the man who spoke English said. "Fahmadi is rounding up young men, Lurs. He is taking from street. No reason. What he do, he make small iron plate. Like this," holding his hands about a foot apart. "Heats with fire. Hot. Metal is glowing red, all red.

"His soldiers bring one Lur man. One soldier standing behind prisoner with a sword. When colonel giving signal, the soldier swinging sword. As sword hitting neck of Lur man, Fahmadi yelling, 'Run!' Man's head falling to ground, but colonel pressing red-hot plate on back of neck. Body with no head taking two, three, maybe more steps before falling. Body not knowing is dead."

"My God," Carrie whispered.

"Is more bad. Fahmadi is bringing another Lur prisoner. Colonel is making bets with soldier men. How many steps each man can go with no head? Record is thirteen steps, *dooshizeh*. This is Fahmadi."

"When he go Tehran, shah is making him General Fahmadi," the driver said. "Even today, Lur mothers is telling children, 'Be good or Namir Fahmadi will come,'" the driver said.

They came up on a road sign in Farsi. Carrie spelled it out. SHIRAZ, 60 KM.

A few hours later, the men in the SUV dropped her off at a large shopping mall, with gardens and lighted fountains, in one of the most beautiful cities she had ever seen.

The city of Shiraz had modern streets flanked with trees and gardens at the foot of a long, high mountain. In the mall, she saw young women mostly in *rusari* head scarves and normal clothes, not chadors. Carrie checked the dead drop, a loose board in the wall of a changing room in a women's clothing store on the third floor of the vast shiny mall. Behind the board was a gobbledygook message hand-scribbled on a piece of tissue paper. She spent a few minutes on her laptop decrypting the message.

Robespierre was in Isfahan.

CHAPTER 27

A family of crows had taken up residence in a date palm in the garden. They gathered like a cloud, their droppings staining that portion of the garden. Their loud squawks woke Brody every morning.

Abu Nazir's son, Issa, was afraid of them. He wouldn't go into the garden when they flocked together on the palm.

"Why are you so afraid of them?" Brody asked.

At first, Issa shrank away and wouldn't answer. But one day, when the boy was standing at the door, afraid, he said to Brody: "They bring bad *hadh*, Nicholas. Sometimes I think I'm going to die."

"Don't be afraid. You're young. You won't die," Brody said, but he couldn't convince Issa.

Brody borrowed a pocketknife—he was trusted enough now for that—and whittled a slingshot like he had used back in Pennsylvania as a boy, playing with Mike. He and Mike had used marbles and small rocks to kill birds and mice and squirrels till something told him, "Don't." Because it was too much like Gunner Brody, he thought. That's exactly what Gunner

Brody would do—and the last thing on earth he wanted to be was anything like his father.

Issa loved his father, Abu Nazir.

Brody gave Issa the slingshot and taught him how to use it. The first time, using a small stone, with his third shot, Brody killed one of the crows. The boy was afraid to touch it. Brody picked up the carcass and he and Issa walked to the edge of the slope and tossed it into the wadi.

They stood at the top of the slope to watch.

At first, the other crows gathered around, cawing loudly, touching the dead crow as if trying to nudge it awake. The next day, they began to eat it.

Brody stood by the boy's side when he killed his first crow with the slingshot.

"*Subhanallah!*" Issa cried in joy. Praise Allah! They hugged, a moment that bonded them forever. But Issa wouldn't touch the crow's carcass, so Brody threw it into the wadi.

"Are you still afraid of them?" Brody asked. "You can kill them."

"Yes, Nicholas, now I can kill them. But I still don't like them," Issa said. His English was getting better all the time. Much better than Brody's Arabic, which sometimes caused both of them to laugh at his mistakes.

"No, a line of things, like cars, is *saff*, Nicholas. A line between two points on a paper is *khatt*." Issa laughed, making Brody laugh with him. "English is difficult, one word can mean many things. In Arabic, each thing has its own word."

Issa was going to the madrassa on the Baradash road that led from Aqrah south to Baradash and, if one continued far enough, to Mosul. Akjemal, the Turkmen girl, had told him there were American troops in Mosul. The U.S. Army First Cav. He tried not to think about that.

Every day Brody walked with Issa to the madrassa and waited outside the stone fence to walk him home. While waiting, he noticed a Jewish star carved over the door of the old stone building.

"This was a place of Jews, wasn't it?" he asked Issa as they walked along the road that paralleled the wadi, green with trees and brush.

"Once, long ago, they say," Issa said. "Now it is ours. Besides, our teacher says the Holy Quran talks of the *Tawrat* of the Jews, given by Allah into the hands of the prophet Musa. The book of the Jews is also holy."

They talked every day this way. If Brody was his teacher for English and about the Western world, Issa taught him Arabic and about Islam. In a way, Issa was the best friend he'd had since Mike. In this world, so far from home, his only friend.

Sometimes they played soccer in a flat space in the compound, Afsal and his AK-47 never far away. Issa was good, quick with the ball for his age, and the two of them sometimes laughed at Brody's clumsiness.

"We didn't play soccer so much in America when I was a kid," Brody explained.

"You make no sense, Nicholas. The whole world plays football," Issa said.

"What are you learning?" Brody asked him one day. They walked in the hot afternoon sun till they found a tree stump in the shade and sat, drinking Fanta juice drinks. A flock of tiny birds flew in a line, a *saff*, toward the green mountainside. They were so pretty against the blue of the sky, it hurt to look at them. Paradise. This is Paradise. But I'm a prisoner. The Jean Valjean of Islam, remembering something from high school. No, he'd read the CliffsNotes in high school. I'm the CliffsNotes Jean Valjean, he thought.

"We learn Quran. We try to understand. To be a good Muslim, you have to memorize a lot, Nicholas."

"And what did you learn today?"

"Of jihad. It is the best thing a man can do, Nicholas."

"What do you mean?" Brody asked, feeling a little uneasy. Was this how people became indoctrinated?

Issa nodded. "To die fighting for Islam is the most wonderful thing you can do. Our teacher said the Messenger of Allah, peace be upon him, said that he wished he could die over and over in battle for Allah. This is how good is jihad, Nicholas."

"So killing is good? I can't believe that."

"No, killing is *haram*. Forbidden, Nicholas. But killing infidels in battle, this is very good. I want to be brave enough when I am grown."

"I was a soldier, a Marine. But I didn't like killing," Brody said. "And you! You can't even touch a dead crow."

"You're right, I must be braver, Nicholas. You must help me," Issa said.

That night, lying in bed, the window open, Brody heard the sound of Abu Nazir's men outside. Daleel, Mahdi, Afsal, some of the others. Earlier, he had seen them preparing their weapons. AK-47s, RPGs, explosives for IEDs. Something was about to happen.

At dinner, with Abu Nazir, Issa, and Nassrin, even though no one spoke of the pending action, Brody could sense the tension. He looked at Issa, whose eyes indicated not to say anything.

He couldn't sleep. So much time with Issa made him think of Dana and his own son, whom he barely knew, Chris. Did Chris even remember him? He was so young when Brody left Virginia. Or was Brody now just a photo on a wall or dresser. *That's my father. He was a Marine, MIA. Never came back from Iraq.*

Maybe now there was another man in his life. Someone

who took him to ball games, read to him before he went to bed. Someone who didn't treat him like shit—like Gunner Brody—or ignore him altogether, like I did, Brody thought.

Why not? Jessica was a gorgeous woman, even more beautiful as an adult than in high school.

Oh God, high school. Was that you, Allah? Did you intervene that night and me too stupid to know it?

Junior year. The night of the game against Allentown Central Catholic. He dropped a pass in the end zone. One second it was dancing on his fingers—he had it—and the next it was on the ground. In the end zone! And it was as if something forced him to turn his head, some power outside himself, forced him to turn and look up into the stands. To look for the one person in the world he didn't want to see, and sure enough, there he was in the crowd. He had been smiling before when Brody had caught a nineteen-yard pass for a first down and pride surged through Brody. But Gunner Brody wasn't smiling now.

He could see the look in Gunner Brody's eyes. The disgust. The rage. And he knew, with every fiber of his being, if he came home, he wouldn't live through the night. If he didn't come home, there was a chance his mother, Sibeal, wouldn't live through it either.

After the game, he sat in front of his locker, not wanting to get dressed. Only one player, Demaine, punched him on the shoulder as if to say, It happens, bro', *but no one else. Everyone feeling crappy after the loss to their rivals—and that touchdown would've made the difference. He had lost the game for them.*

Finally, Mike came over.

"Jessica's outside, man. She's waiting." And then he knew what he had to do. He hurriedly got dressed and came out into the cold with Mike. He pulled Jessica aside.

"Will you come with me?"

"Where?"

"*I don't know. Anywhere. Away. Tonight.*"

"*What are you talking about?*"

"*Jess, I saw his face after I dropped the pass. I can't ever go home again. He'll kill me.*"

"*You don't know that.*"

"*Jess, listen to me. I love you, but it's now or never. I know him like I know nobody else on earth, and trust me, if I go home tonight or anytime, one of us is going to die. It's murder. So either you leave with me now, or I'm gone. You'll never see me again.*"

"*Brody! What are you saying? I'm a sophomore. I can't go. My mom and dad would kill me. I can't.*"

"*Oh, Jess. I love you, but I can't stay here. Bethlehem's dying anyway. This city's done. Everybody knows it,*" he said, turning away.

"*Brody, stop, for God sakes. I'll come home with you. I'll stay with you every second. He can't kill you with me there.*"

"*I'll come too,*" Mike said. "*He'll have to kill all three of us.*"

In Mike's car, Jessica ran her fingers through his hair.

"*I'm sorry you dropped the pass, Brody. I thought you had it. I was screaming, but you know what? I don't care. I'm going to face your father. He doesn't appreciate you,*" she said.

"*You don't get it, either of you.*" Brody shook his head. "*You think he's a dad like your dads. He isn't.*"

"*What is he?*" she asked.

"*He's a son-of-a-bitch Marine. He's a killer,*" he said.

But when they got back to the house, his mother, who never came to any of the games as if she had a premonition, something Irish, of what would happen, was outside, waving at them.

"*Nicky, we have to go to the hospital.*"

"*Why? What happened?*"

"*Your father's been in a car accident,*" was all she would say.

Later, they found out Gunner Brody had smashed into another car while speeding around to the back of the football stadium toward the *team locker room, his fourth DUI, and he'd shot himself in the knee with his own service .45 pistol, which he'd been holding on his thigh.*

As they drove to the hospital, Jessica looked at Brody, stunned, finally realizing that he hadn't been exaggerating. His father—his father!—had been on his way to kill her boyfriend and God knows who else, maybe even her. She was trembling. Except a minute later, there was Brody, putting his arm around her shoulder and grinning like he had just won the lottery.

"What is it?" she whispered.

"Don't you see?" he said, a big shit-eating grin on his face. "I don't have to leave."

"What do you mean?"

"His knee's smashed up. I'm almost as big as he is now. The cops'll take his gun away for evidence. He won't be able to move so good. When he gets out of the hospital and jail or whatever, it'll even the odds, the son of a bitch. And then we'll go away," his eyes devouring her.

She felt as if he were looking right into her soul. She nodded.

He grinned again.

"I thought this was the worst day of my life. Turned out to be the best."

"This was God's doing, Brody," she said, and kissed him.

"If you say so," he said.

Was that you, Allah? Was it? And Jessica. What about her? Six years of waiting for a ghost that wasn't coming back. Bound to be men hitting on her. Come on, Brody. Tell the truth, she's human. She thinks you're dead. Give the girl a break. There's bound to be someone. Maybe even someone you know.

What about Mike? Your buddy. The best friend you ever had. Wasn't there ever a moment . . . Suddenly an image forced itself into his mind. That time at Virginia Beach.

They were coming from the beach with the kids, tired,

sunburned, sandy, and there was Mike, big as life, grinning, bringing toys for the kids, Megan just a step behind him. And just for a second, a fraction of a second, was there a look between him and Jessica?

Was there? Had he really seen it?

Jessica and Mike. No, couldn't be. Not Mike. Besides, he was married to Megan. She was also a good-looking woman. Still, he had to face the fact that it had been six years and Jessica didn't even know he was alive. It was hard to imagine that there wasn't someone new in her life.

Except I'm not dead yet, am I? Not yet, you son of a bitch. Not the same, though. Not the same Nick Brody, son of Gunner Brody, true-blue United States Marine. Semper fi, believing all the bullshit lies. I'm a Muslim. I've surrendered myself to Allah.

What was it Issa had said his teacher told him, some quote from the Quran? "Allah knows, and you know not." It's true. None of us knows anything. Only Allah—and he's not telling, is he? So who are you, Nick Brody?

I don't know. Not the old, not the new. I'm some half creature, living in limbo, waiting for light. *Bismillah*, show me the way, Allah. What I must do. Thy will be done. Amen.

CHAPTER 28

The NSA software locator on her laptop made it possible for Carrie to track de Bruin (she couldn't think of him as Robespierre). He was staying at the upscale Abbasi Hotel, which locals claimed was the oldest hotel in the world. It was located across from the Hasht Behesht Palace and gardens in Isfahan.

But he wouldn't meet anyone there, she thought. Not de Bruin. He'd keep it clean, away from him. A restaurant, a teahouse, a garden. And she couldn't afford to let him see her, which made surveillance, never easy in Iran, next to impossible.

Using a fake Iranian ID that Saul provided, she booked a room for backup at the Dibai House, a small hotel in the Old Quarter. And another room at the Safir Hotel, on the fourth floor, with a window view of the front entrance to the Abbasi, catty-corner across the street.

Waiting. The penalty box of the intelligence game. That's the part they don't show in the movies, the glamorous lifestyle of CIA spies, Carrie thought, sitting beside her hotel window, peeking out from the side. How much time a CIA agent spends waiting. In public restrooms or cars or like now, sitting alone in a hotel room like a character in a Russian novel.

In the morning, she spotted de Bruin leaving his hotel and getting into a taxi. She raced from her room to the elevator. It was going to be a wait for the elevator, so she ran four floors down the big spiral staircase to the lobby. With any luck, she'd be able to grab a taxi from the stand outside before his disappeared.

But just before she made it outside, she saw de Bruin through the lobby window, getting out of his taxi in front of her hotel. That son of a bitch had done a quick circle around the Hasht Behesht Palace grounds to spot any tails. He was coming up the steps to the hotel's front entrance. Another couple of seconds and he'd see her.

Luckily, there were columns around the circular lobby atrium. She quickly moved behind one and put her cell phone to her ear. With her back to the entrance and wearing a modest black chador and head scarf to cover her blond hair, she hoped he wouldn't spot her.

She whispered an imaginary conversation in French into her phone, counting seconds, then peered from around the pillar. De Bruin had entered the elevator. As soon as the doors closed, she came out.

The elevator went down. Why down? she wondered. Unless he was going to the swimming pool or the spa? Wait, the hotel had a *hammam*, a public hot bath. Men only, that sneaky bastard. That's where he was having his meeting.

She couldn't go into the men's *hammam* and she couldn't hang around outside its door without being spotted. Not without being invisible, she thought. How was she to find out who he was meeting with?

But there are people who *are* invisible, aren't there? People no one ever really looks at, she thought, like a hotel maid. She went floor to floor, looking for one. On the third floor, she found a door open and a cleaning maid inside. The young Iranian woman—

she wore a gray hotel uniform tunic over jeans and a black *rusari* head scarf—was cleaning the room. Carrie went in.

"*Bebakhshid*, I must have the wrong room," Carrie said.

"No problem, madam," the maid said.

Carrie told her a quick story about a philandering husband, then asked how much she made.

"Four hundred thousand rials, *khanoum*," the woman said, calling her missus. About forty dollars, Carrie calculated.

"I'll give you a million rials if you'll lend me a uniform, so I can catch that lying son of two fathers," Carrie said. About a hundred dollars.

Twenty minutes later, she was in uniform, pushing a mop in the hallway near the door to the *hammam*.

Waiting. Pushing the mop and a pail up and back the same corridor. She was right about one thing. No one looked twice at her. Invisible. Cell phone in her hand, its camera ready. She would only have a second, if that, she thought.

Finally, de Bruin came out of the *hammam*, dressed in the same shirt and slacks he had worn going in, skin a touch redder. He glanced left and right as he walked toward the elevator.

She kept her eyes down at her mopping. She didn't need his picture. It was who he was meeting that was of interest.

Ten minutes went by. Still no one came out. Then a small Iranian man wearing wire-rimmed glasses and a suit, no tie, emerged. He glanced at her, then the instant he turned away, she snapped the photo. And a second snapshot, from the side rear as he walked to the elevator.

She stayed with her mop till he was in the elevator, then ran back to the small supply-utility room, where she disposed of the mop and uniform and quickly changed into jeans and a top, with a black *rusari* to cover her head. Now all she needed to do was get the photos to Saul and her job in Iran was done.

Previously, she'd located an Internet café on Taleghani Street, near the Bab Al-Rahmat mosque. It was only a twenty-minute walk away. Send it off and she could head for the airport, she thought, taking the elevator to her room. After getting her backpack ready, she wiped down any surface she might have touched and checked that she hadn't left anything.

When finished, she took the spiral staircase down instead of the elevator, to ensure she didn't run into anyone who might be interested in her. Pausing for a second to catch her breath, she headed from the elevator to the hotel's front entrance, where she caught a taxi, getting out at a bus stop a block from the Internet café.

She went inside the café, and a couple minutes later, the photo images were on their way to Saul via the CIA freight-forwarding-cover-company website server in Hamburg. She logged off, then plugged in the NSA thumb drive to cover her tracks, and was about to leave the café, when she heard the sounds of people coming in and turned around.

Two big men, one with round button eyes, wearing a suit, followed by two blue-jacketed Iranian policemen carrying batons came into the Internet café, which instantly grew silent. She looked away, back at the computer, ready to reboot it.

It didn't work. The two policemen grabbed her and pulled her to her feet.

"*Komak!*" Carrie screamed. Help! She looked around desperately, but the other people in the café, mostly young men, just stared at her as the man with button eyes—she didn't doubt for a second he was VEVAK, Iranian security—ordered the policemen to put her in the van at the curb.

One of the policemen handcuffed her hands behind her. The other hit her in the thigh with his baton, causing her to cry out and crumple to the pavement before they tossed her into the van.

She sat handcuffed on a bench inside the van between the two policemen, facing the VEVAK man in the suit. Her thigh throbbing, she watched the street recede through the van's rear window. They passed a vast public plaza and a domed blue-tiled mosque.

This is how my life ends, she thought. Screaming under torture, because that's where this was going. Who had spotted her? she wondered. Was it de Bruin? Had he recognized her despite the maid uniform and the *rusari*? Did he give her up after all?

Or had someone in the VEVAK, going over everyone who'd checked into a hotel yesterday, discovered her false ID? She remembered something Saul said once. "In every operation, there are thousands of variables. It only takes one to go wrong for the train to leave the tracks. Perfect isn't a goal. Perfect is survival."

Through the rear window, a wide boulevard and light traffic. The van was moving fast, siren blaring. You don't have to hurry, she thought. My life's over. She was a CIA spy in a country where they hated nothing more and the punishment for far lesser crimes was death. Take your time. I'm not going anywhere.

Wherever it was they were going was a long way. It took almost an hour to get there. In a far northern suburb, if she could judge by the afternoon shadows. The van stopped, then drove a bit farther and stopped again. A heavy steel gate set in high stone and concrete walls closed behind them.

It's a prison, she thought, heart sinking, catching a last glimpse of blue sky as they took her out of the van. Sucking it in, thinking, I'll never see sky again. Oh God, Saul, Maggie, Dad.

They brought her into a massive building. It was old, with peeling walls, smelling of bad plumbing and despair. There was discussion with someone behind a desk, after which she was brought through a series of steel doors, each of which had to be unlocked by hand, into what she assumed was a women's section of the prison, because she was handed over to four female guards, all wearing the same shapeless gray uniform and black *rusaris* on their heads.

The female guards screamed at her in Farsi, slapping her into a small room, where she was stripped and searched. They dressed her in a white *rusari* and coverall, shapeless as a sheet, manacled her hand and foot, and brought her into a room with only two chairs, both bolted to the floor, facing each other. Near the wall was a wooden table, with a couple of towels and a metal bucket. As they put her in the chair, she spotted at least one hidden video camera and a microphone in the ceiling corner.

Oh God, she thought, her heart beating wildly. She hadn't taken her meds in at least thirty-six hours. Already, her skin felt like it was burning with a bad sunburn. I can't do this, she thought. Not this, Saul.

An Iranian man, one she had never seen before, came in. He was vaguely attractive, in a good suit, white shirt, no tie—which seemed to be a kind of uniform for government agents—with a close-cropped graying beard and well-groomed graying hair. Clearly, the senior person. For a long moment, he just stared at her.

CIA protocol when captured by the enemy: sooner or later, everyone talks. But you don't have to make it easy for them. Agency trainers emphasized the onion approach. Force them to make you reveal things by peeling off layers. The real stuff is hidden deep under the other layers. Her Iranian cover would go quickly. Next was her fake cover ID: Nancy Williams, a stringer for the *L.A. Times* based in Kuwait. Then her ID from

Syria: Jane Meyerhof, travel agent from Cincinnati. Don't give them that for as long as possible.

If you can.

"*Salam*," he said, lighting a cigarette. "You are in Dastgerd Prison. I am an officer of the Iranian Ministry of Intelligence and National Security. Some call us the MOIS," he continued in English.

"*Khahesh mikonam*," she whispered. Please. "There's been a mistake."

"The mistake was yours. You are a CIA spy. You must understand, the penalty for this in the Islamic Republic is death. There is no reprieve. The fact that you are a woman will not save you. You will die."

Her heart sank. Although she knew it was coming, hearing it out loud made it real. Saul, she thought. What am I doing here? Why did we have to go the extra mile? Why was it so important? Dammit, Saul, I don't see it. If I have to die, why?

"Nothing here is in your control," the Iranian went on calmly. "Except one thing. You have a single choice: die by hanging without . . . great discomfort." He exhaled a thin stream of smoke. "Or die in agony, a broken . . . animal. But make no mistake, madam—you will die. Very soon."

"I'm an American diplomat with immunity. I demand you contact the Swiss embassy in Tehran," she said, feeling like she was playing a deuce in a high-stakes poker game where everyone was showing higher cards.

"Yes, we found your passport in your pack, madam. Nancy Williams. A journalist from Los Angeles, a classic CIA cover ruse, using an Iranian woman's ID card? And of course, your country has no diplomatic relations with the Islamic Republic, so you have no diplomatic recourse. All of which is irrelevant. You are a spy," he said. "What is your real name?"

Here we go, she thought.

"Nancy Williams."

"As you wish." He shrugged, getting up.

Almost instantly, the door opened and three male guards rushed in. They lifted her onto the table. As two of them held her down, the third put a towel over her face. When she tried to turn her face away, someone pulled her hair through the *rusari* so tight she screamed. They held her head immobile under the towel. She couldn't move.

"Waterboarding," she heard the MOIS man say. "You Americans taught us this trick. They say it feels exactly like drowning. Of course, most people don't drown over and over. So terrible."

She heard a metal scraping sound and water sloshing. Someone had picked up the water pail.

"First question," the MOIS man's voice said. "What's your name, you filthy whore? Your real name."

CHAPTER 29

At that moment, Saul was sitting in the tea lounge in the Sheraton Kuwait Hotel. The hotel was located in a Manhattan-like area of skyscrapers near the First Ring Road beside the waters of the bay.

The lounge was clubby English; mahogany-paneled walls, stuffed armchairs, roses in small flowered vases on the tables. He was looking at his Go board, set up on his table beside a Wedgwood china teapot and scones, but he wasn't thinking about the game. He was thinking about Carrie.

She hadn't touched the dead drop in Isfahan. A flower bed in the formal garden of the Chehel Sotun Palace. She was supposed to check in every twenty-four hours, leaving a thumb drive or a note or something in a box under the dirt, three bordering bricks to the right of a chalk mark. Not checking the drop meant she'd been arrested. She was probably being interrogated, tortured, right this second, while he sat there in air-conditioned comfort over tea and scones, he thought disgustedly.

It all hung on her. It always had. The last piece in his strategy: the entire Iraq War for a war-weary American public and maybe the entire Middle East. Not to mention the bloodiest retreat in American history if she didn't pull it off. Hard to imagine what she was going through. Harder than any combat soldier who gets his chest covered with medals, because she was on her own, utterly alone. And he had done it to her.

I'd do it again, he thought. What choice do we have? Otherwise the whole war, the lives of those American soldiers, the money, will have been for nothing. Worse, the bloodbath to come in Iraq if she didn't do it. What was one life against that?

Don't quote Talmud to me, Dad, because the image of his father—wearing his suit and *tallit*, the way he looked, Saul's last view of him, before they closed the coffin—popped into his mind. Not now. How a single life is the equivalent of the entire universe. Mira was right. He should've quit the CIA back in Tehran all those years ago. God, this spy game, this life is hard, looking around at the empty lounge.

A waiter came over to freshen his tea. Saul waved him away.

Lieutenant Colonel Larson, wearing civilian clothes, came into the lounge. As Larson passed Saul's table, he murmured, "Room 1605," and sat at another table, well away.

Saul took another sip of tea, waited a minute or two, then put the Go board and stones inside his messenger case that also held his laptop, got up. and went out to the hotel lobby. He took the elevator to the fifteenth floor, walked up one flight to the sixteenth, and checking the corridor to make sure it was clear, knocked at the door of room 1605.

General Demetrius, in civilian clothes, opened the door. He had a Go board on a table in his junior suite, Saul noticed.

They sat down across the board from each other.

"They say mathematically there are more moves in Go than there are atoms in the universe," General Demetrius said, placing a black stone.

"I've heard that," Saul said, placing a white stone.

They played for a few minutes.

"Your female operations officer, she's in Iran?" General Demetrius asked.

Saul nodded.

"Has she been arrested? Be careful, you're in *atari*. Next move, that stone will be captured," General Demetrius said.

"Yes," Saul said, placing a white stone to create an "eye" in a different group. "The game isn't about capturing; it's about who wins at the end."

"What she's doing . . . if she were in my command, she'd get a medal," the general said.

"We don't get medals. Just a black star on a wall inside Langley, no name, if we die."

"Will it work?" General Demetrius asked, putting down another stone.

"Maybe. If she can hold out a bit," Saul said. "Most can't."

"Do we know who's running this?"

"Not yet. Before she was arrested—I believe that's what's happened—she was able to send me a photo of who Robespierre met with in Isfahan. I immediately passed it to Bill Walden. We'll know something soon. But that's big picture. Right now, apart from her, the most immediate fire is your war."

"How much time do we have before the attacks?"

"Two days."

"Hell of a way to fight a war," the general said, placing a stone.

"It's not your kind of war."

"No, it isn't. When do you leave?"

"As soon as I win this game," Saul said, putting a white stone down to complete the encirclement of the general's biggest group on the board.

Later, pretending to inspect accessories in the Harley-

Davidson shop at Kuwait International Airport while waiting for his flight, Saul thought about Carrie. And Mira. Unbidden, something she'd said at the airport before she left Tehran, all those years ago.

"Saul, that's such a biblical name."

"My parents." He shrugged, thinking the intel he was getting from Javadi had trapped him. It was too important or he'd quit the damn CIA and be leaving Tehran too, every fiber of him wanting to get on the plane with her.

"He was a king, wasn't he? A failed king," she said, her eyes boring into him. That too, he thought. The king who wasn't good enough. Who was so jealous he hunted the king God wanted: David. Do you have to throw that at me too? he thought.

"You can't make me feel worse than I already do," he'd said.

"Did it ever occur to you that I need you too?" she said, turning to go.

"Do you?" he said, but she was already handing her boarding pass to the attendant.

Just hang on a little, Carrie, then let go. Please stay alive, he thought, and used the prepaid cell phone he'd just bought at the airport to text Mira in Mumbai.

"miss, need you," he texted. Please answer, he thought. Don't leave me.

Just before he boarded his flight, she texted back: "Me 2. When?"

"soon," he texted, breathing again. He shut off the phone as he boarded the plane. All he could do now was hope Carrie was still alive and that his plan would work.

CHAPTER 30

Dastgerd, Isfahan, Iran
29 April 2009

She was sentenced to death. Out there in the courtyard, where they had a scaffold. Or maybe in a small room with a bullet in the back of the head. The MOIS man had let her know. His superiors had given the final word. She would be dead within the hour.

They had gotten it out of her. All of it. Her ID, Saul, the CIA, Iron Thunder. The plan for an attack on Iranian Revolutionary Guards and Mahdi Army elements in Baquba, possibly the last American action of the war. Because—and this was the deepest secret they had pulled out of her, gasping for air while vomiting out water—attacking Baquba and blocking Iranian support for the Shiite Mahdi Army wasn't the object of the exercise.

She had lost count of how many times they'd drowned her. Impossible to hold her breath. Almost the instant they began pouring water on the cloth, her gag reflex kicked in, and she knew she was drowning, dying. She struggled against the men holding her down, but it was impossible. She was breathing in the water, and just as she was blacking out, they stopped.

Gasping and coughing, vomiting water on herself, urinating because she had lost all control of her body. Until she caught her breath for a second.

At which point, they put the cloth back on her face, even as she screamed, "Wait! I'll tell!" But it was too late. The water was pouring, she was gagging and screaming for air, inhaling more water as the cloth sucked into her mouth and nose.

They did it a third time, before he asked her again for her real name.

This time she told him. Jane Meyerhof. And yes, she worked for the CIA. Kuwait Station.

"Who is your station chief?" the MOIS man asked.

"Charley Brown," she said.

They waterboarded her twice more. This time she truly thought she was going to die. She blacked out. When they brought her around, she gave it up. Perry Dryer in Baghdad. The CIA setup at the Republican Palace. Iron Thunder.

"Why are you in Iran?" they asked.

She told them. Robespierre. De Bruin. Tracking him as the mole. Holding back on Arrowhead and Warzer and Karbala.

"Stupid. You're lying," the MOIS man said. "Whatever military action they take, we'll be ready. They're walking into a trap. And even if they did smash some Revolutionary Guards' forces, what's to stop us from sending more forces and arms the very next day?"

"I don't know," she whimpered. "Please, no more. I'm just an ops officer. Please. Please."

The MOIS man leaned close. His face would be the last thing she would ever see, she thought. Even if she lived, she would never forget it.

"You're lying, Jane Meyerhof. We both know it, don't we?"

He signaled to the others to waterboard her again.

"No—" she wailed, then, even before they poured the water, gagged as they put the cloth over her face.

This time, she told them almost everything.

"It's a trap. Predator drones and Apache helicopters will take care of any resistance. But that's not the point," she gasped, barely coherent.

"Tell me and I'll stop," the MOIS man said. "Truly, I take no pleasure. *Khahesh mikonam*, Jane." Please, tell them anything. Just don't say "Carrie."

"No more," she moaned. "I can't any more. Please."

"Say it. Just say it and we're done."

"Baquba. They'll prove it was Revolutionary Guards, Iranians killing Americans," she sobbed. "We don't care about Iraq. It's about Iran's nuclear program. An excuse to attack your facilities. Not just Arak. Not just Natanz. We know about Fordow. And why it's near Qom. We know the name 'Fordow' is sacred to you, like 'Gettysburg' for Americans. Because of all the casualties during your 'Sacred Defense Era,' the Iran-Iraq War. Putting your centrifuges there is no accident. Fordow is holy to you. And it's linked to Qom and the coming of the Twelfth Imam. The Mahdi, destroyer of infidels. We understand. We get it!" she cried.

"So Baquba is a trap for Iran?" the MOIS man asked. "Tell me, whore!"

"Yes!" she cried. "We know. We know this is jihad. We know what Fordow is and what it means. Iron Thunder is the excuse for the Americans and the Israelis to destroy your nuclear facilities once and for all!"

"Quick!" the MOIS man shouted to the others. "Shut her up! Get her out of here!" He looked at them hard. "No one is to speak of this. No one!"

They brought her, face still covered with the wet towel, to

a tiny concrete cell, manacled, and dropped her on the floor. She lay there, dry-heaving and crying. She had told them everything except her name. Betrayed her country, everything she believed in.

When she sat up, she felt strange. Her skin tingling like electricity was running through her. She'd gone too long without her meds. She found herself staring at a crack on the wall. It was growing bigger. She could see into it, as if with a microscope. All kinds of things, bugs, bacteria the size of her hand, were crawling out of it. They slid across the floor, flowing toward her. She could feel them swarming all over her body. They were feeding on her, like a million tiny needles. She tried to shake them off, but couldn't.

It's not real, some part of her brain insisted. She was going crazy; the thing she had feared most, even more than torture, since the day back at Princeton, when she learned of her disorder. Focus, Carrie. They're going to kill you. Go to hell, you bastards. I don't give a shit.

The bugs were eating her inside, hollowing her out. They couldn't kill her, she thought. She was dying, already dead. She lay on her side on the concrete floor and fell asleep.

Sometime later, she had no way of knowing how long, it could have been an hour or a day, the MOIS man entered with two male guards and said she'd been sentenced to death. He just looked at her.

"The women will come and change your clothes. They will put you in a cotton sheet for modesty," he said, and left, followed by the guards. She heard their footsteps moving down the corridor. A guard peered into her cell through a slit in the door. They would watch her till they came to take her away, she thought.

She had nothing left. If only she could see her family one

more time. Her father, Frank. Her sister, Maggie, and Maggie's kids. She would never see them grow up. What would the CIA tell them? Not much. Died in the line of duty, if that.

It's all bullshit. Whatever they said didn't matter. All that mattered was that she was gone. Would anyone care? Warzer? Saul? Virgil? Perry? For someone who traveled so much, her world was really small.

She would simply vanish. Gone forever like her mother, who disappeared the day Carrie left for college. Never heard from again. A wisp of smoke. Finished.

So I end just like you, Mom? All that work for my country, for my career, myself, was it worth it? Just to end like you. Someone who suddenly wasn't there anymore.

And Saul, blinking at her like an owl through his glasses. Is this enough, Saul? You've taken every last bit of me, you bastard. I have nothing. Not even self-respect.

Two female guards came in; one of them looked at her with pity, and dressed her in a black head-to-foot chador. They took away her still-wet clothes and the door clanged shut. Someone down the corridor screamed and continued screaming until Carrie heard the sound of guards and blows, of a vicious beating, the woman still screaming and then, nothing. The screams that were no longer there, echoed in the silence. She's mad, Carrie thought. I think I am going mad too.

Now she heard them coming for her down the prison corridor. Without her meds, she felt more alert than she had ever felt in her life. She could see everything, feel everything. Don't kill me now, she thought. Not now, not when I'm finally completely alive.

They stopped outside her steel door. She heard the sound of a key in the lock and the door opened. Two guards came in and blindfolded her. She just managed to catch a glimpse of the MOIS man's face. Then darkness as the blindfold covered her eyes.

They hurried her out of the cell and down the corridor. There were more doors, turns, and more grabbing and pushing her to move faster.

All at once she was outside. She could sense the change of air. So they were going to hang her in the courtyard. Oh God, she thought. Please don't let me take too long to die.

She couldn't feel the sun. Was it night? The air felt cooler. They had taken her watch when they brought her here and she had no idea what time it was. She was shoved into a seat in a vehicle, still manacled and blindfolded, and belted in.

That struck her as funny. Keeping me safe with a seat belt in order to hang me. That's really funny, and despite herself, she smiled inside the hood. There was a sound of something heavy being tossed into the back of the vehicle. It sounded like a body. What was going on? Her heart was beating very fast.

Someone, a man, spoke in Farsi and she thought he sounded like the MOIS man. All very *Alice in Wonderland*. Curiouser and curiouser, feeling her body sway as the vehicle began to move, someone grabbed her arm to keep her upright, because she started to faint.

The car was moving fast now. They were on some kind of highway, oddly not for long, it seemed. The car slowed and came to a stop. Someone fumbled with her manacles. Suddenly her hands were free. From outside, she heard the sound of a jet plane coming in for a landing.

"Say nothing," someone—was it the MOIS man?— whispered in her ear in English and removed the blindfold and manacles. They opened the door and pulled her out of a Mercedes van, its windows tinted almost black. As she got out, she spotted a black body bag in the back of the van. There was someone in it.

She was at an airport. Isfahan Airport? Men she didn't know were lifting a coffin from the back of the van and putting it on a trolley. They wheeled it away as two men in rumpled suits hustled her into a modern terminal building and up an escalator. One of them flashed an ID and walked them past a number of checkpoints and gates, no one stopping them, to a small private room.

The room had no windows and was empty, except for a small institutional-style table and four metal folding chairs. A functional room for quick body searches and official conversations; nothing more.

Someone sat her in one of the folding chairs and left. She was alone. It occurred to her she could get up and walk away, but she didn't believe they would let her. Was she dying and hallucinating all this? Her bipolar? None of it seemed real.

The door opened and the MOIS man walked in. He was carrying her backpack and clothing, folded neatly, in his hands. For a moment, she could only stare at him.

"Who was in the body bag?" she asked.

"You," he said.

"I don't understand . . ." she started to say, and then she did, as the door opened and Saul Berenson walked in.

CHAPTER 31

Carrie started to sway. Saul rushed over and put a steadying hand on her arm.

"I'm so sorry. There was no other way," he said, looking around the room for hidden cameras. He turned in a 360-degree circle, holding up a handheld electronic sweep unit to verify there were no bugs. He looked at the Iranian MOIS man. "She held out, didn't she?"

"Unbelievable," the MOIS man said, coming forward. "You were incredibly good, miss."

Carrie shrank away from him and he stopped, his face twisted with concern.

"We don't have much time. They'll be boarding our flight in twenty minutes," Saul said, checking his watch. "Let me introduce you—"

"We've met," Carrie said.

"You think you've met. This is Pejman. Pejman Khanzadeh. And yes, he's a senior MOIS officer. I've known his family a long time," Saul said, turning to Khanzadeh. "It worked?"

Khanzadeh nodded. "I got it off to my superiors less than an hour ago. I've already been ordered back to Tehran." He looked at Saul. "We have to be quick. This is very dangerous for me. More than Abu Dhabi."

"You think they'll believe her?" Saul asked.

"When they see the video of her being waterboarded, they will have to take it very seriously." He exhaled and looked at Carrie. "I regret very much, miss."

"What about them being able to identify her? They saw her face?"

"Her face was covered with a cloth during the interrogation. They won't be able to identify her. I also sent them her American passport with the altered photo. They will believe her real name is Jane Meyerhof. No one will know her real identity," Khanzadeh said, indicating Carrie.

"Who's in the body bag?" Carrie asked.

"A young Iranian woman. Not by us," Khanzadeh said. "The VEVAK. They are brutal." He looked around. "I have to go soon. I'm supposed to be on my way to bury the body in the desert. My superiors in the MOIS have been told it is Jane Meyerhof. Since she was of the CIA, they know there will be no inquiries from the Americans."

"And the repercussions?"

"In Farsi we say, 'The water doesn't move.' You understand? No repercussions. Jane Meyerhof, the CIA spy who gave us the intelligence on Iron Thunder, is no more. She did not survive interrogation. But they will see the DVD of her interrogation and believe. The water is still." Making a flat motion with his hand.

Saul pulled his cell phone out of his pocket and brought something up on it. He showed it to Khanzadeh.

"You've seen this before?"

Khanzadeh nodded. "It was on her cell phone when we arrested her."

"This man is the one whom Robespierre met here in Isfahan. Do you know who it is?"

Khanzadeh nodded. "His name is Kaebi, Jalal Kaebi. He is a courier, little more. But this is not MOIS, not VEVAK. He is of the Al-Quds Force of the Revolutionary Guards. We don't talk to them and they don't talk to us. In Iran today, there is no trust for anyone. But this I know," he said, looking at Carrie. "The video of you will go very high. Perhaps even to the Expediency Council itself."

"What will they do?" Carrie asked softly.

Just then, a public loudspeaker outside announced boarding of the Emirates flight to Baghdad.

"That's our flight," Saul said.

"What would you do? If you learned of a terrible trap being set for you?" Khanzadeh said to her.

"I'd stop. I wouldn't go there," she said.

"Let's hope the Iranians feel the same," Saul said, handing her a fake passport with Iranian entry and exit stamps in it and a ticket. They started moving to the door. Khanzadeh watched them.

"You will get me out? You promised. I will go to America?" he asked.

Saul turned back to Khanzadeh.

"As soon as you confirm that everyone accepts that Jane Meyerhof is dead, so no one will ever know that this one," indicating Carrie, "was ever in Iran. We'll smuggle you out the same way we smuggled her in. You'll be an American. And your mother? Will she come too?"

Khanzadeh smiled. "She says she will never leave North Tehran. It is her world."

"What if they question her?" Saul asked.

"She says she will say, 'I am an old woman. My son, my children never tell me anything. Do yours? What can you do to me?'"

"But she is well?"

"She remembers," Khanzadeh said, hands folded in front of him, apparently planning to wait till they left.

"So do I," Saul said, opening the door to the terminal hallway for Carrie.

CHAPTER 32

Hart Senate Building, Washington, D.C.
29 July 2009
01:51 hours

"What the hell is this? This is crazy! Since when does the CIA and the vice president make decisions about war and whether we attack another country or not? This is way over the line, Bill. I'm gonna have this thing investigated if it kills me. Who the hell do you people think you are?"

"I'm sorry, Bill. This is completely unacceptable. I can't believe you allowed this. I really can't allow this kind of thing."

"Excuse me, Mr. President, Senator. But what the hell are you talking about? We made no decisions. We did nothing."

"But this testimony, Carrie on video, talking about us using the Iranian response to our Iron Thunder attack on Baquba as an excuse to attack Iran and risk war. This is something that can only be decided on the highest levels, by me, as president. And I'd bring the leaders of Congress, both parties, into it in secret before we'd ever do anything like this. What the hell did you people think you were doing?"

"What attack, Mr. President? Senator? There was never an American attack on Iran. Never happened! As for this video testimony, which the Iranians have, not us, in secret, what is it? A video

of an American female CIA agent who under torture blurts out something. Who the hell cares what she says? She's not the president or the National Security Council or the Congress. She is just a female operations officer who under severe torture says something that isn't true. She lied to the enemy. So what? That's what we train them to do. It's her job, dammit! And she did it well, using the identity of someone, Jane Meyerhof, who never existed and whom the Iranians themselves believe is dead. And under unbelievable circumstances— and in the process, saved the Iraq War, the administration's policy, your policy, Mr. President, and probably, tens of thousands of lives. We crossed no lines, Senator. We did nothing. A woman under great duress told a lie. Well, whoop-de-freaking-doo!"

"He's right, Mr. President. When you think about it, nothing happened."

"Even if it ever came out, we've got total deniability. And let's get real, they would never dare show a video of them torturing a woman. Especially one they think they tortured to death. Brilliant, Bill. This was all Saul, wasn't it?"

"Now you know why I couldn't fire him, Mr. President. Even when he's being his most difficult, he keeps saving our ass. As for the girl, what she put herself through . . ."

"You're right. She's no traitor. When you look at what she did— all through this whole thing—I don't know how she did it."

"Frankly, Mr. President, if she were a soldier, you'd be pinning a medal on her."

"So why did the polygraph say she was a traitor?"

"Honestly, Warren, I'm not sure. You have to remember, the polygraph doesn't measure absolute truth. It measures what a person thinks or feels is true. Inside. It might be that even though she knew what she did was the right thing and she was just doing what Saul had told her to do, maybe subconsciously, just by revealing something, even a lie, to the enemy, made her feel—deep inside—like a traitor.

Maybe that's what the polygraph saw. Her weakness under extreme interrogation. Who the hell knows?"

"And it worked?"

"At the very least, it was a shot across the bow to the Iranians. When it came to priorities, what to protect—a temporary halt in their subversion of Iraq versus their nuclear program—which do you think they chose?"

"And Saul knew that? This was some bluff, Bill. Remind me never to play poker with this guy."

"He plays a different game, Mr. President. You have to remember how tricky the situation was: the mole, the war, Abu Nazir, al-Qaeda, the Iranians. It required something way out of the box."

"Iron Thunder?"

"Yes, sir. Iron Thunder."

"And the young woman? Surely after all she had done, he sent her back to that job in Langley."

"Actually, he didn't send her anywhere, Warren."

"Why not?"

"Because as Saul was about to learn, she went off the reservation. On her own."

"What happened?"

"Karbala, Mr. President. Where all hell was about to break loose."

CHAPTER 33

When the plane cleared Iranian airspace, Saul ordered tequila shots over ice for both of them. Through the window, Carrie could see only open Iraqi desert below. It would be a short flight to Baghdad. Saul raised his plastic glass as if to toast, but she ignored him and drained her glass.

"The MOIS guy, Khanzadeh. You're going to bring him to the U.S.? New start, new identity?" she asked finally.

"Part of the deal. If anyone ever asks any questions, he can't be there," he said. "Besides, MOIS isn't the real power in Iran."

"You mean the Revolutionary Guards?"

"Exactly."

"Why did you ask about his mother?" she asked.

Saul exhaled. "Bad day," he said. So much came back to that day. "During the revolution in Iran, things got—" He stopped. The worst mistake of his life. He'd been trying to get his agents out of Iran, but needed a place to hide them in the meantime. He had trusted his most important agent, Majid Javadi, who told him about a SAVAK safe house. "It was chaos.

I trusted someone I thought was a friend," he continued. "I found all four of them dead. Shot in the back of the head. One of them was a professor of political science. Sanjar Hootan. He wanted so much to see Iran become a modern state that could be a beacon . . ." Saul looked away for a second. "He had a sister, Sepideh. Khanzadeh is her son. What he's doing for us is their revenge, although why they still trusted me, I don't know."

Because people want to believe in America, Carrie thought. Even when we let them down. Because without America, what is there?

"He said I would be executed. I thought I was going to die," she said.

"I'm sorry."

"Bullshit! That's bullshit! You keep saying that, Saul, but it doesn't mean a goddamn thing anymore. Do you know what they did to me? First Syria, now this," she hissed in a whisper. "They stripped me. They tortured me. I thought I was going to die. You wouldn't use the lowest whore in the street the way you used me."

"I couldn't tell you everything," Saul said, his eyes incredibly sad. "What if, under pressure, you blurted something out, looked at Khanzadeh for help, anything? I couldn't take the chance."

Her hand holding the plastic glass was trembling. She steadied it with both hands, looking at Saul to see if he had noticed. He'd turned away for a second. She was starting to feel light, as if she were made of helium. Soon she wouldn't need the plane to fly. Some part of her realized that if she didn't get her meds soon, she was going to be in serious trouble. She could almost hear the plane's intercom announce: "Will someone please see to the crazy lady in Seat 12A?"

"I don't think I can do this anymore," she said. "I told them everything."

"No. You told them what you were supposed to. And in a way that will absolutely convince them, even if, as Khanzadeh suggests, it goes all the way up to the Expediency Council and the Supreme Leader himself. You prevented a war and the bloodiest retreat in American history, Carrie. Saved I don't know how many lives. And no blowback. You were never in Iran. No one knows but us," he said. "We just need one more thing in Baghdad and we're done. You'll come back to Langley."

Not looking at him.

"Maybe I don't want to. What we do, the things I do . . . I feel dirty, Saul. And do you know what's worse? Not what they did. What I did . . . do. I think about that Iranian girl in the body bag. What about her?"

"It's almost done," he said.

"I don't want to be a martyr, Saul. A jihadi for America. Because then what the hell's the difference between them and us?"

"One difference," he said quietly. "It's what keeps me going."

"What? Because I swear I don't know anymore."

"They want to kill people. We want to stop killing."

She stared at him; the beard and glasses, the glint of ruthlessness in his eyes that sometimes only she saw. The Rabbi Pirate.

"We kill too. We lie, we cheat," she whispered. "What do you file that under?"

"It's a slippery slope," he admitted, then tried a smile. "But look at a globe sometime. The whole damn world's on a slant."

"Give me a break," she said, shaking her head. "What about the others? Perry? Virgil? Warzer?"

"They're good. We haven't heard from Warzer in Karbala, but—"

"What do you mean you haven't heard? Day after tomorrow's the—" She stopped herself, a thrill of fear going through her. "Where's Warzer?"

"I don't know."

"What the hell do you mean, you don't know? Where is he?" Her heart was fluttering. The way she'd parted from Warzer. What if something happened to him? The horrible thing she'd said. She had to fix it.

"We haven't heard. The assumption is he's hooked up with IPLA's Abu Ghazawan in Karbala. Warzer's a Sunni from Anbar, a Dulaimi from Ramadi. Abu Ghazawan is a Salmani, a branch of the Dulaimi. He'd accept Warzer as al-Qaeda."

She stared at Saul.

"You assume? You're going to sacrifice Warzer too? You used me up; now Warzer?"

"Carrie, Warzer wanted Karbala. He came to me," Saul said, twenty centuries of Jewish sadness in his eyes. "I don't think he was happy." He left it unsaid. He didn't have to say it. *Warzer wasn't happy about what was happening with you, Carrie.*

"Go to hell, Saul. Jesus."

"Carrie . . ." He sighed. The seat-belt sign came on. He ignored it. The plane began its descent for landing in Baghdad. "You talk like we have a choice. We're like the little Dutch boy. If we don't keep our finger in the dike . . ." His voice trailed off.

"I'm going to Karbala, Saul. Don't try to stop me."

"Knowing you, what choice do I have? But if you get yourself killed, I'm really going to be pissed," he said, securing his seat belt.

An Army helicopter, a Black Hawk, reminding her of the mission in Otaibah that started it all, brought Carrie, along with two Army officers, to Security Station Hussayniyah, the joint U.S.–Iraqi Army base in the northern part of the city of Karbala. She'd taken a clozapine before she boarded the helicopter at Camp Victory in Baghdad, but wasn't sure it was working. She wasn't sure anything was. Saul's plan was so complex and she could only see a piece of it. She had to trust him—and trust isn't what spies do, she thought grimly.

In a ladies' room at the base, she changed into a clean black chador that covered all but her face. This was how she would dress in Karbala, she decided. Like a good Shiite woman, showing her ID to a guard at the base gate, who just stared at her, studying the photo on her U.S. passport and then at her several times. Finally, shaking his head, he let her pass. She went to the street outside the base and caught a taxi.

Riding into the heart of Karbala down a wide boulevard, palm groves on one side, a canal on the other, she went over what Saul had told her about the Sunnis, the Albu Mahal tribesmen that Sheikh al-Rashawi of Ramadi had sent for her to liaise with. In this most Shiite of cities, they would have to be extremely wary. As would the IPLA group of Abu Ghazawan they were hunting. Everyone would be lying low till the anticipated attack tomorrow at the Friday sermon at the shrine, which would be overflowing with pilgrims.

Was Warzer undercover with Abu Ghazawan? she wondered. Was that why they hadn't heard from him? Either that or he was being held captive, or quite possibly dead. Not Warzer; he's too good. He must have gotten close, which is what Saul wanted him to do.

But that's why she was here. The one thing she could do that the Albu Mahals couldn't. Spot Warzer instantly, anywhere, even in a massive crowd, such as those expected for the sermon of the Grand Ayatollah al-Janabi at the Imam Hussein Shrine. The ayatollah would speak to the crowd tomorrow at the noon

Dhuhr prayer. And then she had to hope that Warzer could bird-dog them to Abu Ghazawan. Otherwise, there was no way to stop whatever it was that Abu Nazir had planned for Karbala.

Even though it was still early morning, just after six, and a day early, the crowds were already heavy on Al-Moheet Street that ran alongside the plaza around the shrine. Behind the walls, she could see a golden dome and gilded minarets gleaming in the sun. People were already lining up to form a procession. The men were dressed in black; the women, standing in a separate group, wore black chadors. She was right in style, she thought.

Some of the men carried hand-painted signs that read in Arabic BISMILLAH (I Place My Trust in Allah) and YA HUS-SEIN! (O Hussein!). And WE WILL DIE FOR YOU, HUSSEIN! All for Hussein, the martyr buried in the holy shrine. Along one side of the street, vendors were setting up booths and tents, with fruit drinks, kebabs over charcoal braziers, and religious paraphernalia for sale. The turnout tomorrow would be huge, she realized. In the tens of thousands, maybe even hundreds of thousands. A terrible sense of urgency gripped her. She and Saul had left it very late, a taste like metal in her mouth.

The taxi skirted the procession and drove past the plaza, dropping her off at a corner of the Al-Tarbiyah roundabout, with its odd monument in the center that looked like a frozen yogurt. She made her way to a side street off the square, unable to shake the feeling of being watched, pausing for a second by a poster of Iran's Ayatollah Khomeini to check. No one. But the feeling didn't go away.

Then she spotted the building, identifying it by the faded blue door she'd been told to look for. A dilapidated three-story, pocked with bullet holes like other buildings on the block. She crossed the street, checking for watchers. A curtain moved at a second-story window of the building on the opposite side of the street. Shit.

I hope these guys have had a sighting of Warzer or Abu Ghazawan, she thought, walking to the building, a creepy feeling at the back of her neck, knowing she was being watched. She opened the door and went inside. The entrance hallway was dark; it smelled of fried fish and cigarette smoke. She had to wait for her eyes to adjust. There was a wooden staircase on her right. Before she took two steps, she felt hard metal against her neck and a man's voice said, *"U'af."* Stop. She froze.

"Go up the stairs," he told her in Arabic.

She did, the gun at the back of her neck. They went up a narrow wooden staircase in the dark, Carrie feeling her way forward. The man with her knocked at an apartment door. A second Arab, with a fierce hawk's nose and coppery skin, dressed in the uniform of an Iraqi Security Forces officer, opened the door. He held an M4 carbine in one hand, pointed straight at them. When he saw Carrie, he smiled.

"Salaam aleikum," he greeted her.

"Wa 'aleikum es salaam," she murmured back.

"I am Ali Ibrahim. I am your brother. You must be Carrie," motioning her inside. "Come, we have much to do, and only a short time, little sister."

He introduced her to the others. Four of them, including Big Mohammed, the man who'd put a gun to her neck. And Little Mohammed, a short man with a harelip not disguised by a sparse mustache, who grinned at her like a teenager from the couch where he was checking an RPG grenade launcher. The other two were Emad and Younis. Like Ali, they were dressed in ISF uniforms. All of them, she learned were of the Albu Mahal tribe. Ali and Little Mohammed were cousins.

"The house is being watched from across the street," she said.

"We know. A Shiite woman, Mrs. Fawzi. She thinks we're from the Shiite Badr Brigade here to protect Grand Ayatollah al-Janabi tomorrow," Ali said.

"How do you know?"

"We saw her watching, so we gave her that story. We know she believes. She told Emad she will watch the street for us."

That doesn't prove anything, she decided.

"Have you seen Warzer Zafir?" she asked, holding up the photo of him on her cell phone. She knew they were aware that Warzer was originally from Ramadi, of the Dulaimi tribe, of which the Albu Mahal was one of many branches.

"Just once. Little Mohammed thinks he saw him with three men in the Al-Shafaa neighborhood. It was at a distance—and all we had to identify him by was a cell-phone photograph, so he's not sure it was him."

"Did we locate their safe house?"

Ali and the other men nodded.

"They stay inside, like us," Ali said.

"Who's watching them now?" she asked.

"Another of us. Ismail. There's a bakery, on that street. He got a job helping the owner, an old man who lost a leg in the Iran-Iraq War, for a few days. He calls us from the back, by the ovens, on his cell phone," Ali said.

"If we go there, I can recognize him," she said, biting her lip. She had a sickening feeling about Warzer, the way they parted, the IPLA attack Saul believed Abu Nazir had planned for tomorrow. She had left it too late, she thought. Glancing around the apartment, empty of anything that would suggest some person had ever actually lived there, she began to think it was too late for all of them.

"We know. It's good you have come." Unsaid, that she'd come so late they must've thought she wasn't coming, that this mission, which could cost them their lives, would have been for nothing.

"Please excuse me for coming so late to Karbala," she apologized. "What of the men Little Mohammed saw?"

"They were all armed with pistols and AK-47s. Everyone there is Shiite, so the people of the neighborhood must believe they are of the Mahdi Army. If anyone in that district were to think they were Sunnis, like us, they would be dead," Ali said, pouring tea into glasses from a metal teapot.

Carrie asked for a map of the city. Big Mohammed put one on the table and she studied it. He pointed out the Al-Shafaa district. It was near a highway. That meant they were thinking of quick movement, possibly even escape after an attack, she thought. It had all the earmarks of an Abu Nazir–planned attack.

The two of them, Ali and her, sat over tea at a table, partially covered with the remains of breakfast, *khubz* bread and a small dish of butter, dates, honey, and also bullets and magazines for the carbines and other weapons.

"You must know, it is strange for me to sit thus with a woman," Ali said, putting his hand to his heart. "But you are from our friend Sha'wela, Saul, whom we know can be trusted."

"He is lying. He sits thus with his sister, his wife. Also his mother, who still tells him what to do," Little Mohammed said in Arabic, to general laughter.

"With your wife too," Younis called out to Little Mohammed, to more laughter.

"How many of them are there?" Carrie asked, smiling.

"We're not certain. We've spotted three SUVs. All white Toyotas. Perhaps ten men. Perhaps fifteen. There may be more. But this is what we saw in Al-Shafaa. We watched them put jerry cans of gasoline in the SUVs," he added.

Car bombs, she thought. Three vehicles. Multiple simultaneous attacks. Practically a signature of Abu Nazir. And although things were easing up, there were still queues for gasoline in Iraq, which meant they had been planning this for months, accumulating the gasoline. And Warzer was in the middle of it.

She said it out loud. What they were all thinking.

"Car bombs. Where? In front of the shrine?"

"Near the gates, yes. But if they want to destroy the tomb, someone must go inside on foot to get close to the sepulcher of Hussein itself," Ali said.

"If someone were to succeed in blowing up the tomb or damaging the remains of Hussein, would it be war?" she asked.

"Not just in Iraq. The whole world," Big Mohammed said, and the others nodded. "Every Shiite would become a martyr."

The question was, how could they approach the tomb tomorrow, when there would be a hundred thousand people clamoring to get close? The only way, she and Saul had agreed, was if Abu Ghazawan's men went there ahead of time. They would blow it up tomorrow to maximize casualties, but Abu Ghazawan would have to get inside today.

Ali answered his cell phone. He listened, saying "*na'am* . . . *na'am*," yes and yes, and little else. He hung up. They looked at him expectantly.

"They're moving," he said.

"Then we have to go," Carrie said, getting up.

"You must stay close," Ali said, gathering his weapons. "My task is to protect you."

"*Inshallah.*" God willing, Carrie said. "But you know yourself what will happen if they harm the shrine. We have to stop it."

The apartment filled with the clicks of weapons being loaded and checked. Everyone made sure they had each other's number in their cell-phone contacts. All of them using prepaid phones purchased for today only.

The men were dressed as Iraqi Security Force militia, carbines slung over their shoulders. Carrie checked her compact Glock 26 pistol and stuck it in a holster she placed in the front of her jeans and belt, by her groin, the last place any Muslim should touch, which she wore under her chador. When they were ready, Ali walked around, checking the men's uniforms

"If we live, each of us will make his way back here separately. Make sure you are not followed. If anyone follows even one of us, we are all lost. If one of us is wounded, he is lost. We cannot stop," he said.

"So what should one do?" Little Mohammed asked.

"Don't get wounded," Ali said.

They got into two small cars, a Nissan and a Honda, and headed for the shrine. Carrie squeezed into the backseat, as befit a woman in a chador, with Little Mohammed. As they approached the neighborhood close to the shrine, the traffic became heavier and they had to navigate through crowds arriving on buses and on foot.

Little Mohammed shook his head as they moved slowly up Qabla Street toward one of the gates in the stone wall that surrounded the shrine. Ahead, Carrie could see there were already several hundred people beginning to fill the vast open plaza outside the walls.

"It's funny. A joke I never would have believed," Little Mohammed said to her in Arabic.

"What?" she said.

"We are Sons of Iraq." He grinned, his harelip spreading in a way that gave him a toothy rabbit look. "We are Sunnis. And here we are, about to die to save a Shiite shrine. This is a big joke. We're all crazy." He leaned closer. "Sometimes I think Allah created this world as a place for all the crazy people in the universe."

"I think you're right." She grinned back. Inside she was scared to death. Little Mohammed was right. It *was* crazy. And would she be able to spot Warzer in the crowd?

Ali, driving, turned into a narrow side street. It too was crowded with pedestrians and parked cars, some with wheels partially on the sidewalks. There was no parking space. They drove slowly to a small tobacco kiosk, selling cigarettes, sundries, and lottery tickets, with crates placed in the street in front to hold space for customers' cars. He honked the horn twice, then twice more.

A thin, balding man in a Manchester United T-shirt came out, acknowledged Ali with a look, and moved the crates away so Ali could park the Nissan in the space at an angle.

"He's also of the Albu Mahal," Ali said of the tobacconist.

"A long way from home," Carrie murmured.

"Aren't we all?" Little Mohammed said, grinning like a wicked rabbit.

CHAPTER 34

Imam Hussein Shrine
Karbala, Iraq
29 April 2009

The grounds of the Imam Hussein Shrine encompassed two ancient domed mosques, the Al-Abbas mosque and the Imam Hussein mosque, each surrounded by its own high wall with a long
tree-lined promenade between them. A temporary chicken-wire
fence had been erected in front of the blue-tiled Qabla Street gate
that led into the courtyard of the Imam Hussein Shrine.

Carrie, along with Ali and the other Albu Mahal tribesmen dressed as Iraqi Security Force soldiers, crossed the wide
plaza. The air was hot, still. The shrine's golden dome and
gold minarets gleamed in the bright sun. Already, the faith-
ful had begun to gather at the entrance to the Imam Hussein
mosque and in the courtyard, where loudspeakers were being
set up for the anticipated crowds who wouldn't be able to fit
into the shrine.

While Ali spoke with an officer of the shrine security
guards at the entrance, Carrie studied the layout, her eyes
scanning the crowd, searching for Warzer.

Why hadn't he contacted Virgil or Perry? She'd narrowed

it down to only two explanations: he had gotten close to Abu Ghazawan, which meant no cell or Internet communications, or he was dead.

If he was alive, she would see him today. If they had a chance to talk again, she didn't know what she would say. Whatever she'd done with de Bruin had poisoned a well that was already going dry. But what if Warzer was dead?—feeling sick to her stomach. He couldn't be, she thought. Not now.

She and the Albu Mahals had moved a day early because Saul was betting that while a terrorist attack like a car bomb could occur anywhere, anytime, given the crowds, the only way Abu Ghazawan and his IPLA attackers would be able to get near the tomb would be to set up a day ahead. Tomorrow, Friday, the day of the Grand Ayatollah al-Janabi's sermon, the crowds and security would be so massive that it would be almost impossible for Abu Ghazawan and his men to get anywhere near the sepulcher chamber.

Everything was predicated on the notion that the tomb and sarcophagus of the martyr was the target.

Shortly after they had left the apartment, Ismail had called Ali to alert him that Abu Ghazawan's men were on the move. The Toyota SUVs had left, filled with men. He wasn't sure if there were others or whether Warzer was with them. As for tracking Abu Ghazawan's cell phone, according to Virgil back in Baghdad and per Carrie's laptop, it hadn't been turned on in a week. Abu Ghazawan had gone fully operational; no cell phones. But Carrie now knew that Saul had been right. They had chosen today to get close to the tomb, where they would wait overnight and, for maximum effect, attack tomorrow.

She'd worked out a set of hand signals with Ali. If she covered her eyes with her left hand, she'd spotted Warzer. If she raised her right hand to her eyes, she'd identified Abu Ghazawan. Although no one knew what he looked like, she knew that if Warzer was anywhere around and saw her, he would indicate Abu Ghazawan to her. If she spotted both and/or IPLA suicide bombers, she would raise both hands to her face and hit the ground, because that would be a trigger for action.

The shrine officer Ali had been talking to motioned them inside the massive pointed-arch entrance, where they removed their shoes and, at a fountain basin, washed their faces, hands, and feet. They went inside the shrine, entering a decorated hallway opening to a vast *musalla*, or the mosque's open area for prayer, lit by crystal chandeliers and lined with a long row of intricately detailed pointed-arch doorways under an elaborately patterned crystal ceiling.

As a woman, Carrie had to separate herself from Ali's men. She padded on bare feet to a place near the doorway of the sepulcher chamber and peeked in. It was a smaller room than she expected. There were pilgrims standing in prayer around a gold-topped, cagelike metal sepulcher within which lay the gold sarcophagus of the Shiite martyr. Through the crisscrossed metal mesh of the sepulcher, she could see its triangular-shaped top.

Other pilgrims, some dressed completely in black, sat legs crossed, against the wall or crowded behind others to get as close as they could to the sacred sarcophagus. Many were praying. The room was filled with murmurs.

Warzer wasn't there. She saw no one who might be one of Abu Ghazawan's men. They had beaten them to the shrine, she thought as Emad and Younis took up guard posts by the door to the sepulcher chamber. Big Mohammed had stayed outside the shrine's wall to watch for SUVs, which might be used for car bombs. When Ismail got there, he would stay outside with Big Mohammed.

Ali and Little Mohammed positioned themselves against the wall opposite the *mihrab*, the niche that designates the direction of Mecca for prayer. Carrie waited at the edge of the women's section of the hall, turning so she could face the *mihrab* while taking in the entrance hall of the mosque.

With each minute more people filed into the mosque. Men, women, families, all prepared to wait twenty-four hours to hear the words of the Grand Ayatollah al-Janabi. They sat waiting for the call for the noon *Dhuhr* prayer. But it never came.

Instead, Ali signaled her with his eyes. He must've gotten a cell-phone signal from Big Mohammed outside, she thought, her body tensing.

Suddenly a stir as some fifteen policemen, dressed in SWAT-type military gear of the INP, the Iraqi National Police, came four abreast into the prayer hall.

"There's been a bomb threat. We're here to protect the shrine of the holy Imam Hussein," one of them shouted in Arabic. The third policeman in the front row was Warzer. She tried to catch her breath and couldn't. Here it comes, she thought.

The INP policemen marched toward the sepulcher chamber of the Imam Hussein. People moved out of their way like water parting. The INP policemen came fast, menacing and bulky in their blue uniforms and Kevlar vests, any one or all of which could be concealing suicide vests. Warzer was wearing a bulky vest, bulkier even than the Kevlar would suggest, and suddenly Carrie understood what he had done.

Of course. He had volunteered to Abu Ghazawan to be a *shahid*, a suicide bomber. One of those who would die destroying the tomb of the Imam Hussein. That's how he had gotten close to Abu Ghazawan and why he hadn't contacted Virgil or Perry. He was too close. In the inner circle. And about to die, one way or another, no matter what he did. She had to stop him.

Carrie stood, the lone standing figure among the women. She put both hands to her eyes, peeking through her fingers, to signal to Ali that they were IPLA men, but it was already too late. Three of the IPLA men in front, including Warzer, were marching straight toward the sepulcher. The two guards, Emad and Younis, stood, not moving. They were going to react too late! A half dozen or more of the IPLA men had started to split off from the main group of policemen, heading right toward Ali and Little Mohammed.

She dropped her hands from her face and stared openly at Warzer, willing him to see her. Their eyes locked. He looked at the man on his left, as if pointing him out. A short, bearded Arab of no particular age—maybe in his fifties, maybe forties, impossible to say—with longish yellowing teeth—like a rat in a SWAT helmet.

Abu Ghazawan. It was him. It had to be. Except that the man had caught Warzer's look, taking in Carrie, Warzer, Emad, and Younis guarding the door to the shrine.

Mrs. Fawzi, Carrie thought despairingly as she dropped to the floor, her hands scrambling under her chador to find her gun. The old woman had blown the Albu Mahals to Abu Ghazawan.

She saw it happening, all the moving pieces, as if in slow motion. Abu Ghazawan turned his head, somehow spotting the connection between her and Ali, then turned toward Warzer. At the same instant, she saw Ali's eyes as the IPLA men in the front row knelt to aim their AK-47s, the row behind them also aiming while the rows of "policemen" behind them scattered. As Shiite worshipers suddenly became aware of what was happening, screamed and scattered, she caught Warzer's desperate look. He must have realized that Abu Ghazawan had spotted his signal to Carrie and was trying to take off his suicide vest.

Two of the other IPLA men with bulky vests ran toward the pointed-arched entrance to the sepulcher. They were going to blow it up. But before they could take another step, Ali and Little Mohammed fired their M4s, cutting them down. Ali and Little Mohammed then turned to fire at the other IPLA policemen. Emad and Younis swung their weapons into position, but the IPLA men in the first two rows shot in the same instant, wounding Little Mohammed and instantly killing both Emad and Younis.

Warzer ripped off his outer SWAT vest. Under it was a second vest with rows of bulging pockets and wires. He fumbled to unhook it. Get it off, Carrie prayed. Take it off. Shots were popping off everywhere. She watched as Warzer managed to unhook his vest and toss it behind him toward his fellow attackers, at the same time pivoting to a kneeling position to fire his AK assault rifle at them.

Ali and the wounded Little Mohammed each dived in opposite directions, still shooting. They killed two of the policemen in the second row who had kept on coming as the other IPLA policemen took cover behind pillars near the rear of the prayer hall. The remaining IPLA policemen hit the floor or took cover behind pillars or people that they used as human shields, firing back in long bursts.

Bullets flew everywhere. They smashed the crystal chandeliers, one of which came crashing to the floor, scattering razor-sharp shards. The rain of bullets shattered tiles on the walls and ripped into people running, cutting them down. Women were screaming, children were crying, while some of the male worshipers ran to the women and children to shield them. People were running and crawling toward the entrance. A woman who'd tried to get up next to Carrie was shot down, part of her face gone and bloody. Carrie squirreled behind the woman's body, which quivered again when another bullet thunked into it.

There was blood everywhere. The prayer rugs were getting soaked with it. One of the IPLA policemen raised an RPG. He aimed it at the open archway that led to the sepulcher, but a shot from the wounded Little Mohammed drilled into him. As the IPLA policeman crumpled, he fired the RPG down into the floor. It exploded instantly, blasting him and the IPLA men around him into a circle of scattered bodies and arms and legs, like some ghoulish apocalyptic painting.

Two IPLA policemen came toward Carrie. Oh God, she thought, they knew who she was! Before she could raise her gun to shoot, shots rang out beside her. Ali, firing his M4, brought them down, then grabbed her by the arm and yanked her toward one of the arched doorways. An explosion rocked the hall from the spot where Warzer had thrown his vest. Carrie felt the heat and a force of air from the blast, followed by a cloud of black smoke. The prayer rugs were on fire.

Out of the corner of her eye, she spotted Warzer. He was running. Abu Ghazawan was running after him. Abu Ghazawan fired a shot at Warzer, who had shoved his way into a crowd of worshipers trying to exit the prayer hall.

Warzer was trying to protect her, Carrie realized. Trying to lead Abu Ghazawan away. She couldn't tell if Warzer had been hit, but she thought he was still running. As she and Ali ran through an alcove to a side door, a shattering explosion from outside the mosque shook the walls, knocking them both off their feet.

Car bomb. Dear God, there were hundreds of people there, she thought as she and Ali got up and ran out a side door into the courtyard. The sunlight was blinding. All around, people were scurrying like ants, running and screaming. In the distance, she could hear the sirens of fire engines.

Suddenly another car bomb went off in the outer plaza outside the walls around the shrine complex, causing the ground to shake so that she and Ali almost fell down again. She spotted Warzer, sprinting toward the gate that led to the plaza outside the shrine walls. Abu Ghazawan was running after him.

Abu Ghazawan was less than a hundred meters behind Warzer, firing at him as he ran. Abu Ghazawan's face was contorted in a strange smile. He looked like a madman. One of his bullets hit a woman running with a little boy. She went down and was still. The boy stood there, staring blankly at Abu Ghazawan as he ran by.

Warzer was in a crowd of people, many of them pilgrims dressed in black, crowding to get through the main gate. She saw Abu Ghazawan stop for a moment, strip off his uniform helmet and vest. Underneath, he wore a black *thaub*. Now he looked like an ordinary Shiite pilgrim, Carrie thought. A sickening feeling formed in the pit of her stomach.

Abu Ghazawan dropped his AK-47 and ran to the gate, disappearing into the crowd. Next to her, Ali fired two bursts, taking down two more IPLA policemen leaving the mosque. He turned, and together, he and Carrie ran to the gate, squeezing through a crowd, fighting to get through the gate to the plaza.

The crowd was pressed so close together she could hardly breathe. She was lifted off her feet and and carried through the gate. Once outside, she managed to keep her feet and ran. She sensed Ali close behind her.

She and Ali stopped to catch their breath by a vendor's stall in the middle of the wide plaza. The stall was filled with religious souvenirs of the shrine, but the vendor had run away. They ducked behind the stall, hiding from Abu Ghazawan and any of his men who might be coming from the mosque. They could hear the sounds of police and fire sirens and also small-arms fire coming from inside the shrine.

"Stay here. I have to go back. Make sure the sepulcher's safe," Ali panted.

She nodded and watched him run back to the gate, slamming a fresh magazine into his M4 as he rushed inside. Suddenly screams erupted from one of the streets leading into the plaza.

A Toyota SUV—it had to be one Ismail had mentioned—emerged from that street. It was driving right at the main gate to the shrine, knocking over anyone in its way. Another car bomb!

Carrie could see two men in the SUV. They ran over a teenage boy who screamed as both sets of wheels passed over him. Someone was shooting at them. They were coming closer to where Carrie was hiding. If they blew themselves up now, she wouldn't stand a chance.

Big Mohammed and Ismail were in the bed of a pickup truck parked on the periphery of the plaza. They were firing at the SUV. An IPLA man in a police uniform was firing at them from behind. Ismail turned to fire at him and dropped, clutching his stomach. Big Mohammed continued to fire his carbine at the truck that suddenly swerved toward Carrie. A hail of bullets followed the truck, then fell silent. Carrie could no longer see Big Mohammed on the truck bed.

The truck was coming closer to the vendor stall where she was hiding. No time to run, and if it exploded, there was no way to outrun the explosion. That only happened in the movies. Then she saw the truck was slowing. It bumped against the stall, pushing it hard against Carrie, who dived away headfirst. The truck stopped. Both men in the cab were slumped over. Dead.

Fear, like an electric shock, ripped through her. What about Warzer?

She ran into the street. There was a mob forming, a sea of Shiite men, waving their fists. Some in black, some carrying guns.

"*Ya Allah*, it's him!" she heard someone cry out in Arabic.

She saw Abu Ghazawan. He had climbed onto the trunk of a car and was pointing.

"He's one of them! He attacked the holy shrine!" Abu Ghazawan shouted.

"He's lying! It's him!" Carrie screamed in Arabic, pointing at Abu Ghazawan, but no one seemed to hear.

The mob surged forward across the plaza. They surrounded a man in a sea of bobbing heads and black clothes. It looked like they were beating him. There were guttural screams and someone cried out. Although she couldn't see and it might have been anyone, she knew, with a certainty impossible to explain, that it was Warzer.

Holding up the hem of her chador, she ran toward them. She spotted Abu Ghazawan searching for her in the crowd. She didn't care. It was Warzer. The mob was beating him, dragging him somewhere.

"*U'af!*" she screamed. Stop!

They dragged Warzer to one of the intersecting streets, where a temporary metal pedestrian bridge had been built over the road because of the rush of pilgrims coming for Friday's sermon.

For a second, the way through the crowd was clear and she saw Warzer. He'd been beaten bloody, the side of his face bruised almost beyond recognition. His hands were tied behind him and men were tying a rope around his neck.

"*La! La! La!*" Carrie shouted. No! No! No! "It wasn't him!" she cried out, trying to push through. Several men shoved her back, glaring at her.

Just before they hanged him from the pedestrian bridge,

someone splashed liquid on him from a big can. Even at the back of the crowd, Carrie could smell the gasoline.

"*La!*" she screamed. "Don't! He's innocent!"

They threw the rope over a beam and two men began hauling him up. Someone tossed a match and suddenly Warzer was a writhing, kicking torch, blazing just above the heads of the crowd. For what seemed like an eternity, but must have been only thirty or forty seconds, he jerked and kicked, filling the air with smoke and the smell of burned meat. And then he was still. Swaying slightly, a charred pendulum dangling from the rope, smoldering and black.

Carrie stood there, unable to move. She could see what was left of his face. It was unrecognizable, the flesh of his mouth burned away, his teeth white in a charred black mass. An image she knew, even as she saw it, that she would never get out of her mind.

"She's with him! She's one of them!" someone shouted in Arabic. She whirled and looked into the eyes of Abu Ghazawan, pointing, coming straight at her. He was the one who'd shouted. Without thinking, she turned and ran. Carrie, the 1,500-meter runner, raced down the street on bare feet faster than she'd ever run in her life.

There was a small women's clothing store near the corner. Dresses, chadors, hijabs in different colors. Some instinct made her run toward it. She didn't know why. Maybe thinking these men never went into a women's shop. *Haram*. Forbidden. She ran inside and raced to the back, ignoring the saleswoman's "*Salaam, al-Anesah*" greeting her. Another woman, a customer in the shop, just stared at her.

"I need help, O sister," Carrie cried out in Arabic to both of them, not stopping.

There was a tiny dressing room behind a curtain at the

back of the shop. She opened the curtain, pulled it closed behind her, and squatted down, cowering.

She had never been so terrified. They were coming and she had no doubt they were going to kill her. They would hang and burn her just like Warzer. She couldn't get the image of him hanging there out of her mind.

The same mouth she had kissed, she didn't know how many times, now black ash, burned flesh and teeth. Or that it was going to happen to her too.

She raised her Glock pistol and aimed it with both hands at the dressing room curtain. Even though she held the gun with both hands, it was shaking.

She heard a man come into the shop. Demanding in Arabic, "Did she come in here?"

"What are you doing? Stop! This is for women!" she heard the saleswoman say. The woman's voice trembled with fear. She heard the man coming closer.

"She came in. She must be here," she heard him say in Arabic.

"There's no one," the saleswoman said.

"What's back there?" the man said. His voice pinned her like a moth to a board. Abu Ghazawan. She recognized his voice.

"Stop. This is for—" Then a tiny cry, "*Ya,*" from the saleswoman. A thud like a body falling to the floor—and nothing more from the woman. The bastard, Carrie thought, tensing, aiming.

She could hear, almost feel him. He was close, within inches, on the other side of the curtain, though she couldn't see his shoes. As soon as he opens the curtain, he'll shoot, she thought, aiming at where his chest would be.

She held her breath. She could hear him breathing and

fired four shots into the center of the moving curtain. Two bullets were fired back, whizzing over her head. If she'd been standing, she'd be dead. Then she heard a body hit the floor and a hand with a pistol in it appeared at her feet.

Screaming like a madwoman at the top of her lungs, she ripped open the curtain. Abu Ghazawan lay on the floor at her feet, crumpled, bleeding, still holding a pistol with a sound suppressor in his hand. He stared at her and tried to raise the gun. She fired again, the shot hitting him in the throat. He gagged, blinked, and went still, his eyes glaring. She shot him in the head.

Almost collapsing, she tried to think of what to do. You're a trained CIA ops officer, she told herself. Do something useful. She dropped to her knees and began searching his pockets, her hands shaking so much she could barely control them. She found a cell phone in his trousers and dropped it into her pocket.

What am I thinking? she said to herself, and using her own cell-phone camera, took a trembling photograph of his face. No good, she thought, and pressed her hand against the wall to steady it and took another snapshot of his face.

A mob of Shiite men, some wearing the black of pilgrims, burst into the shop. She wanted to run, but where? We might need DNA too, she thought, dipping the sleeve of her chador into Abu Ghazawan's blood, pooling beneath his head and neck, then stood up to face them.

The Shiite men stared, blocking any way out. Most were armed, with clubs or knives or guns.

"She's a blasphemer. A whore. Kill her," one of them said.

Five or six men, their faces twisted in fury, aimed their AK-47s directly at her.

CHAPTER 35

"This man is al-Qaeda. He's the one who attacked the holy shrine," Ali shouted in Arabic from the back of the crowd of men. "Look!" he cried, pointing at Abu Ghazawan's body. "Look at his shoes! His trousers! They are of the INP, the Iraqi National Police. They wore such uniforms when they attacked the shrine. He didn't have time to change."

There were murmurs, but none of the men in the Shiite crowd moved. Ali fired a shot from his M4 in the air, then pushed his way through, Big Mohammed beside him. Thank God, he was alive too, Carrie thought. The two men stood protectively in front of her, facing the crowd, weapons ready.

"What about the woman? We don't know her. She's not one of us," an older man said. He held an old shotgun that he kept aimed toward them. Carrie put her pistol on the floor next to the body and raised her hands over her head.

"Why is she wearing a chador?" someone shouted.

"Truth! What is she doing here?" said another, a heavyset man. He came forward, a pistol in his hand aimed at Carrie. "Who is she?"

"Don't touch her!" Big Mohammed warned, pointing his M4 at the man with the pistol.

"You want killing? In the name of Allah—" the heavyset man shouted.

"Wait!" Ali cried. "She's American. She came to try to stop the attack. The tomb is secure. No harm has come to the tomb of the holy imam."

"We hate Americans," the heavyset man said. "Imam al-Sadr has said they are our enemies."

"Use your heads, you fools!" Ali shouted. "The Americans are leaving. The last thing they want is to have a civil war between Shiites and Sunnis now. That's what this attack was meant to provoke. Think. Why else would an American come? A woman?"

More murmurs in the crowd.

"She's not an American. She's a Sunni spy!" someone yelled out.

"Kill the whore!" someone else shouted.

Two more men aimed their AK-47s at Carrie.

"Pull off your hijab!" Ali cried to Carrie.

Carrie pulled the hijab off her head. The men stared at her long blond hair.

"You know us, brothers! Everyone knows nearly all the Iraqi Security Forces are Shiites. We are of you," Ali lied. "We saved the shrine. She warned us."

Ali didn't wait for the Shiites to react. He and Big Mohammed began muscling their way back through the crowd, Carrie stumbling between them. All eyes were on her. And now, without the hijab, on her obvious American face.

Inside, she was wondering if her bipolar had finally pushed her over the edge, if any of it was real. This is insanity. My life saved because I'm a blonde?

Outside, in the bright sun, she nearly collapsed. Ali and Big Mohammed had to hold her up. From the street, they could see the open plaza around the shrine wall. People were running toward the shrine while others fled. There were a number of police cars and two fire engines. Scattered around the plaza were bodies and the smoking wreck of what was left of an SUV. The klaxons of ambulances and Iraqi Security Forces vehicles sounded over the cries of people calling for help.

She could see smoke billowing from behind the shrine wall. A woman came stumbling toward them, her face covered with blood. In the center of the open space, near the vendor stall Carrie had hidden behind, the same small boy still stood beside the body of his mother.

Warzer's dead, she thought, unable to make herself look in the direction of the street and the pedestrian bridge. Then she couldn't help herself. His blackened body was still hanging from the bridge. She tried to think of something else, but couldn't. The image of him was burned in her mind. She was going down into a dark place. Don't, she told herself. There's more to think about. The others. Little Mohammed, Emad, Younis. Iron Thunder. Perry. De Bruin. Saul. Somehow, none of it mattered.

"Warzer's dead," she said numbly.

"Cover your head," Ali said, shoving the black hijab into her hand. "We have to get out of here."

A large mob of men, brandishing weapons and waving their fists, shouting "Death to Sunnis!" in Arabic, came from the direction of the souk.

"Long live Imam Hussein!" and "Death to blasphemers!" they cried as they marched toward the plaza, where people were still running outside the walls.

"Death!" they chanted, their numbers growing as they neared the Qabla gate.

"More killings," Ali muttered as the three of them headed toward the long promenade between the shrines. They made it to the promenade, walking between the double row of trees toward the Abbas mosque, which was untouched.

"You came back for me," Carrie said.

"I gave Sha'wela my word," Ali said, walking quickly.

"What of the others? Your friends?" she asked, trying to think. But there was only Warzer's body hanging in her mind. I did it, she thought. If I hadn't treated him the way I did, he wouldn't have gone alone, so deep undercover, looking for Abu Ghazawan on his own. I drove him to it. I killed him.

"Dead," Big Mohammed said. "All of them."

Although she'd seen them get shot, his saying it hit her again.

They hurried her along, half carrying her as they turned away from the crowds and headed down Abbas Street, filled with small shops and people coming out of their houses onto the sidewalks, Iraqi Security Forces vehicles and trucks carrying armed Shiite militiamen, honking their horns nonstop as they rushed down the crowded street toward the shrine.

In all the turmoil, the two armed men half carrying a blond woman in a chador seemed almost normal.

"You can turn on your cell phone now," Ali told her, when they got to a quieter side street. They stopped at a small stand for fruit drinks. The vendor handed Carrie a glass of date juice, but although her throat was parched, she couldn't drink. Her legs were trembling. She wasn't sure how she managed to remain standing.

"Did you come from the holy Imam Hussein Shrine?" the vendor, a bearded man wearing a white kaffiyeh, asked them in Arabic.

"Yes, thanks be to Allah," Ali answered.

"You saw the attack? You were there?"

Ali nodded. The vendor looked at them curiously.

"Some say it was the Americans. Others the Sunnis," the vendor said, looking at Carrie.

"It was al-Qaeda. The Sunnis," Ali said. Nothing about the way he said it gave away that he was a Sunni.

"Now there is only killing. They are caught in this like we are, poor devils. In this city, once we were neighbors with Sunnis. Allah willing, different fish may eat each other, but all are caught in the fisherman's net," the vendor said, looking at Carrie.

"Yes," she murmured. "All of us."

"*Ma'a salaama*. May Allah go with you, brothers," the vendor said as they paid and left.

They moved on, but wherever they walked, people were peering out of shop doors and women in windows watched the street. The entire city was on edge.

"The sooner we leave this place, the better," Big Mohammed muttered.

"We must get our little sister away from here. Our friend Sha'wela has been trying to reach you," Ali said to her. "He says to tell you it is from Alabama."

The code word they had agreed on for an emergency. Except she couldn't think about anything anymore, except Warzer's smoldering body, hanging over the street. What bigger emergency was there than that? No more, Saul, she thought.

She nodded at Ali and they moved to another street, working their way to where they had left the SUV. People who saw them saw only victims from the attack. Two ISF soldiers, one wounded, and a woman in a chador, barely able to put one foot in front of the other, their faces blackened and bloody from the attack.

Go to hell, Saul, she thought. Except she now had critical intel. Abu Ghazawan's cell phone and his blood, his DNA. Maybe with that they could finally locate Abu Nazir.

But it would be too late for Warzer. The question is, Carrie, some devil inside her whispered, is it too late for you?

CHAPTER 36

Back in her apartment on Nasir Street in the Green Zone, Carrie opened the window and breathed in Baghdad. A smell composed of diesel fumes, fried fish, death, and the river. If she were blindfolded for a thousand years, she thought, she could breathe in that smell and know where she was in an instant.

Saul was in Baghdad too. Ali and Big Mohammed had dropped her off outside the base in Karbala. From there, she'd flown back to Baghdad on the same Black Hawk helicopter she'd come to Karbala in, the entire way not saying a word to anyone, holding the cell phones and the bloody hijab in her hands.

She went directly from the helicopter pad in Camp Victory to the CIA station headquarters in the Republican Palace. Saul and Perry started to debrief her in Perry's office—and the second he saw how she was sitting there, vibrating like a tuning fork, Saul stopped it. With a look at Perry, who excused himself and left, he went over to the console and took out a bottle of Glenlivet and poured them both a stiff drink.

They sat drinking, not talking, occasionally glancing at the office-window view of the grounds: the columned swimming pool with its fountain, the manicured lawns and palm trees at the back of the Republican Palace. Babylon, she thought vaguely. Saddam was a kind of king. We've been living in the Bible and didn't know it. Maybe when they were living it, the people in the Bible didn't know it either.

She wanted to talk about it with Warzer, feeling a pain like a knife at the thought of him, because she immediately saw him in her mind, hanging from that iron structure. Warzer would have understood.

It felt strange, him not being there. First Dempsey, now Warzer. Everyone she touched, every man she'd been attracted to, gone. She looked at her hands. What was happening? There's only a few of us left, realizing even as she thought it that she was teetering on the brink of a deep black hole, the downside of her bipolar. Don't, don't fall into it, she told herself. Step back from the edge, Carrie.

"I pushed you too far," Saul said finally. " 'Sorry' is such a feeble word." He shook his head. "I know it doesn't mean anything this minute, but maybe later . . . About Karbala, your instincts were right."

"Warzer's dead," she said.

"I know," Saul said. "There was no one else, you know. There are hundreds, maybe thousands of American families who won't be grieving for their loved ones, and tens of thousands of Iraqis. More than this stinking war has already cost. They'll live, Carrie. They'll never even know how close they came. No one will, except you and me. That's the game."

"If I died, you would have found someone, Saul. You always do," she said, looking away.

"We would've failed. You knew Warzer. You could identify him no matter what the disguise, knew his every glance, every gesture, better than anyone. If that shrine had been blown up . . ." He paused. "You didn't just go for Warzer, Carrie. You knew. Subconsciously, you understood. Warzer had to get in deep with IPLA and Abu Ghazawan for the same reason. He knew it too, Carrie. Because otherwise we were totally screwed."

He took off his glasses and rubbed his mouth and beard. "But after Iran, I saw how it was," he went on. "Listen, I've seen tough men, Navy SEALs, Delta guys, you wouldn't believe, destroyed for life, empty shells of the men they were, who didn't do half of what you did. I should've made you go back to Langley, but you insisted on Karbala. You're right. I used you. And if you're crazy enough to go on, I'll do it again."

For a time they didn't speak. She finished her drink. He went over to the console and picked up the bottle of scotch.

"Should we get drunk? Poor Perry," he said, coming over and freshening both their glasses. "Drinking all his scotch. Single malt is hard to come by in these parts."

Neither spoke. They sat listening to the hum of the air conditioner. Outside, the air was blisteringly hot. It was going to be another killer summer in Iraq, she thought.

"What about Abu Ghazawan's cell phone? His blood?" she asked.

"We're working both. Walden's got Langley on it. We'll have something shortly. Maybe help us learn his real identity. Fill in the missing pieces. Like who told de Bruin—sorry, Robespierre, about the upcoming raid on Otaibah." He took a breath. "What about Robespierre? Has he contacted you since he got back from Isfahan?"

She nodded. "I got a couple of voice-mail messages marked urgent. Texts too. Once I turned my regular cell phone back on."

"You don't have to do this," he said. "What happens now with Robespierre, with Arrowhead/Ali Hamsa, all that; it doesn't have to involve you."

"I'm already involved, Saul," she said, swallowing more scotch. "I like him, okay?" She clapped her hand to her mouth. "My God, must be the scotch. I can't believe I said that out loud."

"I'm glad you did," he said, glancing at the window, the afternoon shadows of the trees lengthening on the grounds where U.S. Marines guarded the building, then at her. "If you stay, you might save his life."

"And if I go?"

He didn't say anything. She stared at him.

"God, you can be a bastard. No wonder Mira left you," she said. As with Warzer, the instant the words were out of her mouth, she wished she could pull them back. She had never seen his face like that. He looked lost, like a little boy without a mother. "I didn't mean that. I'm sorry."

"It's true," he said softly. "I shouldn't have asked. Go back to Langley, Carrie. Take the promotion, see your family. You deserve it."

"I can't," she whispered.

"I know," he said, coming over and putting a hand on her shoulder.

Back in her apartment, she was eating a cup of ramen noodles, gazing out the window at Nasir Street, dusted gold by the setting sun, when de Bruin called.

De Bruin sent a car for her. He was waiting in his villa in the Khafat district. The little Peruvian, Estrella, opened the door, her dark eyes unreadable. As always, Carrie wasn't sure how to play him, but the second she saw de Bruin standing in the living room, big and solid as a Babylonian monument, they came together like oppositely charged magnets. Afterward, she told herself as she kissed him. Because one way or another, everything would be decided tonight. Pillow talk is when he's at his weakest, she thought, knowing she was lying to herself.

She kissed him deeply, pressing herself against him. She wanted this as much as he did, feeling him pressing back, then picking her up and they were on the bed, taking off their clothes, his lips touching her.

Later, he lit a cigarette as they lay naked, spent, like castaways on a beach.

"Where's Dasha?" she asked finally.

"She's gone. Why? Do you miss her?" he said, with a faint wicked smile.

"What happened?"

"You," he said, taking a puff and exhaling smoke. "I sent her away, but I wouldn't worry about Dasha. I gave her a nice chunk of money. She's probably taking over half of Kiev and seducing the country's president."

"No," Carrie said.

"No what?"

She put her hand on him and felt him stir. What game am I playing now? she wondered.

"No, I don't miss her," she said.

Estrella came in with two drinks topped with white foam in martini glasses. She stood there for a moment looking at their naked bodies, then served the drinks without expression and left.

"What's this?" Carrie asked.

"Pisco sours. Estrella makes them."

"I'll bet she poisoned mine."

"Entirely possible, cheers," he said, drinking.

After a moment's hesitation, Carrie drank hers. It was the most refreshing drink she'd ever had after sex.

"Cheers. If it doesn't kill me, this could be habit forming," she said.

"I've been trying to reach you for a couple of days. Where were you?" he said.

"Where were you?"

"Touché." He grinned. "I guess neither of us wants to talk about what we do. I thought about you."

"Likewise," she said. "What do you want to do about it?"

"We could go away maybe. Someplace where the palm trees don't come with IEDs. Mallorca. Bali. Why not? I have money."

"Bali sounds . . . unbelievable," wondering, What game were they playing now? What life would be like if they were completely different people. Maybe he'd reveal something useful, she thought.

"There's this place in Bali by Mengiat Beach, the water bluer and clearer than anything you've ever seen. White sand, green trees, and except for the Balinese who take care of the place, not another living soul. You'd like it, *bokkie*." He finished his drink and wiped the foam off his lips. "We're never going anywhere, are we?"

She shook her head. Playtime was over.

"Who gave you the information about the raid on Otaibah?" she asked. An image of the party here at the villa the night they met flashed into her mind. The amazing guests, the artist, the archaeologist . . . Then it hit her. Shit, it had been right in front of her all along. There weren't only Iraqis at the party. There was an American official too, sucking at the teat of de Bruin's money. "Was it Sanderson?" Eric Sanderson, the deputy chief of mission at the U.S. embassy. Was he the mole? "You two meeting at embassy gatherings, taking a sidebar at meetings, stepping out for a smoke. Maybe parties with Ukrainian and

Chinese girls and nice fat deposits into a Zurich bank account for him, was that it, *bokkie*?"

"Sod off, Lady Anne. We're not doing that. Come on, get dressed," he said angrily, standing and tossing her clothes at her. He started pulling on his own clothes, stopping only to take out his SIG Sauer pistol from a hidden drawer that pulled out from under the bed frame.

She stared at the gun. They'd made love on top of it. As she pulled on her clothes, Estrella appeared in the doorway. Carrie could swear the little imp had a faint smile on her face as de Bruin grabbed Carrie's arm and marched her outside to his Mercedes parked in the driveway. The Peruvian she'd seen the first night and the time they'd picked her up from outside the Republican Palace now stood beside the car, his gun drawn.

Carrie got in the back with de Bruin, the Peruvian with the gun in the front passenger seat. Estrella and another Peruvian bodyguard got into a compact sedan behind the Mercedes. Carrie realized that wherever they would've gone, even Bali, Estrella and the Peruvian bodyguards would have gone too.

"Where are we going now?" she asked.

"The racetrack. Not far, on Basra Street."

"Is that what we're doing? Betting on horses?"

"There's no race, *bokkie*. Just a big open space for a helicopter. I'm leaving."

"What about me?"

He shook his head.

"Sorry, not this time. What was that line from *Seinfeld*? 'No soup for you.'"

"Don't," Carrie said, playing for time. "Not like this. I'll take Bali. I will."

"Can't, *bokkie*," de Bruin said, motioning to the driver to go. "The thing is, we're two of a kind, you and me. Business has to trump pleasure for us, doesn't it?"

The car moved down the short driveway, stopping to let the automatic steel gate in the blast wall open. As they started out into the street, a big black GM SUV moved right in front of them, blocking their way. The driver, muttering Arab curses, started to honk. Suddenly the Mercedes was lit by bright lights, flashlights shining on the windows, blinding them.

A dozen U.S. soldiers in Kevlar vests and helmets surrounded the car, shouting "Hands up," their carbines pointed at de Bruin and the Peruvian through the windows. Virgil, dressed like the others in a Kevlar helmet and vest, rapped on the window next to de Bruin with a Colt .45 pistol.

"Open up," Virgil said.

De Bruin looked at Carrie. Again, she couldn't read his face, but for the first time in the glare of the flashlights, she noticed tiny webs of wrinkles at the corners of his eyes. He was getting older. So was she, she thought. She had turned thirty, her birthday three days before they hit Otaibah. She felt him tense, about to do something.

"De Bruin, don't!" she said. "I don't want you to die."

CHAPTER 37

"Caracas? What the hell is in Caracas?" Carrie said.

Saul and Virgil had picked her up at her apartment on Nasir Street in the SUV that morning. When Saul wasn't looking, she slipped her supply of clozapine pills in with her underwear and laptop in her carry-on, taking one of the pills without water. Maybe it would make her feel more normal, because right now she felt numb. Out of body, as if watching herself from another place. See Carrie talk. See Carrie run. See Carrie extraordinary-rendition de Bruin to interrogation in some third-world country.

She'd been up all night, figuring it out. This whole thing started with Abu Nazir, and that's where it had to end. Now was the wrong time to leave Iraq.

"Change of scenery is good. You need a break," Saul said.

"I'm staying, Saul. We have a lead to Abu Nazir."

"What are you talking about? We've been checking the cell phone you took from Abu Ghazawan in Karbala, but nothing definite so far."

"What about northern Iraq?"

"There was one call in the north we knew about, which is an outlier," Saul said from the backseat, eyes flicking over at Virgil driving.

They were on the Qadisaya Expressway on the way to Baghdad Airport. Three lanes in each direction, land flat as a table, and nothing to be seen along the sides of the road but palm trees.

"The hell it is. Remember the first location we ever got on Abu Ghazawan was up north? In the Kurdish-controlled area of Iraq? Of course we dismissed the idea because why would Abu Nazir go from Syria to Kurdistan, but last night it hit me."

"You stayed up all night?" Saul said, exchanging a worried look with Virgil in the rearview mirror that Carrie caught.

"I'm fine, Saul. Listen to me, Kurdistan. It's pure Abu Nazir. He does the unexpected; that's what he always does. You have to let me follow up. I need to finish this. You owe me."

"For what? Doing your job? You're a CIA field operative, and right now you're going through a bit of post-traumatic stress, which, given everything you've been through and the fact that de Bruin was on the verge of killing you, doesn't seem out of order."

"Saul," she said, twisting her body to face him. "Let me do this."

"Carrie, you listen. You've just been through a war. We've taken casualties. And there are going to be repercussions. I'm doing you a favor. If I sent you back to Langley now, that's a different kind of war. Bureaucratic bullshit that'll drown you. And frankly, questions you'd be asked that I really don't want answered."

"He's right, Carrie. You go back to Langley now . . . I give you two weeks, you'll wish you were back in the Sand Pile," Virgil said.

"This is nuts. Why Caracas?" She watched the procession of palm trees go by as they drove along the Airport Road, the highway shimmering in the morning heat like a mirage. Leaving Iraq, bad as it was, was like leaving a piece of herself. So much had happened here. What part of her was left to leave?

"Think of it as a break. Something different. You'll touch base with the station chief, Alvin Gladwell, but you'll report directly to me. Take some time off. Go to Macuto Beach."

"I don't need a freaking break, Saul. Listen to me, I finally figured it out last night. Just me and a map and my last bottle of tequila. Abu Nazir is in northern Iraq. But he's not in Mosul."

"How do you know?"

"Are you kidding? The Kurds are there. We're there. He'd have to be in hiding and disguise himself every time he went out for a cup of tea. That's not his style. He likes a place to himself, where he can have his inner circle with him. When we hit Otaibah, I saw with my own eyes. There must have been at least twenty, thirty people, men, women, children, living in that compound. Trust me, he'd want someplace he can make himself at home, but where we wouldn't look. And the original reading came from a Korek Telecom cell-phone tower north of Mosul, which eliminates places like Kirkuk and Tal Afar."

"So where is he?"

"You have to think like him. A lot of the area north of Mosul is desert and mountains. Pretty barren. There's only one place where he wouldn't be hunted by the Kurds, because there are Sunnis who have started moving into some of the local mosques and madrassas: Aqrah."

"All right, I'll bite. Why Aqrah?"

"Think about it. Aqrah's out of the way. Sunnis, Kurds, Assyrians mostly leave each other alone there. And Abu Nazir always needs a way to escape. Otaibah taught us that. If he had to escape from Aqrah, he could either go up into the mountains by the Turkish border, where it would be murder to find him, or worst case, he could make a quick run down the road to Mosul."

"We'll check it out. I promise," Saul said as they pulled up to the airport checkpoint. After their vehicle and IDs were checked, they were allowed to proceed to the drop-off at the terminal.

"Take it easy, Carrie," Virgil said as she got out, Saul with her. For a moment, the two of them stood awkwardly on the sidewalk outside the terminal building in the blazing heat.

"About de Bruin," he started uneasily, unable to see her eyes because she had put on her sunglasses. "Did you have feelings for him?"

She shrugged.

"Let's not make this a Valentine card. He liked sex and the illusion of being an intellectual, a warrior poet. I just liked the sex." She hesitated. "If push came to shove, he'd have sold me out for a dollar and given you change."

"But you liked him?"

"He was sexy. Women think about these things too, you know."

"Why? You like bad boys?"

She half smiled. "That sounds funny coming from you. You know why girls like bad boys, Saul? Because it gives us an excuse to be bad all the while convincing ourselves we're saving them. Will he be all right?"

"We'll extract intel from him first. Afterward . . ." He shrugged. He helped her with her one roll-on suitcase and she pulled the carry-on inside the terminal, where the air-conditioning hit them with a wall of cold air.

"What about Abu Nazir?" she asked.

"Perry will be on it. And you'll be back yourself in a few weeks to follow up. What you did . . . I won't forget," he said.

"I'm all right, Saul," she said.

"I know." As she turned to go to the security gate, he said: "Give my regards to El Niño."

"You're shitting me? That's his name?"

She handed her passport and boarding pass to the Iraqi security official.

Going through the metal detector, she felt lucky to have Saul. In a strange way, he was closer to her than anyone. Saul Berenson, the Rabbi Pirate.

As she waited in the Baghdad International Airport terminal for her flight to be called, she wondered, Now what would the sisters at Holy Trinity, her Catholic high school, think of that?

CHAPTER 38

It was a perfect day. Two days earlier, Brody had gone with Issa and some of his classmates up to Musa Laka, high in the mountains. They had driven up the winding mountain road out of the desert.

It was a place like no other in Iraq. Fertile fields in the wadis and in the mountains, green trees and clear, rushing streams, waterfalls cascading over sheer rock faces, shepherds with flocks of sheep and goats on the steep slopes. A land time forgot.

Best of all, Musa Laka, a town perched on the top of a sheer flat-top mountain. The village was its own world, a Middle Eastern Shangri-la. Once a refuge for Jews and Assyrians, its heights perfect for defense, now there was a mosque, where Brody, along with two of the teachers and the boys from the madrassa, performed *wudū'*, washing themselves before prayer in a clear mountain pool.

They recited the *Durood*, "O Allah, let your Blessings come upon Mohammed and the family of Mohammed," and the *Ayatul Kursi* prayer, "His throne includes the heavens and the earth," then prayed in the mosque.

From this place, Musa Laka, it was said the Magi, the three kings who came bearing gifts to witness the birth of Jesus, had come. The town, perched atop its mountain midway between heaven and earth, was holy ground. From its gardens, they looked out over the green mountains and wadis, an eagle soaring in a clear blue sky, birds in trees singing against the backdrop of a stream tumbling over the rocks.

Thank you, Allah, Brody prayed. At last, I understand your promise. Why I had to make this journey. I am yours. Use me.

Now, two days later. He walked Issa to the madrassa in the perfect morning. They were close, he and the boy. The wadi was green with life. Small birds twittered in the trees and it felt good to breathe and talk, to feel alive.

"Sometimes I can tell you things I can't say to my father, Nicholas," Issa said as they walked along the side of the road. They spoke in English, better than Brody's still limited Arabic.

"Your father can be fierce. Sometimes fathers have to be," Brody said, feeling a twinge, because the conversation reminded him of his own children. Dana and Chris. Had he been fierce with them? Most of the time he'd ignored them, left it up to Jessica. What a fool he'd been. If he ever got out of this, he vowed, he would do better. Pay more attention, be more understanding, more patient with them.

He breathed in the clear air, felt the warm sun on his face. He was going to get out of this. He was certain of it. Allah wouldn't have brought him all this way for nothing. Allah loved his creation.

"We're at war. That's why. My father has had a setback," Issa confided. "I don't know what it is. He tries not to show it, but I can see."

"You'll be close with him. The war won't last forever," Brody said.

"You're wrong, Nicholas. There are so many infidels. They hate us." He looked at Brody. "I hope we'll be warriors together, Nicholas. You're a good friend."

Brody felt the twinge again. He was the enemy, his family, his country. Semper fi. *Ya Allah*, how foreign that world seemed. How superficial. Especially after Musa Laka, where he felt surrounded by Allah's peace.

A big black crow flew by, cawing loudly. Brody felt Issa flinch beside him. The crow landed on a tree close by and cawed again.

"Do you still fear them?" Brody asked about the crows.

"Not since I killed one with the slingshot. You remember?" Issa said. But Brody heard the quaver in his voice.

"*Yahhhh!*" Brody screamed at the crow, waving his arms. But the bird sat there, turning its head to eye them. Something bad's going to happen, Brody thought, unable to suppress a shiver down his spine. "Stupid bird," he told Issa, and the boy laughed.

They came to the entrance of the madrassa. Brody told him he'd pick him up after school, patting his shoulder. As he did so, he felt the boy tremble.

"The crow is nothing," Brody said.

"*Ma'a salaama*," the boy said, touching his chest. "I know, Nicholas."

He went inside. For a long moment after Issa was gone, Brody stood there, staring at the old stone building, the garden, and the Jewish star over the doorway, though he didn't know why.

That day, he tried to keep busy working in the garden. When it got too hot, he came in and Nassrin gave him a glass of date juice.

He decided he would ask for a rifle. He would teach Issa to shoot like a Marine. They would kill the crows once and for all. It would make Issa proud for his father. He spoke about it with Nassrin.

"It is coming," she said. "To be the mother of a son is to face the day he must become a soldier for Allah. I fear it, Nicholas, though I know it is needed."

"It's only crows we'll shoot," Brody said.

"Talk about it with my husband. But something has gone wrong," she whispered.

"What is it?"

"I don't know. I hope we won't have to leave this place. This is a good place, isn't it?"

"Very good," Brody said. In an odd way, thinking of Bethlehem and Gunner Brody, and now, his captivity—his Babylonian captivity—the struggles he and Jess had in Virginia, when they were barely keeping their heads above water, tough as those times were, they were the best he'd ever known. But peace, grace, had only come here, in captivity.

He sat under a tree in the garden reading his Quran. Elsewhere in Iraq, it was burning hot, but here in the mountains, the air was still and clear, the temperature perfect. As he waited for the time to go pick Issa up from the madrassa, he looked for the crows, but they were gone.

Good, he thought. That's good.

It was the last thought he had before the loud clap of an explosion rattled the garden door and shook the ground beneath him. Turning toward the sound, Brody could see a column of black smoke rising over the trees. Somehow he knew it was the madrassa. Without thinking, he tore open the garden gate and began to run.

Running along the road, he could smell the explosive. As he got closer, he saw a tree on fire. At first he couldn't comprehend what had happened. Then he understood. It had to be. There was no other explanation. A Predator drone. An Unmanned

Aerial Vehicle (UAV), as the Marines called it, remembering his training; the Pentagon's primary antiterrorist weapon. He squinted up at the sky as he ran. Of course he couldn't see it, he told himself. It could hover over a target for hours and fire Hellfire missiles with a twenty-pound high-explosive warhead from twenty-five to thirty-five thousand feet high, too high to be seen or heard from the ground.

Brody slowed as he approached the building, flames roaring up from its center. Black-and-gray smoke mushroomed out of the madrassa. He couldn't believe his eyes. The ancient stone building that had endured for centuries was gone. All that was left were burning timbers and stones scattered on scorched earth. Books, bits of furniture, bodies and parts of bodies were everywhere. Impossible that there were so many bodies. Brody looked down at the ground. There were parts of people, arms and legs and pools of blood. Then he thought of the boy.

"Issa!" Brody screamed.

He ran into the burning ruins searching for the boy, jumping over a flame rippling across what had been a wooden beam. Everywhere he looked there were bodies. Nearly all were boys, of various ages and sizes. Many were burned or scorched by the blast. One body was torn in half. Only a headless trunk remained. Could it be Issa? he wondered, getting close, gorge rising, but there was no way to tell.

He scrambled across a mound of bodies and shattered rocks, stepping through pools of blood. There were arms, legs, even a boy's head, the face untouched, seeming oddly surprised, lying on its side on a pile of smoldering rubble. Brody stepped on something and recoiled. It was a boy's hand, palm up, barely half the size of his. O Allah, he thought. What have you done? What have you allowed?

"*Musaad'eeda!*" Help! he screamed, racing from body to body, a dozen of them tossed in a stack, bleeding, missing limbs. He tore through, looking at their faces. No Issa. Where was the boy?

"Issa! Issa!" he called, stepping past a boy groaning on the ground, twisted at an angle that suggested his back was broken. Then he saw a boy's dark hair under a scorched desk. He flung the desk aside. It was Issa.

At first, the boy appeared untouched. Maybe he was just in shock, Brody thought, shaking him.

"Wake up! Issa, wake up! It's Nicholas!" he shouted. Then he saw the wound in the side of his neck, the blood leaking out. And when he tried to raise Issa's head, his hand, lifting the back of the head, became wet and sticky. Brody tried to find a pulse, but felt nothing. He wrapped his arms around the boy's shoulders, pulling Issa to him.

"Don't die," he pleaded. "Don't."

Issa was dead. Brody picked him up and carried him back to the road. All around, people were running, coming from the village and out of houses along the wadi. Women in abayas screaming, covering their eyes, weeping; men rushing, some carrying AK-47s, their faces unbelieving. People shouting, calling out the names of their children.

Then came wailing and ululating sounds from women like he had never heard, unbelievably eerie and despairing. Like cries from the damned in hell. And with it came an odd memory, some Catholic sermon about hell from when he was a kid. He shook it off.

Now there were swarms of people climbing over the wreckage, looking for people, lining up bodies, searching for wounded survivors. From what Brody could tell, almost no one in the school had survived the direct missile hit.

Brody, carrying Issa, staggered along to the road. As he did so, he saw Abu Nazir himself running toward him, followed by a dozen of his men, Afsal, Daleel, Mahdi, and the women, Nass-rin and others. Daleel's wife, Heba, had found her son dead too and was screaming "Allah, Allah, Allah" over and over.

Brody stopped, panting, holding the boy in his arms as if offering him to Abu Nazir.

"I tried, *ya Allah*, I tried. I'm sorry, I'm so sorry," he said.

"Is my son dead, Nicholas?" Abu Nazir said, his face stricken.

Brody nodded.

Abu Nazir stood there, his face twisted.

"Now do you see, Nicholas? Now do you see who is the true enemy? Who makes war on children. On children! My son!" he cried.

Brody was stunned, ashamed, sick to his stomach. His country had done this. America. Someone in a room thousands of miles away pressed a button. Because they could. How could it happen? Why? For the love of Allah, why?

He handed the boy to Abu Nazir, who slumped to the ground, cradling his son, rocking him like an infant, saying in Arabic, "Now you're with Allah, my beautiful son. Don't be afraid. You're a good boy. You've always been a good boy."

Brody looked around. The road, the sky, everything seemed different. As if every molecule in his body had suddenly realigned. If there was a mirror he could look at, he was certain he would look changed. All his life, he had been playing a part. Brody the football player, Brody the family man, Brody the Marine. That was over. He was filled with a hatred he hadn't felt since a child, hating his father, Gunner Brody, with his entire being. Now he hated again. Allah had preserved him for a reason. He was beginning to see why. America had lost its way. Allah had saved him to help America find its way back to God.

At last he understood.

CHAPTER 39

Hart Senate Building, Washington, D.C.
29 July 2009
02:41 hours

"This drone strike, Bill. What the hell happened?"

"What do you mean, Warren? There's nothing new here. This administration, like the one before it, has a standing policy to eliminate the leaders of al-Qaeda, which in case anyone's forgotten, attacked the United States on September eleventh."

"Take it easy. No one's forgotten. But this report, eighty-two children killed. Is that possible? How could we ever authorize such a thing?"

"First of all, let's be clear, Warren. This drone attack was approved by the president's national security advisor and the NSC. The target was Abu Nazir, the leader of the IPLA and al-Qaeda in Iraq and number three on our most-wanted-terrorists list. We had a solid lead—which, by the way, was developed in the course of Iron Thunder by the same CIA field operative, Carrie Mathison, that we've been talking about—that Abu Nazir was located in a jihadi masjid in the town of Aqrah, about a hundred and twenty kilometers northeast of Mosul. The NSC approved and we executed the attack with a single Hellfire missile from a Predator drone. And we didn't kill any children. End of story."

"Did we get him? Abu Nazir?"

"We're not sure. We're confident we got some IPLA terrorists in the attack. We have Predator images of three adult casualties. Abu Nazir was not confirmed among them. These images—here are two of them I printed out—confirm the casualty count. As you can see from the photos, there were no children killed. The number eighty-two is absurd."

"Let me put on my glasses. All right, it looks like three bodies. Frankly, I can't tell from this whether any were children or not. So where the hell did this story about so many children casualties come from?"

"There was a staged photograph put out by al-Qaeda that purported to show a smoldering building, a madrassa, and a photograph of many dead children. First of all, the count in the faked image is only forty-one bodies. And our experts tell us this so-called photo was clearly Photoshopped. This image was displayed on a number of jihadi websites along with the number eighty-two. It's a phony. Have a look."

"So this was faked?"

"Look, al-Qaeda can never defeat us militarily. Their war is waged via the media. That's where they win or lose. They've become very sophisticated. So they had a bunch of kids splashed with fake blood lie on the ground, They Photoshopped in some additional duplicate bodies, which we noted here, and here, and—bingo! You've got eighty-two dead kids killed by those nasty Americans. It never happened. But if you hold a Senate hearing on this, Warren, this crap all comes out and we'll spend the next ten years fighting the media, our allies, and a million new jihadis who will have signed up because of this. You'll be doing al-Qaeda's job for them, not to mention you'd be snatching defeat from the jaws of victory."

"Everything Bill says is true, Warren. This was a by-the-book drone strike approved by the NSC. Yes, there's been noise on the jihadi channels about children killed. But that's all it is, noise. What Bill is showing you are actual Predator camera images. You mustn't

ruin the international standing of the United States by giving our enemies a platform for these ridiculous lies. The damage would be irreparable."

"Point taken, Mr. President. Getting back to this Carrie Mathison, she obviously had no knowledge of the drone strike and she's certainly no traitor. If anything, she's a hero. She should be honored, not censured or investigated."

"Warren, here's a handwritten note from General Demetrius to Saul. Note where he says that if she were in his command, he'd be proud to pin a medal for valor on her. For whatever reason, something to do with her psyche or whatever, the polygraph was off."

"Clearly. Will that letter go in her file, Bill? I'd like to write one myself."

"I'm sorry, Mr. President. I saved this to show you and the senator, but I'll have to destroy it. In fact, I'd like your authorization to destroy the entire file. This Iron Thunder operation was Special Access Critical. Saul did it outside normal CIA channels. That's why it worked so well and how we were able to catch de Bruin and Sanderson. That's why we didn't want to tell you about it in the first place, Warren. Putting this or something from the president in Miss Mathison's 201 file would break security. In terms of her career, it doesn't matter. Perry Dryer, the Baghdad Station chief, knows what she did. So does Saul. So do I, but I'll never say a word."

"So that's it, Bill? There was no Operation Iron Thunder? It was all a ploy invented by Saul to catch a mole?"

"It never existed, except in Saul's head. And he convinced everyone. Because of it, the Iranian Revolutionary Guards withdrew their Al-Quds forces from Baquba, aborting a civil war. And now no one will ever know what really happened, except the three of us in this room."

"What about our moles? Sanderson? And this Arrowhead, Ali Hamsa? What about them?"

"The same night we grabbed de Bruin, Saul had SOG teams pick them up. Eric Sanderson is currently being held in the Metropolitan Detention Center in Brooklyn, New York, where he's been charged under the 1917 Espionage Act. I'm told he's cooperating fully."

"And Ali Hamsa?"

"After questioning, Warren, we turned him over to Sheikh al-Rashawi, leader of the Sons of Iraq. He betrayed his fellow Sunnis, it seemed best to let them deal with him. His mutilated corpse was found a week later on the banks of the Euphrates River in Ramadi."

"What happened with the Iranian MOIS officer, Khanzadeh; the one who questioned Carrie?"

"He's in Omaha. He has a new identity to protect his family back in Iran. I understand he's applied to study petroleum engineering at Texas A and M."

"And this character de Bruin? Where is he?"

"We extraordinary-renditioned him to an Agencja Wywiadu site in northern Poland, Warren. So far he's being cooperative. He still asks about Carrie, if you can believe it."

"She got to him. Perhaps it was love after all."

"I don't know what it was, Mr. President. These people live so far out on an edge, I'm not sure they know themselves what they feel."

"What about Saul? Where is he? Back at Langley? I'd like to meet him."

"Actually, Mr. President, he's taking some well-deserved time off. He and his wife, Mira, are at a secluded resort in the Philippines. They're probably snorkeling in the Sula Sea or clinking mai tais this second."

"They're together again?"

"So far as I know. The truth is, I'm not sure how serious the problem was between them. It might've been that she really did just go back to India to see her family. That's the thing with Saul, you never know."

"*He plays the game.*"

"*As do we all, Mr. President. So, are we done? No investigation, Warren? No Senate hearing? And no one will ever know of this meeting or anything we discussed?*"

"*You have my word, Bill, Mr. President. But you were wrong about one thing.*"

"*What was that?*"

"*I wasn't doing it for politics, or for grandstanding. Well, maybe a little. I won't be running for reelection. I'm retiring. The thing is—and I'm asking you to keep it as confidential as I'm going to keep everything I now know about Saul and Miss Mathison and Iron Thunder—I have prostate cancer. It's spread. I won't be able to campaign in the midterms even if I wanted to. And I don't. I want to use what time I have left for myself, my family.*"

"*I'm so sorry, Warren. Truly. So who gets the committee chair next? Andrew Lockhart?*"

"*Probably. And if it is Andy Lockhart, you won't find him as accommodating. He has a thing about the CIA. Personally, I think he wants to be director, Mr. President. But you didn't hear that from me.*"

"*I hear you. Damn, what time is it?*"

"*Almost three, Mr. President. We've been at it for hours.*"

"*God, I've got an eight A.M. dog and pony at some company in Pennsylvania on the economy. I'll have bags under the bags under my eyes. Are we done?*"

"*We are, Mr. President. Senator, we have your word, none of us will ever speak of any of this again. This meeting never happened?*"

"*What meeting?*"

CHAPTER 40

Observatory Circle, Washington, D.C.
29 July 2009

Riding in a town car back to his official residence at the U.S. Naval Observatory, Vice President Bill Walden rubbed his eyes. The meeting had gone on longer than he'd wanted and he was bone tired.

The good news was that Senator Warren Purcell was shutting down the inquiry. No one on the Senate Select Committee or anyone else would ever hear about Saul, Carrie Mathison, or Operation Iron Thunder. The only loose end was the drone attack and the Photoshopped photographs he had shown Purcell and the president.

How the hell were they supposed to know that the target building they'd been told was a jihadi mosque in Aqrah was actually a damn religious school full of kids? He'd thought of putting the blame on the girl, Carrie, even though she hadn't picked the target, just the town, but decided against it because she was the heroine of the story he was selling to the president and Purcell to get them to shut it down. And he couldn't put it on Saul Berenson, because he needed him at Langley, he thought as the town car drove up Connecticut Avenue, the streets dark and empty this early in the morning .

So the only loose ends were the drone pilot, Lieutenant Chris Chandler, and the CIA technician, Jake Azarian, who'd substituted the photos of a strike on a compound in Helmand Province in Afghanistan for the real drone photos of Aqrah.

The first thing he'd done after the drone strike was to order Lieutenant Chandler from Cheech Air Force Base in Nevada to his office in the Pentagon, where he laid it out for the young lieutenant. Either a career-ending dishonorable discharge and possible prison time or a promotion to captain and a reassignment for him and his family to Washington.

"A mistake was made," he'd told Lieutenant Chandler. "Either the whole country pays for it, especially you, or we accept the idea that in war there is sometimes collateral damage, and get on with the job of defending our country."

After Chandler swore he'd never utter a word to anyone about Aqrah, not even to his wife, as long as he lived, he'd told the young man, "Congratulations, Captain. I'm sure you and your family will like Washington. Oh, and if you ever see me in the halls of the Pentagon or anywhere else ever again, you don't know me. This conversation never happened."

As for Azarian, he was pure CIA. He knew better than to ever say a word. The original photos and digital records of the Aqrah drone strike were destroyed and replaced with the Photoshopped ones and the digitally revised records he'd shown Senator Purcell and the president. No one would ever know.

After Dupont Circle, the town car turned up Massachusetts Avenue, Embassy Row, heading toward the Naval Observatory. From his official residence he had a view of the observatory grounds and buildings, but the view he wanted was the White House Rose Garden. If the economy didn't pull out soon, even if the president ran for reelection, there was a chance the party out of desperation might look elsewhere. In which case, good old Bill Walden was ready to step in. A lot of people in the party owed him favors, he thought, smiling to himself as they passed Rock Creek heading who knows where.

CHARACTERS

(in order of appearance)

Caroline Anne Mathison, nickname "Carrie"; cover names "Mingus," "Billie," "Jane Meyerhof," "Anne McGarvey," "Nancy Williams"; operations officer, Baghdad Station, NCS (National Clandestine Service division), CIA (Central Intelligence Agency).

Warren Purcell, senior senator from Indiana, chairman Senate Select Committee on Intelligence, Washington, D.C.

The President of the United States.

William Walden, nickname "Bill"; Vice President, former director of the CIA, Washington, D.C.

Abu Nazir, real name unknown; origin: unknown; current status: leader of IPLA (Islamic People's Liberation Army); current location: unknown.

Perry Dryer, code name "Dallas-One"; Baghdad Station chief, NCS, CIA; current location: Baghdad, Iraq.

Warzer Zafir, Iraqi national; origin: Ramadi, Iraq; U.S. embassy translator and liaison to the CIA's Baghdad Station; current location: Baghdad, Iraq.

Saul Michael Berenson, Middle East Division chief, NCS, CIA.

Lieutenant General Mosab Sabagh, code name "Cadillac"; executive officer, Presidential Guard Armored Division, Syrian Army, Damascus, Syria.

Chris Glenn, code name "Jaybird"; CIA SOG (Special Operations Group) team commander; formerly captain, U.S. Army First Special Forces Operational Detachment—Delta, JSOC (Joint Special Operations Command).

Nicholas Brody, sergeant, 2nd Battalion, 7th Marines, United States Marine Corps; captured by forces associated with al-Qaeda outside Haditha, Anbar Province, Iraq, May 19, 2003.

Jessica Brody, née Lazaro, wife of Nicholas Brody; mother of Dana Brody and Chris Brody; current location: Alexandria, Virginia.

Mike Faber, captain, 3rd Battalion, 7th Marines, United States Marine Corps; childhood friend of Nicholas Brody.

Megan Faber, wife of Mike Faber; current location: unknown.

Marion Brody, aka "Gunner Brody"; chief warrant officer 02 (retired); father of Nicholas Brody; current location: Bethlehem, Pennsylvania.

Sibeal Brody, wife of Marion Brody and mother of Nicholas Brody; current location: Bethlehem, Pennsylvania.

Thomas Walker, nickname "Tom"; scout sniper, 2nd Battalion, 7th Marines, United States Marine Corps; captured with team member Sergeant Nicholas Brody by forces associated with al-Qaeda outside Haditha, Anbar Province, Iraq, May 19, 2003; presumed killed by Nicholas Brody, some days after initial capture.

Orhan Barsani, CIA asset; origin: Syrian Kurd from Hama, Syria; current location: Damascus, Syria.

Aref Tayfouri, Syrian Kurdish businessman and friend of fellow-Kurd Orhan Barsani; location: Damascus, Syria.

Mira Berenson, née Bhattacharya, wife of Saul Berenson; origin: Mumbai, India; current status: director, Children's Rights Division, Human Rights Watch organization.

Sanford Gornick, nickname "Sandy"; specialist 2, Iranian Desk, Middle East Division, NCS, CIA.

Christopher Larson, nickname "Chris"; lieutenant colonel, CENTCOM commander's headquarters staff, United States Army; location: Tampa, Florida.

General Arthur Demetrius, CENTCOM commander, U.S. CENTCOM, United States Army; location: Tampa, Florida.

Akjemal (last name unknown); Turkmen woman; location: Tal Afar, Iraq.

Alan Yerushenko, deputy director, OCSAA (Office of Collection Strategies and Analysis), Intelligence Analysis Division, CIA; briefly Carrie's supervisor in 2006.

Abd al Ali Nasser, director of Syrian Mukhabarat, the *Shu'bat al-Mukhabarat al-'Askariyya* or Military Intelligence Directorate, the equivalent of the combined Syrian CIA and DIA.

Aminah Sabagh, wife of Lieutenant General Mosab Sabagh, location: Damascus, Syria.

Jameel Sabagh, son of Lieutenant General Mosab Sabagh, Syrian Army; location: Damascus, Syria.

Syarhey Lebedenko, cover name "Marcos Haroyan"; businessman/senior sales director, Belkommunex, TAA, front company for Russian KGB (later remade as SVR and FSB), Minsk, Belarus; origin: Belarussian.

Virgil Maravich, CIA specialized skills officer ("Black Bag" technical specialist), Middle Eastern Division, OTS (Office of Technical Services), NCS, CIA.

Dar Adal, deputy chief of staff, Black Operations Team, National Clandestine Service, CIA; origin: Druse; born: Baakleen, town in the Chouf region, Lebanon.

Kamal Jumblatt, former Lebanese minister of the interior, founder of the Progressive Socialist Party and later the National Struggle Front; winner of the Lenin Prize; leader of the Lebanese Druse community; father of Walid Jumblatt and mentor to Dar Adal. He was assassinated in March 1977. Suspicion for his murder fell on the Syrian Assad regime or Syrian adherents in Lebanon; origin: Lebanese Druse, born: Deir el Qamar, Lebanon.

Gerry Hoad, consular officer and MI6 intelligence officer, British SIS (Secret Intelligence Service), British FCO (Foreign and Commonwealth Office), British Grand Consulate, Istanbul, Turkey.

Sally Rumsley, senior political reporting officer, British FCO, British Grand Consulate, Istanbul, Turkey.

Simon Duncan-Jones, consul general, chief of mission, British FCO, British Grand Consulate, Istanbul, Turkey.

Alina (last name unknown), trafficked female; origin: Chişinău, Moldova; current location: Manama, Bahrain.

Nassrin (last name unknown); wife of Abu Nazir, leader of IPLA, mother of Issa; current location: unknown.

Issa (last name unknown); son of Abu Nazir, leader of IPLA.

Dana Brody, daughter of Nicholas Brody; current location: Alexandria, Virginia.

Christopher Brody, nickname "Chris"; son of Nicholas Brody; current location: Alexandria, Virginia.

Marius de Bruin, code name "Robespierre"; president and CEO, Atalaxus Executive, Pty, a South African registered private military company; origin: Johannesburg, South Africa; current location: Baghdad, Iraq.

Dasha (last name unknown); female model and companion of Marius de Bruin; origin: Kiev, Ukraine; current location: Baghdad, Iraq.

Eric Sanderson, deputy chief of mission, U.S. embassy, Baghdad, Iraq.

Estrella (last name unknown), assistant/servant of Marius de Bruin; origin: Puno, Peru; current location: Baghdad, Iraq.

Abu Ghazawan, real name Haidar al-Salem; follower of Abu Nazir; origin: Fallujah, Iraq (Salmani tribe); current location: Karbala, Iraq.

Sheikh Ali Hatem al-Rashawi, leader of the Albu Mahal tribe and the Sons of Iraq, a Sunni militia, Anbar Province, Iraq.

Ali Ibrahim, aide to Sheikh al-Rashawi, officer in Sons of Iraq; origin: Albu Mahal tribe, Ramadi, Iraq.

Ali Hamsa, code name "Arrowhead"; assistant to Iraqi Vice Prime Minister Mohammed Ali Fahdel, leader of the Sunni faction in the Iraqi parliament; location: Baghdad, Iraq.

Tal'at al-Wasi, smuggler and prominent member of the Bani Assad tribe; location: Shatt al-Arab, Basra, Iraq.

Majid Javadi, captain in the SAVAK, the shah of Iran's internal security force. This organization was subsequently transformed into VEVAK, the Iranian Republic's Ministry of Intelligence and Security; current headquarters: Tehran, Iran.

Namir Fahmadi, colonel, later general of the Iranian Army under the shah; past location: Borazjan, Iran; current location: unknown.

Pejman Khanzadeh, officer of MOIS (Ministry of Intelligence and National Security), the Iranian equivalent of the CIA; origin: Tehran, Iran.

GLOSSARY

(in alphabetical order)

100X1—CIA expression; the number before the X indicates the number of years before a document may be declassified; i.e., one hundred years. The $X1$ designates classification level; i.e., Top Secret.

Aardvark—CIA designation for messages or reports of the highest urgency; typically indicating an emergency situation.

Agencja Wywiadu—Also called AW; the secret intelligence service of Poland, the Polish equivalent of the CIA.

Alawites—A Shiite Muslim religious group, an offshoot of the "Twelver" branch of Shi'a Islam, primarily located in western Syria. The Alawites began as a sect that followed the teachings of the eleventh imam, Hassan al-Askari, in the ninth century. In the centuries that followed, they achieved notoriety as warriors. Alawites represent only a small percentage of the Syrian population and might have passed unnoticed were it not that Syria has been ruled for more than forty years by a single Alawite dynasty, the al-Assad family, who placed Alawites in positions of power. Bassam al-Assad, son of the founder of the modern Syrian state, Hafez al-Assad, was the president of Syria in 2009, the period in which this book is set. As Alawite Shiites, the al-Assads, father and son, allied Syria with the other two anti-Western Shiite powers in the Middle East, Hezbollah and Iran.

Al-Qaeda—The global international militant terrorist organization. Founded in the late 1980s by Osama bin Laden, a wealthy Saudi jihadi, in part as a response to the Soviet war in Afghanistan (1979–1989), al-Qaeda (the name means "the Base") is a combination militant Islamist terrorist network, stateless military force, and radical Sunni Muslim movement advocating global jihad. As Salafist jihadis, al-Qaeda is intolerant of all persons of other religions or philosophies except strict Salafist Sunni Muslims. This includes intolerance toward other Muslims, such as Shiites, Sufis, or even Sunnis, who in their view do not practice a sufficiently strict Salafist Sunni version of sharia law. The organization achieved worldwide notoriety for its attack on the World Trade Center in New York and the Pentagon on September 11, 2001. Since then, although it has lost much of its early leadership, it has developed offshoots in other parts of the world, including, among others: AQAP (al-Qaeda in the Arabian Peninsula), the Harkat-ul-Mujahideen in Kashmir, AQIM (al-Qaeda in the Islamic Maghreb, North Africa), Jemaah Islamiah (a Southeast Asian Islamist terrorist group), and AQI (al-Qaeda in Iraq).

AQI—Al-Qaeda in Iraq; the Iraqi branch of al-Qaeda; the international Salafist jihadi militant organization founded by the Saudi terrorist Osama bin Laden. AQI was started in 2003 as a reaction to the American-led invasion and occupation of

Iraq. It was first led by the Jordanian militant Abu Musab al-Zarqawi. After his death, in the *Homeland* version of events, AQI or an offshoot, the Islamic People's Liberation Army (IPLA), was led by a mysterious man with the *kunya*, or nom de guerre, of Abu Nazir. By 2009, when this novel is set, the American war effort in Iraq is winding down and AQI has lost much of Anwar Province due to a combination of actions resulting from the U.S. military surge and actions by the Sons of Iraq and other Sunni tribesmen who turned against AQI. In this novel, in order to retain relevance, the IPLA, under Abu Nazir, plots one last attack in the hope of triggering a civil war in Iraq that will force the Americans to withdraw with heavy casualties under fire, leaving the U.S. mission a failure.

CENTCOM—Acronym for the U.S. military's Central Command; its areas of responsibility include the Middle East, North Africa, and Central Asia, which in recent times includes the two U.S. wars in Afghanistan and Iraq. The commander of CENTCOM has the responsibility of all U.S. military forces in those areas.

CIA—Acronym for Central Intelligence Agency; the U.S. federal agency primarily responsible for foreign intelligence; headquartered in Langley, Virginia. Thus the terms "CIA" and "Langley" are often used interchangeably.

CID—Acronym for Criminal Investigations Department of the Abu Dhabi Police Department; responsible for the investigation of crimes and counterintelligence in Abu Dhabi and the United Arab Emirates.

COMINT—Acronym for Communications Intelligence, i.e., intelligence derived from the interception of electronic or voice communications; also see *NSA*.

DCIA—Acronym for director of the CIA.

DIA—Acronym for the Defense Intelligence Agency, the primary U.S. foreign military intelligence organization. The agency's objectives encompass the collection and analysis of defense-related foreign political, economic, geographic, and other types of intelligence; although the majority of its employees are civilians, it is operated as an agency of the Pentagon.

Dorogoi—A Russian term of endearment; sweetheart, darling.

Drop; aka dead drop—CIA term for a secret location where a message or other material can be left in concealment for another party to retrieve. This eliminates the need for direct contact between two agents in hostile conditions. Typically, a mark, such as a chalk mark, a bit of colored thread, etc., is left nearby to signal that there is a message or item to pick up. The person picking up the material normally erases or eliminates the mark to indicate that the material has been retrieved.

FISA Court—Foreign Intelligence Surveillance Act Court; a U.S. federal court established under the Foreign Intelligence Surveillance Act of 1978 (FISA) to meet in secret in order to evaluate requests and issue surveillance warrants against suspected foreign intelligence agents or terrorists operating inside the United States. Post-9/11, the court's powers and scope were expanded to address a wide range of federal actions involving classified material or as deemed necessary for national security.

Flash Critical—CIA term for a message or operation of highest urgency.

FOB—U.S. military term for Forward Operating Base. Each such base is typically designated by a letter of the alphabet, e.g., FOB Alpha, FOB Bravo, etc.

FSB—Acronym for the Federal Security Service of the Russian Federation; *Federal'naya Sluzhba Bezopasnosti*; a successor agency to the Soviet-era KGB, it is responsible for counterintelligence and domestic security. Like the KGB, it is headquartered in Lubyanka Prison in Lubyanka Square in Moscow.

GO—Acronym for a General Order; in the U.S. military a General Order is a directive issued by a commander that applies to all units in his/her command. It is considered general because it is an order not directed at a specific person nor does it necessarily require a specific action, but rather delineates a policy or overall action, such as an attack. Failure to obey a GO is punishable by court-martial.

Green Zone—A ten-square-kilometer (approximately four square miles) section of central Baghdad aka Oz (after the Emerald City of *The Wizard of Oz*); it had been the center of government and the area where the most important government officials lived under Saddam Hussein. It subsequently became the governmental center of the U.S.-led Coalition Provisional Authority. Heavily fortified during the height of the Iraq War and subsequent insurgency, it remains the seat of the Iraqi government and the primary locale of the international community in Baghdad.

GSD—the Syrian General Security Directorate, *Idarat al-Amn al-Amm*, the brutal agency in charge of internal and external security for the Syrian government. In addition to suppressing internal dissent and security threats against the Assad regime, the GSD is involved in intelligence work outside Syria, such as coordinating intelligence activities and information with Hezbollah and the MOIS, the Iranian CIA, both allies of the Assad regime in Syria. In order to work undercover in Syria, Carrie's greatest danger would be in coming to the attention of the GSD, which would have no compunction about imprisoning, torturing, or even executing her.

HUMINT—CIA term for human intelligence, i.e., intelligence gathered from and by human sources; traditional spycraft sources.

Hijab—Arabic word for head scarf, frequently worn by Muslim women for modesty; called a *rusari* in Iran.

IED—Military acronym for Improvised Explosive Device, e.g., a roadside bomb or other explosive booby trap.

Imam Hussein Shrine—Located in Karbala, Iraq, on the site where the battle of Karbala took place on October 10, 680, when the overwhelming forces of Yazid, the Ummayad caliph, defeated and slaughtered the companions and family of Hussein ibn Ali, leader of the Shiite faction. The killing of Hussein, grandson of the Prophet Mohammed, caused the final irreparable rift within the Islamic world between Shiites and Sunnis. The shrine consists of two ancient domed mosques separated by a promenade: the Imam Hussein mosque, which is the burial site of Hussein and also contains a mosque for prayer, and the Al Abbas mosque, the burial site of Abbas, Hussein's flag bearer and bravest warrior companion. For Shiite Muslims, the shrine is, after the Kaaba in Mecca, considered to be the holiest site in Islam. As suggested in this book, an attack that destroyed the sepulcher and remains of the martyr Hussein would have profound repercussions among Shiites around the world.

INP—Acronym for Iraqi National Police.

IPLA—Acronym for the Islamic People's Liberation Army. In the *Homeland* universe, the IPLA is a dangerous affiliate of al-Qaeda headed by Abu Nazir, one of the CIA's most wanted terrorists.

ISF—Acronym for Iraqi Security Forces; a U.S. term for the military and police forces of the federal government of Iraq, including the Iraqi Army, re-formed after the U.S.-led invasion in 2003.

JWICS—Acronym for Joint Worldwide Intelligence Communications System, a containerized Internet-like data communications network for Top Secret CIA communications.

KDP—Acronym for Kurdistan Democratic Party; also known as PDK, *Partîya Demokrata Kurdistan.* The KDP is one of the two main Kurdish parties (the other being the PUK) that dominate the area of northern Iraq under autonomous Kurdish control. This region is unofficially called Kurdistan.

KGB—Acronym for the Committee for State Security, *Komitet Gosudarstvennoy Bezopasnosti,* the foreign and domestic security intelligence service of the Soviet Union and its satellite nations during the Soviet era, headquartered in Lubyanka Square in Moscow. After the fall and breakup of the Soviet Union (1991), it was re-formed in Russia as two new agencies: the FSB, responsible for domestic security and counterintelligence, and the SVR, responsible for foreign intelligence, i.e., the Russian equivalent of the CIA.

Komidashi—In the game of Go, black always goes first, which is a significant advantage. To compensate, agreed-upon points are awarded to white (6.5 points is standard under Japanese and Korean rules; under Chinese and AGA rules, 7.5 points is standard). This compensation to help equalize the game is called *komidashi* or *komi*, for short. By offering a "modified *komidashi*," Saul is giving the general fair warning that he, Saul, is an accomplished Go player.

Kunya—Arabic word for a nom de guerre or wartime cover name adopted to hide one's true identity. Often, the name "Abu," father of, is used (following an Arab custom for a father to adopt the name of one's oldest child; thus if one's firstborn child is named Mohammed, the father might adopt the name Abu Mohammed). The second name of a *kunya* often references a heroic character in Arab history or myth, or a derivation of a name with meaning. Thus, Abu Nazir is not the real name of the terrorist Carrie hunts, but is his *kunya* or cover name; its meaning in Arabic is "father of one who gives victory."

LNM—Acronym for the Lebanese National Movement, a Druse-led coalition of Druse, Palestinian, pro-Syrian, and leftist parties and militias during the early years of the Lebanese Civil War (1975–1990). In speaking about it with Saul, Dar is suggesting that his time as a guerrilla fighter in the LNM during that war was his school.

Lurs—An Iranian ethnic minority (population estimated at approximately nine million), who primarily reside in southwestern Iran. Most Lurs speak Luri, a language related to both Kurdish and Farsi. As a tribal people, Lurs are closely related to the Kurds. They generally follow the Shiite Islamic religion, although some incorporate elements of the Ahl-e Haqq faith, characterized by a belief in reincarnation. Historically, they have been discriminated against by the Persian majority, who sometimes regard them as a more primitive ethnic people.

Mahdi Army—An Iraqi paramilitary force created by the Iraqi Shia cleric Muqtada al-Sadr in June 2003. The group initiated attacks on Iraqi Security Forces and U.S.-led Coalition Forces as well as fighting actions against Sunni extremists and insurgents during the Iraq War. It opposed the U.S. presence in Iraq and was known for its use of IEDs. The group was subsequently linked to the Iraqi police forces.

MCCUU—Acronym for Marine Corps Combat Utility Uniform—the camouflage combat uniform of the United States Marine Corps.

MI6—Acronym for the British Secret Intelligence Service aka SIS, of James Bond fame. It is headquartered in Vauxhall Cross in London. The terms "MI6," "SIS," "Secret Service," "Vauxhall Cross," and "VC" are used interchangeably.

MIT—Acronym for the National Intelligence Organization of Turkey, *Milli İstihbarat Teşkilatı*. The MIT is responsible for intelligence and security both within and outside Turkey, making it the Turkish equivalent of a combination CIA and FBI.

MOIS—Acronym for Ministry of Intelligence and Security, the Iranian agency responsible for foreign intelligence and counterintelligence, i.e., the Iranian equivalent of the CIA. Also see *VEVAK*.

MRAP—Military acronym for Mine Resistant Ambush Protected, used to describe armored personnel vehicles introduced into Iraq in 2008 to replace Humvee vehicles in order to help reduce U.S. casualties caused by roadside IEDs (Improvised Explosive Devices). Also see *IED*.

Mukhabarat—The Syrian foreign and military intelligence service, *Shuʻbat al-Mukhabarat al-ʻAskariyya*, is the Syrian equivalent of both the CIA and the DIA in the United States. As director of the Mukhabarat, Abd al Ali Nasser would report directly to President Assad of Syria, which would make him the most important and powerful intelligence person in Syria.

NOFORN—CIA acronym for No Foreign Nationals, i.e., no one who is not a native-born American may view this document.

NSA—Acronym for National Security Agency; the NSA is the U.S. intelligence agency primarily responsible for COMINT (Communications Intelligence, see above), cryptanalysis, and computer intelligence and security.

NSC—Acronym for National Security Council, the White House's primary policy and decision-making forum for issues involving U.S. national security. The NSC is chaired by the U.S. president and includes the president's national security advisor, key intelligence and cabinet officials, and the chairman of the Joint Chiefs of Staff at the Pentagon.

ORCON—CIA acronym for Originator Control, i.e., the originator controls dissemination and/or release of the document.

PDB—Acronym for the President's Daily Brief; a written summary provided to the president of the United States every morning by the DNI, the director of national intelligence. The PDB is a condensed summary of the most important and critical intelligence information gleaned from all available sources, including potential terrorist and other threats to the nation. The PDB is based on input from all U.S. intelligence agencies, including the CIA, the NSA, the various Pentagon intelligence services including the DIA, the FBI, the NRO, the Department of Homeland Security, the State Department, the Treasury Department, the DEA, etc.

Persona non grata—Latin phrase for a person who is not welcome, it is formally used as the designation for a nonnative person who is being expelled by the government of a foreign country. Informally, it is used to describe someone whose continued presence is not welcome at a particular gathering, event, or place.

PFLP—Acronym for the Popular Front for the Liberation of Palestine, a radical paramilitary movement advocating the liberation of Palestine, with a Marxist base philosophy. It has initiated terrorist attacks, hijackings, and attacks on Israel and has been designated a terrorist organization by the United States, Canada, the European Union, and Israel.

RPG—Rocket Propelled Grenade launcher, a weapon that fires explosive grenades, typically modeled on the Russian RPG-7.

RSSMF—Royal Saudi Strategic Missile Force, the branch of the Saudi Arabian military responsible for the kingdom's ballistic missile, air, and missile defense operations.

Rusari—Farsi word for head scarf, frequently worn by Muslim women in Iran for modesty; called a "hijab" in Arabic.

SAVAK—The Organization of Intelligence and National Security, *Sazeman-e Ettela'at va Amniyat-e Keshvar*, the secret police arm and domestic security and intelligence service established by Iran's shah, Mohammad Reza Pahlavi, during his more-than-two-decades-long reign, which ended with his overthrow in 1979. Part of Iran's hostility against the United States stems from the fact that the CIA helped put the shah on the throne in Iran and also helped him create, supply, and train the SAVAK. Also see *VEVAK*.

Shiites and Sunnis—The origin of the conflict between Sunnis and Shiites dates back to the year 632 when the Prophet Mohammed died without leaving a son or heir. Two claimants vied to replace him as the leader or "caliph" of the new religion: the Prophet's closest male relative by blood, his cousin and son-in-law, Ali, whose followers called themselves Shiat Ali, the followers of Ali, or Shiites for short; and the Prophet's father-in-law, Abu Bakr, whose supporters, called Sunnis, believed he would be best able to manage the rapidly expanding Muslim empire. Abu Bakr was chosen, creating the initial rift. The split between these two groups became final and irreparable when Ali's son Hussein (who was not only Ali's son, but also the grandson of the Prophet Muhammad) challenged the legitimacy of Yazid, the Sunni Ummayad caliph. Ali, his forces outnumbered, was killed at the battle of Karbala in Iraq in the year 680. Many of his male relatives were slain with him. The Imam Hussein Shrine was built on the site where Hussein and his flag bearer, Abbas, fell in battle. The massacre of the Prophet Muhammad's grandson along with most of his male relatives sent shock waves across the Muslim empire that reverberate to this day. It led Shiites to adopt a feeling of martyrdom as part of their faith, exemplified as they saw it, in the actions of Hussein, whose sacrifice is still commemorated on the Shiite holiday, the Day of Ashura. Throughout history, while acknowledging that they are fellow Muslims, Sunnis and Shiites have viewed each other with suspicion. The conflict continues to this day, often played out violently and through surrogates, such as Hezbollah (Shiite) and al-Qaeda (Sunni), and in countries with mixed Sunni-Shiite populations, such as Syria, Lebanon, and Iraq. The civil war in Syria, which began as an Arab Spring movement, has devolved into a Sunni-Shiite conflict.

SOG—Acronym for Special Operations Group, a CIA paramilitary team used for special operations. Members of a Special Operations Group are typically CIA personnel who are veterans of U.S. special military units, such as the U.S. Army Delta Force, Army Rangers, Marine Corps Special Operations Command, and the Navy SEALs.

Souk—Arabic word for market or bazaar.

Special Access Critical—A level above the highest security classification (Top Secret), a Special Access Program is a Top Secret operation that may be designated by the director of the

CIA to deal with an exceptional threat or intelligence action for which access to information on the operation is limited to as few Top Secret clearance personnel as is absolutely necessary. "Critical" is the highest level of operational urgency.

Special Operations Group—See *SOG*.

SVR—Acronym for the foreign intelligence service of the Russian Federation, *Sluzhba Vneshney Razvedki*, a successor agency to the Soviet-era KGB. It is the Russian equivalent of the CIA, headquartered in the Moscow suburb of Yasenevo.

Top Secret—The highest U.S. government security classification; also see *Special Access Critical*.

UAZ—Russian four-wheel-drive military vehicle; roughly equivalent to a U.S. Humvee.

Vauxhall Cross—See *MI6*.

VC—See *Vauxhall Cross* and *MI6*.

VEVAK—The Ministry of Intelligence and National Security of the Islamic Republic of Iran, *Vezarat-e Ettela'at va Amniyat-e Keshvar*; the internal security and secret police organization of the Islamic Republic, primarily responsible for counterintelligence and internal security. It is a successor organization to the shah's SAVAK, which was initially purged and disbanded during the Iranian Revolution in 1979. Also see *MOIS*.

WMD—Acronym for Weapons of Mass Destruction; refers to weapons that have a wide mass killing effect, such as nuclear weapons, poison gas, and biological weapons.

NEW FROM ANDREW KAPLAN